To Cassie — thanks for ~~~ ~~~~~~
and thoughts — hope ~
lovely to meet all of
Vicbledor!

# PALLADIUM

1/12/22

Immortal Works LLC
1505 Glenrose Drive
Salt Lake City, Utah 84104
Tel: (385) 202-0116

© 2022 Leigh Turner
rleighturner.com

Cover Art by Rebecca Barney
barneydesign.com

This book is a work of fiction. Names, characters, businesses, organizations, places, events and incidents either are the product of the author's imagination or are used fictitiously. Any resemblance to actual persons, living or dead, events, or locales is entirely coincidental.

ISBN 978-1-953491-38-1 (Paperback)
ASIN B09Y5CC6J8 (Kindle)

*To Gözde, a Turkish woman with a hard head*

# NOTE TO THE READER:
## CONSTANTINOPLE AND ISTANBUL

Greek colonists founded Byzantium, the city now known as Istanbul, in 667 BC. After 330 AD, when the Roman Emperor Constantine made the city the new eastern capital of the Roman Empire, the name "New Rome" became widespread. But in the following years the city became known as Constantinople, after its founder. Some people called the city Byzantium until the Turkish conquest in 1453.

Arabs and Armenians used the names Stamboul and Istanbul, probably derived from Greek phrases meaning "the city" or "to the city," as early as the 10th century. The name Istanbul became common in the Ottoman Empire after the conquest. The Ottoman constitution of 1876 named the capital of the Ottoman state as Istanbul.

In March 1930, Turkey asked other countries to use Turkish names for Turkish cities, and the name Istanbul spread around the world. Although some people still refer to the city as Constantinople, I have used Istanbul except in a historic context.

# MAPS

*Map 1: Istanbul lies on the Bosphorus between Europe – top left – and Asia – lower right.*

*Map 2: The Old City is on the European side. The Asian side is lower right.*

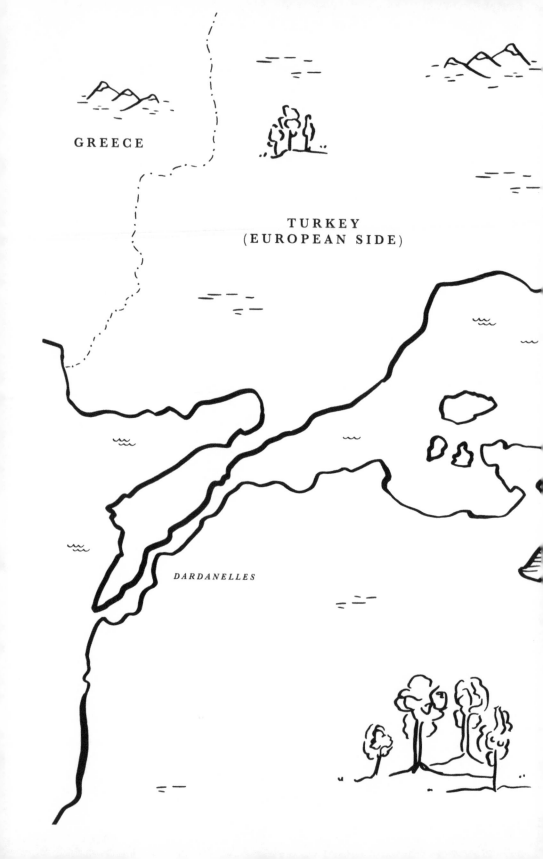

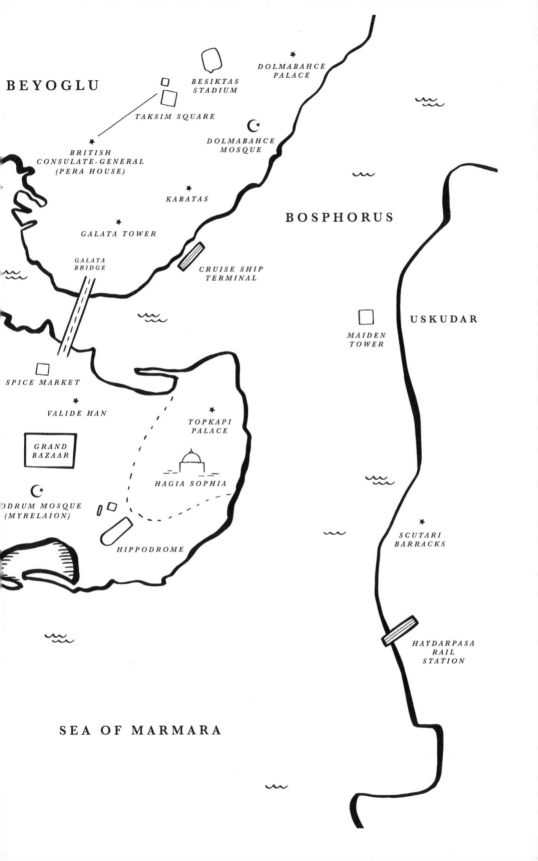

AN INTERNATIONAL THRILLER

# PALLADIUM

## LEIGH TURNER

IMMORTAL WORKS
Salt Lake City

# PART I

## COME HITHER

# 1

## 1453

The Janissary warrior, Yusuf Ali-Bey, had triumphed in countless battles. He had slain numberless foes.

He had never known horror such as this.

Today, Constantinople, great capital of the Christians, would fall. Glory would rain down on him. But only if he, the commander, fulfilled a task so strange he could scarcely believe his orders.

In the darkness, Yusuf gazed at his goal. His hand went to the *nazar* around his neck, beneath the chain mail.

The rotting bodies of his fallen comrades blackened the towering, thousand-year-old walls of Byzantium. Torches on the battlements and guttering flames amidst the rubble cast shadows over the myriad dead from a siege that had lasted an impossible fifty-three days.

Yusuf flinched as a hell-bellow of thunder roared behind him. Sultan Mehmet's cannon, Basilica, forty spans long and cast of bronze full one span thick around the barrel, had spoken. Already, the giant iron ball had smashed into the walls, pulverising masonry, corpses, and the blackened hulks of burned-out war machines left by past assaults. Screams rang out from the Byzantine, Genoese, and Venetian defenders on the ramparts.

They were right to be afraid.

Yusuf smiled. The roar of the great cannon was an omen. By the time the sun had risen and set, every soldier on the walls would perish.

From the crest of the parapet, defenders swarmed down ropes and ladders to begin repairing with wooden beams and barrels of earth the damage wrought by Basilica.

Now.

Drumbeats rang out and a cacophony of pipes and trumpets erupted. Irregular bashi-bazouk forces, Christian slaves and mercenaries from Albania, Hungary, Germany, Genoa, Venice, and even Greece, in the service of the great Sultan Mehmet, rushed towards the walls with fresh siege ladders and grappling hooks, yelling their battle cries.

Behind them, Yusuf and his men slipped into the darkness, cloaks masking their captured Venetian armour.

# 2

---

Orhan Mutlu and John Savage stood on a balcony above the Bosphorus on the Asian side when Elif's fear reached out for them over the water.

"The future of Turkey lies in Asia." Orhan's hand rested on the grip of his holstered pistol. "We should stick with the winners."

"Istanbul grew up European," Savage said. "Look where it started."

Shrieking seagulls circled over the white-capped waves. A rust-streaked bulk-carrier, holds piled high with Ukrainian grain, steamed past the Golden Horn. On the European side, the morning sun painted pink the domes, minarets, palaces, and towers of the Old City of Istanbul, still girt by the walls of the Roman Emperor Theodosius. Out to sea, a vast military vessel steamed towards the city, flanked by two destroyers bristling with weaponry.

"Look at that aircraft carrier," the burly Turk said. "The *Gerald R Ford*. The United States of America bringing one hundred thousand tons of its most concentrated killing power into the heart of Istanbul. Outside powers always try to dominate Turkey. But we are fighting back. As you know, to your cost."

"I don't want to dominate your bloody sister." The sun shone hot on Savage's neck. "What fool would even try?"

"A Turkish woman is a match for any man. Except for a Turk." Orhan squared his shoulders.

"Elif and I were together. Now we are apart. End of story."

"She will do better without you."

Savage wiped a trickle of sweat from his forehead. Across the water, Elif would be in her tunnel, excavating ancient relics. On site she wore shorts and a baggy shirt, her hair tangled, her bare calves flecked with sweat and dust. He smiled as the tune to Sam Cooke's *Working on a Chain Gang* came into his head.

"She is racing to find the famous Palladium," Orhan went on. "Arzu Pasha has threatened to bury her in concrete."

"The Palladium is a Greek myth. Elif told that US journalist she would be more likely to find Achilles down in a catacomb, polishing his sword."

"You imperialist powers pretend arguments are won by logic. In reality, strength decides everything." Without warning, Orhan slapped Savage on the back. "That is why tonight, we shall teach you a lesson you will never forget."

Savage whirled round and seized the Turk's wrist. "Don't hit me."

Orhan stepped back, cradling his arm. "Elif told me you were crazy. I was only talking about the soccer."

Inside the room, two managers faced a battery of TV cameras.

"We expect two thousand fans for tonight's game," the Liverpool boss said. "I know the Turkish police will keep them safe."

Orhan shook his head. "Still no news of terrorist threats from your secret channels?" he said to Savage. "Or are you keeping the best stuff for yourself, as usual? Excuse me." He pulled out his phone.

"What is it?" Savage said

"It is a message from Elif. I must go." Orhan signalled to his deputy, who was watching the press conference with a sour expression. "Call me if anything comes up. My sister needs me."

"Show me." Savage tried to grab the phone, but the intelligence cop shook him off and strode towards the exit.

"Nothing frightens Elif," Orhan said. "Something nasty must have happened."

Savage stepped beyond the Turk, his body braced in the doorway. "You want to leave? Show me the bloody text."

Orhan's eyes narrowed. "You really are a psycho." He held up the screen.

*Come quickly.* Elif's text was in Turkish. *I am afraid.*

Savage looked up to meet Orhan's dark gaze. "I'm going too," he said.

"Oh, yes? I thought you had Liverpool supporters to look after?"

"Elif needs help," Savage said. "I don't trust you to protect her."

# 3

## 1453

The commander, Yusuf, led his men in single file along the hidden path through the darkness. All along the land-walls of Byzantium, from the Blachernae palace to the north, past the Mesoteichion, down to the Golden Gate and the Marble Tower where the stone ramparts plunged into the Sea of Marmara, tens of thousands of bashi-bazouks fought their way up the mounds of rubble beneath the battered walls.

High on the battlements, Genoese and Venetian archers rained arrows and crossbow bolts on the attackers. Catapults hurled jagged rocks into the massed ranks of the advancing troops. Yet still the bashi-bazouks trudged on up the ramp of broken stone, adding their bodies to those over which they climbed. As men fell dead, more rushed forward to fill their places, shields held over their heads, drawing the defenders' fire down on themselves.

Further back, out of range, the main force of the Sultan's crack Janissary regiments massed in the darkness, harbouring their strength for the final assault at dawn. Yusuf's friend, Hasan, waited with them —a giant of a man, and a master of satranç, the game of tactics also known as chess. Hasan had sworn to win the Sultan's prize for the first soldier to penetrate the stockade and plant the Ottoman colours within the city.

Around the sea-walls too, the Sultan's fleets fought their way towards the shore, harassing the defenders, firing cannon, and landing troops to divert the city's defenders from the land assault.

But unless Yusuf succeeded in his mission, all these attempts to penetrate the city would fail; and Hasan, and every other soldier in the Sultan's vast army, would go unrewarded.

Yusuf lifted his arm, one finger raised.

One finger meant move ahead, in silence. A fist, stop. An arm thrown forward, an all-out assault.

Like Yusuf, the eleven Janissaries in his team uttered no battle cries. Their feet and armour were wrapped in cloth, their bright Venetian blades greased and sheathed. They moved like wraiths across the marshy ground through the shadows at the foot of the walls.

Together, they turned north towards the tumult of the assault.

# 4

Orhan's unmarked car stood on a patch of bare earth a city planner had meant to be a garden. A cat slunk away from the shade of the vehicle as they approached.

"In London you would have been clamped, or towed. Probably, both," Savage said.

"In Istanbul we have rules about carrying members of the public in official vehicles." Orhan took a pair of handcuffs from his belt and strode towards Savage. "Put these on and get in the back."

"You are kidding."

"I am in trouble even travelling to the European side instead of alerting colleagues there." Orhan dangled the cuffs. "I have many foes in the Intelligence Department. If my boss learns I have broken the rules, I will be in handcuffs myself."

"You see invisible enemies every-bloody-where. It's like the Welsh Secret Service. Anything that good at concealing its existence must have power beyond comprehension."

"This is no laughing matter. Do you want to cross the water or not?"

"Orhan, if you want to cuff me you will have to do it by force. And I don't fancy your chances." Savage slammed the roof of the car with the palm of his hand. "Let's go."

"At least sit in the back. We have to make this look right. Hurry! She may be your ex-girlfriend, or ex-lover, or ex-*sex buddy* or whatever you call her, but she is my sister. My blood."

A stink of sweat and worse rose from the hot, plastic seats in the back of the vehicle, choking the stale air. The doors had no handles and the windows did not open. A yellowing barrier of transparent plastic between back and front seats created a secure cell.

"Put your foot down," Savage said.

"Put your seat belt on."

Vehicles and pedestrians packed the steep, narrow streets of Uskudar, on the Asian side of the Bosphorus. Orhan steered with one hand as he shouted into his phone. As the car hurtled downhill, lights flashing and horn screeching, people ambled out of the way, filling the road as soon as the vehicle passed.

"Where are you heading?"

"Police dock." Orhan leaned on the horn as a delivery truck pulled out in front of them. "Quiet in the back." He turned on the radio.

The voice of Rauf Toprak, the veteran left-wing firebrand, rang out. "*It is a knife in our backs. Another betrayal by the dark forces that conspire to destroy the power of Turkish workers.*"

"He belongs in prison," Orhan said.

"*They are rallying their most powerful forces.*" On the radio, Toprak's voice had sunk to a stage whisper. "*Three imperialist nuclear-armed warships will dock in the heart of Istanbul. The US puppet governments of Greece and Turkey are acting out a charade of peace talks. Arzu Pasha, champion of hyper-capitalism, is excavating the so-called Palladium, a superstitious Greek icon that supposedly has been in Turkey for two thousand years.*"

"I hope Elif isn't listening to this bollocks," Savage said. "It would drive her insane."

"It is dating you that has driven her insane," Orhan said.

"*We call our supporters to rally at Taksim Square today.*" Rauf Toprak's voice rose. "*We will PARALYSE the city. We will SHOUT the will of the people. We will FIGHT the imperialists. I call on one million Istanbullus to attend.*"

Orhan changed the channel to Radio Eksen and the sound of Def Leppard filled the car. "Heaven help the riot police."

They roared past the tall towers of the Scutari Barracks, once home to Florence Nightingale. The waters of the Bosphorus bristled with white and yellow passenger ferries, excursion boats, cargo ships, and water taxis. The camouflaged bulk of the US carrier loomed in the centre of the channel as the vessel prepared to dock, immense against the outline of the Old City.

"This is it." Orhan braked, wheels screeching on the sun-softened surface of the road. "Don't say a word." He turned onto a narrow track between two chain-link fences topped with razor wire. Ahead, a guard raised a red and white barrier. The car plunged across an expanse of broken concrete towards a row of bollards where the land ended. In the water bobbed a police patrol boat, flying the inevitable Turkish flag.

Orhan stepped out of the car. A police officer in immaculate uniform appeared on the boat and climbed ashore. Orhan addressed her. She shook her head.

Savage clenched his fists. Fourteen minutes had passed since Elif's text. Since then, silence.

What had Elif and her team of archaeologists uncovered? Why rush, on a site that had lain untouched for hundreds of years?

*Come quickly.*

On the quay, Orhan jabbed his finger at the chest of the uniformed officer. With his heavy build and shaved head, the plainclothes cop looked more like a prize-fighter than an intelligence operative. But the policewoman kept her hands in her pockets. She shook her head again and shrugged.

Sweat soaked Savage's shirt. The heat worked on the plastic seats, filling the airless cell with the stench of ancient fear.

Sixteen minutes had passed.

Elif faced danger.

*Savage stood at the edge of the clearing in the wood outside Moscow. He counted the steps to the abandoned arch in the snow. He searched for his agent, codename Upturn. His breath made clouds in the air. Nothing moved.*

With a roar, Savage leaned back, braced himself against the seat, and planted a heavy kick against the opposite door.

The car rocked. Orhan glanced towards the vehicle, frowned, and resumed his argument.

This was no time for polite discussion.

Savage stripped off his shirt and took from his pocket a heavy bunch of keys. They included a long spike of steel that had once fitted the ignition of a Toyota Landcruiser.

Diplomats did not bear weapons. But Savage had carried the Toyota key for years, in Moscow, Kyiv, and now Istanbul. He had used the stiletto in self-defence more than once.

He gripped the bunch in his right hand so the spike protruded down, and wound the shirt around his knuckles for protection.

*Eat this.*

The first blow against the rear window of the car achieved nothing except to make both Orhan and the uniformed officer spin towards him.

The second blow delivered a narrow crack in the glass and a spasm up Savage's arm. The pain filled him with fresh energy.

On the third blow, the shaft of the key penetrated the rear window, sending a web of cracks across the bowed surface of the glass.

Orhan and the policewoman ran towards the car. Savage struck again with all his strength. This time the glass fractured and a shower of fragments fell onto the concrete outside.

"Stop! Stop!"

Savage looked up to see Orhan and the police officer standing outside with their service Berettas drawn. Orhan pointed his weapon at the ground. But as Savage moved to strike another blow, the uniformed officer raised her pistol in a single-handed grip and pointed through the glass at Savage's chest.

# 5

1453

Yusuf led the way, still cloaked by darkness, up a mound of shattered rubble. Smoke and the stench of corpses filled the gloom. Ahead, the battle raged. His men climbed behind him. Each picked his way on padded feet amongst the broken masonry. Every man sought refuge in the shadows.

The clash of arms ahead could have raised the dead.

Yet if a single sound betrayed their presence, or one person glimpsed them too early, their mission would fail before it even started.

The din of the battle drew closer. In the gloom, thousands of bashi-bazouks grappled with the Venetian and Genoese defenders in a chaos of grunts, blows, and screams. Yusuf held up his fist and tried to understand the ebbs and flows of the battle. If only he had more light!

As if in response, something whistled past and burst into flames, lighting up a mass of attackers fighting their way up the lower slopes of the rubble. Dozens of men dropped their weapons and screamed, scrabbling at the sticky, burning liquid that clung to their bodies and armour.

*Greek fire.*

Yusuf stood, transfixed. How could any assault succeed when the defenders wielded such magical, potent weapons?

Close by, the front line of the bashi-bazouks faltered. The defenders surged forward, hacking and stabbing their panicking opponents.

A hand gripped Yusuf's shoulder.

His deputy, Sinan, pointed to the fresh troops who had joined the defence. They wore the high-quality armour, helmets, and chain-mail of elite Venetian forces.

Yusuf threw his arm forward. As one, his men threw off their camouflage and rushed from the shadows into combat.

Yusuf targeted a stout Anatolian mercenary with no head protection and rudimentary armour. The man must have been fearless to advance so far with such primitive protection. He seemed astonished to see this new peril threaten from such an unexpected quarter. Yusuf's Venetian blade sliced through the Anatolian's leather singlet, and the man's blood gushed forth.

Yusuf had never killed a Turk in battle. It pained him to see the light die in a comrade's eyes. The poor bashi-bazouk never knew his death served a higher purpose than he could imagine.

Close by, a tall Venetian grappled with two attackers in full armour. Yusuf swept his sword across the unprotected backs of their ankles, sending both tumbling to the ground.

"Thank you." The Venetian, seeing a comrade, spoke to Yusuf in his own language.

"It is my honour," Yusuf replied in the same tongue.

The assault fell back against the powerful counter-attack. But some still fought. Yusuf gasped as a crossbow bolt slammed into his chest, but his Venetian chain-mail stood firm.

"The archers can complete this work. We shall regroup on the outer wall of the Mesoteichion." The tall Venetian raised his sword. "Back! Back!"

Along the line, dozens of armoured defenders disengaged from the enemy. Of his own eleven men, Yusuf counted six still standing, all in the distinctive Venetian armour and weaponry they had captured in the battles of the last month.

Sinan lived still. Karaca, a simple man but unstoppable in battle, survived too. The wild boar, they called him. Nasuh, the Albanian, sheathed his sword, his motions quick as lightning. Yazid, the Arab boy who had grown up in Greece, stepped alongside, silent but faithful. Keen-eyed Halil scanned the dark night for enemies. Evhad, one of the swimmers, wiped blood from his brow, his teeth white in the darkness. Yusuf breathed a sigh of relief. He must keep Evhad alive at all costs: Kemal, the second swimmer, had fallen.

Sword in hand, Yusuf led his men in retreat alongside the Venetian forces with whom they had merged, towards the interior of the city.

## 6

"I am telling you, Misty. Get out!"

Elif Mutlu grabbed the woman's shoulder and pulled. She repressed a smile: her hand, filthy from the excavation, left a dark smudge on the American's arm.

"Hey. Easy, sister. Don't you know about freedom of the media?" Misty Anderson took a step back and brushed at her diaphanous swirl-patterned blouse. Her hair was dyed red and brutally short, matching the slash of lipstick that lent colour to her pale features. "We are friends, aren't we?"

"We will brief the media tomorrow," Elif said. "But today, we must finish our excavation. We have to find—"

"The Palladium?" The journalist unslung her camera. As she interrupted Elif, she took a shot of her.

Elif stepped back, disoriented by the flash in the twilight of the tunnel. As she blinked, shapes seemed to form like ghosts in the air above the tombs.

She needed rest. But only a few hours remained to uncover the secrets of these tunnels, before Arzu Pasha buried them forever in concrete.

Misty Anderson leaned forward, her green eyes glittering. "You know the Palladium is here, I know you do. This site has been a treasure trove from the start. The whole city is waiting. Today is the day."

"There is no Palladium. Every minute you get under our feet, we lose time."

"Elif. Take it easy." Dervis Basturk unfolded his substantial body from the shadows, where he leaned against a stone arch. Had her pious colleague lost some weight, or was he dressing better? A new earring dangled from his ear. "We shall find every relic on this site by the end of today. Maybe we can dig out some more Byzantine relics before they close us down: the tooth of a saint, or some breast milk of the Virgin Mary in a jewelled case. But now, we need to dig."

On each side of the tunnel, twin rows of arches linked a series of antique vaults, each supported by thousands of thin red bricks set in a generous layer of mortar. Many of the vaults contained decorated marble tombs. In others, empty niches revealed smooth stone floors of close-fitting rectangular slabs. In some stones, iron rings lay flush in the centre of the masonry. A thick layer of earth and rubble insulated the underground passages from the traffic-choked highways of the city, creating a silent capsule of the past.

Nearby, the four young interns worked with fine tools and brushes on areas where they had raised the flagstones. The American student, Chloe, wore a red baseball cap with a matching shirt that emphasised her slim build. Lars, the long-haired German from the university of Aachen, worked close to Chloe. He glanced her way from time to time, eyeing her tight jeans. Stuart, the paraplegic Scottish boy, sat on a cushion, wielding his dust-brush with infinite patience. Olga, the young Russian with the blonde hair and the encyclopaedic knowledge of Scythian history, picked at something with an archaeology trowel.

Elif smiled. Then she caught her breath as a machine growled.

A steel cable with a hook came snaking down through a hole in the roof. Two thick-set workmen stumped down the passageway between the tombs, wearing yellow hard-hats and boots, followed by a clean-shaven man with a brilliant white shirt and tie under a fluorescent orange jacket. Even his construction boots looked fresh out of the box.

"Elif, good afternoon," the man in the tie said. "I would like to tell you that Arzu Pasha wants to know how the treasure hunt is going. But the truth is, she does not care. She has sent us to collect the rest of the sarcophagi and any other relics. She has ordered the engineers to start pouring the foundations at dawn. Your time is up." He kicked one of the stone tombs and jerked his chin at Misty Anderson. "I also have instructions to remove this idiotic American journalist. Where is your fat friend, Dervis, by the way?"

Elif looked around. The archaeologist had vanished. "I have no idea. Maybe he nipped up to ground level to use his phone."

Misty Anderson held her camera up in front of her like a shield. "Mehmet Ozdemir. Your boss, Arzu Pasha, is an animal."

Ozdemir withdrew a document from his pocket. "We have the permits we need to pour concrete today if we want. Would you prefer that?"

"But the whole world is waiting to see the mysteries these vaults conceal," the journalist said. "Surely, Elif must have told you about the inscription?"

"The whole of Turkey is full of inscriptions," Mehmet said.

Elif gritted her teeth. "Can you both clear off and let us excavate?"

"This inscription is different." Misty raised her voice. "The next slab Elif raises could reveal the most fabulous treasure in the world."

"No-one gives a toss what these dust-huggers dig up." Ozdemir seized the journalist's shoulder. "As for you, this is a construction site. Turkish law requires you to wear a helmet." He called the two workmen. "Kindly accompany Ms Anderson to the exit. Then get cracking on the sarcophagi."

One of the workmen frowned. "The what?"

"These stone boxes. They contain human remains. We have to remove them. No-one wants bones in their foundations."

"Mehmet." Elif fought to control her voice. "Some of these sarcophagi are over a thousand years old. For the love of human history, only trained archaeologists should move them."

"She's right!" Misty Anderson shouted back down the passageway as the workmen hustled her away. Her skull gleamed through her short red hair. "Wait until I publish my article about you burying the Palladium!"

The surveyor turned back to Elif. "Why not let us help you? I do not think you and your student friends are big on heavy lifting. We, on the other hand, have a winch."

"What difference will a few days make?" Elif gritted her teeth. "Leave us alone."

"Uh, Ms Mutlu." The German student, Lars, spoke from the floor where he knelt. "Take the help. These guys have muscle and machines."

"He's right. We took a day to raise the last sarcophagus lid," Chloe, the American, said.

"Thank you, Lars. Thank you, Chloe. Get on with the dig, will you?" Elif rotated her shoulders to ease the ache building there.

Ozdemir straightened his tie and lowered his voice. "Get out as fast as you can. Arzu Pasha would do anything to get rid of you. She is angry."

Dervis Basturk stepped out of the shadows. "Do not threaten us, Mehmet."

Elif started. Where had Dervis sprung from?

"Misty is right, this is something extraordinary," she said. "When Arzu Pasha first sent her bulldozers in, they uncovered ancient vaults and tunnels, crammed with bodies. Men, women, and children crowded up against each other, carrying gold, or holy relics. Perhaps they were hiding, then suffocated. Or burned. Maybe in one of the fires that followed the conquest in 1453."

"Let me see this stone with the inscription the American journalist keeps writing about." Ozdemir picked a speck off his white shirt. "What do you think is underneath?"

Dervis Basturk shook his head. "Misty Anderson has to make everything a sensation. For all we know, the bodies could be people hiding from the Christian crusaders when they sacked Constantinople in 1204. They were as bloodthirsty as anyone."

"The inscription is intriguing." Elif knelt down and shone a light on one of the rectangular stone slabs, carved with fine chisel marks and inset with an iron ring. "See here. It is in Greek."

Her finger traced the black letters scrawled upon the stone:

$$\text{δεῦτε αὖθι}$$

Ozdemir laughed. "So what? This was a Greek city for over a thousand years. Maybe it says *help*, or *I need a shag*."

"No. It means *Come hither. It is here.*" Elif brushed the slab with her fingertips. Touching the cool, dry stone seemed to restore her sense of calm. "Something special lies in this sarcophagus."

"Maybe the Palladium." Dervis Basturk shrugged; a self-conscious gesture. "Misty Anderson is not the only one who thinks we will find it."

"No-one serious believes in the Palladium!" The words came out louder than Elif intended. She stared at Dervis. Why was he creeping around in the dark, recycling Misty's stupid theories?

"I must go." Ozdemir looked at his watch. "But believe me, you will have more trouble than you can imagine if you are not out of here quickly. I would leave now, if I were you." He strode off.

"Get out, he says." Dervis watched Ozdemir disappear. "He may be right."

"Why did he rush away?" Elif said. "I do not trust him, or Arzu Pasha."

"We must be quick." Dervish glanced back up the tunnel.

"What are you so worried about?"

Dervis bit his lip and took a deep breath. "I am afraid, Elif *hanim*. We are unleashing forces we do not understand."

Elif wrapped her arms around herself and shivered. Had the temperature dropped in the tunnel? "Come on. Let us lift that slab. But first, I am going to text Orhan. I would like to have him here."

"Good idea," Dervis said. "Text that butch boyfriend of yours, too. You know what they say about the English. They always have a secret plan." He winked at Stuart, who sat with a trowel on the cushion next to a shallow excavation.

"Scottish. It was the Scots who built the British empire," Stuart said.

"Ex-boyfriend," Elif said. What had Savage told her last night? *I don't even know if love exists.* "I am going upstairs to text Orhan. Can you ask these workers to use their winch to lift the stone? As soon as I am back, we will move it."

"Elif. Be quick," Dervis said. "I want to know what is under that stone as much as you do. And then I want us all to leave."

# 7

1453

The bashi-bazouks Yusuf Ali-Bey had slain this night, in his disguise as a Venetian soldier, could have been sons of those warriors of the Sultan who, ten years earlier, had seized Yusuf himself, a boy of ten who spoke Greek and Venetian and went by the name of Pietro Goldini, from the Kingdom of Negroponte to the north of Athens.

Yusuf, like all Janissaries, was an elite fighter enslaved by the Ottomans as a Christian child and raised as a Muslim *Askeri*, the Sultan's fiercest and most loyal troops. Many of Yusuf's team spoke Greek from childhood. All spoke Venetian dialect. Their garb and weapons, stripped from corpses and prisoners in the past weeks, made them indistinguishable from the defenders with whom they had merged.

Chaos ruled on the summit of the battlements. A wilderness of destruction filled the Peribolos between the inner and outer wall: bodies, rubble, and the wreckage of war lay everywhere. Beyond rose the inner wall, black and forbidding in the night sky, its crest manned by sharp-eyed archers.

If the Janissaries penetrated this far, the Greeks and their Venetian allies would mow them down.

The Venetian infantry who had retreated from the hand-to-hand combat on the ramp of broken masonry ran into new positions atop the outer wall, while archers and gunners picked off the enemy beneath. The tall officer who had ordered the retreat directed fresh Byzantine reinforcements. Greeks, Genoese, and Venetians streamed out towards the battle, heads held high, through a postern gate at the base of a nearby tower.

Perfect.

Without breaking step, Yusuf led his men through the small gate and into the city beyond. No-one even glanced at the disciplined squad of Venetian soldiers as they set off across the open fields within the walls, towards a destination none of the defenders could possibly have imagined.

S avage stared at the barrel of the Beretta and, taking care to make no sudden movements, raised his hands.

"We don't have time for this," he said in English. "We must—"

"*Shut up!*" It was not the uniformed officer who barked the Turkish words, but Orhan Mutlu. "Out of the car. Hands behind your back. And nothing stupid, or so help me." The intelligence cop cracked the butt of his pistol into the roof of the car and yanked open the door.

Savage kept his face blank. "Okay, Okay." He stretched his long body out of the cramped space and turned towards the car, his arms held out behind him, palms up. "Mind the circulation," he murmured in English. "I need these hands later."

"Quiet!" Orhan ratcheted the cuffs tight and turned to the uniformed officer. "I have to deliver this guy to the Police Intelligence HQ in Eminonu," he said. "The MIT have questions for him."

"Better get a move on." The policewoman took a step back at the mention of the *Milli Istihbarat Teskilati*, Turkey's powerful National Intelligence Organisation. "I guess he will tell them what they want to know soon enough."

Orhan gripped Savage by the arm. "Come on, scum. Onto the boat with you. You won't like it where you're going, that's for sure."

Savage trudged towards the police boat, head bowed, the cuffs biting into his wrists. To submit to being rendered helpless contradicted every aspect of his training. What if Orhan double-crossed him? What if something happened to Orhan? But they must reach the European side of Istanbul fast.

Savage grunted as Orhan shoved him towards the quay. He stepped on board, smelling the fresh tang of the sea as the water lapped below the hull. Across the water rose the Old City, crowned by the Haghia Sophia and the great mosque of Sultanahmet.

Why had Elif called for help?

# 9

1453

Silence enveloped the band of disguised Janissaries as they moved away from the Theodosian Walls.

Behind them, the din of battle faded. Yusuf, the commander, led his men in a fast march down a paved track towards the city.

Had the inhabitants fled? To either side lay fields of mud and scrubland, filled with carts of war supplies and tethered horses. The doomed city of Constantinople lay ahead, hidden by the night.

The orders Yusuf and his men had sworn to execute would seal the fate of the great capital of the Christians.

Yusuf kept his hand on the hilt of his sword, scanning the darkness. No-one must thwart his mission.

Two weeks earlier, fate—or Allah—had brought the Greek officer into the hands of the Zagan Pasha.

After six weeks of attacks, despite the giant cannon, Basilica, and the reckless bravery of the bashi-bazouks and Janissaries, the Ottoman assault had faltered. Even the young Sultan Mehmet's miraculous transport of the Ottoman fleet across the heights of Galata into the Golden Horn had not achieved a breakthrough.

All the while, rumours abounded that the Hungarians had crossed the Danube to relieve the beleaguered city; or that a powerful Venetian fleet could arrive by sea, bearing supplies and thousands of fresh troops.

Zagan Pasha, on the Sultan's orders, had brought in German silver-diggers from Serbia to tunnel beneath the towering walls and destroy them with explosive mines.

To the dismay of the besiegers, even this strategy had failed: the Byzantines had dug counter-mines, intercepting and slaying the opposing tunnellers far beneath the surface. They said the Byzantine Emperor Constantine himself, seized of the threat the miners posed to the walls, had ordered his elite Greek squadrons into the tunnels to extinguish the danger.

That act had been the Emperor's undoing.

For during a counter-attack in the blackness of the tunnels, the Janissaries had captured a Greek officer, Panteleimon Metochites. When tortured, Metochites had revealed a secret that turned the conflict on its head.

The siege, Metochites had said, could never succeed. Even if the Sultan had a million troops and a thousand Basilica cannon, he could not take the city. A divine force protected Constantinople.

Zagan Pasha had laughed at the bravado of the captive officer. What mystical protection could stand against the might of Allah, the true God? Even the Virgin Mary, whose shape was said to appear on the battlements of Constantinople at times of crisis, had abandoned the city to its fate. It was told her icon had fallen to the filthy ground when paraded through the streets of the city a week before. No more awful omen could assail a city.

Yet Metochites had answered with the pride of a man who knows death is nigh but believes his cause will live forever. A force more ancient and potent than Allah or the Virgin, he said, guarded Constantinople. Even as his eyeballs lay shapeless on the beaten earth and fragments of his own teeth choked his throat, the Greek remained stalwart. Constantinople, he said, was protected by the Palladium: a holy relic, carved by the hand of Athena herself, Greek goddess of war and wisdom and defender of ancient Troy.

So long as the Palladium shielded Constantinople, the Greek said, the great city could never be harmed.

E lif Mutlu walked back down the tunnel. When would Orhan arrive? He had crossed to the Asian side this morning. Something to do with football, he had said. He must have received her text and puzzled over the urgency of the message. But what more could she have written?

What did Mehmet Ozdemir mean by his threats? Arzu Pasha's errand boy had hurried off, his orange fluorescent jacket brilliant in the lights of the underground excavation, as if his life depended on it. Did the property tycoon plan to close down the excavation by force?

The way Dervis kept disappearing, and his anxious glances into the darkness of the tunnel, unsettled Elif even more. The archaeologist had changed in recent weeks, as though he harboured his own set of secrets.

Maybe Arzu Pasha was right. Elif should let the tycoon bury everything in concrete. Sealing the site would settle this nonsense about the Palladium forever.

Back at the excavation, the workmen secured the steel hawser to the ring set in the slab. Dervis tied a cloth around the rusted metal to prevent damage to the stonework and the inscription.

*Come hither. It is here.*

What lay beneath the stone? Following the discovery of the pitiful bodies huddled in the vaults, the Turkish media had competed to come up with more graphic theories about how so many people had met their end. Had they died in an accident? Had someone sacrificed them in an ancient ritual? Might an antique potentate have committed an atrocity? If the latter, who had carried out the slaughter?

The fact many of the dead men, women, and children had clutched to their bodies items of immense worth had fuelled the hysteria.

The first body Elif found was a warrior, clad in Venetian armour, holding to his chest an exquisite silver reliquary box. A woman, her head on his shoulder, had worn around her neck a gold cross, inlaid with jewels. Others had taken with them to their death secular treasures: gold and silver coins, or a box crammed with gems and fragments of bone and teeth set in precious metals.

Elif and her team had sent all these discoveries to the workshops of the Archaeological Museum to be examined and, later, displayed in the new extension funded by Arzu Pasha. Did the property magnate feel shame for destroying Istanbul's heritage? Or did she think her public relations campaigns could persuade the people to give her credit for rescuing a few trinkets as she annihilated the ancient heart of the city?

Elif cared less about gold, silver, and holy relics than for the secrets the dead carried in their heads. How had they lived their lives? Who had they loved, and hated? What had pursued them when they gathered their most precious possessions and, in vain, sought refuge?

She thought she knew the answer. Before dispatching her discoveries to the museum, Elif had studied the coins.

The ancient money Elif raised from the crypt had included some singular prizes. Few coins compared in value and rarity with the gold Hyperpyron and Histamenon pieces, dating from the eleventh century. But dead hands also clutched more modern coins—silver Stavraton from the fourteenth century.

Those dates corralled the truth.

Dervis had been right to describe the sack of Christian Constantinople by the Fourth Crusade in 1204 as barbaric. The Crusaders had violated every church, convent, and monastery in the city.

But no-one taking refuge from a rampage in 1204 could have carried with them coins dating from centuries later.

Elif believed the people in the vaults had sheltered from the siege of 1453, when the great Mehmet the Conqueror terminated the thousand-year reign of the Byzantine Empire.

From the positions in which she had found them, none of the dead seemed to have died violently. They must have taken refuge in the basement of a church or monastery, only to be overcome by smoke or fumes when flames consumed the building. Silenced forever in their hiding place, the dead had been forgotten, like so many other subterranean mysteries of the ancient metropolis.

She placed her hand on the silent stone. What secret lay beneath?

"Here we go." Chloe held up her phone to record the scene. "The last sarcophagus in Istanbul."

"Cool." Lars held his phone up too. But he filmed Chloe. The semi-circle of young people couldn't tell the difference between a rock concert, a birthday party, or an archaeological dig. They recorded everything to experience later, instead of living in the moment. Elif sighed. In the shadows, Stuart, the young Scot, watched from his cushion. How he must long to put his shoulder to the slab and push! His wheelchair stood folded in one of the vaults nearby.

The workman tested the steel hawser. The cable held firm. Dervis leaned forward, his face almost fearful in its anticipation. Elif took a deep breath. What if nothing lay beneath?

*Come hither.*

She cleared her throat and spoke to the workman. "Okay. Lift."

"Lifting now." The workman depressed a button on an electric cable. The steel hawser tightened.

The great stone slab rose.

# 11

1453

Inside the walls, Yusuf held up his clenched fist. His companions fell silent. Around them, fields stretched, punctuated by overgrown ruins. Nearby, two tall columns rose, wreathed in ivy. To the north, near the walls, loomed buildings vaster than Yusuf imagined possible. Their goal lay to the east, close to where the Church of the Holy Wisdom rose above the city, still shrouded in darkness. Here, further west, trees grew through the roofs of many buildings, and birds nested in cold chimneys. Houses lay shuttered and abandoned, emptied not by the Sultan's siege but by some other, more ancient, crisis.

An ox-cart drew alongside them, picking its way towards the city. A woman drove the animal. Two small children huddled in the back.

Yusuf's men stirred at the sight of the defenceless woman. But they held their discipline.

"Where are you going?" Yusuf said.

"To the Holy Wisdom," the woman said. She urged the ox forward, eyeing the group of soldiers in the gloom. "It is our refuge."

They stood back and let the cart trundle on eastwards. Yusuf glanced up at the sky, but low clouds hid the stars he needed to navigate. He stared ahead. The greatest Christian church in all the world must come into sight soon: the landmark showed the way towards a goal he had never seen, in a city whose every inhabitant wished him dead. By nightfall, the church would be the world's mightiest mosque. All those seeking refuge within would perish or face the Sultan's mercy.

But only if Yusuf fulfilled his task.

In the distance, Basilica roared again. Reloading the huge gun took three hours. One hour remained before Hasan led the dawn attack. Yusuf led the men off the road into the rough, wet ground that marked the course of the River Lycus as they drew closer to the heart of the city.

# 12

"What the hell happened to you in the car?" Orhan Mutlu braked to avoid a boy no more than six years old who had darted into the road brandishing a stick stacked with *simits*, Istanbul's ubiquitous bagel prototype. "You were thrashing around like a madman. You could have been shot."

"You would never have got past that plod at the dock." Savage never spoke of Moscow. Even inside MI6 or the Foreign Office, few people knew what had happened in the Russian capital. "Now, we're across the water."

"I can tell when a man is lying. I know you do not care about Elif. If we are to work together, I need the truth. Otherwise, you can walk." Orhan Mutlu brought the unmarked police car he had picked up at the dock on the European side to a halt. "I shall be faster without you." He shook his head at the child, who approached the car window with his *simit*-stick. "Tell me, or get out."

"What are you waiting for? Elif needs us."

"Why do you care?" Orhan held his muscular arms crossed in front of him.

"She would rather die than ask for help," Savage said.

The car stood motionless. Ahead, the boy wandered into the middle of the traffic, brandishing his *simits*. One lane further across, two more boys stood selling bottles of water from crates at their feet. Cars shot past, barely missing the urchins. Sweet, choking fumes from Istanbul's diesel buses filled the air.

Both men sat, staring ahead as the traffic flowed around them.

Orhan glanced in the rear-view mirror, turned to Savage, then looked back at the mirror. "Tell me why you went crazy in the back of the car."

Savage closed his eyes. The muscles in his neck grew tight as his upper body tensed. "Get this car moving, or I'll break your bloody neck."

Orhan Mutlu shrugged and turned the ignition key.

"You will tell me about your strange behaviour eventually, I assure you. But now, we have to find Elif."

He gunned the engine and the car shot ahead, swerving up a crude concrete ramp to mount the curb, leaving the road and bumping across a patch of scrubby ground. Advertising billboards showed mock-ups of the towering apartment blocks to be built on the empty lot.

"You're a fool." Savage slammed his hand against the dashboard. "We lost over a minute."

"I had to stop so we could take this route," Orhan said. "Otherwise, the police car behind us would have pulled us over, and that really would have wasted time. Once he had passed by, I took off."

With a jolt, the car descended a second curb onto an unpaved track between two tall half-built office blocks swathed in scaffolding.

"If anything happens to Elif," Savage said, "I will kill you."

Orhan shook his head. "John. No-one cares about Elif more than I do. Least of all a dirty foreigner who wanted my sister for sex."

He switched the siren on and accelerated. The car barrelled into the entrance of a construction site. Without warning, the paved road ended and they skidded out of control across a quagmire of mud and water. Straight ahead, the ground dropped away, a raw-earth cliff edge into oblivion.

# 13

## 1453

The sky grew lighter in the east. Within the walls of Constantinople more buildings became visible. Yusuf placed his hand on the hilt of his sword and scanned the ruins for foes. What if Metochites, the captured Greek officer, had lied about the Palladium?

Yusuf's grandmother had lit up his imagination with tales of ancient Greece, year after year, during his childhood in Negroponte. He had asked her to tell him the story of the relic that made a city invulnerable again and again.

Mystery shrouded the origins of the Palladium. Legend said the virgin goddess Athena had fashioned the statuette out of sadness at killing her foster sister and best friend Pallas, daughter of the sea-god Triton, in a playful fight. The resulting image, representing the slain Pallas, was called a *Xoanon*: a statue not made by human hand.

Zeus, the king of the Greek gods, threw the Palladium to earth at Ilios, close to the straits of the Dardanelles. The city of Troy rose on the spot: the Trojans revered the Palladium, and housed the relic in the temple of Athena.

To a true Muslim like Yusuf, the Greek legends belonged in the mouths of shamans and storytellers.

No god existed but Allah.

Yet everyone knew the powers of heaven and earth surpassed all understanding. Just a few days before, darkness had blotted out the moon at its fullest glory for three long hours—an evil omen for one side or the other. The defenders of the city, for all their supposed Christian faith, believed Constantinople could only be conquered when the moon waned, as now. Since the siege began, earthquakes had shaken the walls; hailstorms had lashed the city; an unseasonal fog had risen from the Sea of Marmara; and strange lights had danced around the dome of the Church of the Holy Wisdom itself.

Who knew what mystic, ancient power lived in a sacred object?

Every soldier and strategist knew no besieging force had ever conquered a city housing the Palladium.

No wonder they called the relic The Luck of Troy.

Greek forces had besieged the city for ten long years before Odysseus and Diomedes stole the sacred *Xoanon* from the temple of Athena and smuggled it beyond the walls.

Within a year, the victorious Greeks had razed Troy to the ground.

From Ilios, the Palladium travelled to Greece. Then the *Xoanon* disappeared. Some said the Romans had stolen it. Others said the desecration of Rome and the long, slow decline of the Western Roman Empire proved the Palladium had never reached the great imperial city.

Under torture, Panteleimon Metochites revealed the truth. The Roman Emperor Constantine the First had removed the Palladium from Rome in the year 330, when he founded the new capital of the Eastern Empire on the Bosphorus.

No wonder the Goths and Vandals had sacked ancient Rome a few years later.

No wonder Constantinople had stood unconquered for a thousand long years.

Constantine, Metochites said, had hidden the Palladium at the base of a tall porphyry column built in the heart of a circular forum named after himself, close to the Church of the Holy Wisdom. A golden statue of Constantine crowned the column, his crown blazing with glory in the rays of the rising sun.

Metochites had sworn to reveal no more about the Palladium to his captors. Two days later, the removal of his fingers, toes, eyes, ears, and other parts of the Greek's anatomy, proven to have an effect in loosening even the most stubborn tongues, persuaded him to reveal all he knew.

As the vast Ottoman fleets and armies surrounded Constantinople, Metochites sobbed, the Emperor—the eleventh man to bear the name Constantine since the city's founding—had begun to fear one thing above all else. He dreaded Ottoman spies entering the city, as Odysseus and Diomedes had crept into Troy, and stealing the Palladium.

Without the protection of the relic, the walls and armies of Constantinople meant nothing.

Four weeks before, in the silence of the night, a team of workmen had excavated the Palladium from its resting place of a thousand years at the base of Constantine's column. They had moved the relic to a more secure, hidden, location.

The Sultan's torturers had persuaded Metochites to reveal that secret place.

But had he told the truth?

# 14

In the vault, the stone slab inched upwards. A sliver of age-dried dirt flaked loose and fell to the ground. Dust shimmered in the floodlights.

Black shadows sprang up beneath the stone.

"Slowly!" Elif's throat was as dry as the swirling dust. "Lars, Chloe. Put those stupid phones away and get ready to push the slab laterally. Mind your fingers. It weighs over a ton. Olga and Stuart, watch and take notes on what you see."

Lars, the German, scowled as Chloe pocketed her phone.

"Keep up to date," he said. "Your pal, Misty Anderson, has put another story on-line saying you are about to find the Palladium. She has been writing about the 'Lost Treasure of Troy' for days. She has published a picture of the inscription."

"I can't stand that woman, and I don't care what she writes." Elif licked her lips. "Push the stone. And lose the phone."

Lars propped his device on a ledge across the passage to continue filming. "We do not want to miss the climax, do we?" he said. He knelt close to Chloe and put his shoulder to the marble.

"Wait until it is free of the base." Elif held up her hand. The chiselled lower edge of the slab rose into view. The fine stonework was a monument to the expertise of whatever long-dead Byzantine craftsmen had designed and built the vault. A little more...there. At last, the stone hung clear.

"Get ready to push!"

The excitement made her voice rise. Like a schoolgirl. If only John Savage were here to witness this moment. Elif stamped on the idea. *I cannot care about you,* he had said last night. At least Orhan would be here soon. She stepped forward, breathing deeply, looked up at the workman with the winch control, and made a throat-cutting gesture. "That is high enough."

The steel hawser froze. Elif knelt alongside the two young archaeology students. "Now," she whispered. "One, two, three...push!"

Suspended from the cable, the great slab moved aside more smoothly than Elif expected. The other workman left on site by Mehmet Ozdemir had looped a length of rope around the hawser. He pulled hard, boots braced against the earthen floor, then secured the rope to a rusted iron peg set in the wall.

"Thanks," Elif said. The pressure of the slab eased against her shoulder.

"No problem," the workman said. He pushed back his yellow construction helmet as if to signal he had completed the hard part of the work. "Go on. Why not take a look underneath?"

Elif blinked. The workman was right. Why look at him, rather than explore the void beneath the slab? Why must one of Mehmet's men help her focus? Did she fear what lay beneath?

Or did she fear finding nothing?

By trailing whatever lay beneath the stone as the *Lost Treasure of the Byzantines*, Misty Anderson probably wanted to help. Maybe the journalist hoped to use publicity about the so-called Palladium as a weapon to slow down Arzu Pasha's efforts to bury the site under a shopping mall. But if the dig revealed nothing, Elif, not Misty, would end up looking a fool.

*Come hither. It is here.*

Why write such an inscription, if the finely-wrought slab hid nothing special?

Or was the scrawl someone's idea of an elaborate Byzantine joke?

She took a deep breath, switched on her helmet-lamp, and peered into the void.

*Oh, no.*

A deep, broad, rectangular space carved from a single piece of fine, white marble lay beneath the raised slab. A wealthy Byzantine citizen must have commissioned the sarcophagus as his or her final resting place. In other, similar voids, she had discovered Byzantine chests filled with valuables.

But the void gaped, nearly empty. At one end, a couple of earthenware dishes and beakers stood together, as if set out for a meal. At the other, a bundle of rags and clothing lay bunched up into a ball. The remains reminded her of something.

Elif leaned forward, her arms opened wider. "Wait! Back. Everyone. I need more light."

The object at the end of the sarcophagus was not a random clump of fabric. The mummified body of a child lay curled up in a foetal position, clutching something to its breast.

Clutching—what?

# 15

1453

The testimony of the captured Greek officer, Metochites, had launched Yusuf on his mission.

A cock crowed as the Janissary peered ahead. What if he risked his life, and that of his men, for nothing? What if Zagan Pasha had based his strategy on the incoherent ramblings of a man ready to say anything to end the torment racking his body?

The dome of the Church of the Holy Wisdom lay due east.

"Where is everyone?" Yusuf's deputy, Sinan, whispered in his ear in the Venetian dialect, although the street was deserted. "I thought this was a city of millions."

"They must have fled when they heard us coming." Yusuf licked his lips and forced a grin. "All the men are on the ramparts. The women are taking shelter. Soon the men will be dead, and the women will be ours."

A walled group of buildings rose on the left. A church or monastery, Yusuf guessed. They must be close.

They entered a public square so magnificent that Yusuf and his men stopped, dumbfounded. To the east, an arch marked the path of a broad avenue. Other wide streets led south and west. For hundreds of paces on every side, archways and porticos stretched, filled with stone figures. Some lay prostrate where trees and bushes pushed apart the masonry. In the centre of the square stood four blackened metal legs, perhaps the remains of an ancient statue of an animal. Nearby, a figure dangled from a gibbet.

The Forum of the Ox.

Their destination lay only a few minutes distant.

"Giants must have built this place." Sinan gestured towards the stone figures. "And the devil filled every span with icons."

"Ignore them." Yusuf gazed east. "We must go two hundred paces beyond the arch. Then one hundred south."

"We will be slaughtered like chickens if they find us here."

"We had better keep moving, then, hadn't we?"

An old man sat beneath the archway, holding out a hand. Yusuf hesitated between giving the beggar alms to show the generosity of his people, and putting him out of his misery before the city fell. Instead, he hurried past.

They entered a wide avenue lined with tall, stone-built houses, shops, and public buildings. More people appeared: women and children gazed from doors and windows as he and his men passed. They seemed relieved to see the Venetian soldiers. Little did they know they witnessed their own doom, penetrating the heart of the ill-starred city.

## 16

G azing into the open sarcophagus, Elif Mutlu held her breath. A bubble of calm surrounded her, containing only herself, the child in the tomb, and whatever the infant had protected.

Elif leaned into the sarcophagus and, with the fingers of one gloved hand, eased a strand of hair away from the child's face.

A soft, rounded profile looked back at her, set in an expression of extraordinary serenity.

A girl.

Elif understood.

The child had fled whatever catastrophe had overtaken the city. When a desperate band of fugitives gathered in the vault, she had persuaded the others to seal her in a sanctuary within a sanctuary: inside the sarcophagus itself, along with a pathetic last meal.

To keep safe the object she held clasped to her breast.

Had the girl, or those around her, sensed she protected something unique? Was that why someone had scrawled a message on the lid of the sarcophagus?

Perhaps as they did so, noxious smoke had penetrated the space, filling the passageways and consigning the tiny refugee to oblivion, along with those who had hidden her.

What had the girl protected, to persuade her fellow fugitives to hide her beneath the great stone slab?

"What's the big secret?" Lars stepped forward, pushing the hair out of his eyes, and stood above her staring down into the tomb. "Oh." The German frowned. "More bones."

*"Stand back!"*

The vehemence of her reaction astonished Elif. In a single sweep, she pushed back hard against the tall student's legs. In the crowded corridor, Lars stumbled back onto the upright edge of a wooden sieve tray, catapulting the opposite side upwards into the back of his own knee. With a yelp, he toppled backwards into the darkness.

Ignoring the laughter and scrabbling sounds behind her, Elif leaned forward, focusing the light of her helmet on the curled-up body in the tomb. A blanket or scarf, stiff with age, covered the lower abdomen and legs. Elif lifted one side of the fabric with the corner of her trowel.

A foot appeared. Then a tibia, still covered with dried-up remnants of skin and flesh. Finally, the all-important femur.

She took the measure from her pocket and stretched the tape from one end of the thigh-bone to the other. A fraction under thirty centimetres. A standard calculation made the girl one hundred and twelve centimetres tall. She must have been six or seven years old.

Was she a high-born princess, or an emperor's daughter, allocated a special hiding place?

Yet where the girl's clothing had crumbled, no gold or other ornament remained. The earthenware at the far end of the sarcophagus did not resemble the bejewelled precious metals associated with the late Byzantine dynasties.

Perhaps the bundle the child clutched offered a clue. Had she taken to her death a relic? Or a doll?

Elif stretched her hand into the tomb. Whatever the girl clutched was the reason for her being in the sarcophagus.

Her arms must shield a relic.

She reached down and eased her fingers around the package. It came away easily, as if the girl had wanted to offer the object up to her, rather than Elif taking the bundle from long-dead hands. The mummified face of the child seemed almost to be smiling.

Elif shook her head. One mystery and her imagination had run away with her. Mediaeval Christians had ascribed mystical powers to countless fragments of bone, wood, or indeterminate substances scattered across the region, their origins lost in the mists of time. They had venerated alleged saints' teeth, holy bones, or pieces of the True Cross for their healing powers or protective properties.

Other fabulous prizes, such as the legendary Holy Grail, had remained forever over the horizon.

Elif felt the weight of the object through its wrapping. Something solid pressed against her hands, too large for any supposed fragment of the True Cross.

If only she could examine what she held! But if the relic were fragile, the object itself could be entangled in the fabric that had protected it for hundreds of years. The very act of removing a covering could damage beyond repair a delicate piece of wood or leather.

A pattern ran around the edge of the cloth, embroidered, or perhaps woven.

The experts from the Archaeological Museum would want to examine the relic in their laboratories. Elif must ensure she was present in the room when the time came; and that she received the proper credit for her discovery.

Without her, Arzu Pasha's bulldozers would long ago have sealed the whole site in concrete forever, undiscovered.

Elif let the bundle rest in her hands. A sacred cloth or scroll weighed less; a gold or silver relic, more.

That left wood or ivory. Again, the strange certainty washed over her. The substance must be one or the other. A wooden relic could mean anything from iron-hard, aged timber to a meringue of insects and mould ready to crumble to dust. Ivory might be better preserved. Perhaps she could glimpse something in the folds of the fabric without unwrapping it. She peered at the object. The light on her helmet penetrated the shadows cast by the protective fabric.

"Hey!" Lars again. If only the boy could keep quiet. "What do you think—"

A loud click cut off the German's voice.

Something fell to the ground. Behind Elif, someone screamed.

Holding the ancient package in her arms, Elif Mutlu turned towards the sound.

# 17

## 1453

Two hundred paces beyond the Forum of the Ox, Yusuf and his men reached an alley on the right. Yusuf entered. Straight ahead, the Sea of Marmara glittered, waves black beneath the dark sky.

"Halt! Who goes?"

Two men stepped from the shadow of an arch. Both wore the insignia of Greek infantry and spoke their language.

"My name is Pietro Goldini, of Venice," Yusuf said. "We are assigned to strengthen the defences at the harbour."

The shorter of the two men spoke in a commanding voice. He wore his hair in a white mane. A broad, well-fitting metal breastplate covered his chest. An old soldier. The other, more boy than man, wore a farmer's smock and carried in his hand a spear too long to use in the confined space. As his stout-chested companion stepped forward, the boy's eyes widened and he tightened his grip on the spear.

"Return to the Mese and go west," the older man said. "None shall pass here."

"Very well." Yusuf turned as if to go, then whirled around, sword drawn, to strike his helmless opponent in the neck.

But the white-haired man, for all his years, moved like lightning. He ducked to his left, pushing his companion behind him, and unsheathed a short, gleaming sword.

"Enemies!" he cried. "Fetch help!"

## 18

Ali Aydin, the Controller, knew a display of strength marked the first step to achieving authority. The Protocol stated you must never use firearms lightly. Guns spewed out a torrent of forensic evidence, like a patient on an operating table vomiting blood: from ballistics and serial numbers to powder burns and oil traces. To discharge a firearm was like making an unscrambled call using a registered phone with the GPS switched on.

But the single shot from the silenced pistol in the tunnel under the building site established Ali's mastery of the archaeological dig better than any lesser show of force.

Power surged through his body.

The unexpected use of the winch to raise the coffin lid had saved the archaeologists hours of work, forcing Ali to bring forward the first phase of today's operation. The shot compromised the pistol. But by tonight the weapon, together with Ali, everyone else present in the tunnel, and even the tunnel itself, would be annihilated.

Ali's first shot had struck in the heart a student in a red cap named Chloe: an American, by her accent. In addition to the corpse and the two targets, Ali counted five people. His Makarov PPM pistol held eleven further rounds.

The plan remained on track.

Ali gestured with two fingers towards the exit tunnel. Hussein, wiry and athletic, his face hidden by a black silk mask, moved to block the path. He kept his large-calibre AKM assault rifle trained on the terrified group of archaeologists and workers.

They could not know Hussein had no intention of using the automatic weapon except *in extremis*.

Too noisy. More evidence.

Hussein stepped closer to the tunnel wall, away from Ali's firing line. He held the long barrel of his weapon steady.

"Who are you?" Target One spoke with a soft, calm voice. Like a teacher in a classroom rather than a helpless woman facing two masked gunmen. She spoke in English: a good guess, but random. For all she knew, Ali could be French, from an Arab country, from Italy, Russia, Turkey, or practically anywhere.

He did not reply. The spoken word could be evidence, too.

Words took time. They created distraction. Words could kill: now, or years later.

Ali took a deep breath, captured the scene in his mind, and prepared to act. With himself and Hussein in place, they had brought the situation under control, despite the early start. Nothing must stand in their way. He owed this duty to his God.

Ali fired the Makarov, squeezing the trigger in a regular, familiar rhythm, aiming to kill.

One: the squat building worker whose position at the rear of the group made him the hardest shot if anyone moved. Two: the second worker, a heavily-built man Ali rated the most likely to disrupt his plans. Three: the male German student, Lars, who had interrupted Target One as she sought to complete her excavation. Four: the second young male, with the crippled legs. Five: the second female student, her pretty face framed in blonde hair turned towards him, pleading in a language Ali did not understand.

All six bullets, placed in the chest, caused fatal internal bleeding. Ali never missed. All his shots struck the heart or organs close to it.

But, as planned, his ammunition clip contained six more shots.

In his life, Ali had experienced more deaths, even of the faithful, than he could bear. Now, thanks to The Protocol, he could redeem himself.

He nodded to Hussein. *Hold your position.* He held up his hand to Targets One and Two. *Do not move.* Target Two, his face swarthy, a jewel glistening in his ear, raised his trembling arms above his head.

Target One clutched to her body with one hand the object she had taken from the tomb. She held her other hand in the air, loosely, as though she did not believe he threatened her.

Wrong.

She faced an unimaginable terror.

Moving lightly for his size, Ali stepped forward, picking his way between the bodies, and shot each victim again, once, in the head. He nodded to Hussein, moved behind Targets One and Two, and prepared to initiate the next part of The Protocol.

# 19

In the narrow passage, only the commander, Yusuf, could engage with the veteran warrior who blocked their way. The man's sword could not match Yusuf's Venetian armour; the first blow of the Janissary's blade connected with the Greek's bare neck, producing a deep cut and a bellow of rage. The man fell towards Yusuf, grabbing him around the waist.

A searing pain shot through Yusuf's thigh.

The Greek must have held a knife in his left hand. He had buried the short blade in Yusuf's leg at the top of the protective steel.

He had sacrificed his life to delay Yusuf and his men.

The second Greek disappeared down the passageway, leaving his absurd spear behind him. Yusuf raised his sword and thrust the blade deep into the back of his white-haired assailant. The man's body went slack.

"Quickly." Yusuf struggled to stand, bracing himself against a low arch in the wall. He waved Sinan past. "Catch that boy, or our quest is lost. Evhad! Not you."

The others surged past. Blood soaked Yusuf's leg. Numbness crept down his thigh. The limb refused to bear his weight. He grabbed the boy's spear and tried using the shaft as a makeshift crutch. But he could not move.

"Come." The swimmer, Evhad, placed Yusuf's arm around his shoulder and helped his commander limp around the corner. A small, brick-built church stood in a wide square.

Sinan returned. "We could not catch him." Yusuf's deputy gasped for breath. "We have a few minutes. No more. What are we to do?"

"We must retrieve the Palladium," Yusuf said. He gestured towards the church. "We are at the Myrelaion. The icon lies beneath."

## 20

A li Aydin motioned towards the exit tunnel. Hussein paced ahead, relishing his role as the muscle in the operation. He paused where daylight entered the shaft. Ali motioned to Target One and Target Two to follow Hussein.

The woman did not move.

"He wants us to go, Elif." Target Two spoke Turkish, which Ali understood. "It is a kidnap. Do as he says." The man's bushy eyebrows rose in a parody of fear. Was he a homosexual? Why did a pious man wear an earring?

"They will not shoot us. They would have killed us already if they wanted to." Target One spoke in her teacher's voice.

Ali had planned for everything. He ejected the spent clip from his pistol and reloaded, pressing the fresh ammunition into place with gloved fingers.

"Who has paid you to commit this atrocity?" the woman said. "Arzu Pasha? I despise conspiracy theories, but this—"

Ali fired.

The sound of the silenced pistol was no louder than a door closing.

But Target One fell silent.

Ali aimed his shot a fraction above the raised hand of Target Two. An injured captive posed a series of problems, even if the wound were not life-threatening. Injuries, too, left evidence: traces of blood, fragments of flesh or bone.

Target Two jerked his hand away as though Ali had shot off a finger.

"For pity's sake!" Target Two's voice trembled. He gesticulated at the bodies on the ground as he addressed Target One. "Do you want us to end up like them?"

"We may as well die here as somewhere else." Still the woman sounded calm. "The trick is to delay. Do what they don't want."

Ali shook his head. He raised the pistol again, aiming slightly lower.

Target Two flinched. He turned and stumbled down the passageway. "You die here if you want," he said. "I am staying alive as long as I can."

"Why us?" Target One said. Moving without haste, she followed her colleague, still addressing Ali. "Why so much death? Can you not speak behind those masks?"

Ali said nothing. Ahead, Hussein approached the ramp to the surface, his AKM relaxed and ready in his arms.

The woman cradled the object from the grave like her own child. Did she realise she had it?

He checked his watch. The interventions of the German student and the woman's resistance meant they had waited in the tunnel five minutes longer than planned. Before that, the construction workers' use of cables had forced Ali to start the day's events hours ahead of the time The Protocol specified. Even now, a delay increased the risk of failure. What if the security forces intervened?

Ali eased his muscular shoulders and touched the pistol at his waist. The police knew nothing.

Hussein climbed the ramp ahead. He beckoned the others. At the rear, Ali glanced back. In the tunnel, the bright lights of the excavation illuminated a still-life of corpses, like a Rembrandt. Plenty for the forensic team to waste their time on.

Target One and Target Two reached the surface. Ali followed, his pistol drawn inside his jacket. The yellow stolen taxi with the fake plates stood where they had left it.

Sixty seconds of walking lay ahead, across the broken ground of the construction site.

Sixty seconds of exposure.

Ali's boots picked up clumps of mud as he walked. He glanced around the building site, ahead to the captives, up at the windows overlooking them.

Hussein reached the taxi, shepherding Targets One and Two ahead of him. Ali had nearly caught up. A drop of sweat trickled down his brow. He exhaled and reached to open the door of the yellow car.

*Whoop-whoop-whoop.*

Ali froze.

How could anyone come so quickly?

On the far side of the construction site, between two half-completed buildings, an unmarked police car raced towards them, siren wailing.

# 21

## 1453

Yusuf stood at the entrance to the square at the Myrelaion with his deputy Sinan and the swimmer, Evhad. On the far side, the remainder of the disguised Janissaries clustered around the alley leading south.

"Is that it?" Sinan stared at the tiny church. "Why here?"

"It is because of what lies beneath." Yusuf hobbled into the square, supported by Evhad. A trail of blood followed him, coursing down his injured leg.

"Your time has come," he said to Evhad. "You, others," he shouted to the Janissaries. "Guard the entrances."

Stocky Karaca, the wild boar, crossed to the north to stand guard at the entrance to the courtyard. The remaining three, faithful Yazid, keen-eyed Halil, and Nasuh the quick, took up position at the mouth of the south alley, down which the boy had fled to seek help.

In front of the church stood an ancient well. Carvings adorned its marble sides, so worn with age that Yusuf could not tell whether the designs depicted icons or simply decorations. The round base rose from titanic stone slabs, each three paces or more in length.

The shaft of the well disappeared into blackness.

"Is this the place?" Evhad, the swimmer, looked down into the dark.

"This is it." Yusuf glanced at Sinan, who took an oil lamp from his tunic, lit it, and placed the trembling flame in the bucket of the well. The guttering light illuminated Evhad's beardless chin and thin lips.

"You are strong," Yusuf said. "The Sultan will reward you."

"I am strong." Evhad's voice was no more than a whisper. He

slipped off his clothes. His shallow chest rose and fell as he braced himself on the lip of the well, staring down into oblivion.

"The co-ordinates are four north, two east," Yusuf said.

"I know this." Evhad gazed at Sinan, then at Yusuf. His young eyes shone bright with courage. "Goodbye."

He turned, climbed into the well so his hands supported him on each side, and let himself drop into the darkness.

## 22

Savage braced himself as the vehicle slewed sideways towards the deep excavation at the entrance to the construction site. Orhan spun the steering wheel one way and the other and the car recovered traction, shooting forward into a water-filled ditch and throwing up a wall of brown sludge before coming to a halt.

Both men leapt from the car. The site looked more like an open-cast mine than an archaeological dig. Ahead lay an immense pit lined with steel pilings, its base populated with brightly painted construction machinery. Battered eight-wheel trucks loaded with rubble ground their way towards a ramp, toy-like in the distance. Nearer to them, small-scale equipment rose from a wilderness of low, broken buildings and exposed stone arches. That must be the dig. Beyond, a group of people surrounded a yellow city taxi.

Three men and a woman.

The woman wore shorts and a baggy khaki shirt.

"Orhan!" Savage hissed. The Turk reached into the car and pulled out a pair of binoculars.

One of the men carried a weapon. Some kind of Kalash. He and the other man pushed the woman into the back seat of the car. She struggled. Then she slumped. Had the second man struck her? Could that be a pistol in his hand? The third man walked around to the other side of the taxi and climbed into the front passenger seat. He looked more like a third kidnapper than another hostage.

Orhan stared at the taxi through the binoculars. "Fiat taxi," he said. "Istanbul plates. First two letters are TE something. But they will be fake." He threw the binoculars back in the car and ran across the building site, zig-zagging between construction machinery, shafts, and concrete pilings.

Savage ran alongside, his feet sinking into the soft earth. "Can you call it in? Seal off the road? Are you sure the plates are fake?"

"It is certain. Istanbul taxis have registration numbers on their doors. The sides of the taxi are bare, because they have stripped off the numbers. The plates will be fake. I think the woman is Elif."

"Elif and three men, one with an AK."

Orhan clutched his Beretta. "I could hit the car from here. But Elif is inside. Too risky."

"Is the fastest route across the site through the excavation?"

"Yes." Orhan pointed to a pile of rubble by a large generator and sprinted towards it.

They splashed through mud towards an incline that descended into darkness, then plunged down the slope into a passage with vaults leading off to both sides.

Ahead, lights blazed.

"Oh, no." Orhan stopped.

Bodies lay strewn across the ground. Savage counted six: two young women and two young men, one lying across a kind of cushion. Further back sprawled two older men in construction workers' overalls. In the glare of the construction lights and the shadows in between, the bodies looked posed, like some macabre artwork. "Chest and head shots," Savage said. "Executed."

Orhan shook his head. "Who would shoot a bunch of archaeologists?"

"Wait," Savage said.

On a ledge across the passage stood a white smartphone, propped up as though observing the scene.

Orhan peered at the phone.

"The screen is blank." The intelligence officer took a cloth from his pocket and picked up the device by its sides. "It could be recording. We will need a code to access it."

"Leave the forensics to the lab. Our job is to catch the bastards." Savage moved towards the exit.

"I must call an ambulance." Orhan took out an evidence bag and slipped the phone inside. He knelt down to feel the pulse of a young man, his body lying half across a woman.

"Quickly." Savage grabbed Orhan's arm. "They have Elif."

The Turk shook him off. "These people have rights, too."

"Rights? They're corpses. Your sister could still be alive."

"You are correct. They are dead." Orhan stood. "We have to stop that taxi." They picked their way through the bodies and ran up the steep ramp beyond.

In seconds, they reached ground level. Orhan cursed.

They had emerged at the spot where they had seen the gunman forcing Elif to enter the yellow taxi. Nothing remained but tire tracks in the mud.

# 23

1453

Yusuf stood at the well outside the Myrelaion. A splash came from the darkness below.

"I am here." The voice of the swimmer, Evhad, seemed to echo in a vast space. "Give me light."

With a steady hand, Yusuf's deputy, Sinan, lowered the bucket with the oil lamp. For a few spans, the flickering rays illuminated the smooth stone sides of the well. Then, nothing but water, glistening in the light of the lamp like a subterranean lake.

"Yes. I see a cistern. Columns." Evhad's face gleamed pale in the water. "Where is north?"

Yusuf pointed. Without a word, Evhad swam out of sight.

"Away from that well!"

A tall Greek emerged from the passage to the north, a crossbow in his hand. The body of brave Karaca lay at his feet, an arrow in his neck. He must have fallen while Evhad's cries distracted them.

Without another word, the Greek steadied the crossbow and fired. The projectile hit Sinan in the eye. He tumbled backwards, releasing the rope. Yusuf grabbed at it, but the bucket struck the water, extinguishing the oil lamp

From across the courtyard, Nasuh rushed at the Greek, who dropped the crossbow and fled back up the alley.

"Stay." Yusuf tried to shout, but could only croak. "We must keep together."

He looked around the courtyard. Two entrances. Both harboured enemies. A spasm of pain shot down his leg.

"Evhad!" he cried down the well. "Do you have it?"

No reply.

"Evhad! The light is out. Come to my voice."

Only the swirling of the water answered him.

"Evhad! Come."

"I am here." The voice sounded from below him. "I have it. Raise the bucket."

Behind Yusuf, the clash of arms rang out in the passageway. He hauled up the rope, wincing as pain shot through his leg. The container was too light. Had the prize slipped into the water?

At last the bucket reached the lip of the well.

He reached inside the damp pail.

There.

A hard block, wrapped in some kind of cloth or leather, no more than a span or two in length, thinner at one end.

Yusuf leaned against the edge of the well and clutched the object to his breast. He had accomplished his mission. He held in his arms the statue of Pallas, carved by the hand of the Goddess Athena.

## 24

E lif Mutlu opened her eyes and fought for breath.

Something obstructed her mouth. A blanket.

She remembered.

They had forced her down into the space behind the front seat of the car, her face against the foul-smelling rubber floor mat, and thrown something over her.

Before the taxi even moved, she had tried to jump up and open the door.

Her captors had rewarded her with a terrific blow to the head from a hard object. She had fallen back, dazed.

Beneath the blanket, Elif blinked. A car engine rumbled, but nothing moved. Something dug into her chin. She eased her head to one side. A fat roll of silver duct tape lay on the rubber mat.

They had not yet bound her.

Something had disrupted her captors' plans. A police siren had sounded in the distance as they bundled her into the taxi. Could Orhan have come to save her?

Her brother had once told her twenty thousand yellow taxis plied their trade in the city. But Istanbul traffic could paralyse any street. Orhan might still catch them.

From outside, the taxi looked like any other.

She must draw attention to the vehicle. But how?

She gritted her teeth and drew in a breath of foul air. How could Dervis be sitting in the front seat? In the tunnel at the building site, her devout colleague had seemed consumed by fear. Each time one of their captors waved a gun, he had jumped. The terrorist had nearly shot his hand off.

Both attackers had worn masks. The man with the pistol, overweight perhaps but muscular and full of authority, must be in charge. The second man was taller, slightly built, and moved like an athlete. When the taller man had shoved Elif down into the car, she had glimpsed Dervis standing on the opposite side, shaking his head.

He must have been in shock.

Since then, she had seen nothing of her friend and colleague.

Inside the taxi, no-one spoke. The radio spat bursts of static. Underneath her body, the object from the sarcophagus dug into her. Did her attackers know she had carried the relic to the taxi? They had not referred to it.

It could not be a coincidence that two armed men appeared the second she lifted the cloth-wrapped bundle from the tomb. How had they timed their arrival so perfectly?

Could Ozdemir have summoned the terrorists after he left?

Or had Dervis called them, when he disappeared from the tunnel for a few minutes?

Their captors must need her, Elif, alive. The kidnapping must be something to do with the relic. But what?

None of it made sense.

The pain pulsed in her head. She raised her hand to check for blood, then arrested the movement, lest she prompt another blow. The taxi inched forward. They must have turned right, heading towards the Old City.

Why drive into the most congested part of Istanbul? Afternoon traffic choked the streets, from construction trucks to taxis, city buses, scooters, and tourists out to explore the Grand Bazaar, the Burnt Column, the Hippodrome, or other wonders of the ancient district. Some tourists might even be searching for the Bodrum Cami: a tiny mosque, converted from a Byzantine church, which sat atop a sixth century Roman water cistern.

The Greeks had called it the Myrelaion.

The taxi stuttered forward and stopped again.

The attackers had shown ruthless efficiency in the tunnel. They must have foreseen the traffic. What did they plan next?

Elif closed her eyes. The bundle pressed against her body, solid and reassuring. The pain in her head faded. Did the hostage-takers plan to make for the teeming warren of the Grand Bazaar? But police always stood guard at the entrances to the Ottoman structure. The crush of tourists and traders would make any kind of coercion impossible.

Ahead, past the Hippodrome, lay the Blue Mosque, the Haghia Sophia, and the Topkapi Palace: the heart of Istanbul's tourist zone.

Beyond lay the Bosphorus, the deep channel of ocean water that separated Europe from Asia.

The Bosphorus. Her captors must be heading there.

She must stop them from reaching it.

Her captors wanted her alive. That gave her power.

Nearby, Orhan and a force of Istanbul police officers could be combing through the gridlocked traffic, searching each yellow taxi for anything suspicious. Had Orhan told John Savage she had vanished?

Why should he? Savage did not give a damn either way.

Any moment now, the traffic might ease. In seconds, the taxi could vanish into the twenty-million-strong city of Istanbul.

Elif might never get another chance.

The duct tape lay ready.

The idea of being bound, helpless, by her captors made her nauseous. Yet she must act.

Flexing her aching leg muscles, Elif pushed herself up from the seat-well, hammered on the window with the palm of her hand, and scrabbled to open the door of the taxi.

Her hand grasped thin air. They had removed the door handle.

Outside the window rose the side of a white delivery van, advertising a brand of pet-food. No police. No pedestrians. No other driver to see her plea for help.

She twisted around. Dervis sat in the front seat, looking ahead.

Could he be drugged? Or dead? Or a part of all this?

"Dervis," she said.

Strong hands seized her head front and back, a wet cloth covering her face.

*No air. Cold.*

She took a deep breath through her mouth. Nausea rose and her throat convulsed. In response, the pressure on her face eased and she took a second, reflex breath through her nose.

*Sweet. Faint.*

Elif did not feel the strong hands forcing her back into the seat well then covering her head with the blanket.

She did not hear the slick strip of the duct tape as the band unspooled from the roll.

# 25

## 1453

Yusuf stared, transfixed by the bundle from the well by the Myrelaion. What other man had touched an object crafted by a goddess?

As if in answer, an immense calm and certainty descended on him.

He, Yusuf Ali-Bey, had retrieved the Palladium.

He had accomplished his mission.

The fate of a city lay in his hands.

"The rope!" From the cistern below, the voice of the swimmer, Evhad, cut through his reveries. "Haul me up!"

Yusuf turned, clutching the precious statue. Sinan lay at his feet, a crossbow bolt in his eye. The wild boar, Karaca, too, had met his fate. How could Yusuf rescue his comrade from the dark water? Nasuh had disappeared up the north passageway. That path lay open.

The enemy could be upon them at any moment.

Yusuf clutched the Palladium to his chest. He could not haul up Evhad on his own. He could barely hold his own body erect.

Far to the west, Hasan led the Janissaries against the Roman walls. The assault could only succeed if Yusuf achieved his mission. He and his men could not rescue Evhad. Allah must decide whether the brave swimmer lived or died.

Yusuf called out. "Yazid. Halil. Help me. We must flee."

Seconds later, with faithful Yazid supporting him and Halil guarding their rear, they hurried away from the Myrelaion, leaving behind their dead, and still living, the swimmer, Evhad.

They emerged into a busy street. On every side, armed men hastened west towards the land walls from which they had come.

"You. Where are you going?" A Genoese commander stopped them. "The enemy is seeking to break through the Mesoteichion. All forces are gathering there."

Without a word, Yusuf turned west with his two companions. He pictured Evhad, his energy ebbing as he fought to stay afloat in the darkness of the cistern. The Palladium pressed against Yusuf's body. What to do with it? He had imagined returning to the encampment outside the city and kneeling down before Zagan Pasha with the precious statuette in his hands. But in this chaos, he might as well fly to the moon. Should he destroy it? What had Odysseus and Diomedes done at Troy? They had nullified the protective power of the *Xoanon* by carrying the relic outside the city.

Yusuf must do the same.

The Luck of Troy must leave Constantinople.

Allah would guide him.

He paused, leaning on Yazid's solid shoulder, and looked around. The road passed close to the sea walls. Beyond them lay the harbour the Greeks called Eleutherios. Freedom. Could they find a way to leave the city there?

Two gates led to the harbour. The St Aemilianos lay further west. The Jewish Gate must be closer, to the east of the harbour. Might the gates be open? The city's inhabitants must be fleeing the tempest that descended on them.

They limped south. Ahead, the sea wall rose. At the summit, soldiers gathered around a kiln heating some kind of liquid. Could they be mixing Greek Fire, to attack any Ottoman ships that approached? He scanned the wall, trying to see where the towering stone barrier met the road they followed.

At last Yazid gripped his shoulder. A tower stood guard over a low opening, flanked by sentries. Heavy wooden gates, strengthened with steel, stood ajar at each end of the passage through the wall.

Throngs of people surged in both directions, as if fleeing enemies both within and outside the city walls.

Yusuf clutched the arm of faithful Yazid and allowed himself to hope.

The doors of the Jewish Gate lay open.

## 26

S avage sprinted through the mud of the building site towards the
highway. Crowds of pedestrians, seeing the traffic immobile,
pushed across the road, threading between cars, buses, and trucks
and dodging the motorcycles hurtling through the gaps.

"Nothing is moving. We can still catch them. Orhan. *Orhan.*"

He looked back. The police intelligence officer stood motionless,
peering at his phone.

"This is no time to check your Facebook," Savage said. "Elif is
close. In five minutes, she could be gone forever."

"Elif's phone has GPS tracking. I am sending her number to HQ
in case it is still turned on. Go ahead. See if you can find them. But
remember you have no power of arrest."

"Every second you waste playing with your phone makes it less
likely we'll ever see Elif again."

Orhan whirled round, his face dark. "No-one wants to save my
sister more than I do. You, she tells me, have least of all to say." He
spat. "I must call in the murders. The dead have families, too. If I did
not, the Police Intelligence Department would think I had taken
leave of my senses."

Savage stared at the Turk. What had Elif told her brother? Last
night, she had called Savage a monster to his face. Could she be right?
He had failed many women, starting with his agent, Upturn.

*He had found her at the far side of the snowy Moscow clearing, her
thin figure hunched against the bone-numbing cold. Weeks later,
Savage's pregnant wife, Clare, had wrapped her car around a tree.*

He must not fail Elif.

He ran, feet pounding on the hot asphalt. In the centre of the highway, he paused. Six lanes of stationary traffic baked under the sun.

The layout of the junction meant the killers must have turned east. In that direction, not a vehicle moved.

Terrorists could get stuck in traffic, too.

He ran towards the nearest taxi. Forty or more of the yellow vehicles studded the sea of hot metal. Which hid the killers?

Elif had a lean, muscular physique. She ran for an hour every morning from her home in Bebek along the shore of the Bosphorus, her dark hair wild in the wind.

She never submitted. Not to anyone. No matter what the threat.

They must have harmed her.

Savage cursed and charged forward between the traffic.

A middle-aged woman with a tattoo drove the first taxi. A multi-generational family packed the second, the women in headscarves, the men with bushy moustaches, the children sat on laps or stood on the seats. Ahead, a man in a Jaguar blocked the way. He held out his hand for a *simit* from a boy who had manoeuvred his brightly-coloured cart into the stream of traffic. Savage pushed past, drawing a string of obscenities, and aimed for the next splash of yellow.

Horns blared everywhere. A bus revved its engine, enveloping him in diesel smoke. A motorcycle ridden by two men wearing white robes and bushy beards careered towards him between the lines of traffic, swerving aside at the last moment.

He peered inside one cab after another. Nothing.

The traffic moved. Streams of vehicles in both directions jerked forward. Dozens of taxis jostled for position. One, a dark streak across its side, accelerated.

Was that mud from the building site? Or blood?

Savage darted between two black limousines. The taxi changed lanes, accelerated, and braked as another vehicle pulled in front.

He closed the gap.

The heat of the road surface rose through his shoes. The traffic lights changed to green. The taxi surged, overtaking less aggressive drivers. Savage passed the lights. Some vehicles slowed to turn, but the taxi powered straight ahead.

His breathing deepened and he extended his stride into a measured, powerful pace. The driving beat of the Supremes' *Nathan Jones* seized his consciousness. He could run for hours at this speed. But the taxi accelerated away.

A battered eight-wheeled construction truck, its body heaped with a mountain of excavated earth and rock, lumbered towards the main road. Mud caked its corrugated metal sides. As the juggernaut climbed the slope, a torrent of black sludge spewed from its rear.

The construction truck did not have right of way. It toiled across the building site towards a gap in a chain-link fence that led to the public highway. The driver did not slow as he approached the busy street, diesel fumes belching from the exhaust. He knew everyone else on the road made way for forty tonnes of earth, rock, and rust-streaked steel. The driver's left arm dangled from the open window, a cigarette between two fingers.

Vehicles on the highway took evasive action as the truck approached. An expensive sedan pulled to the left, triggering an explosion of brake-lights. A purple city bus wheezed to a halt. Pizza delivery motorcycles wove through the shrinking gaps in the traffic. The truck, as if oblivious, continued its trajectory. As the wheels thudded down onto the dual carriageway, lumps of earth fell from its sides and exploded against the road surface.

The taxi with the dark streak pulled up, hemmed in by a dozen vehicles.

Ahead, the truck ground onto the empty street. Traffic eased forward.

Savage sprinted. In twenty seconds, he drew level with the taxi. *Use the door-jamb for protection.* He pulled open the passenger door with his left hand, crouching low to present as small a target as possible.

A man shouted in Turkish. "Close the door. This taxi is taken."

In the back seat, two women huddled together, putting distance between themselves and the violent intruder.

Two women. Both wore traditional Turkish clothes and headscarves.

The driver, a stocky man wearing a flat cap, shook his head and put the car in gear as if men assaulted his taxi every day. "Shut the door! You are scaring my passengers." He gestured at the meter and raised his chin, tut-tutting.

Savage slammed the door and stepped back. Traffic flowed in both directions.

Elif was gone.

# 27

## 1453

Keen-eyed Halil led the way. Yusuf stumbled behind him, supported by Yazid's strong arms, towards the Jewish Gate. People passed through the arch in both directions: porters dragging handcarts loaded with supplies; soldiers, sweating in their heavy armour; civilians desperate to enter, or leave, the city. Near the sea wall, a wealthy merchant and his family stood next to a handcart, arguing with a heavily-built slave. Trunks and boxes filled the cart.

The numbness in Yusuf's thigh grew. Yazid grunted as the commander leaned on him more heavily. Halil glanced behind for any sign of pursuit. They reached the inner gate. A gust of sea air banished the stink of smoke and fear. On the walls above and to each side of the gate sentries stood guard: mostly white-haired reservists, their faces wreathed in fear. They paid no attention to the three men in Venetian uniform.

Yusuf's heart pounded as they passed through the inner gateway. He slipped his hand inside his tunic and touched the object. In the passage under the wall, between the city and the sea, surrounded by the jostling crowd, he hesitated, a sense of peace coming over him. He had almost reached his goal.

He stepped beyond the outer gate and pulled out the Palladium, still protected by its fabric covering.

The sea stretched before him, black and endless. To one side, vessels packed the harbour, loading or unloading goods. On the other stretched the sea wall, framed by sky and waves.

Yusuf, Yazid, and Halil paused, overcome with their achievement. The Luck of Troy had abandoned Constantinople.

In the distance, a bell rang out. More bells, spreading across the city.

Someone shouted.

"The city has fallen! The city has fallen!"

## 28

Savage stared at the traffic. Yellow taxis hurtled in every direction. Elif and her captors could go anywhere via the network of motorways, bridges, and tunnels that linked the Old City to Asia and to Europe.

In Istanbul, even the underground railway spanned two continents.

But if the kidnappers wished to flee, why had the taxi set off east, towards the Topkapi Palace and the Grand Bazaar, instead of south, west, or north to hit the arteries out of town?

Their destination must lie in the city.

"John." Orhan jogged towards him, grim-faced. "Did you find no sign of Elif?"

"Nothing. They got away." Savage eyed the traffic. "Heading east, for some reason."

"Yes. I gave HQ the details of her phone."

"They will ditch it. You saw how they executed six innocent people. The attackers are organised and well-trained." Savage looked around, as if he might glimpse the killers committing some atrocity as he spoke. "Whatever they plan, this is not the end of it."

"They may be good. But everyone can make mistakes. Do not forget they have Dervis to handle. He is big and strong. Elif will fight to her last breath." Orhan checked his phone. "There is more. This idea she unearthed some mythical Greek relic has gone viral. There could be a connection to the kidnapping."

"Terrorist archaeologists? I don't think so."

"Worse. Look at this." Orhan held up his phone.

The screen showed a tall, hook-nosed man with a stubble of

white hair, a white beard, and piercing blue eyes addressing a battery of microphones at the foot of some aircraft steps. Savage recognised the Greek Prime Minister, Sophas Papakostas. Overhead, the sun blazed in a brilliant blue sky. Papakostas jabbed his finger at the air as he spoke.

A white-on-red ticker across the foot of the picture screamed *GREECE SAYS: READY FOR WAR.*

"*It is an act of aggression,*" the prime minister said. "*I came for peace. The people of Greece reach out the olive branch of friendship. But if Turkey wants war, we are ready.*

"*First, they keep secret that for months they have been excavating the most sacred relic of Greek history.*" The prime minister's blue eyes fixed on the camera. "*Today, they tell us the relic has been uncovered, but it has vanished. The Palladium itself. The Xoanon. The Luck of Troy. It belongs to Greece. I demand an explanation.*"

Savage wiped his brow with the sleeve of his shirt. "Looks like the Reconciliation Summit has got off to a good start," he said. "But what does this have to do with Elif?"

"Everything. Papakostas and half the Greek government arrived in Istanbul this morning to discuss a lasting peace between Greece and Turkey. Do you not think it is weird that the most famous icon in Greek mythology is discovered, and lost, right under their noses, the day they show up in the city?"

"Bullshit alert." Savage shook his head. "How could an archaeology professor—your sister—dig up a relic, and be kidnapped, because a Greek politician is visiting Turkey? Who organised it? Where's the evidence?"

"John, your naivety astonishes me. Asking for evidence, or facts, shows how little you understand about our culture. Where are you standing, right now? In ancient Byzantium. Every conspiracy theorist in Turkey, and there are eighty-five million of them, will have a hundred ideas about why Elif and Dervis have been kidnapped, or whether they have even been kidnapped at all."

"You and I saw six dead bodies. You checked that young bloke's pulse. How could that be a fake?"

"By tomorrow morning, half of the Turkish media will be saying no-one died in the tunnel. Or Mossad is responsible because they want to weaken Turkey, and the bodies came from an Israeli morgue. What matters is you and me, John. We have to make the right decisions fast if we want to see Elif alive again. We cannot rely on anyone else." A triangular dent appeared on Orhan's forehead as he stroked his tiny, trimmed beard with finger and thumb. "Are you with me?"

"Only you could even consider the need to ask that." Savage breathed deeply.

"You have to keep that crazy temper under control. You cannot deploy violence here. You are a guest in Turkey."

"Just watch me." Savage fought the urge to punch Orhan in the face.

The Turk's cell-phone rang. He answered, holding up one finger to silence Savage. He listened, spoke one or two words, and terminated the call.

"They traced the phone," he said. "It is switched on. If Elif and the phone are still together, my sister is less than two kilometres north of here, and they are heading for the Golden Horn."

# 29

## 1453

S tanding by the sea wall outside the Jewish Gate, the Palladium in his hands, Yusuf smiled and closed his eyes. The first light of day turned the waves from black to blue. Behind him, across the city, church bells rang. Right now, the giant figure of his friend Hasan would be leading his fellow Janissary warriors up the ruined walls in a final assault, the Sultan's standard in his hand. Thanks to Yusuf and his fallen comrades, nothing stood in the way of victory.

"Look!" Keen-eyed Halil pointed out to sea.

Yusuf opened his eyes. A sleek Ottoman war bireme approached from the south. The slaves manning its twin banks of oars never faltered as they drove the prow onto the foot of the walls to the east of the Jewish Gate. Black-clad archers picked off defenders along the ramparts.

Halil raised his arm and shouted "Stop!" in Turkish. His reward was an arrow in the heart.

A ball of fire exploded inside the ship, illuminating the war platform at the rear of the deck. Men with buckets ran to extinguish the flames, but the water seemed to spread the conflagration, which climbed the platform towards the archers gathered there. *Askeri*, dressed in light armour and brandishing curved scimitars, swarmed ashore over the prow.

"They will kill us all." Faithful Yazid reached out to support Yusuf. "Come inside."

The defenders tried to push shut the heavy doors as Yazid helped Yusuf to enter, but a dozen Ottoman troops surged inside, hacking at the people bunched within. The merchant turned to flee, shepherding his family ahead of him, abandoning their cart of treasures. Yazid fell. Yusuf tumbled with him, unable to stand on his wounded leg. He lay in the mud beyond the gateway, the package clutched to his breast. Fresh Byzantine troops arrived to repel the Ottoman raiding party. Something struck his head. A blinding light flared and went out.

## 30

S avage breathed deeply as he and Orhan pounded back along the road towards the building site. A bus shot past them, horn blaring.

"How fast can you drive us to the Golden Horn?" Savage yelled. "Won't the local cops get there quicker?"

"Elif is not their family," Orhan said. "For all I know, my police colleagues are working for the same dark forces that have seized my sister."

"You're nuts. Is this the Welsh Secret Service again? How could anyone set something up so quickly?"

"No-one has to organise anything. They already know what they are trying to achieve. They have immense resources." Orhan slowed as they entered the construction site. "See how many have come."

Beyond the bare-earth landscape that cloaked the murder scene, half a dozen emergency vehicles had gathered. Two ambulances boxed in Orhan's unmarked car. Behind, the police drivers had parked their cars at odd angles, as though seeking to show an aggressive lack of co-ordination. A fourth manoeuvred to allow a boxy control-centre truck to enter the crowded parking space. Orhan could not move his car without shifting the ambulances and every other vehicle on the site.

"Who did you call?" Savage said. "They've sent in the whole bloody cavalry."

"This is a mass shooting," Orhan said. "Six died, including what look like foreigners. Of course, they suspect a terrorist plot. Maybe with a link to the Reconciliation Summit at the Dolmabahce Palace."

"But why would terrorists kidnap Elif and Dervis?"

"Who knows? We have not heard their demands, yet." Orhan strode through the sticky mud. "Listen. If they ask about the phone we found, say nothing. I want to check it myself, in case it tells us something about Elif."

A giant plainclothes officer with a broken nose, thick neck, and shoulders like sandbags jogged forward to meet them. He towered over Orhan, ignoring Savage.

"Are you Orhan Mutlu? We need to talk."

"I have reported everything I know to HQ," Orhan said. "One of the hostages is my sister. My instructions are to track her down."

"Do not lie to me," the plainclothes man said. "My name is Tarik Korkmaz and I am in charge of this counter-terrorist operation. Two separate squad cars have been dispatched to intercept the suspect taxi."

"It is my sister." Orhan's voice rose.

"I do not care if they have your mother, your girlfriend, your wife, and your baby daughter. I need you to answer some questions. How did you know to come here? When you crossed the Bosphorus, illegally, in an official police vessel, the shootings had not yet happened, yet you were already on your way. Did you know what they had planned? When you arrived, you say you found six bodies and a phone that happened to be filming the scene. You can give me the device, for a start. Why did you remove it? We need to get it to forensics right away."

Savage's phone rang. He stepped away from Korkmaz as he continued to berate Orhan.

"John, it is Ram. Come right away. The Consul General wants you. Also, I have a report you will wish to see."

"I can't come. Elif has been kidnapped."

"The Palladium killings? Someone took Elif? There are survivors? How many?" Ram Kuresh, the senior spook in the Istanbul office of the Secret Intelligence Service, would be taking notes as Savage spoke.

"Six died. Archaeologists, students, and workmen, so far as we could see. Two missing: Elif, who you know, and Dervis Basturk, another archaeologist."

"I do not like coincidences," Ram said. "A shooting and kidnapping in Istanbul, on the same day we have thousands of Brits arriving in the city for the Liverpool-Besiktas match, and a US aircraft carrier in town. Some reports say a British student was at the site."

Savage hesitated. Only dead bodies had lain in the tunnel. Should he have abandoned his pursuit of the kidnappers and Elif to check the identities of the victims? Once the police arrived at a crime scene, consular teams could wait hours or even days to establish the names of the dead.

He had failed.

Ram Kuresh had mentioned a report Savage must see. He meant a piece of intelligence. If the experienced SIS officer linked a report to the shootings, it must highlight a threat.

But how could Elif be involved?

Savage glanced around. Orhan was still squared up to the bull-necked counter-terrorist cop. A squad of officers in forensic suits headed for the tunnel.

A terror attack at an archaeological dig. Six people killed. But not everyone.

The kidnappers wanted Elif or Dervis for something.

They needed them alive.

"The report, Ram. Have you told Braintree?"

"The Consul General has seen the report and is, in the vernacular, shitting bricks. He is asking where you are and what you are doing. We have briefed the Ambassador, but she is on leave near Lake Van without secure comms, so she cannot do too much. We have passed a sanitised copy to Turkish liaison. But I want you to see it. With your background—"

Ram meant Savage's career as an SIS officer, before the incident in Moscow that had forced him to leave the service.

"I'd like to see it. But first I must find Elif."

"Now, John. Come."

"You can't order me around anymore. You know that."

Raised voices drowned out whatever Ram said next. Savage terminated the call. Orhan shouted, his veins standing out on his forehead, the tendons at his neck like cables. Opposite him, Tarik Korkmaz, the house-sized counter-terrorist cop, did the same, but from a greater height.

Orhan fell silent. He pulled from his pocket a phone in a plastic evidence bag. He waved the phone in Korkmaz's face, then turned the bag upside down, ejecting the device onto the ground. The phone smashed against a rock, glass and plastic splintering, and splashed into a muddy puddle.

"There!" Orhan shouted. "There! It's all yours!" He raised his foot and stamped on the phone. "Are you happy now? You have the evidence! Take it!"

Korkmaz stared at the ground, his mouth hanging open. "You will rot in jail for this," he said to Orhan. "Or maybe I will kill you and save the courts a case. Who are you working for?"

"You should examine the crime scene, not hassle me." Orhan's breath came in sharp bursts. "And while you do your job, I am going to find my sister." He half-turned to Savage. "I don't think Mr Korkmaz wants us here." He sprinted away across the building site.

## 31

## 1453

Yusuf opened his eyes. Moisture beaded his face. A pool of dark liquid gathered by his head.

He lived. That much he knew. For how many seconds, or minutes, he knew not.

The fighting had raged past. Outside the gates, Ottoman soldiers roared their battle cries and hammered on the stout wood. Yusuf lay alone, life ebbing away into the mud.

Why did he feel no fear?

He pushed his arm downwards. His body had become heavy. On the third attempt, he rolled onto his side.

Yazid lay next to him, his truest ally, the Arab boy who had grown up in Greece. Dear Yazid had been faithful to the last. He lay on his face, two Ottoman arrows planted in his back like black flowers.

Yusuf closed his eyes. The first man he had slain today had been the Anatolian mercenary. The fighter had fallen on the rubble at the Mesoteichion when Yusuf and his men first joined the fray on the side of the Venetians. A Turk, slain by a Greek Janissary, pretending to be a Venetian. No wonder the man had seemed astonished as Yusuf's blade brought his blood gushing forth.

Yusuf's grandmother was long dead. At their home in Negroponte, she had sat him on her knee to tell him tales of ancient Greece. Perhaps he would see her again, in the afterlife. He smiled. The mud of the alleyway seemed warmer. Welcoming.

All feeling had gone from his legs.

The package pressed against his chest.

Lying in the filth of the street, Yusuf opened his eyes and looked at the bundle. With his last strength, he fumbled to open the embroidered covering. Within, he found a soft wrapping of oiled leather. This, too, he opened.

The face of a goddess looked at Yusuf. Serene. Forgiving. Eternal.

# 32

A vibration against her right buttock awoke Elif Mutlu.
A text message.

She tried to reach for the phone but her arms did not move. They had bound her. When she opened her eyes, she saw nothing. Had they blindfolded her, too? When she breathed, she smelled the sweet, sour scent of the ether. In that instant, a red-hot spike of iron drove into the top of her skull. She tried to groan, but her lips were sticky with the duct tape. She flexed her body and something shifted, allowing a little light to penetrate. Her face pressed against the floor of the car.

Elif remembered everything.

*Stay still.*

The phone in her pocket held out hope. Maybe a location tracker appeared on the screen of a police computer at this very moment. Maybe a commander was passing the data to Orhan or a police commando unit.

Elif swallowed and steadied her breathing. Staying silent was easy. They had sealed her mouth. The police might be following the taxi with a helicopter. Orhan and every other cop in Istanbul knew two multiple killers had seized her.

"Do it."

The voice came from the driver's seat.

For the first time, one of the kidnappers had uttered a word. He spoke Turkish, in the low, controlled tone of a man accustomed to giving orders. Elif could not identify his accent. The vehicle slowed.

*Do it.*

Something touched her. Someone moved his hand down her

body, touching her neck. Her arm. Her breast. She flinched, but could not move away. The hand lingered there for a second, exploring the curve of her helpless body, squeezing her. The probing fingers moved on towards her waist.

He was looking for her phone.

In a spasm of movement, she tried to jack-knife her body, to stop him, to keep her lifeline safe.

Instead, she cracked her head against the metal support of the front seat. The hand, moving faster, located the slim device and pulled it from her pocket.

The car stopped.

In the struggle, the blanket covering her head had shifted. The car door opened. Everywhere people hurried to cross roads and descend from buses and taxis, but no-one looked down into the space behind the driver's seat in the taxi. A tram stood at a stop, its doors open. The legs of a man climbed down from the car, unhurried, and mounted the steps onto the tram. Then he climbed back down, approaching the car. Blue jeans. Black shoes. His face was out of sight. Behind him, the tram doors closed. The huge vehicle rumbled off along the rails. The jeans climbed over her, he did not step on her. The taxi door slammed shut, obscuring her vision.

The man's hand reached down again to touch her buttock, patting her on the spot where her phone had been.

# 33

## 1453

Calm descended on Yusuf Ali-Bey. He blinked and gazed at the face of the statuette. Athena was the goddess of war. Of course. She had sent an emissary to fetch this warrior home.

A dull ache grew in his side. Someone kicking him.

"What you got there, mister?"

A gang of children clustered around the merchant's cart, plundering what they could reach. The merchant and his family had abandoned the possessions of a lifetime. Perhaps they had escaped onto a ship. A little Greek girl, no more than eight years old, stood over him. He shuddered to think what fate awaited her.

"Take this." Yusuf held out the statuette. He could barely breathe or speak. "Make haste. Throw it in the sea. Then get on a boat. You must escape."

"I'll take it." The girl snatched the Palladium from Yusuf's trembling hands and gazed at the face of Pallas. "It's pretty. I will show it to my friends."

"The boat," Yusuf croaked. "The sea." The place where the object had lain against his breast grew cold.

The girl wrapped the cover around the statuette and rocked the bundle against herself, like a baby. She smiled down at Yusuf, as if inviting him to join in her game. He tried to return her smile, but his lips did not obey. She turned away.

Not towards the sea. Away from the water. Back north, towards the Myrelaion.

"No!" Yusuf tried to shout. "The sea!"

She did not seem to hear him.

Blackness fell.

The last thing Yusuf Ali-Bey saw was the girl, holding the Palladium, running back up the lane into the doomed city.

## 34

Savage took a step away from Korkmaz. Orhan dodged between vehicles as he put distance between himself and the big counter-terrorism cop. Why the evasive action?

*CRACK.*

Korkmaz had drawn his service Beretta and fired in the air.

Orhan went on running. He closed on a group of pedestrians, making himself an impossible target even if Korkmaz were prepared to gun down a fellow police officer. Then he vanished.

The superintendent lowered his gun and turned towards Savage.

"Who the hell are you?" he said in Turkish.

Savage raised his head to hold the man's gaze. Korkmaz might have a broken nose and a wrestler's build, but his deep-set eyes glittered with intelligence.

Every step of the day, people had placed obstacles in Savage's path. Now this. He fought down his anger. "Please do not shoot me," he said in Russian. "I am a Russian diplomat with immunity." He repeated the words in Turkish. *"Diplomat. Dokunulmazlik."* *Diplomat. Immunity.* Without another word, he turned to flee.

He expected his words to make Korkmaz hesitate. But the big Turk reacted with extraordinary speed. He lunged after Savage, grabbing empty air. "Stop!" he shouted. "Police!"

Savage plunged down a street lined with brightly-coloured restaurants towards a decrepit building with a red plastic sign advertising doner kebabs. A mustachio'd waiter emerged, smiling, to welcome him, but stepped aside, still smiling and nodding, as two fit, muscular, men barrelled towards his restaurant.

Korkmaz kept pace with Savage despite his bulk. What did these

Turkish cops eat for breakfast? Savage threw himself inside the restaurant and slammed the door behind him.

Inside, rows of tables with fresh white paper coverings waited for the day's first customers. Savage ran into the kitchen, where a man in a filthy white apron and chef's hat sat with his feet up on a table, reading a newspaper and smoking a cigarette.

When Savage burst in, the man leapt to his feet and grabbed a meat-cleaver from the counter, baring his teeth and hopping from foot to foot, as if terrified yet ready to defend himself against a superior adversary.

Savage raised his thumb as if to acknowledge the cook's bravery. "A crazy man is coming," he said, spreading his mouth into a manic grin. He dashed through into the yard.

Ahead, a sheer concrete wall marked the rear of a building site. To the right, razor wire topped a high fence. On the left rose a corrugated iron partition, fixed onto invisible supports with flush bolts. Nothing he could scale.

What about the fourth side?

Savage turned. The back of the restaurant stood two storeys high, its windows barred with ornamental grilles.

Perfect for climbing.

Years of fat deposits from the kitchen coated the metal. But his Clarks work shoes gripped the treacherous surface. In thirty seconds, he swung himself onto a first-floor balcony.

"Got you." An irresistible force slammed Savage into the wall of the terrace, blasting the air out of his lungs. Someone gripped him around the upper body, pinning his arms. Savage responded instinctively, twisting and raising his own arms to break the grip. He turned to face Korkmaz.

Do not strike back.

You are in control.

You will not use violence.

*He had run across the snow-filled clearing in Moscow to reach*

*Upturn, her back hunched against the tree in twenty-five degrees below zero.*

He could not lose another woman he cared for.

Savage shook his head. "*Nyet. Nyet,*" he said. He repeated, in Turkish: "*Olamaz.*" *It cannot be.* He feinted jumping back over the balcony into the courtyard, then ducked past the bigger man back into the restaurant, pulling the glass door closed behind him.

This time the key was in the lock. Savage turned it and sprinted down the stairs.

"*Spasibo,*" he said in Russian to the waiter, still smiling and nodding outside the front door. He darted across the main road to enter an alley that sloped down towards the Sea of Marmara.

Ancient buildings lined the narrow passage. The layout of these streets had not changed for centuries. A café colonised a low arch to one side. Tourists drifted in every direction, studying guide books or gazing at their phones.

Savage bent his head to lose height and picked his way through the crowd. Ahead, water glittered. He ducked and turned left.

A choice confronted him. On one side a steep flight of concrete stairs climbed upwards; on the other a stone-framed doorway opened, surmounted by an ancient Greek inscription. He turned, ready to sprint up the stairs if anyone followed, then stepped into the cool darkness of the doorway.

Within, columns marched across an underground void lined with finely-carved stone. Perhaps he had entered an ancient church or *hamam.*

Between the columns, stores sold cheap sneakers or clothing. Piles of cardboard shoe-boxes lined the walls. High overhead, fluorescent strip lights illuminated a vaulted ceiling, braced with rusting steel supports.

An old man poked his head out of a shop and pointed at a column.

"Look," he said in English. "Very old."

In the white marble of the capital a carved cross stood out, its extremities smoothed by time.

"What is this place?" Savage asked.

"This is cistern beneath Bodrum Mosque," the man said. "Greeks called church here Myrelaion."

A cistern. The Byzantines had built the space in which he stood as a circular, subterranean space, filled with eternal darkness—and with drinking water for the city of Constantinople.

Savage stepped into the shadow of a column and made a call.

*"Efendim?"*

"Orhan. Why the hell did you smash the phone?"

"Did you not hear that ape Korkmaz ask who I worked for, as if I was some kind of double agent? Was it not your Shakespeare who said *'suspicion haunts the guilty mind'*? I think there is a reason he is investigating the abduction of Elif so slowly."

"Not the paranoia. The phone. Why?"

"I know you think all Turks are stupid, but credit me with some intelligence. I always carry a spare phone in case I have to make a private call. I sacrificed it to get Korkmaz off my back."

In the gloom of the cistern, Savage grinned. *"Chapeau.* I owe you a beer. Where is the phone from the tunnel?"

"I have sent it to a friend in the Intelligence Department. He says he can crack it in about an hour."

"Any more on Elif?"

"The police have tracked her heading towards Kabatas and the Dolmabahce Palace." Orhan paused. "That is where the summit with the Greeks is happening at half past eleven. But what do you care about my sister?"

What did he care? Savage bit back a glib answer. "No way the killers would leave a phone in her pocket."

"Do you not think the presidents of Greece and Turkey would make an attractive target for terrorists?"

"Istanbul also has about twenty million other targets."

"John." Orhan spoke as though addressing a child. "Terrorists have kidnapped my sister. Her phone is heading towards a summit meeting. Of course, I am going there." He paused. "I need your help."

"Did you just ask me for help?"

"I am not joking. Come now. Please."

Savage closed his eyes. The kidnappers had taken Elif because she knew something or could do something they needed. Could the intelligence report Ram Kuresh wanted to show him shed light on their goals?

"Orhan. I will see you at the Dolmabahce Mosque at eleven. Someone I know has information that could help us find Elif."

"This had better be good."

"It will be." Savage rang off.

First, he had to get to Ram. He looked around the cistern. Where the columns met the high, arched ceiling, two more white marble capitals bore crosses and Greek inscriptions. The city had synthesised east and west for thousands of years. Long might such tolerance continue.

A water cistern, the man had said; ancient, beautiful, and invisible. What had he called the place? The Myrelaion. A Greek name.

At last, Savage found what he needed. He dug in his pockets and held out some money to the delighted stall-holder.

## PART II

## ISTANBUL RISING

## 35

A yellow plastic sign on the unmarked door showed a phone crossed out and the words *NO PHONES* to prevent any confusion. Savage hesitated and left his in a slot marked *GUEST*.

What if Orhan received news about Elif and could not reach him?

At the end of the corridor, he rang the bell next to the key-pad. Before Moscow, he had always known the code.

Ram Kuresh appeared. He wore a diamond ear-stud.

"John. Thanks for coming. Stashed your phone?"

"Of course."

"Come in. Nice hat. Is that shirt new too?"

"Checked shirts and baseball caps are in this year."

"Evading surveillance?"

"It's a long story. Where is the report?"

Kuresh beckoned him inside. "What changed your mind about coming?"

"No-one can find Elif. Orhan thinks the police are deliberately not finding her, or are in on the plot." Savage shook his head. "He's brilliant at problem-solving, but a total conspiracy junkie. What have you got?"

"Before I show you the report, we must look at the threat scenarios. Have you seen the latest from the ultra-rightists?"

"I don't have time for this, Ram."

"I know you want to find Elif. Listen, please." Kuresh did not need to raise his voice to convey authority.

"You have one minute."

"You know Rauf Toprak plans to lead his Trotskyist rabble onto

Taksim Square. In response, Nasim Kaval has called out his National Rebirth thugs. Istanbul is a tinderbox. Kaval and Toprak want to light a spark and dump petrol on the flames. The demonstrations will also provide a target for terrorism."

Kuresh stepped into a side office equipped with televisions and internet-enabled terminals. The room had the musty smell of a space cleaning staff could not enter. A notice said: *Speech in this room is not secure.* Kuresh peered at a terminal and clicked on a link.

On the screen a tall, thin-faced man in a dark suit with a white shirt and matching handkerchief and tie appeared. His lips brushed the microphone as he spoke.

"You can say what you like about the Turkish far right, but Nasim Kaval has a good tailor," Kuresh said.

"*Turkish brothers! I promise you this,*" Kaval's voice was silken, "*we will never allow the money merchants of Wall Street and Tel Aviv to tell us how to live our lives. Are we not men? Why must we offer our arses like Greeks to the heathen gods of Athens?*"

Kaval stood straighter and raised his fist. "*Will our National Rebirth martyrs stay silent while the communist quislings of Rauf Toprak parade? The Greeks want the Palladium—a relic that belongs to Turkey. I call on all true martyrs to march on Taksim to resist the so-called Trotskyists and fight calls for a surrender pact with Greece.*"

The crowd roared its approval. Ram Kuresh muted the sound. "Both communists and nationalists have called rallies at Taksim at two o'clock. We can expect the usual tear-gas and water cannon from our police friends. But if terrorists target either side, the damage will be immense. Mysterious attacks on political protesters in Turkey are almost a tradition."

"A terror attack on a demonstration." Savage chose his words carefully. "Does the report you mentioned back that up?"

Ram nodded. He led the way to the secure facility. A single sheet of paper in plain-format text lay on the table. The report, topped and tailed. Savage longed to see the sourcing data that accompanied the original. But he no longer enjoyed the clearance to see where the intelligence had originated.

"HQ hoped you would have some insights," Kuresh said.

Savage scanned the text. "Can we speak freely in here?"

"As much as we can anywhere."

"This says fifteen operatives of an unidentified terrorist group have been assigned to Istanbul *to strike a mortal blow against the infidels and the apostates who destroyed the caliphate.*" Savage frowned as he read the quote. "Fifteen is a huge team. They must plan a complex attack, or multiple attacks. Timing is today."

"Quick thoughts. What could the target be?"

"Have we told the Turks?"

"We passed them this version."

Kuresh meant that if a more highly classified version existed, Savage did not have clearance to read it. "If the people who took Elif are part of this," Savage said, "there must be one or more larger groups somewhere else in the city."

"HQ believe the reference to the apostates means a Turkish target," Kuresh said. "Under the leadership of Ataturk, modern Turkey ended the Muslim caliphate in 1924. A bit like the Pope turning atheist and abolishing the Vatican. Or admitting he gets it wrong sometimes." Kuresh pushed his hand through his black hair and took off his thick-framed glasses. "But what about the infidels? Come on, John."

"Istanbul has a reputation as the home of secular values in Turkey. The city is also the business capital, full of people from all over the world. Both the nationalists and the communists hate religion on principle, so their slug-fest could be a target. Or the so-called Reconciliation Summit of the Turkish and Greek presidents. What about the *Gerald R Ford* and its escorts? But attacking an aircraft carrier would be a tough target for any terror group." Savage looked up at the intelligence chief. "You have something else, don't you? Show me."

Kuresh laid his glasses on the table. Blood vessels criss-crossed the whites of his eyes. "The internet is full of chatter. The computers analyse traffic from suspected terrorist sources to try to pin down potential threats. But the most dangerous operatives know the importance of radio silence."

"Tell me."

"We are seeing a surge of traffic, both encrypted and open source, around something they are calling *the end of all evil*. There is even a hashtag, #endofallevil. Another hashtag doing the rounds is #endofthewest. Ring any bells?"

"It's hard to make sense of psychopaths. What is the West, anyhow? Are Japanese or Brazilians westerners? How about Australians or ancient Greeks?"

"Well, Alexander the Great reached India, and we sent wisdom back to Europe." Kuresh smiled. "Everywhere is west of somewhere else. Perhaps we are all westerners."

"The police think the summit at the Dolmabahce Palace could be a target. Elif's phone is heading that direction. But *end of all evil* sounds more like an indiscriminate attack than a surgical strike."

"Go on."

"What about a mass casualty target? The Champions League match between Besiktas and Liverpool is right next to the Dolmabahce. Thousands of football fanatics are in the area already, including plenty of Brits."

"We also have the cruise ship *Queen Anne* due to moor on the European side this evening, close to the stadium, with six thousand US tourists on board," Kuresh said. "You are doing security liaison for the match tonight, aren't you? Did you find out whether one of the victims in the Old City was British?"

Savage shook his head. "Wait," he said. "Elif connects all this. She was excavating the so-called Palladium. The kidnappers attacked there. What could she have that they need?"

Kuresh shrugged. "I cannot believe you are spouting mumbo jumbo about some ancient statue. We are talking Homeric legends here. The Iliad, I believe."

"Ram. Ideology and terror are never based on facts. They are about what people believe. The Palladium could be the key to this."

"You want me to tell that to Vauxhall? Something about Greek gods?"

"Go ahead. They already think I'm crazy. My best guess is a mass casualty attack in Istanbul in the next fourteen hours, somehow linked to Elif. The Dolmabahce Palace is the first target up. I'm meeting Orhan there."

"John. Do not forget your day job."

"My day job is security for tonight's match. Orhan is my liaison officer. What else is my job, if not stopping a terrorist attack next to the stadium?"

"I am not sure the Consul General will agree."

"Tell him I'm liaising with the Turkish police to investigate a threat to the match. It happens to be true."

The SIS officer rubbed his eyes. "Is this about Elif?"

"No. We finished it." Savage paused. "Tell me if you hear anything new."

"You will have to come back here. I am not going to read you classified information over the phone."

"Ram. If we want to prevent a major terrorist attack in Istanbul in the next few hours, we will have to put our heads above the parapet."

## 36

Saif al-Din, the captain, relished the harsh roar of the engine. Sea-spray bit his face as the bow of the tiny boat smashed against a wave.

The Turk smiled and licked the salt from his lips. In 1453, the irresistible hordes of the Conqueror, Fatih Sultan Mehmet, had blasted down the crumbling walls of Constantinople. Now a new force of righteous believers came to lay waste to the city of infidels.

His old life as a taxi driver in Istanbul lay far behind him.

"Uzay! Kaan! Are you ready?"

Behind him at the tiller, Uzay raised his hand. The dark-skinned boatman set his square jaw in a ferocious scowl and screwed his eyes tight against the sun's glare. Saif trusted Uzay, the pilot, with his life. But his aversion to wearing sunglasses made no sense. Kaan, the muscle, cradled in his burly arms a long boat-hook with a cruelly-pointed tip as though he longed to wield the spike in anger.

Kaan's aggression was an asset. But Saif must not unleash the attack dog's rage too early.

Thirty seconds to go.

Uzay lifted the handset of the VHF transmitter to his mouth. He had set the radio to Channel 16, the distress frequency. "We have a problem," he said, his voice calm but urgent. "We need help." He made the appeal sound the most reasonable request in the world.

They closed on the bright orange vessel. As they approached, the other boat slowed and its bow-wave sank into the sea. Uzay turned to starboard, taking his time, manoeuvring towards the back of the orange ship. The Protocol said they must present no threat, until the last possible moment. Boarding from the stern, rather than jumping across onto the orange-painted bow section, was a tricky manoeuvre. But the approach gave direct access to the wheelhouse.

"*What is your problem?*" Whoever commanded the orange ship spoke with the sneering authority of a man used to being obeyed. "*We have a schedule.*"

"So sorry, brother. Man injured. Needs painkillers. We will not delay you," Uzay said on the radio. For a man from the Black Sea coast, he could do an extraordinary impression of humility. "Coming alongside now."

Kaan approached the port side, boat-hook ready. Saif stepped up next to him, smart in his matching nautical white shirt and trousers. The months of training at the Turkish Marine Academy had brought a host of benefits.

A boy of about sixteen stepped out onto the rear of the orange vessel. He wore scuffed orange overalls, as if to match the ship. His matted hair and salt-streaked features showed him to be a simple deckhand. Perhaps the arrogant commander had sent him. The boy smiled, displaying a mouthful of crooked teeth. He braced himself against the rail and held up a plastic carrier bag.

"Greetings, brother. Peace be with you. May you recover quickly." He prepared to swing the bag towards them, still displaying his teeth. "We put in two packs of aspirin and a couple of shots of morphine in case it is serious," he said. "How was your man injured? Hey! Slow down!"

The two ships met with a clunk as Uzay slammed the engines into reverse, like an Istanbul ferry captain touching the nose of his ship to a passenger wharf. Kaan reached the boathook across to the orange ship and pulled, bringing Saif and the boy in the overalls face to face.

Under his breath, Saif counted. At three, Uzay stood at his shoulder. Their vessel no longer needed anyone at the helm.

"Your name will be forgotten by tomorrow," Saif said to the boy in the orange overalls. "Mine will live forever." He stepped past him onto the other ship with his pack, followed by Uzay. Kaan came last, with boat-hook and rucksack. The boy stood back to let them pass, scratching at the matted hair on his head.

Saif entered the wheelhouse, Uzay close behind.

The marine VHF set that posed the greatest danger to The Protocol stood next to the wheel, an easy arm's length away. The nearest man wore immaculate naval fatigues. He must be the commander who had spoken to them. One hand on the wheel, he peered round towards the stern. A second uniformed officer looked out of the window at the smaller boat. The two most important occupants of the cabin, dressed all in white, sat in the corner, a backgammon board and two steaming glasses of tea on a table between them.

No-one was close enough to the radio to hit the DSC alarm—the single button designed to send an urgent distress call.

"Thank you for stopping to help us," Saif said. He drew his pistol and fired.

The haughty commander died first. He stood closest to the VHF radio. The low-penetration round exploded in his chest, causing maximum destruction to the target and minimizing the risk of damage to the electronics behind him.

The look of amazement on the commander's face as death took him gave Saif a rush of elation. Not so arrogant now, eh?

Saif had not used a silencer. The Protocol said the muzzle blast and flash from the first shot disorientated the other targets.

He turned towards the two men at the backgammon board.

Both rose and charged him.

They had military training.

They recognized they faced death if they did not fight.

Tea and backgammon board crashed to the ground. The men in white did not run straight at Saif but took different, zigzag courses to present more difficult targets.

Saif took careful aim and fired, catching the first man in the shoulder. The man grunted in pain but his momentum carried him forward, crashing into Saif, his arms spread wide. Saif fell back, dissipating his attacker's speed and power and clubbing upwards into the man's face with his weapon.

Something exploded next to his ear. Uzay had fired at the second man in white, hitting him in the stomach. A red wound blossomed in the man's shirt as he pitched forward, his head striking the deck, hands clutching at his wound.

The hollow-points had done their job. No medical help, much less a man's fingers, could staunch the blood. The first man weakened fast, panting as his right arm scrabbled for a grip around Saif's torso. His left arm hung loose where the massive wound had torn away half his shoulder.

"Who?" the man groaned. "Who are you?"

"We are the men whose names will be remembered," Saif said. He pushed the man's flailing arm away and swung the butt of the pistol at the side of his head. Now to finish the killing.

The fourth man in the cabin stood frozen by the window, his arms raised.

"No need, brothers," he said. "I will do what you want." He tried to smile, his face a mask of fear.

Saif smiled back and pulled the trigger. Hitting a stationary target was easy. He thanked God for the 9mm ammunition, which the manufacturer claimed "shredded violently" in the first six to eight inches but did not exit the target's body or cause any collateral damage.

The advertising seemed truthful. The man slumped to the floor, leaving no signs of damage—no splintered wood or broken glass, not even blood stains on the cabin wall or windows. The vessel must look pristine, at least from a distance.

Saif had become captain of a larger boat.

Outside, two more gunshots rang out.

Saif spun round, gripping his pistol. "Make sure they are dead," he said to Uzay, nodding at the bodies in the cabin. "Any doubt, use a blade. Then take the wheel and set the course."

Uzay sheathed his sidearm and took out a knife. He knelt down by the first body. Saif ran outside, clutching at the railing as the boat rolled in the choppy sea.

Outside, someone screamed.

Kaan, the attack dog, stood over the young deckhand in the orange overalls, the sharp point of the boat-hook raised above his head. Inflamed gristle and bone bulged from the boy's knees.

"Are you crazy? There is a reason we are using low-penetration ammunition. Shoot him in his knees and you harm the boat. And he is still living."

Bright, splintered furrows split the deck where fragments of bullets had ploughed into the wood. A trail of blood and gore led to the deckhand. He must have tried to crawl to safety after being shot.

The boy in the orange overalls groaned.

"Shut up!" Kaan yelled. He turned to Saif. "You said to kill them in the cabin. Not outside. He tried to run. I thought he would jump overboard." He stood a little straighter, clenching his fists to show off his muscular forearms. "Two shots, two hits."

Behind Kaan, the man continued to moan. Kaan raised the boathook.

"No." Saif seized Kaan's arm. "No more damage to the boat. Get the blood out of the body. Cut his throat over the water, and let it flow. When the bleeding is finished, bring him into the cabin. Then, clean up the deck."

Kaan did not reply, but knelt and hauled the injured boy's body into position. The youth screamed. Saif ignored him and checked the surroundings.

The fishing boat they had used to approach the orange-painted vessel had drifted a safe distance away, rolling in the swell.

Far enough.

He scanned the horizon. No sailors or vessels must witness what came next.

A gurgle told that Kaan had completed his work. The boat lurched as the pilot, Uzay, accelerated.

Saif checked his phone and grinned at the strong signal. He pressed the first number in the list of three.

In the distance the fishing boat shuddered and listed. No smoke. No sound. No waste. Two hundred grams of explosives, placed below the waterline, had blown a hole the size of a suitcase in the thin hull. Within sixty seconds the boat half-submerged. Ten seconds more, and the bow slid below the surface.

Later, they would use charges one hundred times larger, to world-changing effect. Saif deleted the number he had used, leaving two others stored in the memory. A simple app meant that by making one call, he could dial up to twenty phones simultaneously.

At his feet, Kaan dragged the lifeless body of the orange-suited boy towards the cabin.

"He is a heavy bastard," Kaan said.

"When you have taken him inside, come back here and clean up the mess you made," Saif ordered. In his earlier life, Saif's high voice had troubled him. Some men, even some girls, had laughed at him when he spoke, just as they had laughed at his short stature and his small hands and feet.

The voice of Saif al-Din, the Sword of the Faith, the captain, was deep and authoritative. "Do it fast," he told Kaan. "You never know when another ship will approach."

Kaan grunted and hauled the body into the wheelhouse.

Saif checked the time. Everything remained on track. He pocketed his phone and turned to face the bow of the vessel.

*No. Were they cursed?*

Straight ahead, the menacing silhouette of a Turkish coastguard fast patrol craft raced towards them. The muzzles of the four .50 calibre machine guns on the front deck rose dark against the sky.

## 37

Savage slammed the door behind him and ran into the grounds of the Consulate General. Six minutes remained before his meeting with Orhan at the Dolmabahce Mosque.

*We will have to put our heads above the parapet,* he had told Ram, to prevent a catastrophic attack.

Savage had never kept his head down.

He sprinted down the ramp to the garages.

He never should have bought the black Triumph Thruxton R motorcycle. He had imagined Elif clutching his waist as he negotiated hairpin bends on the Aegean, ocean views and the scent of thyme. He had pictured himself weaving through the choking Istanbul traffic.

The first fantasy had fallen at the hands of Elif, the previous summer. She had refused to ride pillion. "You kill yourself if you want to," she had said. "I love you, but I am not suicidal. If you want me, get four wheels."

They had spent blissful weeks exploring the coastline between Marmaris and Antalya, pausing to hike sections of the Lycian Way. The Triumph had stayed in the garage in Istanbul.

The city traffic had bitten back, too. Many *Istanbullus* rode scooters. Few owned motorcycles. The muscular 1960s-style road bike baffled the car, truck, and taxi drivers of the city.

Everyone told him conflict was inevitable.

The first time a taxi nudged the Triumph's stationary rear wheel in traffic, Savage had responded by smashing his fist down on the bonnet of the bright yellow vehicle. The driver had climbed out of the car, stared at the bike, laughed, and shaken Savage by the hand.

The second time, the driver had attempted to attack Savage with his fists. Savage had calmed the man without injury to either of them, and the incident had passed off quietly.

The third driver had stayed in his vehicle, locked the doors, and phoned the police. In the absence of visible damage to the Triumph and a large, fist-shaped indentation in the front of the taxi, Savage had only settled the case after months of hassle and an out-of-court payment.

All three incidents had happened within the first week of Savage picking up his new ride. Now, he uncaged the beast on special occasions only.

He opened the garage door and wiped down the leather seat. Could a relationship ever have worked between him and Elif? Could Savage be with any woman, after Moscow? After Upturn? After what Clare had done to herself?

No wonder he and Elif had crashed and burned. But how could Savage live without the Turkish woman's power and beauty?

He looked at the helmet and allowed himself a grim smile. "Elif," he said out loud. "This is for you."

He tossed the helmet onto a pile of tyres at the back of the garage. Then he started the bike and roared up the hill towards the gate.

A figure barred his way.

"Where are you off to? And why aren't you wearing a helmet?"

"Consul General, good morning. I have an urgent meeting with Turkish police liaison."

Christopher Braintree stood tall, with the habitual stoop of a formerly slender man with a recent history of weight gain. His prominent jowls gave him a permanent air of annoyance, perhaps not helped by his rage at being appointed Consul General in Istanbul for his pre-retirement posting, rather than the more senior position of Ambassador to Ankara as he had hoped.

This morning, Braintree's bulging forehead was red, and he held his fists clenched to his sides. The fact he stood in the full force of the sun in a tailor-made three-piece suit could not have improved his mood. Savage fought a smile as the words to *I Can See Clearly Now* by Johnny Nash rose unbidden in his mind.

"Listen, John, I appreciate your taking time off from your NCA work to act as police liaison for the football match. But where have you been for the last two hours?"

"Liaising. With the police."

"When you are fighting modern slavery with the National Crime Agency, you can do what you like. But when you are part of our consular team, I need to know what you are up to."

"Have you spoken to Ram?" Savage meant: *have you seen Ram's latest intelligence report?* He glanced at his watch.

"Ram has briefed me. Another reason I was alarmed when no-one could find you. Can you keep us all in the loop, please? Put your helmet on." Braintree shook his head. "And you, an NCA officer."

"I'll pick it up on the way out," Savage said. "If you'll let me get going."

Braintree sighed and stepped out of the way.

Traffic had backed up from Taksim Square all along Tarlabasi Boulevard. Buses, trucks, and taxis stewed in an aromatic canyon of *kokoreç* stalls selling sweetmeats wrapped in lamb intestines, kebab shops, dust from building works, and exhaust fumes. Savage spotted a space between a purple bus and a blue-and-white armoured police car and twisted the throttle.

In traffic, a car could take an hour or longer to travel the short distance from the Consulate to the Dolmabahce Palace. Savage made the journey in three minutes, slowing for the speed traps as he passed through the tunnel under Taksim and coasting down the steep hill past the Besiktas stadium, venue for the match against Liverpool.

At the base of the hill a muscular white TOMA police riot control vehicle blocked the road, like an armoured bulldozer loaded with ten tons of water, toxic chemicals, and a cannon to deliver them. Two riot control police buses, their windows shielded with wire grilles, stood to each side.

Either they did not care about snarling up the traffic, or they wanted to cause a jam.

Savage counted four uniformed police on foot guarding the TOMA, bulky in bullet-proof vests and carrying Heckler & Koch automatic weapons. He swung in the opposite direction, zig-zagged through the stationary traffic on the coast road, and cut into a car park overlooking the Bosphorus beneath the minarets of the Dolmabahce Mosque. Further south rose the hulks of moored cruise ships, with a strip of empty wharf waiting for the *Queen Anne* to dock that evening.

The Summit between the Turkish and Greek leaders was due to start any moment. The Bosphorus glittered blue in the sunlight. A cool wind whipped across the waves. Seagulls circled overhead. A long, low oil tanker headed south, ploughing between passenger ferries and pleasure craft.

Police had cleared a safety zone for hundreds of paces around the Dolmabahce Palace. The rambling, baroque structure at the water's edge lay hidden behind trees and outbuildings. Beyond the cordon, in all directions, stationary traffic blocked the streets.

Could the police have backed up the traffic as part of the security concept?

Yet Elif's phone had approached the same spot, after the killers had executed six people and taken her captive.

A powerful blow struck his back.

"At last, our brilliant British crime expert has come to help the poor Turkish police. I suppose you think we should be grateful." Orhan Mutlu's shaved head glistened in the sun.

"Poor Turkish police my arse. Your guy Korkmaz is superhuman."

"Korkmaz and his Special Operations team are at Kabatas, towards the Galata Bridge. They found Elif's phone in a tram. No Elif. You were right, it was a long shot. What is your secret information?"

"Everything points to a mass casualty attack, today, in Istanbul.

We have evidence operatives of an unknown terrorist group are in the city."

"How many?"

"SIS have passed the information on liaison channels."

Orhan flicked Savage's shoulder with the back of his hand and stepped closer. "Do not talk gibberish to me, Mr former-MI6-man. Do you think I am not worthy of your secrets?"

The tiny dent appeared again above Orhan's forehead, about where the hair would have started, had any grown there. The Turk's powerful chest rose and fell.

The information Orhan wanted came from an intelligence report. Yet the cop had a point: they needed all the information available to track down Elif.

*We will have to put our heads above the parapet.*

"Fifteen," Savage said. "Enough for a major complex attack. They could explode a truck bomb at the gate of the Dolmabahce here, followed by gunmen storming through the gap. Or an assault on the football stadium. Or a ship. The intelligence talked about a 'mortal blow' against Istanbul."

"We saw two men with Elif. Plus Dervis." Orhan grimaced and glanced towards the palace. "No-one could drive a truck anywhere near here."

"We don't know if Elif's kidnapping is part of this," Savage said. "But I would put money on it."

"Suppose they attacked here. How would they begin?"

"Your guys have set up a good security cordon," Savage said. "Roads closed, a wide perimeter, air cover." He pointed to a helicopter overhead. "Difficult for anyone to deliver a bomb bigger than a man can carry."

"Tell me something I don't know." Orhan shook his head. "Your retro bike is a joke, by the way. Where is your helmet? Perhaps I will give you an on-the-spot fine."

"If you tried that I would kill you. What about the phone on the tram?"

"A passenger says a man boarded at Eminonu, sat down, then disembarked, as if he had forgotten something. We think he planted the phone."

"Description?"

"Tall, slim, light beard, dark clothes."

"Same as half the men in Istanbul. If they sent the phone this way, they've probably gone in the opposite direction, back towards the excavation site. Or somewhere in-between."

"That includes the whole of the Old City. Unless it was a bluff, and they were coming this way after all." Orhan looked around. "I cannot see an attack happening here, John. All traffic is stationary. They have no hope of reaching the Summit. Why would they bring Elif here anyhow?"

"Good question. We're missing something. Any news from the phone at the excavation?"

"My contact in the Intelligence Department has unlocked the interface. He will upload any pictures or videos."

A white coastguard vessel stood guard over the choppy waters near the shore. "What about the Bosphorus?" Savage said. "Could they have transferred Elif onto a boat? No traffic there."

"Wait! The video is coming through." Orhan squinted at his screen and moved into the shade of a withered tree. "Look."

Savage craned forward, his hand on Orhan's shoulder.

A picture sprang into view. Bright lights illustrated a group of people around something set in the ground, like a low, rectangular stone table.

"Elif is on the right," Orhan said. "And her colleague, Dervis—see, with the big eyebrows. Here is a girl. Looks as if the cameraman fancies her."

The image panned down the body of a young woman wearing jeans, heavy boots, and a T-shirt. She in turn recorded the scene on her own phone. A shout came from off-screen, and the view swung round to show a slab of stone, rising into the air.

"Looks like the final act," Savage said.

"Here someone is putting the phone on the ledge. There he is: a young man with long hair. He is stepping in to help push the stone to one side. Elif is looking into the space beneath the stone."

The starkly-lit figure of Elif approached the newly exposed void. Savage held his breath. What could she see?

Dark hair framed Elif's face. She frowned as she knelt down, pushing a strand back behind her ear. But when she leaned forward into the tomb, she seemed to relax.

"She has seen something," Orhan said. "But what?"

The long-haired man stepped towards Elif, obstructing the camera, and spoke. Savage could not make out his words. Braced for an outbreak of violence, he half-expected the man to pull out a weapon. Yet Elif reacted first, sweeping back her arm against the man's legs so he tripped and fell backwards over something on the ground. Everyone in the tunnel laughed.

Except Elif.

What had she found to make her so aggressive—or protective?

Elif leaned forward, her face a mask, and pulled a tape measure from her pocket. She dipped her hands forward, out of sight. Then she extended her whole body into the space. Could she be reaching down for something?

"Freeze it there," Savage said.

Orhan touched the screen. The image showed Elif lifting an object from the tomb. "I can zoom in," Orhan said.

"It looks about the size of a new-born baby," Savage said. "Something wrapped in a hide, or cloth. I can't see the shape."

Elif gazed down at what she held in her arms, her face bright.

"What is that thing?" Orhan said. He restarted the video. "Now she is moving her head. Maybe she can see—wait." He froze the image again as an alert came up. "My friend in the Intelligence Department is messaging me."

Words appeared on the screen. *LOOKS LIKE YOUR SISTER FOUND THE PALLADIUM. BUT SO DID SOMEONE ELSE.*

"The Palladium? That bundle of rags could be anything," Savage said.

"The boys at HQ must be watching the video too," Orhan said. "Maybe they are further ahead." He hit 'play' again.

A commotion broke out in the tunnel. Someone shouted. The sharp detonation of a shot rang out from a silenced large-calibre hand-gun. The figure of the young man who had placed the camera on the ledge spun round, landing out of sight. More shots rang out, but the image showed only Elif, standing immobile, holding her bundle.

"Six," Orhan said. "Six chest shots."

"Why is Elif so calm?" Savage said. "She saw six people shot dead."

The figure of a masked man appeared briefly, a pistol in his hand, before stepping out of sight. Savage registered a heavy build, big hands, rapid, confident movements. More firing. The killer delivering the head-shots. Still Elif did not move. It was as if she, not the assailants, controlled the scene. Someone spoke off-screen. Elif replied.

"That is Dervis Basturk talking," Orhan said. "Something about a kidnap. But Elif refuses to leave." He shook his head. "And you think I am stubborn."

Savage stared at Elif's frozen form.

*When he approached Upturn, he had seen her bare feet, white skin exposed to the Moscow snow. He had known then his world had ended.*

"This is Elif, you idiot! Not some kind of joke!"

Orhan took a step back. "I thought you did not care?"

Savage said nothing. He had told Elif he did not, could not, care. Repeatedly.

Orhan bent his head over the phone. "Watch."

A final gunshot, off-screen. Elif, apparently unhurt, moved out of view. The picture showed the deserted excavation site. At last, he exhaled.

"It cannot be a coincidence the killers appear the moment Elif opens the tomb," Orhan said. "Someone must have tipped them off."

"The shooters never say a word." Savage kept his voice steady. "Well trained. Wait."

The screen burst into life. Savage and Orhan appeared, standing in front of the phone.

*Chest and head shots,* Savage said. *Executed.*

*The screen is blank.* Orhan's voice. The image went black as he picked up the phone and popped it into an evidence bag, but you could still hear the words.

Orhan: *I must call an ambulance.*

Savage: *Quickly. They have Elif.*

Orhan: *These people have rights, too.*

Savage: *Rights? They're corpses.*

"John," Orhan said. "What do you see?"

"My guess is Basturk tipped them off, since everyone else is dead. Elif found something in the excavation and took it with her. The kidnappers need what she found, or her, or both."

"What she found is the Palladium, according to my contact at the lab and half the journalists in Istanbul." Orhan raised his gaze. "The fact is, John, we still have no useful information about where Elif is or where the terrorists are planning to attack next."

## 38

E lif lay in darkness. The back of her head throbbed where she had cracked her skull against the metal seat-base. The engine whined as the taxi lurched forwards and stopped, throwing her head once more against the spot where her raw flesh met the steel.

She had learned the pattern. But that did not make the pain any less. She must have broken the skin the first time she hit her head against the seat support. She had sought to escape the wandering hands of the young gunman in the back seat, as he pawed her body under the pretext of searching for her phone.

Well, power ran two ways down a cable. If some sex-starved wannabe terrorist got his rocks off groping a trussed-up professor of archaeology, his urges gave her a way to control him.

She closed her eyes and fought to lick her lips, held immobile by the powerful adhesive of the masking tape. The car jerked forward and stopped again, rolling her helpless body to and fro.

She could not open her mouth to scream in pain.

Instead, she blew a blast of air and phlegm through her nostrils, bending her legs and torso as she fought to protect her head, but instead jarring her waist against a sharp-edged object on the floor. The killer's gun, maybe. Or some other piece of war-hardware the pathetic, sexually-challenged idiot used to boost his sense of self-worth.

What if the terrorists let her, Elif Mutlu, asphyxiate in the footwell of a Fiat taxi in the back streets of Istanbul without even telling her why they had seized her?

Who would ever know how, where, and why she had died?

She tried again to brace her body against the floor. As she did so, the soft bulk of the object she had lifted from the tomb touched her face.

Elif opened her eyes.

In the darkness beneath the blanket, the wrapping of the relic pressed against her cheek. A cool, spicy aroma of incense, or balm, rose from the fabric, or from whatever lay hidden within.

Why should she panic?

The men who had seized her needed her alive. They seemed to need Dervis, too.

Or could he be allied to them? Why had he disappeared from the excavation when Mehmet Ozdemir appeared with the two workmen?

Maybe he had snuck off to make a phone call. To tell their assailants the dig had accelerated.

Could Dervis have faked the terror that overcame him when the shooting started in the tunnel?

In the claustrophobic seat well, Elif closed her eyes, and opened them. The fact her captives needed her alive gave her power.

She knew what she must do.

Repeated blows against the metal bracket that fixed the front seat to the car frame as the taxi jerked forwards through the traffic had left the back of her head tender and bloodied. Elif rammed her face forwards into the back seat, her nose crushed against the cheap plastic, her cheek burning against the filthy fabric on the floor. She took a deep breath. Then she slammed her wounded head back against the steel support.

*The pain.*

Her mouth tried to scream, lips straining against the duct tape. But the adhesive held fast. Her throat convulsed, sending a great retching gob of bile rushing up, choking her, filling her mouth and her nostrils.

*Now I will choke to death. Drown in my own vomit. Or break my skull. You cannot stop me or defeat me.*

In the front seat, someone yelled. She could not make out the words. A shot of air penetrated her nostrils, making her giddy.

Time to show them how hard-headed a Turkish woman could be.

She folded her face forward and jack-knifed her body, smashing her head back. This time she knew to expect the agony. She could master pain. Elif drew a shuddering breath through whatever vile liquid clogged her nose. Her body tensed as shock flooded her nervous system.

Someone shouted again. Was he speaking Turkish? She understood nothing. A shrilling in her ears, like feedback in a microphone, drowned everything else. Hands reached for her. Too late. She bent her head forward once more.

Her movement grew stronger with each impact. Surely at the next blow her skull would shatter and crack.

Light streamed in as someone whipped the blanket away. A man stared down at her. He had strong features, straggly dark hair, and a light beard, like many of the archaeology students in her university courses. But his eyes blazed, and his mouth was twisted in a snarl as though she, rather than he, had done something frightful. He shoved the muzzle of some primitive gun into her face, as if she cared.

They needed her alive. She possessed the most powerful weapon: her own body.

*Again.*

But as she braced to smash her head back a final time, the man seized hold of her hair and jerked her towards him. Instead of the raw pain of bone against metal, new agony ripped through her as her ruined scalp met the fabric of the seat-back, and the man's grip twisted her neck out of line.

"Bitch!" The man slapped her with the back of his hand. Her neck jerked sideways, her bound hands unable to balance her body.

"Whore! You think you can kill yourself? You belong to us. You will die when we say, not before." He raised his fist, teeth bared, to strike her helpless face.

## 39

That thud again. Target One had learned how to fight back. Ali gripped the steering wheel tighter.

The Protocol said they must remain silent at all times. Silence gave them strength. They needed maximum power to achieve their historic mission, unimaginable in its scale and destructive impact.

Yet the premature start meant Ali and Hussein must stay longer than planned with the hostages. They must improvise. They must communicate.

Hussein's inaction threatened the life of the archaeologist.

"Stop her." Ali kept his voice calm. "We need her alive. Why are you sitting there?"

"What can I do?"

"Grab her! Hold her! Anything but sit there letting her kill herself!"

The traffic opened up ahead. Behind, a horn sounded. The car juddered forward and stopped again.

Did God not wish the mission to succeed? Or was he testing their devotion, as he had tested Ali when everything had gone so wrong at the hospital?

Behind him came sounds of a struggle, then a slap as Hussein tried to stop the woman's self-harm.

"Stuff something behind her head, moron," Ali said. "Do not harm her."

Hussein grunted. Another slap.

"*I said do not harm her!*"

Ali whirled around. Hussein had raised his fist as if to punch Target One in the face.

"I was not going to hit her." Hussein lowered his fist.

"Did you not read The Protocol?"

"Yes. I did not hit her."

Ali turned to face the road, his heart racing. How could they regain control? The Protocol had foreseen seizing Targets One and Two in mid-afternoon and moving directly to the Balat house. Instead, the arrival of the workers with their heavy lifting tools had accelerated activity at the excavation.

Every minute of Ali's training had focused on command. *Take the initiative*, his instructors had told him. *Be ready*. Today, the training had paid off: when summoned, he and Hussein had carried out the operation professionally, despite the unexpected arrival of an unmarked police car.

But half a day remained before their next assignment. They could not yet move to the Balat house. They must occupy the fall-back location. The Protocol said a brother waited for them there.

Could Ali trust such a "brother"? Why should he? The "brother" might not know how to keep his mouth shut, for hours, while Ali and Hussein lay low with Targets One and Two. What if he betrayed them?

To make things worse, they could not reach the fall-back location by car. They must proceed on foot with two hostages, through the alleyways of the Old City, without attracting unwelcome attention.

Behind him, Hussein seemed to have subdued Target One. She fought like a tiger. She must have worked out that her actions lay at the heart of The Protocol. She had tried to destroy their plan by destroying herself. How did she know to do that? By contrast, Target Two had become compliant when he witnessed the executions in the tunnel. He sat rigid in the front passenger seat, his wrists cuffed behind him.

Target Two could be induced to walk a considerable distance, if necessary, by the threat of pain, violence, or death.

Target One might refuse to walk at all.

Ali peered at the navigation system. Every route seemed to be pedestrianised, one-way, or choked with traffic. Every street was steep, narrow, and packed with people.

A vacant lot came into view with a board advertising parking services by the hour or by the day. A boy sat in the shade, cigarette in hand, drawing in the dust with a stick.

Ali knew what he must do.

He turned the wheel and leaned towards Hussein.

"Prepare the ether."

"Two doses in an hour will harm her."

"Do it!"

Ali wrenched the taxi to the side of the street, alongside a derelict, domed structure of reddened brick. Behind him came sounds of an unequal struggle as Hussein applied the ether. Sweet fumes filled the air. They reminded Ali of the antiseptic smell of the hospital.

The vapour would condemn the woman to violent nausea and a head like an inferno when she awoke.

But they need expect no trouble from her until then.

The commotion in the back seat subsided.

"It is done." Hussein's voice had risen a tone.

Ali braced himself. He must take control, as leader.

"Remove the bindings," he said. "Be careful when you take off the tape. Her face must look unharmed."

Ali waited. Next to him the big man, Target Two, stared straight ahead. Even in the crowded street, people did not see inside the taxi. The vehicle made them invisible.

What was Hussein doing in the back?

Ali turned in his seat. The muscle, Hussein, cradled Target One in his arms. He supported her bare neck with one hand and held the other underneath her body, out of sight. He had not removed the silver tape covering her mouth.

"She is beautiful," Hussein said.

"Are you crazy?" Ali reached back across the seat. His big fingers might look clumsy, but years of surgery had taught him to perform the most delicate of actions. He caught the edge of the tape and peeled the fabric away, massaging the skin beneath to reduce the risk of damage.

Hussein's mouth formed a sneer. The ether-soaked cloth lay across his lap. "I am not crazy. But she is lovely," he said. "I want to —" His mouth opened and he licked his lips.

"Leave her be, idiot. Get out. You will bring her. He will help."

Ali gripped the knife. He leaned as though to embrace Target Two in the seat next to him and placed the blade flat against the man's neck, cold steel on skin.

"I cannot kill her," he said. "You, I can. Now. In five minutes. In ten." Ali spoke with a conversational tone. "With this blade, I can cut your eyes. Your tongue. Your nose. Your ears. Your tendons, one by one. I am used to cutting. I can leave you to bleed, here in the car."

"No. Please."

"Silence. If you help us, you will live. You will serve the higher cause you sought. Freedom of religion, for everyone. Our beloved Greek Gods, too, are worth fighting for."

"But you killed—*ah!*"

"I said, silence." Ali slid the blade beneath the man's epidermis. A clean incision. No depth. Plenty of pain. With his other hand he stripped the cover from an adhesive dressing in his pocket and pressed the plaster hard against the invisible tip of the blade beneath the skin.

Target Two shuddered. His mouth opened in a low moan.

Ali withdrew the blade, pressed hard on the exit wound, and smoothed the dressing to stop any bleeding.

"You are serving your God and ours," Ali said. "If you obey."

"I will obey. I, of all people, understand the meaning of belief. The importance of tolerance." Target Two's body still trembled.

The man's fear of pain made him the perfect hostage. A valuable foil to Target One, who seemed resistant to any form of coercion.

Ali undid the man's handcuffs. "Step out. Help him to bring the woman. You." He turned to Hussein. "Walk together, slowly, up the hill. I will follow."

"What about the AK?"

"We do not need it. And we cannot carry a long weapon in the street."

Hussein reached into the back seat and hauled Target One out of the car. He lifted her with his wiry arms, reaching around her upper body so she seemed to be leaning on him. Target Two stood across from him, supporting the woman from the other side. Her hair fell forward as the men took the first steps.

Ali waited as they climbed the hill. No wonder Hussein could not keep his hands off the woman. The khaki shorts revealed her long, smooth legs. Even semi-conscious, her features displayed a curious calm, more like a free woman daydreaming than a hostage living through a nightmare. Her lips hung open. Her grubby khaki shirt hung loose. The sun-hat Hussein had jammed over her brow concealed whatever damage she had done to her head.

Why had she shown no fear in the car?

Even in the tunnel, after Ali gunned down six of her friends and colleagues, she had disobeyed his orders.

He could not tolerate such defiance.

The two men, supporting Target One's slumped form, set off up the alleyway that climbed the hill. They weaved amongst the scooters careering through the crowds of shoppers, men hauling recycling carts, *simitcis* balancing piles of freshly-baked *simits* on their heads, tea-boys darting from shop to shop with trays of steaming tea-glasses, and tourists rooted to the spot by whatever fresh wonder they had encountered.

Ali sat behind the wheel of the taxi and drove onto the patch of waste ground.

The boy minding the car-park jumped to his feet, eager to earn a tip by helping with the taxi. Ali waved him away with a scowl.

First: cover Hussein's assault rifle with the blanket they had used to hide the woman.

Next: ensure his pistol nestled snug in the rear waistband of his jeans.

Last, and most important: gather up the object the woman had retrieved from the tomb.

The fabric wrapped around the object hid what lay beneath. Secrecy trumped curiosity. *Avoid drawing attention to the object,* The Protocol said. *Deliver the relic, and Target One, at the appointed time.*

He placed the bundle under his jacket, paid the boy, and set off up the hill. Ahead, Hussein and Target Two made steady progress through the crowds. They stopped, started, paused as if to look at a shop display, and moved on.

Hussein behaved like a crazed teenager when it came to sex. But his tradecraft was second to none.

The buildings on each side grew older and taller. On the left, a stone doorway led into a pool of shadows. A man sat in a chair, resting on a stick; he looked up as Ali passed, clear eyes set in a brown, wrinkled face. He gestured to a sack of scarves at his side.

"*Buyrun abi,*" he said. Take a look.

Ali gripped the object more tightly under his jacket. He moved closer to Hussein. Their destination came into view: a decorated, monumental structure. They needed five more minutes to step off the street into forgiving shadows of their own.

Until then, their path lay exposed.

A motorized delivery tricycle roared up the one-way street behind him, ignoring the traffic rules like everyone else in the city. Ali stepped aside. Two minutes to go. He had nearly caught up with Hussein.

An overweight policeman stepped out of a café, straightening the trousers of his uniform. A pistol hung in a leather holster at his hip.

Ali kept walking.

Hussein, too, did not pause. But Target Two stopped dead, as though his big feet had been nailed to the ground.

The policeman noticed Target Two come to a halt. He stepped towards the two men, one hand on his pistol, and peered at the slumped figure of Target One.

"What is the matter with your friend? Is she ill?"

## 40

I n the gridlocked mass of cars blocked by the police at the Dolmabahce Palace, temperatures rose. Somewhere in the jam, a driver sounded his horn. In seconds a hundred, two hundred horns blared out.

Savage wiped his brow. The frames of his sunglasses burned his face. In the shade of a café, tourists sipped black tea from tulip glasses by the water, unaware of the vast counterterrorism operation taking place next door.

Orhan Mutlu slipped his phone back into his pocket and rocked to and fro on his heels. A trickle of sweat ran down his temple. He scanned the police lines, frowned at the barricades around the palace, cast a glance towards the choppy blue waters of the Bosphorus, and rounded on Savage. "Where the hell are your fifteen terrorists? Where is Elif? What are we doing here?"

Crowds swarmed down the hill from the direction of Taksim, many disgorged from stationary buses and taxis. A few Liverpool fans explored the city ahead of the match. Savage watched them. Any threat could only approach on foot. No-one could get past the police, and the traffic, to reach the palace.

"Maybe we're wrong," he said. "Maybe a fanatic bunch of archaeology nuts is lining up raids on Troy, Ephesus, and Pergamon as we speak. But I'm sure whoever took Elif is linked to something bigger, right here in Istanbul. Scoping out targets has to be our best shot at finding your sister."

"Sure. So where is she?"

Orhan stared at Savage. The intelligence agent sought to display the slick mix of macho, stubborn, and sophisticated that defined so many Turkish men. Yet the flicker in his eyes told a different story.

Where had the kidnappers taken Elif?

Two weeks earlier, he had sat opposite her at a restaurant in Galata. She had sipped a glass of white wine, wearing a black dress that left her shoulders bare.

The evening had been strained. Elif had discussed the latest finds at the dig and the time pressure from Arzu Pasha. He had described his work with the Turkish police to tackle people-trafficking gangs along the Aegean coast.

Savage had not asked why she had turned down his last three attempts to arrange a night out. She had not volunteered any explanation.

At last, after the waiter had cleared away the main course and brought them each a tiny cup of aromatic Turkish coffee, she had reached across the table and taken his hand. "Do you love me, John?" she had asked.

"What is the point in asking that? I'm English," he had replied. "If I said yes, you would never believe me. I'm not great on romance. But I am reliable."

When she shook her head, her dark hair brushed the brown skin of her shoulders. "Did you just tell me you were reliable? You are beyond unromantic. I would like to say I love you anyway. But I am not sure being harnessed to a cold-blooded English reptile will ever work for me." She had sighed and looked down at her coffee.

"I'm not cold-blooded. You know that for a fact. You are the one who keeps telling me you're too busy to meet."

"Can you not be serious? The dig in the Old City is consuming me. We have two more weeks before we must close the site." She had shuffled her things together and stood. "Let's pause it," she had said, and headed for the exit. "I will not have time to see you anyhow."

"But I want to be with you," he had said to her back.

At the door, she had paused. "Really?" She had left without saying another word.

They had not met again until their disastrous drink last night. Had the killings in Moscow and Sevastopol turned him into a monster, incapable of love? Who could he love, if not Elif? Now she had vanished into the boundless city of Istanbul.

"You are right, this is a long shot," Savage said to Orhan. "I still think the Summit is the likeliest target. But I can't see how they could bring Elif here in this gridlock."

"Two elected presidents," Orhan said. "A reconciliation process. Millions of ordinary Greeks and Turks hate what is happening, let alone terrorist groups. You are supposed to be the man with the operational experience, John. How would you breach the perimeter?"

Savage looked in every direction. Nothing here could threaten the summit.

*Wait.* At the street entrance to the Dolmabahce Mosque, two men supported the limp body of a woman. Had she fainted? A third man hovered behind, as if deciding whether to help.

"Look. Is that Elif?"

The Turk whirled round. "Where?"

"Entering the mosque. They went inside."

Orhan ran. "Good work. Kick off your shoes at the entrance."

"You got it."

Savage threw himself forward, dodging between tight-packed groups of people observing the police operation or heading for the ferry terminals at Kabatas. A few seconds later they stood inside the shady entrance to the mosque. Orhan stepped out of his shoes effortlessly; Savage spent a moment tugging at his laces.

Inside, cool air surrounded them. A ceiling rose high above, lit by circular windows.

A few men stood talking at the rear of the chamber, a handful more prayed. Where had the woman gone?

"Are you sure they came in here?" Orhan lowered his voice. "This area is for men only."

"I am sure."

"Is there another way in?"

"They came in here."

Orhan muttered under his breath and walked out. They paused inside the entrance. Savage held his breath.

Someone whispered behind a curtain to one side.

Might the fabric conceal a passage, or an alcove? He seized Orhan's arm, tapped his ear, and pointed to the curtain. Orhan drew his weapon. He stepped forward and ripped the cloth aside.

An elderly, dark-skinned woman in a headscarf lay on a bed of cushions, her eyes closed. A younger woman fanned her sweating face with a piece of card. Two men stood nearby, watching.

"What is this? Did you just come in here?" Orhan barked the words in Turkish, but shot an accusatory glance at Savage.

The two men flinched at the sight of the gun. The woman on the cushions opened her eyes and stared at the mouth of the weapon. But the younger woman snapped back. "The *abla* fainted in the street. These brothers helped her. Shame on you!"

Orhan stared at the two women, his face working, and sheathed his pistol. "I am sorry," he said. "We were following a tip-off. Peace be with you." He turned to Savage and gestured to the exit with his chin.

Outside, the sun seemed hotter than ever. Orhan shook his head. "Idiot. How could you think she was Elif? An old woman in a headscarf?"

Savage breathed deeply. "I only saw them for a second."

"Think harder!" The Turk struck his thigh with his open hand. "Will they attack here? How?"

To the left rose the bulk of the Besiktas stadium. To the right, two blue-and-white armoured police Land Rovers stood in front of a high iron fence marking the palace grounds. A row of riot police leaned on their shields.

"If it was me, I would attack somewhere else," Savage said. "Or if I had to launch an assault here, I would use a fast boat to land south or north of the Palace. Hard for them to get here any other way, with the roads closed."

"Brilliant theory. A child could have thought of it. The Summit begins in three minutes. I cannot see how a boat could land anywhere near here."

Orhan jogged down to the water. The high palace fence jutted out far over the Bosphorus, the rusty iron spikes festooned with gleaming new coils of razor wire.

"Hey! Back off!"

A riot policeman clutching a high plastic shield, his legs and chest protected by thick curves of body armour, advanced on them, baton drawn. "This is a restricted area. What are you playing at?"

"I am a police officer." Orhan held up his badge. "Take it easy."

The riot policeman lowered his baton. He ignored Savage and addressed Orhan in a low voice. "Sorry. We are on high alert. They are expecting a terror attack. Suicide bombers, maybe." He used the Turkish phrase, *living bombs*. "The Summit is starting already, so maybe it is a false alarm. But I would stand further back if I were you, especially in plain clothes. There are snipers everywhere."

"Sure thing." Orhan led the way back towards a row of bollards separating the car park from the security zone next to the palace fence. High above, two masked soldiers with automatic weapons eyed them from the peak of an ornate bell-tower.

"Congratulations. Now we're suspects," Savage said. They paused next to an empty yellow tourist coach, stranded by the traffic.

"It shows security is good, idiot." Orhan punched his hand.

"Hold on."

Across the street, a young couple holding hands stepped out from the crowd of onlookers facing the police lines. Savage tensed and gripped Orhan's shoulder. Both youngsters wore long, loose jackets. At first they ambled forwards, then they picked up pace. *Towards the police buses.*

"Orhan—see those two people? Call in a warning."

"Where?" Orhan gripped his police radio in his hand.

Everything moved in slow motion. As an armed police officer in a bullet-proof jacket stepped out to intercept the couple, they split apart, each running straight at a police bus.

"*Down. Get down!*"

Orhan reached for his pistol. A uniformed official guarding the police buses raised his automatic weapon.

Savage had failed. Again. *He saw the six-inch nails pinning Upturn's frozen, naked flesh to the pine tree in the Moscow snow, chill fingers of defeat gripping his heart.* Here at the Dolmabahce Palace, nothing could stop the two suicide bombers.

Automatic gunfire rang out. Orhan turned towards the sound, his pistol rising to take a shot. The blast would rip him apart.

Savage's fist connected with Orhan's chin with such power that the blow lifted the heavily-built Turk off the ground. Orhan tumbled to the concrete behind the axle of the yellow coach. Savage threw himself on top of him. The pistol spun away across the asphalt.

Orhan's face contorted in pain and rage. "*What the—*"

Whatever Orhan said next was drowned in twin explosions that shook the ground on which they lay.

## 41

The Turkish coastguard vessel surged forward, white with a bright orange stripe on the hull, edged in dark blue. The stripe, and the prow of the ship, thrust forward as if to highlight the vessel's aggressive intent. The twin .50 calibre cannon sent the same message.

Saif stood his ground.

He, Saif-al-Din, commanded the orange-coloured boat. He must play the part of captain like the most natural thing in the world.

The patrol boat moved closer, bow high in the water, and turned, coasting parallel to the smaller ship.

What could the crew of the coastguard vessel see?

Saif took a step to his left, placing one foot over the biggest bloodstain. He held his breath. Were other marks visible, where Kaan's careless knee-capping of the boy had let spatters of blood soak into the wooden decking?

He gripped the railing. Perhaps his feet covered the blood. His uniform matched the real thing. Should he wave? What was the naval protocol when approached by a Turkish coastguard ship? If only he could consult Uzay.

The hard bulk of the pistol pressed against Saif's waist. After thousands of practice rounds in training, he could hit any part of the coastguard ship he chose. But he had no chance of damaging or disabling the white vessel. The coastguard's .50 calibre machine guns, by contrast, could cut Saif, Kaan, and Uzay to pieces in moments and consign their ship to the bottom of the Sea of Marmara.

Kaan poked his head around the corner of the cabin. "Come inside. Radio."

Saif walked the short distance to the wheelhouse. The imperious voice of the coastguard commander filled the cabin.

"Report anything suspicious. I repeat. Be on high alert. Confidential sources indicate the probability of a terrorist attack today in Istanbul. Report anything suspicious."

Of course. No experienced sailor expected the coastguard to communicate by shouting between their two ships. Uzay, the mariner, kept one hand on the wheel; with the other, he held the speaker set of the VHF unit.

"Roger that," he said. "Thanks for the warning." He nodded to Saif, and turned to look ahead.

"Be alert to any sign of other vessels behaving suspiciously," the coastguard continued. "We had a weak radar signal for a second, smaller vessel in the vicinity, perhaps approaching you. Did you see anything?"

"Negative that." Uzay held his voice steady.

"You enjoy a quiet day." The tone of the coastguard lightened. "What are you planning to do?"

"Work. Eat. Sleep," Uzay said. He turned a questioning gaze to Saif. *Quiet day?*

"Good luck with that. Now they have closed the Bosphorus to water traffic, you could just be sleeping and eating."

"We have our orders," Uzay said.

"Have a good trip. Stay out of trouble." Without warning, the coastguard ship accelerated, its engines boiling the ocean as the bow turned away to port. In a few minutes the menacing silhouette had accelerated out of sight.

Uzay docked the handset on the VHF unit. "They closed the Bosphorus?"

Saif shook his head. "Keep going. The Protocol covers all variables."

Uzay nodded and glanced at the clock. Then he rested both hands on the wheel and let the vessel move forwards at a steady pace.

Now came the time for leadership. Saif al-Din stared out the window as the sea moved past. Kaan hauled the bodies below deck.

Saif nodded his approval.

Had he kept his face impassive? He must not betray any weakness or uncertainty. But his mind raced.

For The Protocol to succeed, the Bosphorus must be open to sea traffic. What could they do now?

# 42

In the cobbled street close to the Grand Bazaar, Ali Aydin, the Controller, stepped closer to the stout policeman confronting Target Two and Hussein a few yards ahead.

"I said: is she ill?" The uniform peered at the slumped figure of Target One, then back to Target Two. The big archaeologist stared straight ahead, like a statue amidst the bustle of people flowing up and down the cobbled street.

The cop frowned, his lips forming a question mark. Should Ali draw his weapon? Impossible: people milled around them in the street. Flight? No. Even if Ali escaped, he could not complete The Protocol without Target One or, if all else failed, Target Two.

The Elders said The Protocol provided for every eventuality. But no-one could forecast the behaviour of each person in Istanbul.

Why did he feel so calm, despite the crisis? The object nestled against his body. He could trust in God. The police officer could not be searching for the kidnap victims, or he would already have raised the alarm. He must have eaten an early lunch while he read a newspaper or chatted with the proprietor over a backgammon board. He could have no idea what he had stumbled over.

His ignorance gave Ali and Hussein a chance.

"She is my wife, sir." Ali took a step forward up the hill. "She fainted in the heat." He indicated Target Two. "This man is my driver." He nodded at Hussein. "He is my security. We need to find a cool place to sit and rest."

The policeman turned towards the newcomer. Ali met his gaze, while taking in his adversary. The cop had a paunch, flabby arms, magnificent leather boots—surely not standard issue—and a heavy growth of stubble. His small eyes flicked between Ali and Hussein; his hand rested on his holstered sidearm.

"Sir," the cop said, "she looks more dead than alive. Her face is like chalk. Has she been ill? It does not look like heat-stroke to me." Again, he peered at Target One. "Hello? Lady? Wake up."

All around them, tourists, shoppers, vendors, and motor scooters pushed up and down the street. A couple of young boys stopped to watch the cop question his suspects. One sucked a lollypop. The sun blazed down, searing the street and everyone who had not found shade.

The police officer bent to take a closer look at Target One. Hussein, the attack dog, glanced at Ali and tilted his head towards his waist, where he carried a short-bladed knife. *Let me finish it*, he seemed to be saying. *Let me kill the uniform.* A tremor in Hussein's face betrayed his agitation.

Hussein could dispose of the cop in an instant.

But in the crowded alleyway in Mahmutpasa, a hundred witnesses surrounded them.

Ali licked his lips and forced a smile. What was a single policeman against the will of the Almighty?

He raised his hand. "Come. Let us step into the shade together. Once my wife can sit down, the driver will fetch us tea." Ali placed his hand on Target Two's back. "Why stand here in the mid-day sun?"

Gently, he pushed Target Two towards the tall, dark structure on the right. The gate stood broad and high, a truck could pass inside. The carved words *Buyuk Valide Han* stood over the entrance. They stepped across a threshold fashioned from worn marble hundreds of years old.

Target Two took a halting zombie-step nearer the doorway.

The police officer scowled at him. "What is the matter with you? Are you going to faint, too?" He took a step back. "Okay, enough joking around. Show me some ID. Easy does it." He pulled out his radio, his other hand still on his gun.

The group of watching boys grew to four, like a tiny Greek chorus. Three of them took a step back, echoing the police officer.

Ali's eyes narrowed. They could not let the cop call in their fake IDs. If he arrested them, or called reinforcements, he signed a death sentence for The Protocol and all those who had worked for its glorious goals.

They must kill the policeman. Ali shifted his hand closer to his waist. But the officer followed the movement, fingers flexing, ready to draw his weapon in an instant.

Ali tilted his head a fraction towards Hussein. *Be ready.*

"My ID is here." Ali made a piece of theatre of opening his jacket to display the inner pocket, aiming to distract the victim. "See, I—"

The unmistakable roar of two explosions, half a second apart, echoed across the city.

Everyone turned to stare down the street towards the Golden Horn and Besiktas.

"*Allah, Allah,*" the police officer said. "A bomb. Two bombs. Here in Istanbul, on the European side." He shook his head and gestured at Ali. "Get your wife inside. This is an evil day for our city."

Without another word, he turned and sprinted up the street, his radio to his ear, dodging between passers-by who stopped to stare in the direction of the explosions.

"Inside," Ali said. He guided Target Two and Hussein into the deep shadow of the *Han*. As he did so, he glanced back to the street.

Who knew what had caused the explosions? The Protocol contained many elements of which he knew nothing.

The police officer had spoken the truth when he said this was an evil day for Istanbul. How evil, he could not imagine. In the next few hours, the cop and every person in the street faced an agonising death.

The suffering of this day had barely begun.

## 43

S avage flinched as a spattering of shattered safety glass from the bus windows fell on him, blunt brittle chunks blown clear by the pressure waves. Next, other fragments from the site of the explosion came raining down. Pellets of metal, thrown upwards by the bombs while others drove laterally into the soft flesh of victims. Scraps of cloth. Small, indistinguishable pieces of people.

Fragments of the suicide bombers themselves. Maybe of victims, too.

Savage lay on the ground. The precipitation intensified, then ceased. His ears rang. Had the city fallen silent? Or had the detonations deafened him?

What if gunmen launched a follow-up attack, seeking to penetrate the gap the bomb blew in the police lines? Did one or two more bombers stand in the crowd, waiting to step forward when the emergency services arrived?

He raised his head from the asphalt and peered under the bus. No-one moved towards the Dolmabahce Palace. He could hear no gunfire.

As if in response, sounds penetrated his consciousness. The chirping of car alarms set off by the blast. The swell of approaching sirens. Seagulls squawking. But no shots.

It didn't make sense.

What made an isolated pair of suicide attackers target a police detachment so far away from the outer walls of the Dolmabahce Palace, without a follow-up plan to do harm to the summit inside?

Had the young couple belonged to the fifteen operators the intelligence report predicted? Or had they acted independently?

Had Orhan survived the bombing?

Savage hauled himself onto one elbow and looked around. Smoke, dust, and the reek of burned flesh stung his nostrils. The Turkish intelligence cop lay motionless, face down. Could the axle of the bus have shielded him? Or had he caught the blast full-on?

He moved on his hands and knees to Orhan's body and did a visual check, examining Orhan's head, trunk, arms, and legs. No external sign of major trauma. No limbs at odd angles.

"Orhan."

No response.

Had the explosions deafened Orhan, too?

Savage slid his arm under the Turk's shoulders, turning him gently in case the blast had damaged the front of his body.

"Orhan. You useless bastard."

The Turk opened his eyes.

"Welcome back," Savage said. He glanced down Orhan's body, checking for injuries. "Hey. Hello."

The intelligence cop groaned and raised one hand to his brow. "My head." He frowned and looked down at his hand. Blood dripped from his fingers.

"Let me see." A patch of vivid red stood out on the Turk's brow. His head must have struck the concrete. "Who am I? Do you know what day it is?" Savage peered into the brown eyes.

Orhan frowned. "I know you are a treacherous English spy, a bomb has gone off, and today is the day we will get Elif back." He paused and touched his chin. "Wait. You hit me!"

"I was trying to put you behind the bus and didn't have time to argue. You're getting a terrific bruise on your forehead. Want me to clean it up?"

Orhan rotated his jaw and blinked. "You saved my life." He rose to his knees and waited a few seconds while blood circulated around his body. "I owe you one." He climbed to his feet. Then he held out a hand. "Thanks. I guess you enjoyed the chance to belt me."

"It was the most fun I've had in months." Savage took Orhan's hand in his.

Orhan held on tight. He took deep, regular breaths. For all his bravado, the intelligence cop was dazed from the blast.

"We must help," Savage said. "It's risky. There could be a follow-up attack on the rescue workers. They're calling that a double-tap too, now, like an execution, the terrorists repeat the trick so often. But we can't hide away."

Orhan stared at him. "Sometimes, John, I think you must have Turkish blood in you."

They stepped out from behind the bus.

Bodies lay scattered across the street. Two ambulances threaded between the victims from the direction of the Dolmabahce Palace. Medics knelt over recumbent bodies, cutting away clothes. Police unfolded crowd control barriers to stop onlookers encroaching. Here and there, figures lay further from the epicentre of the blast. One or two raised a hand, calling for help. Others lay still. Up the hill, four police riot control buses inched their way down a path cleared through the traffic, followed by two TOMA water cannon. Uniformed police ran out from the palace.

Savage surveyed the scene. After the blast, as emergency services gathered, the site of a bombing made a high-value, vulnerable target. The lack of a follow-up attack did not surprise him. The tactic required good logistics and trained personnel. But the omission made the attack itself seem doubly senseless. He grabbed Orhan.

"What was the goal? Of the attack?"

Orhan wheeled around. "You do not see a target? I see dead and injured police officers."

"Why attack the perimeter, if you're not going to follow through?"

"Can you not accept we failed to prevent a deadly attack?"

"The scale of this is wrong. We saw two suicide bombers. Thirteen more are out there, maybe including whoever took Elif."

"See the security convoy descending the hill?" Orhan said. "Those are elite units. They should be guarding Taksim Square."

"The place where the communists and nationalists are about to hold massive rallies. A vast crowd, whose protection is being diverted down here. Maybe the people who took Elif plan a spectacular attack at Taksim."

"Why would they?" Orhan shook his head. "But you were right about the Summit." The Turk hesitated and gripped Savage's arm. "If I were to tell anyone in Turkey an Englishman predicted the site of a terrorist attack, they would tell me you must have planned it."

Savage's phone rang. Orhan, too, reached for his pocket.

"John? This is Christopher Braintree."

"Consul General. I'm here. It's awful."

"It is. Have you seen the reports?"

"I can see at least seven police officers down. Maybe more. The emergency services are here in force."

For a long moment the Consul General said nothing. "What on earth are you talking about?"

"I'm at the site of the Dolmabahce bombing. I can't make sense of the attack."

"What the hell are you doing there? They told me you were a trouble magnet, Savage, but I obviously never grasped the magnitude of the issue. I am talking about a video going viral on the internet of you ignoring the victims of the shooting at the building site this morning. Including a British citizen, Stuart Lamont, who happened to be disabled. You are audible on the video as saying there is no point in trying to help the victims because, and I quote, 'They're corpses.'" Braintree's voice rose a tone. "Why, for heaven's sake, would you say such a thing?"

"Because I saw they were dead. Shots to the heart and head. Meanwhile, we knew kidnappers had seized two hostages from the site a few minutes earlier. We had to give the living priority."

"John, are you a member of a Turkish counter-terrorist unit or a British police liaison officer?"

"I would do anything to save a life."

"Really? What about Moscow?"

"*What?*"

Braintree paused, as if aware he had gone too far. "Have you any idea how this is running in the UK media? Several of our journalist friends have pointed out that you are one of our team in Istanbul responsible for the safety of two thousand British football fans this evening."

"Do you want to talk about Moscow or Istanbul?"

"Who are these hostages? Are they British?"

"Turkish, we think."

"Who are they? Or is that a secret?"

Savage hesitated. "The Turkish Police believe the hostages are Elif Mutlu, the head of the archaeological team at the site, and Dervis Basturk, her assistant."

"Elif Mutlu. You ignored a British consular case to run after a Turkish citizen who happens to be your girlfriend. Do you ever consider the consequences of your actions, John? Or their impact on British interests?"

"Bad people plan something cataclysmic for today. Nothing will serve British—and Turkish—interests better than stopping a bloodbath. I think the Dolmabahce attack is a diversion. Do you know if Ram has anything new?"

He meant, speaking on an open line, *is there any fresh intelligence?*

"In case you have forgotten, John, you are not SIS any longer. I want you to return to Pera House. Immediately. I am calling a meeting to decide whether we should ask the Turks to cancel tonight's Besiktas-Liverpool game."

"A meeting?" Savage gripped the phone. "The Turks will decide whether to cancel the match. The key is whoever seized Elif. The video from the dig shows she found something in a tomb before the kidnappers arrived."

"You have already made a punch-bag of the Foreign Office, John.

Don't make it a laughing-stock. I don't know what you think you achieved in your last job in Sevastopol, or wherever it was, by disobeying orders, but I will not put up with it. If you are not at the Consulate within the next hour, you will be on the next plane out of here. I won't ask–"

Savage terminated the call. He turned to Orhan. The intelligence cop's face had turned scarlet below the swollen bruise on his forehead. The tendons on his neck stood out.

"Let me guess," Savage said. "The Special Ops guy, Korkmaz, has been onto your boss and has summoned you back to base."

"You?"

"I am a disgrace to the Diplomatic Service and if I don't go back to the Consulate, I'm toast."

"They want to take my badge while they investigate. And my weapon." Orhan touched the gun at his waist reflexively. "Getting it back will take months."

They looked at each other. Savage lowered his hand to the saddle of the Thruxton. All around, the great city of Istanbul pulsated with life. Piece by piece, terrorists had dismantled the defences of the metropolis. They had taken Elif alive for a purpose: to harm the city and all who lived there. That harm loomed closer as every minute passed. How could he possibly go back now to sit in a meeting in Pera House?

"I vote we try and find Elif," Savage said. "Will you help?"

Orhan squared his shoulders. "I will not help you. You will help me. This is my country. And Elif is my sister."

Savage eased the Triumph off its stand. The bike started with a throaty roar. "Want a ride to Taksim?"

"Sure. I just hope none of my friends spot me riding on the back of your ridiculous machine."

# 44

In Mahmutpasa, a breeze ventilated the entrance to the *Buyuk Valide Han,* cool after the bustling street. A long-haired blond boy and a slim blonde girl sat on a low ledge inside the archway, fiddling with their phones. Hussein glanced at the girl's legs as they passed.

Ali twisted his lip in a sneer. The tourists must be looking for news of whatever bombs had gone off a few minutes earlier. Perhaps they believed the solid, ancient stones of the *Han* could somehow protect their resting place.

He shook his head. Little did they know that death stood next to them.

The entrance led into an open courtyard. To the left, a steep, grimy staircase climbed to a gallery with a vaulted roof. Hussein and Target Two moved past the couple into the shade, still supporting Target One. Hussein held his arm around the woman's waist, as if to support her. But his arm was bare, and her shirt had ridden up, exposing a stripe of burnt-cream skin.

Had Hussein deliberately brought his arm into contact with the waist of Target One?

Ali frowned. He had no time to deal with Hussein's animal urges. But the man's behaviour threatened to disrupt The Protocol. He should be thinking how to put maximum distance between them and the street, not trying to touch up the woman.

The encounter with the police officer could still bite them. What if the cop learned later about two people missing after the killings at the archaeological site? Might he recall the unconscious woman in Mahmutpasa?

Ali hesitated. The decision he took now, to seek out the fall-back safe house in the *Valide Han* or to seek an alternative refuge, could determine the outcome of the operation. If today's great work succeeded, he and his team stood ready to punish the godless of Istanbul for their apostasy. But what if he failed? Ali looked down at the dusty ground. Many brave men had martyred themselves to make today's action possible. He must not be the one to rob their sacrifice of meaning.

Hussein stood still, his straggly hair falling over his forehead, his hand against the naked waist of Target One, waiting for his leader.

Ali made his decision. He reached across, gripped Hussein's arm, and led the way towards the stairs. As he climbed, the artefact under his coat shifted next to his skin. How could the package from the grave be cool against his sweating body?

The action of moving calmed Ali. He and Hussein had seized the object. They had captured Targets One and Two. Now they must lie low for a few hours, complete The Protocol, and seal the fate of the corrupt city.

Might the police come after them? The Protocol intended the six bodies at the archaeological dig to cast sand in the eyes of a force investigating the wrong crime, in the wrong place. The fact the officer who intercepted them had not recognized Targets One and Two told its own story about police priorities.

Now, with perfect timing, someone had detonated two bombs in the heart of the city—by the sound of the explosions, somewhere near Besiktas. The fat policeman, like the rest of the security forces, had his hands full with whatever havoc those detonations wrought.

Police from all over Istanbul would be drawn to investigate the bombs and the bodies in the Old City. Ali smiled. The rest of the metropolis lay open to attack.

A warren of passageways filled the upper floor of the *Han*, with workshops and stores leading off to either side. Ali turned to the right at the top of the stairs. He ignored a broad passageway that lay ahead, pierced by a shaft of sunlight. Instead, they entered a narrow, shady corridor, lit by dim light from doorways on either side. He picked his way past a workshop where six or seven men sat barefoot on the floor, preparing oriental rugs for sale. A stout wooden door clad in worn metal, pitted with centuries of wear, barred the next opening. Inside a third doorway, a bearded Armenian craftsman bent over a machine, muscular shoulders gleaming, sending a cascade of sparks tumbling to the stone floor as he ground a metal component into shape.

Ali spat and walked on. No doubt the man made a living crafting worthless pieces of junk for the foreign tourists who flooded the city. Why did the authorities even allow Armenians to live in Istanbul, let alone ply their trade unhindered?

Within hours, every Armenian in the city would be dead.

Ali found what he sought two doorways further along. A narrow staircase climbed to the right, sandwiched between rough walls of antique stone. A rusty iron gate set into the masonry on either side blocked the foot of the stairs. The steps looked dusty with disuse.

He seized hold of a bar and shook. The grille stood solid as a mountain.

Ali smiled and flexed his fingers. The bars formed an obstacle only to unbelievers. He looked around to ensure no-one observed them and dropped to his knees, then reached through the lattice.

His hand encountered the rough blocks of the wall. He touched a damp patch. Close by, an iron peg protruded, cemented into the stone.

Nothing else.

Had they found the right staircase? He looked back at the passage, where Target One slumped against Hussein. Her nostrils twitched. Her legs jerked. What if she recovered consciousness or someone saw her, here on the upper floors of the *Han*?

He knelt again and stretched his hand out through the metal lattice. His fingers encountered the iron peg. They scrabbled to explore the hollow behind the rusty metal protrusion. Ali pressed his face into the bars until his jaw hurt, straining against the metal.

*There.* Behind the peg, almost out of reach, he felt a niche hollowed out of the mortar between two stones. Ali eased his fingertips into the dusty space. Something cold lay there. He laid the metal sliver in his hand.

The key looked as old and rusty as the gate. Yet the blade glistened with oil.

Hussein pointed at the face of Target One. The skin of her cheeks showed traces of colour. Her long black eyelashes trembled.

He could not rely upon her to sleep much longer.

They must get out of the corridor before the irrepressible tiger-woman shouted or drew attention to them.

Ali slid the key into the lock of the ancient gate. The mechanism turned smoothly. He pulled the grill open, then paused on the narrow stairs while the others hauled Target One past him. He re-locked the gate and slipped the key into his pocket.

Footsteps climbing towards the sky for hundreds of years had worn a smooth indentation in the centre of each marble step beneath his feet. The stairs curved to the left, perhaps following the outline of one of the domes making up the roof of the *Han*. The light from the passageway faded as they climbed. Ahead, Target Two and Hussein shuffled and panted as they manoeuvred their precious burden up the steps in the darkness.

Then silence.

Ali gasped for air as he climbed into the dead atmosphere of the staircase, holding the object close against his body. He reached out, groping towards the summit of the steps.

His fingers touched the slumped body of Target One. The woman's arms and legs moved in tiny jerks, like a sleeping dog. Hussein gripped her tightly, one hand constraining her arms, the other over her mouth. Her body convulsed and her arms strained against Hussein's urgent embrace. If she woke, she might break loose and scream, or flee at least as far as the iron grille, drawing attention.

Target Two sat against the opposite wall, silent in the blackness.

Between them, at the head of the stairs, rose a solid sheet of smooth metal, unyielding to the touch.

A steel security door, invisible from the foot of the stairs.

Target One intensified her struggles.

They needed to get inside.

Using his fingertips, Ali probed the rim of the flat, cool surface until he reached the metal frame, set flush in the masonry on either side. At waist height, a heavy metal hasp jutted out, secured with a padlock. Did the key open this, too? No, rust caked both the padlock itself and the spring-loaded cover concealing the keyhole.

Ali turned his attention to the spot where the door frame met the stonework opposite the padlock.

There. His fingers encountered a flat plastic blister set under the rim of the metal. He pressed hard and heard the click of a contact closing. Had he rung a bell somewhere?

"Aah. She bit me." Hussein's voice rang out in the cramped, quiet space.

"Help! I–"

"Silence, bitch."

Target One freed her mouth for only a second before Hussein silenced her, curling his wiry arm around her throat and bending her head back. She gurgled and coughed.

"Careful, idiot," Ali said. "Keep her quiet. But do not damage her." Why did the door not open? Ali reached for Target One in the darkness and encountered the bare skin of her midriff. Had Hussein touched her in the dark? In any case, the time had come to silence the non-believing whore. Ali drew back his fist and punched Target One in the centre of her exposed underbelly. She gasped and retched, still restrained by Hussein's choking grip.

A line of bright light illuminated the face of Target One. Skin taut, her features blanched by the ether, the suffocation, and Ali's blow, she did indeed look more dead than alive. Hussein wrapped his other arm around her waist, pressing her buttocks against his groin. No wonder he could not control her. Hussein grinned as he became aware of Ali's gaze and loosened his grip. Target Two lay stretched against the curved wall of the passage, his eyes shut, mumbling a prayer. As if an *Istanbullu* could ever understand the will of God.

At the head of the stairs, the steel door swung open. A woman spoke.

"Welcome. Hey, stop! No! Oh, no!"

He glimpsed a form silhouetted against a flood of light. But the moment the door opened, Target One broke away from Hussein, lurched up into the bright space at the top of the stairs, fell to her knees, and vomited onto a richly-coloured rug that lay beneath an open window.

The woman in the doorway wore round eye-glasses like a 1960's rock star. She had a slim figure, verging on the scrawny, and a lined face framed with wild salt and pepper hair. Tight jeans and a sweatshirt accentuated her boyish physique.

Did she have breasts? Ali could see none.

As soon as they entered, the woman pushed shut the door and turned the lock. As Ali suspected, the rusty padlock and hasp on the outside served no function. They formed a cover you could draw over a modern security lock from inside and clamp shut, rendering entry impossible. The woman slid a metal brace into position and completed the sealing of the entrance by closing a padded, tightly-fitting inner door intended, so far as Ali could see, to insulate any possible noise from within.

What other surprises did the apartment at the top of the *Buyuk Valide Han* conceal?

The multiple locks and gates hinted at a paranoid host, a security freak, or both. Ali needed a bolt-hole as his fall-back location for the afternoon. But only if he could be sure the woman herself posed no risk.

He eyed her frizzy hair, streaked with white. Why had the architects of The Protocol used a woman, and an unbeliever, as their guardian for these crucial hours? He must try to build a relationship of trust.

He stepped forward. "Thank you for hosting us."

The woman walked past him and knelt by Target One, who retched and gasped for breath after Ali's blow to her stomach.

Perhaps she planned to show some sisterly love.

"That is a hand-knotted carpet from the Turkmen Soviet Socialist Republic," the woman said. "It is irreplaceable." She put one hand on the back of Target One and with the other touched the edge of the vomit-stained fabric. "I suppose you macho idiots think a religious ideology justifies the mistreatment of women and the damaging of my rug? Why is it that all the world's most widespread superstitions—I do not say great religions—are invented and administered by men?"

She rose and headed for a kitchen unit across the room equipped with a gleaming stainless-steel hood and a stone work-top. Above the range, a huge window framed the rooftops, domes, and minarets of the city. "I suppose you are hungry, and as it is lunch time you men are expecting me, as a woman, to feed you."

She turned and grinned at Ali and Hussein, her hands raised in a parody of helplessness.

"Well," she said. "You would be right. Because although I think your mystic drivel is so much bollocks, *I support the goals of The Elders.* Anything they do to attack the cancer of global capitalism and promote the rights of the down-trodden and oppressed is good with me. They tell me that today, you are going to give capitalism the mother of all bloody noses."

With a flourish, she turned and busied herself with some vegetables on the immaculate stone work-top.

Ali stared at the woman's back and fingered the gun in the waistband of his jeans. An aura of madness clung to the woman. Did she not know the real goals of The Protocol? How could she view capitalism as the enemy? Or any political belief?

The Protocol aimed to destroy evil, decadence, and godlessness.

The Elders had contacted Ali, too, through the darknet. They yearned to cleanse the world of depravity, starting with Istanbul. If today's events meant Ali's name lived forever, so much the better.

Perhaps The Elders had deceived the woman in order to recruit her.

Could her confused worldview endanger their mission? A single shot in the back of her neck would eliminate a source of unpredictability. Or might they need her to keep them safe in the rooftop apartment for the next few hours? As the woman chopped something on a wooden board, Ali scratched his chin. She seemed harmless enough. How could she hate capitalism and yet live in such a luxurious apartment?

"Here is the deal." The woman turned away from the counter. In her hand she held an old but serviceable-looking snub-nosed pistol. "You don't mess with me, I won't mess with you. No more violence against lover-girl here, for whom I'm guessing skinny trousers over there has the hots." She waved her pistol towards Hussein and flicked off the safety.

Could he pull his own weapon from his waistband and get off a shot before she fired? She seemed comfortable with her gun. Perhaps she had killed more people than he had.

The woman looked down at Target One. "Restrain her if you must," she said. "But any hanky-panky from you two lads and I will shoot you both in the balls and enjoy it. Don't worry, I always aim high. Up here above Istanbul, no-one can hear you scream. Believe me, I know. Behave, and I will feed you and pamper you and send you on your way to create as much mayhem as you can manage." She rubbed her temple with the barrel of the gun. "Although, how you plan to destroy the global economic system with nothing but that pistol in your pants is, frankly, a mystery to me. And what are you hiding under your coat?"

Ali tensed. For a woman, the wild-haired witch was perceptive. He glanced across the room to where Hussein lounged against the brilliant white wall. She was right about his legs being thin. Ali had never noticed before. She had seen, too, that he sat too far away to help Ali.

"It is an artefact we took from the site where she worked." He jerked his head towards Target One, still crouched on the soiled rug. "A superstitious idol, if you like." He snuggled the object closer to his body.

The woman stepped forward, pistol levelled. "My house, my rules. This must be the famous Palladium everyone has been gabbing about. The Luck of Troy. A *Xoanon*, no less." Beneath the white-tinged eyebrows, her eyes sparkled. "A concentrated concatenation of cabalistic crap concealed under your coat. I shall use it for target practice."

Ali backed away. *Avoid drawing attention to the object,* The Protocol said. "No. The relic is holy."

"But it isn't your religion or your relic, is it darling? Unless you are an ancient Greek or a Trojan, which I doubt. Come on. Hand it over."

"Stop." The voice rang out loud and clear.

Ali and the woman turned. Target Two stood facing them, his hands held out, palms up. "He tells the truth. The object is sacred. They are...they said they were believers."

Target Two's chin quivered, and a tear rolled down the side of his nose into the thick dark growth of his moustache and beard. A pitiful display.

The woman frowned. "Believers? In what?"

"They knew about the Palladium. They said they were people of faith. Hellenic polytheists. Worshippers of the ancient gods, like Zeus, or Athena. They said the *Xoanon* should be worshipped, not gawked at by tourists in a museum. I summoned them when we were ready to lift the final stone. I never dreamed they would kill."

On the floor, Target One mumbled something. But the scrawny woman stared at Target Two.

"A man with feelings. A rare thing." She grinned, displaying a mouthful of strong white teeth. "The tissues are on the counter. But these two? Greek polytheists?"

"They contacted me on the internet. I never saw them until they arrived at the dig. Even then, I made no assumptions. Only a bigot would try to bind together faith and race. Or sexuality."

Ali said nothing. The Elders had played Target Two and the witch like puppets. Which other stooges had they bent to their will to achieve the awesome goal of The Protocol?

"Faith and race! You are adorable." The woman waved her pistol at Target Two. "What is your name, sweetheart?"

"Dervis Basturk."

"Dervis by name, dervish by nature. I would like to see that. Well, Dervis darling, I am Meryem. Meryem Shah. Scourge of imperialism. Treat me right and you can come for tea when this is over." She turned back to Ali. "I won't bother asking your name, because you won't tell me. But if you could make yourself useful and chop up some vegetables for our lunch I would be most obliged."

Another groan cut short her instructions. Target One attempted to stand. Meryem hurried to her side. Ali tried in vain to see where the old woman stashed her weapon.

"You. Skinny cute guy. I won't ask your name either." The woman pointed to Hussein. "Come and help me, here. We need to wash this rug before the acid stains the colours. Relax, I'm a pussycat once you know me." She turned to Target One. "Now, dear, let's clean you up. You must be precious to them. Remember that."

She helped Target One into a sitting position and eased her to her feet. The old revolutionary's preoccupation with Target One made her vulnerable. Yet her manic energy and cunning alarmed Ali. He or Hussein could overpower her. But if they failed—he remembered her threat.

"You!" Meryem addressed Hussein, who ambled over to gape at Target One's face. "Rug under the shower, please? Cold water only. Get to it."

She held the gun in her hand again, rock-steady. From where had she conjured the weapon? The woman knew about firearms. Perhaps she belonged to a gun-club, or practiced on a range. A Marxist gun-nut. Did such people exist?

At least she seemed to have forgotten the object. The contours pressed against his body under the coat. He shut his eyes, and calm rose in him. The idea of assaulting their host seemed absurd. She had no intention of using the pistol. Why should she? Her goal, like his, must be to keep all of them safe in the fortified apartment until the time came for them to complete their mission.

How could he prevent the woman using the gun? He and Hussein must exhibit no threat towards her or the captives. They must distract her from her unhealthy obsession with the object.

Ali knew what he must do.

He stepped forward to the work-surface and laid the object, still enclosed in its wrapping of soft fabric, behind a pile of cook-books on the counter. He washed his hands, picked up the sharp-bladed kitchen knife that lay on the chopping board, and sliced the carrots and onions into fine cubes.

## 45

A t Taksim, the sun blazed down on a sea of paving stones Savage guessed must cover an area ten or twenty times the size of Trafalgar Square. Ranks of LED lights on towering masts dwarfed a cluster of spindly trees at one end, lending Taksim the aura of a prison camp or railway marshalling yard. To one side, police crowd barriers fenced off a statue of Ataturk dwarfed by a new mosque. On the other, a flight of white marble steps climbed to a park.

City planners had built the square to make the huge space as exposed as possible. No obstacles interrupted the expanse. If riots erupted, the police TOMA water cannon trucks lined up against the wall could use Taksim as a shooting gallery.

Six buses of riot control personnel equipped with plastic shields and body armour waited for events to kick off. In turn, officers in flak-jackets toting automatic weapons guarded the buses and TOMAs. The armed sentries looked watchful and experienced, as if they had prepared for riots in Taksim Square a thousand times before.

The police wanted to put on a show of force. Yet before the bombing at Besiktas, formations twice as powerful had watched over the rally.

Savage parked the Triumph down a side-street away from the square. Behind him, Orhan cursed and stepped off the bike, rubbing his crotch.

"John. Does it turn you on to crush your balls?"

Savage remained seated astride the Triumph. "Can't you withdraw your testicles into your body? Part of SIS basic training."

"You are kidding. Right?" Orhan shook his head. "I never can tell with you Brits."

Savage said nothing.

The great square filled with people. To one side, close to the hulk of a tall church with a domed roof, people poured from the mouth of Istiklal, Istanbul's main pedestrianized shopping street. Opposite, a row of stainless-steel fountains, like oversized cattle troughs, split into two parts a stream of protesters arriving from the north. The tall red-and-white stands of salesmen selling chestnuts, simits, and corn-on-the-cob studded the square, tempting the crowds with the mouth-watering scent of freshly prepared street food.

Savage scanned the protesters. "How can you tell which are Rauf Toprak's Trotskyist fantasists and which are Nasim Kaval's fascist thugs? Are we rooting for either of them?"

"No. Both left and right in Turkey love conspiracy theories and violence," Orhan said. "They both believe all foreigners are trying to crush Turkey and cannot be trusted. Luckily, I have a good education, including my MBA from Columbia, so I know it is not true that every foreigner is evil. There may be one or two exceptions. But I still do not trust them. Especially ones who have been sleeping with my sister."

"Do you trust Turks?"

"No. We have a saying: *A Turk can only trust another Turk.* But actually, we do not trust each other, either. Except our families. I would die for Elif. She would die for me."

"We will find her."

"How? In this crowd? In this city of twenty million?"

"We were right last time. We identified the target. We could be right again. The bombings at Besiktas are linked to whoever took Elif. I am positive."

"So, where is she?"

"I don't know. But we have to keep looking."

"John. We guessed right last time. But did we stop the bombers? No. Here, at Taksim, half a million people are gathering. Suppose the terrorists do attack. How do we prevent a massacre?"

Savage gazed across the square. What target appealed most to a terrorist? The vast space seemed to offer infinite options. People carrying banners pushed through the throng. He looked again at the food stands, trying to identify a pattern to the distribution of the stalls. The salesmen located their trolleys to intercept the maximum number of pedestrians. How did their stands relate to the multiple entrances and exits of the square?

The layout of the food stalls and the streets came into focus. His pulse raced. Savage seized Orhan's arm.

"Imagine I plan to explode a bomb," he said. "I am here, at Taksim, with my suicide vest. I want to cause maximum casualties. Where do I start?"

"Go where the crowd is most dense, I suppose."

"Look how big the crowd is. With each suicide vest, you kill maybe fifty people. But what if you use the crowd as a weapon? Instead of bombing randomly, you detonate a vest in each of the approaches. People panic and scatter. Imagine a crowd of half a million stampeding, crushing everything in their path. Instead of dozens of victims, you kill thousands."

"Why target a rally?"

"What if the target is Istanbul itself? First, they attack Besiktas to draw the police away from Taksim. They then carry out the main event here, at the heart of Turkey's political culture, the scene of tragedies across the years. A massacre here would be iconic: an assault on everything Turkey stands for."

Orhan touched his tiny beard. "Even if they killed five thousand people, it wouldn't change Turkey."

"The 9/11 attacks in New York and Washington killed less than three thousand people, and they changed history. The dead amounted to 0.001% of the population of the United States. Or an attack at Taksim could be another feint. To distract attention from something even bigger."

"Bigger than killing thousands of people? How?"

"Who knows? In the nineteen-fifties, the British government worried about someone sailing a nuclear bomb into the Port of

London. Maybe the terrorists are planning something bigger than we can imagine."

"No terrorist group has access to nuclear weapons. Maybe the Besiktas bomb was the attack we were waiting for."

"No. Remember the hashtags? #endofthewest? #endofallevil? Their plan must combine Elif, whatever they found at the building site, the bombing in Besiktas, and something else. Remember—the intelligence talked about fifteen operatives assigned to strike a 'mortal blow' in Istanbul. Where are the rest?"

"And where is Elif?" Orhan made a violent gesture towards the crowd.

"Wherever she is, she will be giving them hell," Savage said.

Around them, chaos grew. A stage flanked by stacks of loudspeakers rose in front of the Ataturk Cultural Centre. On the opposite side of the square, a second stage reared up against a background of nondescript hotel buildings. Across the centre of Taksim, police had erected a double barrier of steel to separate the crowd. Riot control squads patrolled the space between, wearing full body armour. Each wore a gas mask around his or her neck or pushed up on the forehead like sunglasses. A TOMA riot control vehicle stood at each end of the barriers. Two more parked in the no-man's land in the middle. Atop the trucks, the menacing snouts of water cannon jerked from side to side as the operators searched for trouble-makers on the TV screens in the cabs.

Crowds of Trotskyists and rightists hurled insults at one another. So far, the police had kept them apart. But people streamed into the square every second.

"We were right at Besiktas," Orhan said. "Yet we didn't save a single life. How can we protect people this time?"

"When do the demonstrations start?"

"Officially? At two p.m. But they are always late."

"The terrorists will strike precisely at that moment. Maximum people, maximum TV coverage, before people settle down and the crowd becomes static. We must identify the spots where they will detonate their bombs."

"We need a better vantage point." Orhan looked around. "What about the upper floor of one of these burger places?"

Protesters packed the restaurants facing the square, refuelling before the rioting started. Orhan pushed his way into an outpost of an international burger chain. At the back, grubby stairs climbed to an open-air terrace.

"The police always have a couple of people up here," he said. "You can see across to Gezi Park and along Istiklal."

They wove between crowded tables to the edge of the terrace. Savage gazed down at the largest group of people he had ever seen in his life.

An ocean of protesters pulsed in Taksim Square like a vast, irregular organism stretching, filling every space except the narrow strip between the barriers. Everywhere, red and white Turkish flags and bright banners bearing political slogans fluttered in the breeze. Steam and smoke rose from food stalls. Here at the edge of the square the smell of kebabs, burgers, and hot fat saturated the air, together with a deafening clamour of chanting, klaxons, music, and public address systems.

"It's like a rock concert. Or maybe two rival concerts, with each set of fans determined to annihilate the other." Savage looked upwards. "Those streetlights. I suppose they have CCTV cameras installed?"

"Of course. Unfortunately, most criminals these days wear headgear."

"We don't need to identify individuals. We don't know what our suspects look like. What we do is use standard police software to distinguish individual people in the crowd, whether by faces, by clothes, or by dress. Once the computer has logged each person, the algorithm can analyse their movements."

"You seem to know a lot about this software."

"It has existed for years. What's new is that better optics and faster processing mean you can use it in real time. They use the same technique at airports. Criminals, whether they are pick-pockets or suicide bombers, tend to move in a predictable way. The computer can spot an individual moving suspiciously and direct security personnel to intercept them before they commit a crime."

"You think we Turks have this technology?"

"You probably invented it."

"But could the software work with a crowd this size?"

"No." Savage shook his head. "No existing technology could identify half a million individuals in real time. But it might work if you ignored ninety-nine percent of the crowd and directed the system to examine the areas of highest risk. We would have to focus on where the suicide bombers were most likely to explode their vests. Look."

He took a pen and a notepad from his pocket, tore out a page, and drew a diagram.

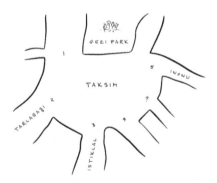

"About eight streets run into Taksim. I never heard of a terrorist attack with more than three suicide bombers. But if we assume the worst, say, five attackers, and the police focus their cameras on the biggest junctions, their chances of spotting something increases dramatically. The bombers could strike any second. If you have, say, one hundred cameras covering the whole square, you could concentrate twenty of them on each—"

A huge force jerked him back from the edge of the terrace and threw him face-down on the tiles. Orhan yelled. Someone seized Savage's wrist and twisted his arm behind him. In the café, a woman screamed. A table crashed to the floor.

The metallic bite of handcuffs closed on his wrists. He brought his arm down sharply to break free, but something held his hand tight behind him, like a huge piece of machinery. A second pair of hands seized his other arm and bent it round behind his back. The handcuffs clicked again.

"Our Russian friend has decided to join us again," someone said behind him in Turkish. "Except this time, he is speaking English with a Turkish police intelligence officer who is under investigation for misuse of official transport, destroying evidence, disobeying orders, and suspected espionage and treason. Let us take a look at him."

Someone slammed Savage back against the floor of the terrace, mangling his bound hands against one another and smashing his head against the tiled floor. For a second, blue sky filled his vision, then someone placed a heavy boot upon his chest.

The broken nose, rounded shoulders, and outhouse physique of Tarik Korkmaz blotted out the blue. The police superintendent who had chased him from the archaeological site grinned and scratched his head. Uniformed police officers surrounded him.

"Nowhere to run to now, is there, my friend?" the giant cop said. "Or should I say, 'comrade'?"

## 46

S aif al-Din sat at the rear of the cabin of the orange-coloured boat. Uzay stood at the helm. The dark-skinned pilot navigated using a kind of electronic map set into the control panel, glancing up from time to time at the horizon. He felt no need to consult Saif, the captain. How could his subordinate, a simple Black Sea boatman, be familiar with sophisticated equipment whose function Saif did not comprehend?

"Tell me." The words came out more brusquely than intended. "What is this device?"

"That is the ECDIS," Uzay said. His hand rested on the wheel as the ship surged through the water. "The Electronic Chart Display Information System. The apparatus is like an old-fashioned nautical chart, but it is computerised and combines with a radar to show us any nearby ships or land. The software links with GPS to set the centre of the chart at our actual position at all times. This ship is also equipped with an AIS."

"What is this? An AIS?"

"An Automatic Identification System." Uzay sighed. "It can track and identify any other ships, like another radar, but based on radio frequencies. So no-one can sneak up on anyone."

Saif frowned. "You mean, when other ships look at us, they see a pilot ship."

"This is a pilot ship, yes. That is what they will see." The boatman's voice oozed insolence.

"Have you located the target?"

"Yes. It is here." Uzay stabbed at the electronic screen. "We will reach her in twenty minutes. Sea conditions are fair. I see no other vessels. The coastguard ship that intercepted us is far away, towards Istanbul. The target is moving in the opposite direction, towards Gebze, two hours east of the strait."

"Good. Our plan cannot fail," Saif said.

Uzay glanced around at him. "We go ahead? With the Bosphorus closed to sea traffic?"

"The Protocol includes a contingency plan," Saif said. "Trust me."

"Of course." Uzay nodded towards the horizon. "Look. Nothing can stop us."

"God willing." Saif gazed across the bright-blue ocean. Far ahead, a red-and-white speck winked in the sunlight. He narrowed his eyes. Could the minuscule vessel be the target? He had expected something larger. Behind, to the north of the Sea of Marmara, mountainous uplands rose from the sea.

The beauty of his country, Turkey, eclipsed all other nations on earth.

Why had the infidels who controlled this land chosen to destroy the caliphate? The obscenity cried out for revenge. Today, the godless city of Istanbul must suffer the consequences.

The prospect of delivering judgement filled him with such joy that he rose up on the balls of his feet. A taxi driver from Istanbul, transformed into the most powerful man on earth. In time, children might learn the name Saif al-Din in their history classes.

Two years ago, Saif had called himself Karim Ahmed. A nobody. Even his wife, Demet, had disrespected him. One day, after Karim had disciplined Demet with his fists for the hundredth time, her brother, Ibrahim, had shown up at their flat in Kasimpasa and slashed all four tyres on Karim's taxi, broken every window, and given Karim Ahmed a beating that still made Saif ache when he remembered the blows.

Two years ago, Karim Ahmed had not understood power. He believed himself a failure. A victim.

Out of the blue, after Karim had surfed sites on the internet where men gathered to vent their anger at injustice of every kind, a group calling themselves The Elders had made contact.

The Elders had explained the world to him. Karim should not consider himself weak. Rather, he should understand the cruel bias of the established order against him and his beliefs. Dark and powerful forces, controlled by the infidel godless, wished to ensure true believers remained powerless and divided. Karim, they said, did not have to suffer injustice in silence. He could join others who wished to fight back and create a new, better world where God's justice ruled and men like Karim harvested the respect they deserved.

The Elders showed discipline and caution. Karim had taken weeks of contacts to convince them of his fervour, his reliability, and his devotion.

At last, The Elders introduced him to The Protocol. They offered to train and support Karim if he joined in their plans.

When he first heard the goal of The Protocol, Saif—or Karim as he called himself then—had punched the air in excitement.

If he believed in The Protocol, The Elders said, he should start by changing his name. That first step showed his commitment. The fresh start also began the process of vanishing from the records of the decadent, corrupt authorities who ruled Turkey.

That same day, little Karim Ahmed became a follower of The Protocol, and changed his name to Saif al-Din, Sword of the Faith. Thus had Saif set out on his path to immortality.

As for little Karim's wife, Demet, Saif put her and her unbelieving, blasphemous family out of his mind. He did not even know whether she still lived in the run-down apartment where he had deserted her. But if Demet and her mother, her father, her sisters, or her cousins were in Istanbul this day, they would be dead by midnight.

"It is done." Kaan poked his head up through the hatch at the front of the cabin. "I have used a timer, set for forty-five minutes. You do not need to remember to make a phone call."

"Good work," Saif said. Was Kaan, too, showing him disrespect?

"I have used the last of our explosives for this job," Kaan said. "What is the plan when we reach the target? We will need fresh supplies."

"All will be well," Saif said. The Protocol stated he must not tell Kaan or Uzay more than they needed to know. "We will have the supplies we require."

Kaan looked at him, his sullen eyes and square jaw incongruous in the smart uniform. He said nothing, but walked to the rear of the cabin and looked out at the wake of the boat.

The attack dog needed action.

The red and white speck grew larger every second, resolving itself into something more recognisable. The vessel still appeared too small. But Saif said nothing. The Protocol specified this target. The dimensions must be adequate for the task.

"How long before we reach them?" Saif said.

"Ten minutes," Uzay said.

"Use the radio. Tell them we are ready to come on board."

The Black Sea boatman prepared to call the target. Uzay's scowl, and the tremor in his right eyelid, did not mark concentration, but fear. The next few minutes decided everything.

The ferocious-looking Uzay did not resemble a professional pilot. But neither Saif nor Kaan looked much like trainees. Their white naval uniforms formed a crucial disguise. They had deceived the crew of the pilot vessel and the coastguard for a few seconds. The ship they approached, in turn, expected a pilot to arrive. The deception must last only a few seconds.

No wonder Uzay's eyelid trembled. If the target did not respond as The Protocol foresaw, they might lose all they had fought for.

Uzay's first contact could determine the life or death of a city.

The dark-skinned pilot propped up a white card with his script on the console in front of him. He scowled at the text one last time, and pressed the "call" button on the handset.

"Calling Royal Lion. Calling Royal Lion." Uzay spoke heavily accented English, limited to a few standard phrases. But he spoke with authority. The training in the Naval College had paid off.

The response came within seconds. "This is Royal Lion, I hear you loud and clear."

"Royal Lion this is Turkish Pilot 80. Request permission to come on board."

"Pilot 80 welcome. We are lowering ladder at starboard side-door and slowing to seven knots. Come aboard."

"Royal Lion, please be aware I will be accompanied by two trainees, boarding first. Three persons in all."

"Roger that, pilot. Three persons."

"I am coming alongside now."

Uzay replaced the handset. A bead of sweat trickled down his cheek. He turned to Saif, and his face cracked into a grin. "We have permission to come aboard."

"Packs and buoyancy aids are ready." Kaan stood at the rear of the cabin, his stocky legs braced against the swell. He had divided the equipment into three rucksacks, each little larger than a day-pack.

Nothing to arouse suspicion.

For the same reason, each of them wore the bulky life-jackets. No genuine pilot could risk dangling from a rope-ladder, in the middle of the ocean, without protection. International Maritime Organisation rules insisted on the flotation devices.

"Everyone get ready," Saif said. "The side-door is on the starboard side below the bridge."

"I see it," Uzay said.

Saif slipped the buoyancy aid over his head and threaded his arms through the straps of the heavy rucksack. "Remember," he said, "it will take two minutes for the three of us to climb the ladder to the side door. During that time, we are vulnerable. Take your time. I cannot afford to lose one of you in the water. Once on board, fulfil The Protocol."

"Prepare to board," Uzay said.

Ahead, the side of the target vessel rose like a cliff. How could he have doubted The Protocol? Never in his wildest dreams had Saif imagined such a monster of a ship. He peered upwards, trying to catch a glimpse of the superstructure. Far ahead, the bow wave of the target rose as the craft turned to starboard to create an area of sheltered water for the pilot boat to come alongside. Uzay turned so the two ships lay parallel to one another, and slowed to match the larger vessel's speed.

"Go forward and get ready to board," he said. "Take care transferring from boat to ladder. I shall set the course to keep the nose of our boat against the target, but once I leave the wheel, our ship will drift."

Saif squared his shoulders and led the way out of the cabin. Uzay giving the orders did not feel right. But the Black Sea boatman controlled the pilot ship. Once they boarded the target, Saif would be master of events.

A stiff wind stung his face as he left the wheelhouse. He clung to the safety rail as he made his way forward to the front deck. Uzay must move swiftly from the cabin to the ladder to ensure the pilot boat stayed snug against the hull of the larger vessel long enough for him to board.

Without Uzay, they could not complete their mission.

The prow of the pilot boat slammed into a wave. Saif shuddered. Ahead, a rope ladder dangled down into the water from a rectangular opening in the hull of the ship high above. Two dark-skinned deckhands peered out, ready to help the pilot climb aboard. One raised a hand in greeting, the other's lips formed a circle as if he might be whistling a tune. No senior officer had come below to welcome them. Saif breathed a sigh of relief: neither he nor Kaan could respond to any detailed questions about navigation or seamanship.

The pilot boat moved alongside the hull, bringing Saif closer to the ladder. He grabbed hold of the ropes with both hands and stepped onto the narrow wooden rungs. The heavy rucksack pressed against his back. Did its bulk look suspicious? The ladder swung to one side. He pulled himself up, rung by rung, towards the side door. The deckhands reached down for him, grinning in encouragement. Again, the ladder moved, this time with a secondary rhythm of up-and-down motion. That must be Kaan, climbing behind him.

Three more steps. Two more. One. At last he reached the door, where a deckhand seized his arm and helped him to step inside. The second man leaned out of the way, whistling a tune Saif did not recognise. Saif ignored him and turned to look back down at the ladder.

Kaan had climbed halfway up. But Uzay still stood on the front deck of the pilot boat. The prow of the vessel lodged against the dull red hull of the target, but the friction had slowed the smaller ship's progress, leaving the ladder dangling out of reach over open water.

"Your coxswain asleep," one of the deck-hands said. "Need to go faster."

Kaan obscured Saif's view, climbing past him into the side-door as the two deckhands helped him aboard. Saif pushed forward. Below, in slow-motion, the pilot boat lost speed and drifted away, leaving the rope ladder further and further out of reach. Uzay took a couple of steps away from the wall of steel and shouted towards the wheelhouse, as though to a hidden helmsman.

But no-one manned the wheelhouse.

Clear blue water had opened up between the two hulls. The pilot boat accelerated as the drag against the larger vessel fell, bringing Uzay closer to the ladder. But the gap stayed wide.

The Black Sea boatman looked up, and their eyes met.

Could he re-enter the cabin and bring the boats together again? No. For Uzay to return to the cabin risked making it obvious he was the only man on board.

Uzay shook his head, as if in frustration, and walked back towards the wheelhouse. He turned, took three great strides forwards, and threw himself over the prow of the pilot boat.

## 47

Savage looked up into the grinning face of Tarik Korkmaz. Behind his back, steel handcuffs cut into his wrists for the second time in six hours. This morning, Orhan had restrained him as a ruse to cross the Bosphorus. This time, the cuffs bit with intent.

"You are wondering how we found you among twenty million people," Korkmaz said. He glanced at the uniformed police officers standing around him as if glad to have an audience.

"I don't give a shit how you found us," Savage said. "What I care about is stopping the suicide bombers who will attack this demonstration in the next fifteen minutes."

"Suicide bombers?" Korkmaz grunted. "My job is to catch the criminals who killed six innocent people at an archaeological dig in the Old City this morning. You were at the scene and fled when I attempted to interrogate you. If that is not suspicious behaviour, I do not know what is."

"Listen to the Englishman." Orhan spoke as though someone had jammed a cloth in his mouth. Savage could not see him. "He predicted the attack at Besiktas."

"An Englishman masquerading as a Russian? Who knew in advance about the Besiktas attack?" Korkmaz peered down at Savage from an immense height. "Perhaps you helped organise the suicide bombs that killed my colleagues?"

"My condolences for the victims. But you have fifteen minutes to stop a massacre here in Taksim. You can be a hero, or you can be the fall-guy." Savage took a deep breath. "If it helps persuade you to listen, I can tell you how you found us. You programmed your face-recognition software to look for two individuals—me and Mutlu. For reference, you used images of him from your records, and data-grabs from closed-circuit TV or the telephone at the construction site for me. When we showed up at Taksim, you got two hits and came to pick us up."

"It turns out you do give a shit how we found you." Korkmaz pursed his lips, his eyes narrowed.

"You need to use that technology to stop the attack here," Savage said. "At five specific areas in the crowd. We don't know who the killers are. But you can use movement analysis to pick up suspicious behaviour. If you turn all your cameras to the spots where the terrorists are most likely to be, you will have a chance."

Korkmaz said nothing.

"The bombers will explode their vests at the start of the demonstration, at two p.m.," Savage went on, "when the place is at maximum capacity. Their goal is to create a stampede that kills a hundred times more people than the bombs. If the Istanbul Police don't have the software, you can leave these cuffs on and throw me in the Bosphorus."

"I would love to throw you in the Bosphorus." Korkmaz tapped his teeth with a pen. "Okay. Tell me: where will the terrorists be?"

"Look on the table, where we stood before you grabbed us. I drew a diagram. Try it. If I'm wrong, you have nothing to lose. I am a British diplomat, and my ID papers are in my wallet in my front left pocket. But don't waste time with me, start the surveillance system working on the crowd, and get your sniper teams ready. Step one: identify anyone whose movements the system marks up as suspicious. Step two: be ready to take them out if anyone looks like a suicide bomber. We only have a few minutes."

For five long seconds the superintendent said nothing. He put his head to one side and held Savage's gaze, his dark eyes steady. "A pretty speech," he said at last. "Perhaps I do have nothing to lose by testing out what sounds like the screwiest theory I have ever heard. What do they say? *The English always come from the other side.*" Korkmaz scratched his thick neck and paused. "But when I look you in the eye, I am almost ready to believe you think you are telling the truth."

He turned and shouted to his men. "Okay. We are going to test the crazy Englishman's theory. Get the plan from the table. Take a photo and send it to whoever is in charge of this operation, from me. Tell him I want to speak to him immediately. Someone else call police HQ in case the commander won't listen. Anyone know who's in charge of the snipers? Good. And check this guy's ID."

Savage lay on his back on the ground. Everything seemed to happen with maddening slowness. Uniformed police pushed together some tables and cleared a space amongst the startled café guests. Others gazed at the crowd with binoculars or spoke into walkie-talkies. Korkmaz seemed to have decided the terrace was too big, and crowded, to clear completely; a line of people watched from behind a tape, some recording the scene with phones. A few clambered onto chairs for a better view, including a woman with short red hair and what looked like a compact high-definition video camera.

Turks had an unparalleled talent for improvisation, if you could release that potential. Unfortunately, they also possessed an unparalleled talent for disbelieving anything you said.

How long had he been lying here? The sun overhead blinded him. He closed his eyes. *Upturn stared at him, her face waxy from the cold of the Moscow winter. She held out her hand. In her palm lay the scalpel, blade gleaming. He had known he could do only what his enemies had planned for him.*

His eyes jerked open. The steel of the cuffs crushed his wrists. What if the bombs exploded while he lay helpless on the roof of a restaurant?

Savage tried to count the seconds. Two uniformed officers came, lifted him off the filthy tiles, and propped him, sitting upright but still handcuffed, against a wall. One of them eased the wallet from Savage's pocket. Savage caught sight of the watch on the man's wrist.

Eight minutes had passed.

Korkmaz stood at the edge of the terrace, a phone in one hand, a pair of binoculars in the other. The booming of chants and counter-chants from the throng in the square grew louder.

At any moment, multiple explosions could rip through the crowd. Savage gritted his teeth, fought to slow his breathing, and braced himself.

A police officer appeared from the direction of the stairs and pushed his way towards Korkmaz. Several officers on the terrace glanced at Savage. The superintendent came and knelt next to him.

Sweat glistened on the big man's forehead. "I don't know what kind of diplomat you are," he said, "but your ID checks out. No time to talk, but we have identified two possible suspects in your zones, near the entrances to the square. So far, the crowd is too dense to approach them or take them down." He unlocked the handcuffs.

"You could use synchronised sniper fire," Savage said.

Korkmaz grunted. "A strange kind of diplomat, indeed. I suppose you are a British spy. Are you ex-special forces?"

"I know something about terrorism. It's up to you whether you listen. You need to hit as many as possible at once."

"You think we do not know that?" Korkmaz's dark eyes flashed. "Of course we will use synchronised fire. Once a bomb explodes, everyone will stampede and a clean shot will become impossible."

"Right." Savage shook his hands to restore circulation as the cuffs came off. "The terrorists will have a timing sequence. Even taking out one or two could make a difference."

"One or two? How many do you think there are?"

"I have no idea. But based on what happened at Dolmabahce, I would guess two, minimum. Maybe three. Four or five maximum."

"Four or five?" Korkmaz swore under his breath.

"Maybe less. Even fewer if you can take a couple down before they can explode."

"In case you have not noticed, this is a democracy." Korkmaz shook his head. "We do not simply gun down suspects in a public space."

"Up to you. Like you say, once the first bomb explodes, it will be too late. You have two or three minutes."

Savage stood. Orhan lay near a table on the opposite side of the terrace, hands still bound behind his back. The intelligence officer grimaced at Savage and gestured with his head towards the edge of the terrace. Savage crossed to join Korkmaz.

The thick-necked superintendent bellowed into his phone. "Yes! Yes! Now! The time is almost two o'clock! You have terrorists in your sights? Take them! Of course it is dangerous. If we get it wrong, we are both criminals. If we are right, we are heroes. Shoot!"

The crowds in the square below had swollen to a mass so tightly-packed, no-one could move in any direction. Protesters, their banners fluttering in the breeze, crammed the fences separating the Trotskyists from the rightists, by the two stages, and at the entrances to the square, where streams of people continued to arrive. Drones hovered overhead. Did the police control them, or the protesters?

The digits on Savage's phone clicked around to two p.m.

The snipers on the roofs of the surrounding buildings had positioned themselves to be invisible against the skyline. But they would be there: three, four, or five teams, ready to strike. Each unit comprised a shooter armed with a high-powered sniper rifle with a telescopic sight, accompanied by a spotter with long-distance binoculars. A single communications system linked the teams, allowing them to share target information.

In a hostage situation, the commander allocated snipers to every target. Each reported back to a controller when he or she saw a clean shot through the sights. When the commander knew at least one sniper had locked onto each hostage-taker simultaneously, so all could be taken out in a single split-second, he or she authorised the shot.

The Turkish sharpshooters at the square faced a task one hundred times harder.

Instead of being confined to a building or a room, terrorists planned to attack at multiple points across a vast area packed with half a million people. Clarity of targeting was near-impossible. Even to hit a single suicide bomber would be a miracle.

Korkmaz stopped shouting into his phone and turned to Savage. "Still only the two suspects," he said. "But the data analysis on their movements is more conclusive every second. We have—" the big man paused and touched his white earpiece with a forefinger. "We have taken the decision. The sniper commander has authorised two teams to open fire as soon as both have a clear shot."

"Good luck," Savage said. "Two is a lot better than none. But if any are left, they will explode their devices as soon as they realise their partners are down."

"Better brace yourself." Korkmaz wiped his brow. "It could be any second."

In the square below, the volume of the hubbub rose another notch. A helicopter hovered overhead, adding to the din. Savage scanned the surrounding buildings. Where were the snipers?

"Shots taken," Korkmaz said. "Two suspects down. Neither has exploded yet." The big man's face hardened. "Damn it. Let us hope we didn't just gun down two innocent protesters. Now we'll see if—"

The shock of the explosion sent Savage and Korkmaz tumbling back onto the floor of the terrace. A plume of smoke rose from the crowd less than fifty yards from the café. Then the screaming started.

## 48

"Open your mouth. You will feel better with something in your stomach."

Elif Mutlu clamped her teeth shut and shook her head. How could she feel any more nauseous than this? The smell of the soup the elderly woman held up to her face made her stomach convulse with a violence that left her faint-headed.

Where had the terrorists taken her, and why? What drove the old woman to jam the soup spoon at her mouth? The owner of the apartment seemed friendly, but behind the round, wire-framed glasses, her eyes burned with passion.

Elif had regained consciousness in a dark place, her arms bound, her head pierced with an indescribable agony. She had tried to flee. In the blackness, someone had struck a terrific blow to her stomach, making her want to puke. She had seen a glare ahead and run towards the light, her head exploding with pain, confusion, and vertigo as if someone had clamped her temples in a vice and thrown her out of an aircraft.

She had vomited, she knew, before finding herself kneeling on the white tiles of a bathroom as spotless as an operating theatre. This same woman had handed her a wet cloth to clean up. But even as Elif dabbed at her cheeks and splashed water on her hair, the woman had threatened her with a gun. She must be working with her captors.

The woman tried to make her eat. They needed her alive for something. Might Elif survive? All hostages faced the same dilemma: how much should you risk to try and escape? Her captors had done everything to render flight impossible. After she left the bathroom, the stockier kidnapper, the Chief, had bound her around the ankles and wrists with gaffer tape.

At least he had left her face free.

In this space, which looked more like someone's smart apartment than a terrorist den, her captors felt no need to hide their faces. That lack of concern must be bad news. The two men had slaughtered all the students and workers at the archaeological site. If the kidnappers did not care that she and Dervis saw them now, they must plan to kill them both.

The Chief had an expressive, alert face with thinning black hair, a healthy complexion, and good teeth. He looked like an accountant or a dentist. His cheeks were clean-shaven except for a little tuft of beard below his chin. He moved lightly; that, his grooming, and his big, delicate hands suggested someone educated. A narcissist, someone preoccupied with his image or the impression he made. Perhaps he had trained as an artist or a sculptor.

The man had also executed six people, kidnapped her and Dervis, and allowed her to be beaten and abused by the skinny kid with the wandering hands—the Groper, she called him. The disgusting animal lay on a couch. Had he hit her in the stomach or had the Chief delivered the blow?

What about Dervis? The pious archaeologist lay slumped across the room, looking at the floor, his face expressionless. Their captors had bound his ankles with tape but left his hands free, as though they thought he posed less danger than her.

Based on his performance so far, they had judged the lack of threat from Dervis correctly. Elif gritted her teeth. She recalled him saying something about Hellenic polytheists. Surely Dervis had not believed these terrorists worshipped the ancient Greek gods? Or had someone targeted him on the internet with a narrative tailored to his beliefs and weaknesses, like an ideological confidence trickster?

Why did anyone believe in any kind of invisible deity? Could they not see that if their god existed, those of other believers could not?

What were the odds that your own parents, in your own country, taught you about the one true God, whereas all the parents of the children of other religions in other countries and continents of the earth happened to be misguided or evil?

Maybe Dervis, with his Muslim beliefs, sympathised with the faiths of others. Or perhaps he had changed, if that were possible. Savage had insisted he could never change, the night she asked him to love her.

As for Elif, her captors had better keep her bound tight if they wanted to stop her trying to kill them. She strained against her bonds and her heartbeat surged. Whatever her captors planned, she had the strength to destroy them.

She closed her eyes again. Had she, the archaeology professor, Elif Mutlu, sworn revenge? In the car she had remained calm, even when jammed into the space behind the front seats. What had happened?

The object. Holding the soft contours in her arms had comforted her. Where had the killers hidden the relic? What might she discover within the fabric wrapping? The Palladium, carved by the hand of the Goddess Athena, could not await her, for the simple reason that the Palladium was a myth and Athena did not exist. Yet the fact the killers had arrived at the precise moment she uncovered the object and had taken it with them, must mean that the artefact from the tomb–together with Elif herself—formed part of their plan.

What, after all, made anything valuable or holy? The belief of human beings.

Her eyes jerked open. Wrinkles creased the face of the woman who held the soup to her mouth. She looked more like someone's grandmother than a terrorist accomplice.

"Do not struggle, my dear. My name is Meryem, and I shall look after you. Our two friends tell me you have been trying to self-harm by banging your skull. Is that true? Or did they hit you with something? For now, I did not want to risk you getting hurt again, so I let them restrain you. Do tell me if you need the bathroom, won't you?"

Again, the woman's eyes burned with emotion. Could she be a psychopath? Meryem, she had said.

"Get some soup down you, sweetheart. You won't get another chance. Did they drug you?"

Elif blinked and opened her mouth to take a sip of hot soup, all the while studying the woman. She looked like a dried-up hippy—a leftist, maybe, from one of Turkey's countless atavistic revolutionary groups. Where her scrawny wrists protruded from her sweatshirt, faded tattoos decorated her wrinkled skin.

One looked like a dove of peace.

How could this old anarchist share the killers' deadly agenda? Did she know their plans? Did she know they had murdered six people?

Maybe the woman viewed extremist politics as a romantic game.

The nausea subsided. Her mind raced and her breathing steadied. The soup tasted good.

Whatever challenges she faced, she needed nourishment to survive.

"Yes," she murmured. "They drugged me. Ether, maybe. My head is killing me."

"I thought so. Beasts. Tip your head back, dear. Drink."

Elif nodded and opened her mouth. Warmth filled her as she gulped down the hot soup. Then a wave of biliousness rose up.

"Easy. Easy." The woman cushioned Elif's head with her hand, tipped her back, held her chin. "That is better, isn't it?"

The soup coursed down her throat. Her stomach convulsed again, but the food stayed down.

What had they done with the object?

Had Dervis triggered their capture? Maybe the terrorists had seen the ridiculous reports of the American journalist about the Luck of Troy and approached the burly archaeologist. How could the followers of an ancient cult be prepared to kill to gain possession of a relic?

Or had Dervis made up the story to mask his allegiance to their goals? Why else had they not killed him in the tunnel?

Perhaps Dervis, not the stocky terrorist, controlled the group.

Elif swallowed another mouthful of soup.

"Thank you," she said. "Delicious."

"My own recipe." Meryem smiled. "Want something to settle your stomach? A shot of Russian vodka? A glass of water?"

"Water. Please."

The wizened woman moved towards the kitchen. Elif scanned the room. The Groper's mouth hung open, his closed eyelids displayed long, delicate lashes. If he slept, he gave Elif the power to wake him up. Dervis gazed into space. The Chief stood near the kitchen counter, watching Meryem.

Why did he stand that way? His pose looked as if he wanted to protect something.

She looked again, and started. The object lay on the kitchen counter, shrouded in its protective wrapping. The woman had talked about using the relic for target practice.

The killer wanted to shield the object.

Elif shifted her gaze from the woman as she filled a glass of water from a dispenser on a giant fridge, to the object on the counter.

If the terrorists wanted to keep the relic safe, she could use that, too, to cause trouble.

"Hey!" Her voice came out as a croak. She took a breath and swallowed. "Hey!" Louder this time. Had she woken up the Groper? She hoped so. "The object from the grave. Can you bring it to me, please? I wish to examine it."

"Shut up." The Chief spoke in an educated Turkish accent, overlain with hostility. "You do not give the orders here."

"She wants to see your *Xoanon.*" The old woman held a glass of water in her hand. "Do not give the relic to her. Let us do the target practice thing." With a smooth movement, her pistol was in her other hand. The surface of the water in the glass remained steady.

"No!" The Chief took a step forward. "The object must not be harmed."

"You are one weird bunch of revolutionaries," Meryem said. "How can you ascribe power to some old relic you find in a hole in the ground? Have you not read your Marx, about the religion and the opium?" She stuffed the pistol back in her waistband and approached Elif with the water. "Why does she get to play with the *Xoanon* if I cannot?"

"She is an expert," the Chief said.

"What a shocker." Meryem squatted down in front of Elif and held the water glass to her mouth. "First, they molest their female hostage, and beat her, and drug her. Then they say she is *special* and must not be harmed. Typical male behaviour."

Elif bent her head to sip the water. "I do not believe these men are revolutionaries," she murmured. "They seek power, like all men. Not change. They will never let you touch the *Xoanon*, simply to show they are stronger than you."

"Hey." The Chief approached. He held a pistol in his hand. "No whispering."

"No sweat, macho man." Meryem rose to her feet. "She was telling me what pigs you all are. No news there. Let me see this so-called object. How do you even know the old piece of junk is the Palladium if you haven't checked it out?"

"No!" Refreshed by the water, Elif's voice rang out. "She must not touch the relic! Bring it to me. Only me."

As she bellowed the last word, the Groper stirred on his couch. Elif smiled and coughed, hoping he might wake.

"What happened to sisterly solidarity?" Meryem grimaced at Elif. "I will ask your sexist brute admirers to gag you again if you don't shut up." She turned towards the Chief. "I told you: my house, my rules. I was joking about the target practice, I would never harm your precious Palladium. But I would love to see a carving Athena herself is supposed to have made. Some actual booty Odysseus stole from Troy. What is the harm in that?"

She took a step towards the kitchen counter.

"I cannot allow you to touch the relic." The Chief placed himself in Meryem's way. "It is central to The Protocol. It must be preserved."

"The Protocol? What the hell is The Protocol?" Meryem held the gun steady, pointing at the Chief. How did she move so fast? Elif cringed away, straining against her bonds.

The Chief, his body between Meryem and the object, did not move. He, too, held his weapon, but in a relaxed grip, the muzzle facing the ground. "Do not threaten me," he said, his lips barely moving. "You cannot endanger the object."

"Cannot? First you mess up my Turkmen carpet, then you start issuing orders. Did nobody tell you power grows from the barrel of a gun? Speaking of which, big boy, put yours down. Nice and slow."

"I suggest you put yours down. Before you are hurt." The Chief did not move. His high forehead creased slightly. He nodded, as if agreeing with her. "I know you have helped us," he said. "I wish to respect your hospitality. But we cannot risk your presence here if you threaten us." He bent his knees and reached out to place his gun on the floor. "Do it."

"Do what?" Meryem said.

Elif had no time to cry out.

The second terrorist, the man she called the Groper, rose from the couch behind the old woman, crossed the space between them, and slammed his right hand down on Meryem's gun arm, smashing the limb towards the floor. A shot exploded, deafening in the confined space. The weapon tumbled to the ground. The Groper pulled back her head, exposing her throat. He hesitated, his eyes trained on the Chief.

The burly killer did not speak but gave a curt nod, as though he had exhausted all other options.

The knife in the Groper's hand sliced deep into Meryem's neck.

Blood poured out, soaking the faded sweatshirt and running down her jeans.

"No. Oh, no." The woman gasped and collapsed into the Groper's arms. He supported her as she fell, easing her shoulders back onto the rug on which she stood.

Meryem's eyes widened, seeming to stare at her own blood ebbing onto the fabric. A stain grew, spreading across the reds, golds, and blues of the antique Persian pattern.

The thin face grew more gaunt. Her wire-framed glasses tilted at an angle, her thin lips fell open, frozen in despair. At rest, the wiry body settled to the floor.

Meryem, the gun-loving revolutionary who had offered terrorists shelter at the *Buyuk Valide Han* in the heart of Istanbul, need never worry about a carpet again.

Elif had helped bring about her death.

## 49

From the side-door of the target ship, Saif al-Din looked down in horror as the prow of the pilot boat drifted clear of the larger vessel to expose a gaping chasm of water. Uzay, the boatman from the Black Sea, could not possibly leap across.

Without Uzay, they could not complete The Protocol.

How could he even move, in his bulky life-jacket?

Uzay turned, took three giant strides towards the prow of the smaller boat, and jumped.

In his mind, Saif knew Uzay's leap over the water lasted a split second. But from his vantage point high above, the boatman seemed to hang in the air for an eternity. His outstretched body looked tiny; his arms, reaching for the rope ladder, too short. The red-painted bulk of the hull rose up, monolithic and smooth.

Uzay landed in the water.

Saif gasped. But Uzay had snagged the rope ladder with one hand. He struggled on his back in the water, the heavy rucksack dragging him down, the buoyancy aid keeping him afloat, waves buffeting him as the great ship steamed ahead. The drag of Uzay's body tugged the ladder backwards towards the stern.

Even at the reduced speed of seven knots, designed to make boarding easier for pilots, the man from the Black Sea struggled to keep his grip. The water surged up over his shoulders as he fought to bring his other hand round to seize the ladder.

He could not reach.

"Your pilot tough guy," the whistling deck-hand said. "He like to swim." He laughed. "I help him."

Without hesitation the short, wiry Asian swung his body out over the sea and descended the ladder at speed, whistling as he went.

The man stopped at water level, his feet resting one or two rungs below the surface. He crouched down, one hand grasping the rope ladder, the other reaching towards Uzay, his lips still pursed to whistle as though he did this every day. But the man from the Black Sea could not turn his body in the water to reach out with his free arm. As the waves battered him, his fingers, wrapped around the ladder, came loose one by one.

Above him, the deck-hand crouched, feet wedged on the bottom rung, swaying like a gull on a buoy as the ship crashed through the broken water, his outstretched arm unreachable.

The next wave could sweep away the man on whom The Protocol depended.

Uzay's fingers opened. A wave crashed over his body, then a swell buoyed him up. As the body of the Black Sea boatman rose, the deck-hand shot out a wiry arm and grabbed him by the front of his life jacket, dragging the sodden bulk round towards the ladder with a strength that belied his slender limbs.

Uzay seized hold of the ladder with both hands. His wet clothes obstructed his movements and weighed him down, yet he persisted, one step after the next, up the side of the hull. The deck-hand climbed behind him.

Saif reached down. "Welcome aboard, sir." Uzay was supposedly the pilot, Saif and Kaan the trainees. "Are you ready to take control of the ship?"

"I am wet. The coxswain of that pilot boat is a dead man. But I am ready."

They stood in the narrow passageway. Behind them, a steel staircase climbed to the main deck. The two Asians bolted closed the side-door, one still whistling his tune. Kaan knelt. His hand, in his rucksack, gripped a silenced pistol.

One false move by the impetuous attack-dog could wreck the operation.

Saif shook his head.

Kaan's face darkened. He pushed the gun back into the bag. Saif followed as Uzay climbed the stairs, leaving the deckhands to re-stow the rope ladder.

The attack-dog wanted to execute the two hands in this secluded corner of the ship. He loved to kill, and the fewer crew members they needed to worry about, the better.

But The Protocol made clear they must control the target vessel for several hours. The ship must remain seaworthy. They must leave alive all the engineers and ratings needed to operate the diesel engines that powered the propellers. They must also ensure as many as possible of the crew members outside the bridge remained ignorant of what happened at the control centre of the vessel.

If someone summoned the two deckhands and they did not respond, or worse still, found their bodies in the well of the stairs, the crew might raise the alarm or demand an explanation of the captain.

Either risked disrupting The Protocol.

The deckhands would never know how close they had come to a violent death.

Their escape did not matter. In a few hours, every member of the ship's crew would perish.

They emerged on deck. From here, the vessel extended to such a distance that sea-spray hid the bow. The yellow-painted mass of the gas storage tanks dominated the centre of the deck, several storeys high, running all the way from the bow of the ship to the rear. At the stern, the white-painted superstructure rose as tall as an apartment block. Their target, the bridge of the ship, perched at the summit. A row of steel masts punctuated the length of the vessel, emphasising the scale of the colossus.

How had he ever thought the target ship could be too small? Of course, The Protocol specified the right size of vessel for the job. They stood aboard the ultimate machine of vengeance.

Saif checked the time. Apart from Uzay getting wet, everything had gone according to plan. He swung open the door giving access to the bridge superstructure.

Once they entered, the three men took off their rucksacks.

"Arm yourselves," Saif said. He closed the metal door and slid home a heavy bolt designed to secure the control centre of the ship in the event of a pirate attack.

The timing of their arrival meant no-one should need to enter the bridge until the end of the shift.

But The Protocol said they must take no chances.

Kaan and Uzay each removed from their bags a stockless Uzi submachine gun and a silenced pistol, with spare magazines for each. They turned to Saif.

"Ready," Kaan said. His eyes gleamed.

"Good. I will lead the way."

"Why no gun?" Uzay said.

The challenge was as clear as if Uzay had slapped him in the face. But Saif remained calm. "You two have all the firepower we need," he said. "I will enter the bridge first. Our goal is maximum surprise."

He climbed the metal stairs. The ship was deserted. Despite its size, the naval architects had designed the vessel to operate with a crew of only twenty, to save money for its godless owners.

A false economy, as Saif and his team planned to show.

Most of the crew members on board consisted of deck-hands or engineers, with assigned duties far from the bridge. Others slept in their cabins, off-shift.

If an off-duty crew member from within the rear superstructure of the ship came up to the bridge unexpectedly, they could blow The Protocol apart. Saif and his team must reach their goal without drawing attention to themselves. If only they could reach the wheelhouse without seeing anyone.

"Hi, there." A dark-skinned man in a white officer's uniform, with thick, tattooed arms, an upright posture, and a body-builder's chest stepped onto the landing ahead.

Saif froze. Praise God he carried no weapon. But what if the tattooed man saw Kaan or Uzay behind him?

"Are you the pilot?" the officer said in English. "I heard you screwed up the boarding."

"We are heading for the bridge," Saif said.

"Two floors up." The man gestured to the stairs.

Saif hesitated. If he went ahead, the man might see that Kaan and Uzay carried weapons. Yet if either opened fire, the din risked alerting the entire crew. Killing the tough-looking officer without using firearms posed challenges.

Making the man accompany them to the bridge, on the other hand, would reduce by one the number of officers they needed to control.

"This is my first time on this ship," Saif said. "Could you kindly lead us to the bridge?"

"First time?" The man shrugged. "Sure. Follow me."

He climbed the stairs ahead of them. A flag decorated the man's socks. Green, white, black, and red. Pan-Arab colours. Saif frowned. The officer could be a Muslim from Palestine. Or from Jordan or Egypt, from Iraq or Syria. Saif had expected American or British officers.

He shook his head. Where the dark-skinned man came from made no difference. If he stood in the way of The Protocol, he must die.

Saif rested his hand on the metal banister of the stairs as he followed the officer. Safety first. He smiled. One flight. Two. Kaan and Uzay followed behind.

"Here you go." The officer in the white uniform opened a door at the top of the stairs. "After you."

"No. Please. You go first." Saif sought to usher the other man though the door onto the bridge. If Saif entered first, the officer might see the weapons.

"The pilot's place is on the bridge," the officer said. Before Saif could stop him, he stepped to one side, away from the door.

The officer turned and stared straight at Kaan, who held his silenced pistol ahead of him.

"Hey! Stop!"

The man's voice pierced the enclosed steel space.

Kaan fired. A red stain appeared in the centre of the broad chest, and the officer slumped to the green-painted floor.

Saif turned towards the door. Another uniformed man appeared from inside, blinked at Saif, and ducked for cover, trying to pull the door closed behind him.

They had lost all element of surprise. Only speed and force remained.

Saif crammed himself into the opening. "Quick. Inside."

Uzay moved fastest. He seized the edge of the door in both hands and pulled, hard. Kaan dodged inside, the pistol extended ahead of him in a two-handed grip, and fired a single shot.

Saif followed, withdrawing his own pistol from his bag.

*They must not hit the controls.*

The door opened onto the back of the bridge. The man who had tried to stop them lay inside the entrance. A waist-high wooden barrier blocked access to the main wheelhouse. Ahead, an array of windows looked out over the deck of the vessel towards the prow. A curved console crammed with electronic equipment dominated the wide, bright space.

The bridge was empty.

Saif stepped forward, Uzay behind him. Kaan moved ahead, stalking round the wooden barrier into the wheelhouse, his pistol held ready.

"One guy," he said, "plus the one who brought us up. Where are the others?"

Saif pointed to two side-doors leading out onto a green-painted deck. A yellow-painted funnel the size of a ten-storey building rose aft.

"Could they have escaped?"

"No-one left the room." Kaan approached the central console.

"Two people must be on duty at all times," Uzay said. "There must be one more man. Maybe two."

"You bastards!" From behind a curtain at the rear of the wheelhouse a heavily-built man launched himself at Kaan. He wore glasses, had long, greasy hair, and carried a fire-axe with a wooden handle. Kaan spun around, firing, but his first shot missed and the man smashed into him. The length of the handle made the fire-axe an awkward weapon. But the impact sent both men crashing to the steel deck, the pistol spinning away out of reach.

"Help him," Saif shouted to Uzay. Kaan's head must have struck the deck; he reached for his assailant's throat, but without strength. Saif aimed his pistol but could not get a clean shot. The long-haired man raised the clumsy axe above his head, struggling to bring the blade down with maximum force on Kaan's face.

Why did Uzay not attack?

The Black Sea boatman knelt on the steel deck. He levelled his weapon and pulled the trigger. The man in glasses fell sideways, his lank hair hiding where the shot must have struck.

For an instant, Saif relaxed. Something moved. A short black crew member with a high forehead rose from behind the console. He must have been hiding there the whole time. Kaan lay motionless. Uzay, kneeling, could not see the new threat.

The black man had no weapon. He made no sudden movement but looked at Saif, his eyes clear and calm, and leaned forward towards a device set into the console. Large red illuminated letters spelled out the word: DISTRESS. To one side a marine VHF set with a telephone handset stood within reach. To the other rose a red, round button protected by a plastic cover.

The DSC alarm.

Before Saif could raise his weapon, the man reached over from behind the console, lifted the cover, and brought the palm of his hand down on the red button to activate the distress signal.

## 50

B lood. In his mouth. And something else.
John Savage knew the taste.

He raised his head from the paving. His ears rang. The hubbub of the wounded crowd grew louder.

In his mouth he tasted failure.

Twice today he had predicted a terrorist target. Twice he had failed to stop a massacre.

Nor had he come any closer to finding Elif.

"You okay?" Orhan rolled onto his back on the floor of the terrace, his arms still bound behind him.

"How could I be? You heard the bomb."

"No pressure wave down here on the floor. Hey! Korkmaz!"

Savage turned. The mountainous counter-terrorism cop knelt at the edge of the terrace staring straight ahead, as if in prayer.

Could the blast have caught him?

A single piece of shrapnel or a steel nut from a suicide belt could kill as surely as a bullet.

Savage ran to the superintendent.

When he touched Korkmaz on the shoulder, the big man turned his head. "You." His voice seemed even deeper than before. "I can't hear too well."

"Me neither." Savage shook his head and looked down from the terrace. The crowd in the square stood still, as if stunned. The bomb had not started a stampede. The noise had died down. Ambulances arrived.

"How about taking Orhan's cuffs off?"

"The traitor? Who disobeyed orders and endangered an

investigation? Why should I? Your pathetic theory didn't even stop the attack, in case you haven't noticed." Korkmaz rose to his feet and frowned down at Savage. A trickle of gore ran down his cheek, mixing with sweat and dust.

Whose blood streaked his face?

Savage looked into the police chief's eyes. Korkmaz must despise him. Everything he touched failed.

"Have you checked the suspects your snipers took down?" A woman's voice, shouting in English. "Did they have belts?"

The woman with the short, dyed red hair and pale skin stood on a chair. She held her video-camera steady, like a part of her.

"He told you where to find the needle in the haystack," the woman shouted. She tapped the camera, whose recording light glowed. "Don't take my word for it, I have the evidence here. The name's Anderson. Misty Anderson. I am a journalist."

"Who do you write for?" Savage said.

"AP. New York Times. Times of London. Stringing, to be honest. But Istanbul is hot right now. Especially the Palladium. Good work, by the way."

*Good work. A needle in a haystack.* The phrases pierced the fog around his brain. *The surveillance system.* Korkmaz had used Savage's plan of Taksim to identify two terror suspects.

Snipers had gunned down those two suspects.

Only one bomb had exploded, instead, perhaps, of three.

Had Savage, by his actions, prevented two further bombs designed to create the stampede and bloodbath the terrorists planned?

*Did they have belts,* the red-haired woman had asked.

The journalist, protected from the blast at the back of the terrace, was thinking more clearly than either him or Korkmaz.

"Give us some bloody credit," Savage said to the police chief. "The two suspects the snipers took out. Did anyone check if they had bombs?"

Korkmaz nodded and rubbed his head. His hand came away

covered with blood, but he seemed not to notice. "Someone is checking now."

"What about Elif Mutlu? The missing archaeologist. Could you programme her into your system? Maybe the cameras can spot her somewhere."

"In this chaos?" Korkmaz gestured towards the vast square teeming with people, ambulances, and police. "No chance."

"At least try. I just saved your job."

"First, we check the suspects. Then search." The big superintendent shouted orders.

Orhan still lay on the ground. How could Savage get the intelligence cop released? His phone vibrated.

"John. Where-the-hell-are-you?" Christopher Braintree spoke each word as if it formed the end of a sentence.

"I am at the scene of the explosion in Taksim. I was on my way back to the Consulate, but I couldn't get through the crowds."

"On your motorcycle. You couldn't get through the crowds. Bizarre."

"So, send me back to London. Istanbul has suffered its second major terrorist attack in two hours. Have we declared a crisis?"

"We set up the crisis centre in the Consulate after the Besiktas bomb. The Turkish media are talking about twelve dead at the Dolmabahce Palace, mostly police officers plus the two bombers. There could be upwards of fifty at Taksim. But our head of police liaison—you—is AWOL. I don't know what the hell you think you are doing wandering around Istanbul looking for your girlfriend, John, but we need you. How soon can you get here?"

Savage hesitated. The moment it seemed Braintree could not be any more pompous, he switched on the human touch and appealed for help. His question about Elif stung. Why had Savage tried to track her down? He himself had buried whatever remained of their relationship.

"She is not my girlfriend. I will be with you in a few minutes, if the police don't lock me up as a suspect. Count on it."

He cut the call, knelt down next to Orhan, and gripped the Turk's hand. "Sixty dead in the two attacks. I am sorry. I must go to the Consulate. How do I get you out of this?"

"How about staying away from me?" Orhan grimaced but did not withdraw his hand. "I was fine until we started working together this morning. If Korkmaz finds two dead suicide bombers with belts in Taksim, he will owe both of us a big favour. If snipers have gunned down two random protesters, things will not look so rosy. You should disappear either way."

"The report I saw talked about fifteen operatives. Two blew themselves up at Besiktas. Add one more at Taksim, plus the two shot by the snipers, if we're lucky. Ten terrorists are still on the loose, including the two who took Elif and Dervis. Plenty enough to do something big–and vile."

Orhan's eyes smouldered. "Could they attack the football match? Over forty thousand fans will attend."

"The city is packed with targets. The *Gerald R Ford* and the two escorting destroyers are moored near Topkapi Palace. All kinds of people would love to attack three juicy US warships. The *Queen Anne* is arriving this evening with six thousand US tourists. And yes, the Besiktas-Liverpool match. Take your pick."

"No, John. I will not pick any of them. The police have all these places locked down."

"Locked down like at Dolmabahce? Or at Taksim? Since the attack at the dig this morning, the killers have spread chaos across the city. Maybe their goal is to soak up police resources investigating attacks and guarding against new ones, while their real target is somewhere else."

"I do not see how even the best-equipped terrorists could attack a fully armed US aircraft carrier. Or bring a bomb within a mile of tonight's game or a cruise ship. Those terminals are guarded like military installations. Of course, they can explode a bomb in a crowd anywhere they want. But is that the spectacular they seek? No, John. I am certain we are looking in the wrong place."

Savage stared into Orhan's calm eyes. All around, the sounds of the crowd grew louder as people began to communicate in the wake of the bombing. Istanbul pulsed like an organism, populated not by millions but by tens of millions of human beings.

Already that organism was healing itself.

Every death through terrorism was a tragedy. A handful of killings could rock a country, from Mogadishu or London to Tokyo or Los Angeles.

Yet Orhan's theory that the intelligence pointed to something bigger made sense. Those hashtags: #endofthewest and #endofallevil, presaged a spectacular, cataclysmic ambition, a new 9/11 attack. A few dozen deaths, however horrific, did not meet that standard.

What atrocity did the terrorists plan?

"Orhan." Savage gripped the Turk's shoulder. "I have to check in at the Consulate. But keep that fine mind of yours on the job. The exam question is: if the attacks so far are diversions, what the hell is the main event?"

"Maybe we could persuade Korkmaz to deploy his surveillance technology and set up sniper teams around likely targets."

"That could be what the terrorists want us to do." Savage rose to his feet. "I asked him to use the tech to try and find Elif, but I'm not holding my breath."

"Did you say Elif? Elif Mutlu?"

The short-haired journalist stood perched on the chair behind the cordon, her camera trained on Savage, her smear of lipstick bright against her face. The red light of the live feed blazed like a malign eye.

Savage pushed past the woman towards the stairs.

"Wait! Stop! I know Elif." She stared up at him, her green eyes bright. "I was at the dig this morning. I saw her."

"You saw Elif?" He seized her arm. "Is your camera still on?"

"Uh, yes." She stabbed at the controls. "Not now."

"What time were you there?"

"Early this morning, about eight-thirty. Hey, take it easy."

"Sorry." He loosened his grip.

"Some workmen showed up," she said. "At the dig. To help lift the cover of the last sarcophagus. The one containing the Palladium."

"The Palladium? Wait. Misty Anderson. You're the one who dreamed the whole idiotic story up, aren't you? What happened this morning?"

"I don't know. They threw me off the site before they lifted the lid."

"Are you sure that camera is off? Let me see."

"Whoops. Sorry. It does that sometimes." Misty Anderson stuffed the camera into a voluminous handbag and placed the bag between her legs on the ground. "There. What can you tell me? Strictly for background?"

"Who threw you off the site? Was it Elif?"

"No. It was a guy called Mehmet Ozdemir. He works for Arzu Pasha. She's the tycoon building the new shopping mall. She owns half of Anatolia."

"Arzu Pasha had you thrown off the site, but she let Elif carry on working? It's as if she wanted her to find something."

"Maybe she did. What do you think will happen next?"

Savage glanced down at the bag containing the video camera and said nothing.

"Don't you want to find Elif?"

For the second time in as many hours, Savage hesitated. Every scintilla of his training bound him to keep secrets secret. Compromising sources killed people. During the war they had said: "Loose lips sink ships."

Yet kidnappers held Elif in their power. Someone could, if the intelligence Ram showed him was correct, be preparing a devastating attack on a city of twenty million souls.

"Off the record? Background?"

"Cross my heart. Maybe I can help you."

"There may be more terrorists in the city. They killed six people at Elif's dig. She is missing. These terror attacks and her kidnapping must be connected. But we can't see what a mythical Greek relic has to do with attacking Istanbul."

The journalist frowned. "Attacking Istanbul? Maybe that's the answer."

"What?"

She bit her lip. "I know you'll say this is crap."

"Try me."

"Isn't the point about the Palladium that the relic protects whichever city it is in? Troy. Then Athens, Rome, and Constantinople. Like the *nazars* you see everywhere in Turkey. Maybe whoever took Elif believes destroying the relic, or taking it outside the city, will weaken the Palladium's protection, or amplify whatever attack they have planned."

Savage shook his head. "Last time I looked, we were living in the twenty-first century."

Misty Anderson stared past him. "People believe weirder shit than that. Look at the internet. An attack linked to a symbol could have more impact. That could explain why they took Elif. She is a world expert on ancient Greek artefacts. They want to assault the entire city."

The journalist ran her pale hand up over her forehead as if pushing back tresses of non-existent hair. She held out a crumpled visiting card. "Call me if you find out more. And think: maybe they took Elif because they need her to interpret the Palladium. Before they launch their final attack."

## 51

Ali Aydin stood at Meryem Shah's picture-window. Outside, Istanbul went about its business for the final time.

Shadows crawled over the red-tiled roofscape of the Grand Bazaar. The hands of the clock over the kitchen counter seemed frozen. In the city, nothing moved. Since the authorities had closed the Bosphorus to shipping, more traffic than ever choked the bridges and tunnels of Istanbul.

Millions of people, criss-crossing the city in ignorance. None of them realising this day was their last.

Ali drummed his fingertips on the windowsill. They should enjoy their hollow, pitiful existence while they still lived.

Around the shoreline and on the Galata Bridge, clouds of seagulls massed. He knew *Istanbullus* tossed fragments of sesame-coated *simits* in the air to attract the bickering birds. How many gulls might survive the day?

Ali pictured every building, every street, and every square of the sprawling city transformed into a wasteland of dust and ashes. A storm was sweeping in to destroy the unbelievers and to return righteousness to Istanbul.

The heat of the day had ebbed. But the luxurious apartment still stank of death.

Ali had ordered Target Two, the pious archaeologist, Dervis Basturk, to help Hussein roll up the body of the anti-capitalist firebrand in her own blood-soaked carpet. They had dragged the corpse into the bedroom, stowed the rolled-up rug in a cupboard, and turned the air-conditioning up to high. But the woman's presence hung over the shiny surfaces of the penthouse.

Why had the anarchist sought to touch the object? What power had drawn her to the relic? Ali frowned at the bundle on the kitchen surface.

He had looked death in the eye. Yet he had felt no fear.

The clock in the kitchen ticked round to three. Soon, their final journey across the city could begin.

Ali's gaze returned to the object. Had Target One encouraged the witch to try to seize the ancient relic, when the two of them whispered together?

Maybe Target One knew how to manipulate a fellow woman. She had exploited the unpredictability of Meryem Shah as a maverick force of female power.

The Protocol made clear any unexpected event, however insignificant, could put the project at risk.

He must not underestimate Target One because of her sex.

The archaeology professor lay on the floor, her head on a cushion, hands bound behind her with tape. Hussein had freed her feet, to make visiting the bathroom easier for her. But she had not moved since Hussein cut the throat of the old anarchist. Maybe seeing the blood gush forth had knocked the fight out of her. Most of the time, she kept her eyes closed. Once or twice, Ali caught her looking around the room, her gaze resting on Hussein, or the object on the counter, or on Target Two slumped in an armchair by the window.

No help would come from that direction. The Elders had chosen Target Two, picked at his weaknesses and longings, and ensnared him in a web of deception.

"Hey."

Target One spoke for the first time in an hour. Ali did not reply or look at her.

"Could you put the television on?"

He hesitated. What did she want to see? The less she knew, the better. Yet Ali liked the idea of activating the television. He might find out more about the bombs that had exploded in the city. The propaganda channels of the infidel state would flounder as they tried to analyse the attack at the archaeological site and the subsequent blasts.

Even as their enemies pored over Ali's actions in kidnapping Targets One and Two and neutralising the students and workers at the dig, someone had carried out bombings further north, on the European side. What further havoc did The Elders plan?

Nothing could stand in the way of The Protocol.

"Did you hear me? Hello? Or do you want me to die of boredom here on the floor?"

Target One spoke with a drawl, as though the ether still paralysed her tongue. Ali looked at the woman and made a decision.

---

Elif studied the eyes of the killer she dubbed the Chief. Her request to watch television had unsettled him, giving her control. The sound from the TV might wake the Groper, transferring to her another fragment of power over her captors.

Whether they put the TV on or not did not matter. Her making the request had boosted her strength.

At last the Chief, moving with an easy grace, picked up a remote from the kitchen counter and switched on the television. He flicked through football, a documentary about wildlife in the Antarctic, and a couple of Turkish police procedurals before finding a twenty-four-hour news channel.

"*The treacherous terrorists have all been neutralised,*" the commentator said. The images showed people streaming across an open space. "*It is reported that three terrorists are dead here at Taksim and two more outside the Dolmabahce Palace. Several police officers and members of the public have been hurt in the attacks. It is believed the same cell carried out an assault at an archaeological site in the Old City at around nine-thirty this morning. The authorities urge the public to stay away from crowded areas.*"

Elif suppressed a moan. Two separate bomb attacks in the heart of Istanbul. How many people had they killed? Could her captors have triggered the explosions? She wanted to shout at the television, *They are here! They still live!* She closed her eyes. Stay away from crowded areas? In Istanbul?

When she opened her eyes, the picture showed a restaurant terrace packed with uniformed police. She blinked. To one side of the shot, John Savage knelt with his hand on the shoulder of Orhan, who lay on the ground. Her pulse raced. Had a blast injured her brother? Could he be dead? No. He raised himself on one side and spoke to Savage, his face screwed up as if in pain. Someone had twisted his hands out of sight behind his back. Who could have done such a thing? Why? Savage's lips moved, but Elif heard nothing.

The image changed. Misty Anderson stared into the lens, her skin pale in the sunshine.

"The police have imposed a news blackout," she said. "But sources say at least three suicide bombers blew themselves up in the heart of Istanbul. The first two, around noon, detonated outside the Dolmabahce Palace, where the Greek and Turkish Presidents had been about to start what was optimistically named the Reconciliation Summit. The third attacker exploded his vest in the centre of a crowd at a political rally here in Taksim Square a few minutes ago. Reports speak of numerous casualties.

"Officials say none of the participants in the Reconciliation Summit were injured. But a planned press conference has been postponed amidst differences over the fate of the so-called Palladium, or Luck of Troy, which the Greek government says the Turkish authorities are hiding from them."

On the screen, Misty Anderson leaned forward.

"Sources report that the Palladium itself was the target of today's first terrorist incident, an attack on an archaeological site in the Old City. Reports say kidnappers seized archaeologists working at the site, together with the legendary relic, and escaped after murdering several people."

Misty Anderson stood up straight. "Controversial property

tycoon, Arzu Pasha, is the owner of the site. We asked her whether the Palladium had been discovered during foundation works for her future *Heart of Istanbul* shopping and entertainment complex, due to open in eighteen months, and where the relic was now."

An attractive, smartly-dressed woman with straight brown hair and full, red lips filled the screen. She wore a stylishly-cut emerald dress whose delicate contours hinted at a slender yet well-developed figure. A barely-visible blemish on one cheek hinted that her apparent youth owed something to cosmetic surgery.

"Arzu Holdings is shocked by the news of a terrorist attack at our construction site," the woman said. "We offer our condolences and hope the two archaeologists can be rescued quickly. But we deny all speculation about alleged religious relics supposedly found at the site. Arzu Holdings has funded an extension to the Archaeological Museum to house the numerous Byzantine objects recovered during the excavation. No item is missing."

How could the tycoon know whether an object had gone missing if Elif had not yet catalogued the find for the museum?

"What the people of Istanbul want," Arzu Pasha continued, "are jobs, entertainment, and retail opportunities, not superstitious claptrap. We shall begin to pour the foundations of the Heart of Istanbul as soon as the police clear the site."

Elif tried to wriggle into a more comfortable position. That three bombs had exploded in Istanbul in the hours since her captors seized her and Dervis in the Old City could not be a coincidence. The attacks, and the threat of further atrocities, had overwhelmed the police. Orhan lay helpless, injured or under arrest, at Taksim. John Savage could achieve nothing on his own. He did not care, anyway.

Yet the sight of the Englishman with his hand on Orhan's shoulder gave her hope.

The television replayed CCTV footage of the bombing at Taksim Square. As the explosion rang out, the Groper stirred on the sofa and opened a groggy eye.

Perfect. The television had woken the sleazy killer from his sleep.

How else could she turn the tables? Or, better still, call for help?

She must keep challenging her captors. Try to keep them off-balance.

A pressure in her abdomen reminded her she had not visited the bathroom since the Groper slit Meryem's throat.

The old revolutionary's death had left Elif the only woman in the apartment.

"I need to use the toilet," she said.

The Chief looked around the room.

*No use looking. No-one is left to help you.*

"Please," she said. "It is urgent."

The stocky terrorist nodded. But instead of coming to help her, he walked into the bathroom. She heard clattering. A few minutes later he emerged, his hands piled with nail scissors, a pack of women's razors, pills, toothpaste—even a glass phial. Perhaps he thought she could break the bottle to use as a weapon or to harm herself. He placed the objects on the kitchen top and opened drawers as if searching for something. At last he found a stout, yellow-handled screwdriver. With this, he unscrewed the locking mechanism and handle of the bathroom door and placed the pieces with the other items on the counter.

At last, he knelt and undid the tape around her wrists. When he pulled her to a standing position, both his strength and his care in not touching her more than necessary struck her. He gestured towards the bathroom door.

Elif tried to appear grateful. Her wrists burned, the blood pounded at her temples. Her aching legs felt cumbersome, as though they had swollen. The Groper stared at her and grinned.

Inside the bathroom, she swung the door behind her. Without the locking mechanism, it glided open again. She placed a towel on the floor to hold the door shut.

The barrier offered no protection. But at least she gained a degree of privacy.

No time to fill the bath. She closed the plug on the hand basin and turned on both taps to maximum. Water splashed against the porcelain. Everywhere in the bathroom, fancy ceramics gleamed. The owner had installed a huge, rectangular basin, with no space for soap or a toothbrush. After thirty seconds, the water had barely covered the bottom of the bowl. With the giant basin came an oversized overflow. The tide of water from the taps looked too puny to defeat it.

She reached for a handful of toilet paper, moistened the wad in the water, and jammed the resulting spongy mass into the overflow pipe. The water rose half-way up the sink. Should she use the toilet while she waited? Or flush, to suggest she had used it?

No, to flush might slow the flow of water into the sink.

Still the water inched up the side of the bowl. She glanced at the door. How much longer would the process take? When the basin had filled to the brim the water would slosh onto the floor and seek an outlet. Somewhere below, as a torrent gushed down into a workshop or café, perhaps bringing down a ceiling, people would come to investigate, then—

"Hey! What are you doing in there?" A muffled voice. Could the Chief suspect something? Or did the Groper plan to burst into the bathroom?

"Hold on a minute." She flushed the toilet. "Give me a second."

"I don't think so."

The bathroom door crashed open, smashing against the bathtub with a crack.

Dervis Basturk stood in the doorway, his wrists still bound with masking tape.

"Elif!" he said. "What the hell are you trying to do?" His face darkened. When he shook his head, the earring glinted against his neck. "You fool."

He turned and shouted into the lounge behind him. "Quick. Get in here. She is trying to flood the bathroom. Come and pull out the plug."

## 52

On the bridge of the ship in the Sea of Marmara, the black crew member raised his hand from the DSC alarm and stood up straight, arms by his side. A warbling signal sounded from the panel.

"Surrender, now." The man spoke almost as though he wanted to help them. "The coastguard are coming."

Saif-al-Din fought to control his breathing. The Protocol stated that above all else, he and his team must prevent anything damaging the ship's controls. As a second priority they must prevent those on board communicating with third parties.

The black officer had breached The Protocol.

"Shall I kill him?" Uzay stood at Saif's shoulder, his pistol trained on the crewman.

"Wait." Saif shook his head. The dignified officer seemed to be of African origin. Perhaps he was a man of faith. How else could he remain so calm in the face of danger? Did he believe God stood guard over him? The Protocol said nothing about the ethnicity or religion of the crew of the target ship. So far, they consisted of a veritable United Nations of races and beliefs.

But The Protocol said everyone on the bridge must die.

The crew member could be a threat if he communicated with others on the ship or on the shore. Might he be useful? Possibly, but they had no resources to keep him alive and restrained.

The Protocol must be right.

"Shoot," Saif said.

Uzay fired. The bullet hit the dark-skinned man in the chest. His expression did not change. "God will judge you," he said. Uzay fired another single shot. The man fell to the deck behind the console. Silence filled the bridge, except for the warbling of the alarm signal.

A new, urgent noise rang out. Like an old-fashioned alarm bell.

Uzay stepped forward. "It is the coastguard on the radio telephone, responding to the distress signal," he said. "Give me a few seconds."

Without waiting for authorisation from Saif, the Black Sea boatman leaned forward to examine the DSC panel. A light flashed orange. Uzay touched a button and the warbling stopped. The radio telephone continued to ring.

Uzay lifted the handset. He grinned at Saif, as if relishing the fact that his supposed boss stood there like a scarecrow.

"This is Royal Lion." Uzay peered at the panel and read out a string of numbers in halting English. "Regret DSC alarm activated in error." He held up his hand to Saif and Kaan for silence, as if they might otherwise have been so stupid as to intervene. "Alarm is URGENT priority, not DISTRESS. Pilot boarding vessel fell into water. We rescue him. He is safe, but wet. I wish to cancel distress call."

Did Uzay believe himself the master of this operation? Saif strode to where the Black Sea boatman stood at the console, the handset to his ear.

Yet what could Saif do? He could not strike, or even speak to Uzay without compromising The Protocol further.

The Black Sea man paused, listening to the coastguard. He locked his insolent gaze on Saif. "We continue course towards terminal at Gebze," he said. "Yes." He paused again. "How awful. I am sorry. Yes. Thank you." He replaced the handset and flashed a grin. "A tragedy. Three bombs have exploded in Istanbul. Many dead, including police officers."

Saif clenched his fists. "What are you doing? You cannot decide your actions for yourself. You must take orders from me."

"And leave the phone ringing? No-one ignores a call from the coastguard. Nothing would make them more suspicious." Uzay folded his arms. "What did you plan to tell them, anyhow?"

"Not that we continue our course to Gebze. That is the opposite direction to where we are going." Saif stared around the bridge. Kaan leaned against a hand-rail, watching the exchange with his small eyes. Did he sense Saif's loss of authority? Outside the window, the bow of the ship was more than a quarter of a mile away.

Command of this behemoth had made Uzay arrogant. Only he could pilot the vast vessel and its cargo, so central to the completion of The Protocol.

"Of course I said we were going to Gebze," the Black Sea man said. "This is what they are expecting. Gebze is our official destination. Our nearly-drowned pilot came on board in order to help us enter and dock at the port. The coastguard know this."

"Next time, you will consult me." Saif stood up straight. Why should he care about Uzay? The death of the Black Sea man lay only a few hours ahead. "Is the alarm signal audible to the crew?"

"No. The signal is designed to alert nearby ships to any problem where we might need help from another vessel." Uzay spoke as though lecturing a particularly stupid child. "The crew cannot hear anything. For the coastguard, what I said is logical: our pilot is safely on board, so we have cancelled the distress call. Everything is back to normal."

"They will watch our progress. They will see we have changed course."

"The risk is low. They are busy. Even if I continue towards Gebze for a few minutes, we will arrive at the destination specified in The Protocol in a few hours. I will turn off the AIS tracking system and turn."

Saif frowned. "The Automatic Identification Signal, right?"

Uzay sighed. "Yes. Like the transponder on an aircraft."

"Will turning it off not attract their attention?"

"The AIS is not perfect. Sometimes a satellite signal is weak, or you can have interference. Even if they do spot us on their radar and ask where we are going, we can say we have received another set of orders." Uzay gestured towards the immense bulk of the ship and shrugged. "Most of all, what action can they take, even if they are suspicious when we near our destination? They can do nothing to stop us."

## 53

"Thank heavens you are here."

Christopher Braintree stood in the crisis centre at Pera House, surrounded by consular officers on the telephone and at computers, checking hospitals for injured British citizens or calling contacts for news. Handwritten notes on a whiteboard showed the names of those killed and injured in two columns, with the nationalities of the victims.

So far, the blue cursive script showed only one British name: Stuart Lamont, the paraplegic archaeology student shot dead at the dig. Other victims included an American, a German, and a Russian. A consular official put down a phone, walked to the whiteboard, and revised the number of Turkish fatalities upwards.

Braintree made a step as if to leave, then stepped back. "Two separate attacks the same day. Maybe three. Get onto your police contacts and find out what the hell is going on."

Savage nodded. Time, heat, and stress had crumpled the Consul General's suit. Dark patches of sweat stained the armpits of his jacket. He also wore a waistcoat and tie. Did the formality make him feel more in control of the situation?

"I have talked to everyone on the crisis team," Savage said. "Their training has kicked in: they know what they have to do. I have set up a connection between the consular crew and Turkish police liaison." He shrugged. "Fact is, the Turks have no more idea what is happening, or why, than we do."

"London are worried the worst is yet to come." Braintree lowered his voice. "Ram says he showed you the intelligence. They think the terrorists are planning something even bigger. Bigger than sixty-three victims so far." He shook his head. "Unbelievable. Poor bloody Turks."

"You get some rest," Savage said. "The shift system is up and running."

"Take a rest? I am supposed to be meeting the head of the Turkish football federation in half an hour. Can you believe the police here want the Liverpool match to go ahead? They say the British fans are all over Istanbul, and they will be safer gathered at the stadium than wandering around the city drinking and getting into trouble. Patricia will be here soon, I hope."

"Pat? At least that's good news." Patricia Worthington was the Deputy Head of Mission, a pillar of common sense. "As for the idea the fans are safer in the stadium than anywhere else, that may well be true."

"You will stay here at the crisis centre until the next shift comes on duty at midnight. I am sorry your girlfriend is missing. I can imagine how you must feel. But the team needs your experience."

Savage did not correct Braintree. The Consul General's ignorance that his relationship with Elif had finished gave him an odd sense of satisfaction. He looked around the crisis centre, where staff worked calmly in the face of events of whose scale, as with every consular crisis, no-one could yet be certain.

"I will do all I can to help," he said.

"Good. We are expecting a call from the mother of Stuart Lamont. You must offer her every assistance." Braintree sighed. "He is the boy you called a corpse, live on camera, before you rushed off. His mum is flying out tomorrow to bring her son's body home to Scotland. Imagine how she feels."

Braintree strode off down the corridor, turned back to enter his office, emerged, fumbling in his pockets for something, returned to his office, and, at last, left the building.

Savage's phone rang. Orhan Mutlu.

"Got your hands free, at least," Savage said.

"No thanks to you," Orhan said. "We have news. The police

found the bodies of the two people they shot in Taksim. Both wore suicide belts. They had positioned themselves where we predicted: on two entrance roads into the square on the side opposite the explosion. If we had not told Korkmaz where to focus his search, we would have had three bombs, not one, and a panicked stampede of half a million protesters. We could have seen hundreds or thousands of people dead. Korkmaz owes us one. My cuffs are off."

"You are free thanks to me. Admit it."

Orhan ignored him. "Two more things. Korkmaz is certain the attacks so far form a pattern. Five terrorists have died up to now. If the intelligence is right, ten more remain on the loose. More than enough to carry out a spectacular complex attack on a target in Istanbul."

"At least Korkmaz is a good listener. We told him all that."

"He thinks the final target will be the American aircraft carrier, the *Gerald R Ford*. We believe the ship carries nuclear weapons—an irresistible target for terrorists–although the Americans refuse to confirm or deny this. The carrier is moored with two support ships at the Kennedy Street wharf near the Topkapi Palace. The attacks in Besiktas and Taksim are perfectly placed to draw attention away from there. Korkmaz has gone to the military dock with thirty armed police to strengthen the perimeter."

"Who would attack an aircraft carrier protected by US marines? They might as well commit suicide."

"I agree." Orhan paused. "But I do not mind Korkmaz going there, because that gives us the opportunity to follow up another lead. A police officer who was on duty near the Grand Bazaar when the first two bombs went off at noon has called in. He saw a TV report about the killings at the archaeology site. He remembered someone who met Elif's description being half-carried into the *Valide Han* near the Grand Bazar. About three hours ago."

"Three hours ago? What do you mean, half-carried? Was she injured?"

"He says he does not know." Orhan's voice sank. "He said the woman appeared unconscious or maybe even dead, and was supported by two men."

"Dead? Elif?"

"It may not be Elif. And the woman could have been alive. The description of one of the men supporting her fits Dervis Basturk. Another guy appeared, saying she had heat-stroke. The uniform was about to ask for their IDs when the bombs went off at Besiktas."

"Three men. Could be Dervis and the two killers. But why would Dervis help them? Where did they go?"

"The cop thinks they entered the *Valide Han*. I am on my way there with a SWAT team. Korkmaz drew a blank using facial recognition at Taksim, as he predicted. This is our first concrete lead since Elif vanished. Come with me."

Savage cursed under his breath. "I can't," he said. "I promised to stay at the Consulate."

"What? Have British citizens been killed?"

"Only the poor Scottish lad at Elif's dig, so far as we know. But more may be out there."

"Are you crazy? How many British police were on duty at Besiktas? How many British tourists turn out at rallies to support Nasim Kaval or Rauf Toprak? I can tell you now, not a single Brit broke a fingernail in either of the bombings."

"You can't be sure of that. I have to stay here."

"I never believed it was really true. You don't care about Elif, do you? I guess I will be better off without you." Orhan cut the call.

The tall figure of Patricia Worthington entered the corridor. She held a laptop computer clamped under her arm and a mug of tea in her hand.

"John," she said. "The CG told me you were here." She looked around the crisis centre and lowered her voice. "How is the team doing so far?"

"Totally professional." Savage gestured towards the whiteboard. "No reports yet of any more Brits killed or injured. The family of Stuart Lamont are flying out tomorrow. Out in the city, no-one knows what will happen next, although I did hear from police liaison they have a lead. Did you see the intelligence? About the number of attackers?"

"The intelligence could be wrong." Patricia Worthington's calm eyes studied Savage as if daring him, an ex-SIS officer, to disagree. "It has been known."

A young consular officer called Deniz approached them. "We have the mother of Stuart Lamont on the line," she said to Patricia. "Will you take the call?"

"I will," Savage said.

"I'm happy to speak to the mum," Patricia Worthington said. "This must be awful for her."

"No. I screwed it up. It's the least I can do."

Savage followed Deniz to her desk. She handed him the receiver.

"This is John Savage at the British Consulate. I work on liaison with the Turkish police. I am so sorry for your loss."

For a moment he heard only breathing on the line. "My loss? Is it certain? He was just a wee lad."

"The Turkish police have confirmed his death, unfortunately. I am so sorry."

"My name is Catriona Lamont." Stuart Lamont's mother spoke with a Glaswegian accent. Her voice rose. "A policeman came to see me. He said Stuart had been killed in a terrorist incident in Turkey. I told him there must be a mistake."

"We are here to help you. I understand you are coming out to Istanbul tomorrow."

"He was a child. In a wheelchair. Who would do such a thing?"

"The Turkish authorities are trying to find out. I am helping them. We expect a coroner's enquiry."

Catriona Lamont paused. "John Savage. Are you the one who was in the tunnel? Who found them? I saw the video."

"Yes. I am sorry I did not stop."

"Mr Savage. You deserve to be sorry. Stuart could be dead

because you did not stop to help him. You may be guilty of manslaughter."

She could not know the killers had executed each of the dead in the tunnel with a chest- and head-shot double-tap.

Savage could not tell her.

"I understand why you are angry. You have every right to be. I should have stopped to check." He paused. Catriona Lamont said nothing. He pictured her standing in the hallway of her house, phone in hand, tears running down her cheeks. "Mrs Lamont. We will do everything we can to help you when you come to Istanbul tomorrow. And I will do all in my power to find out who killed your son and bring them to justice."

"I hope they find them and kill them. But that won't bring my boy back. I saw you on the video. So wicked. Horrible." Abruptly, Catriona Lamont ended the call.

Savage replaced the receiver and closed his eyes. A mother had lost her son. Who could imagine such sorrow?

What could he, Savage, do to help her?

He could track down the murderers.

"John? We have a problem." Patricia Worthington stood behind him with Sedat, one of the security guards, in his uniform of black trousers and a white shirt. "Tell him," she said.

"The police." Sedat, who wore thick, black-framed spectacles, pronounced the word with a respect bordering on fear. "They want to question you. Right away. About the killings at the archaeological site. For their investigation."

"Now? Can't they wait until morning?"

"They are waiting outside the front gate, apparently," Patricia Worthington said. "We have spoken to London. They say you must talk to the police, especially if it is about the death of a British citizen. We would only invoke diplomatic immunity if we thought they were unfairly charging you with something."

"What if it takes a while? I promised Braintree I would stay."

"I can manage here," Patricia said. "We have no reports of any other British casualties yet, apart from Stuart Lamont. We do not want a story about the Consulate refusing to help the Turkish police with their enquiries: every conspiracy theorist from Edirne to Erzurum will say it proves we killed the archaeologists ourselves. If they want you to make a statement, you can go with them to the station. But call me if they accuse you of anything."

"What I would like to do most is help them catch whoever killed that boy."

"Frankly, I would suggest you do what you are good at, and I will do what I am good at." Patricia Worthington's eyes sparkled. "If anyone in this building can help the Turkish police with their enquiries, I think it is you. And you're about as much use around the office as a chocolate teapot. Go on, scram. I'll hold the fort."

Savage left the Consulate with Sedat through the wooden doors, built high and wide enough in the nineteenth century to admit a horse-drawn carriage. Outside, a sultry breeze stirred the leaves on the trees. All around rose the hubbub of cafés, motor scooters, and passers-by in the surrounding streets, teeming with pedestrians and traffic. A plaque on an ivy-covered wall marked the site of the devastating bomb attack on the Consulate in 2003.

"I hope you are not in trouble." Sedat glanced up at Savage. "The police are angry. They say they must see you right away."

"I am angry, too," Savage said. "Let me talk to them."

At the entrance, they passed through the heavy metal security turnstiles. Outside, two unmarked police cars stood, lights flashing.

Orhan Mutlu strode forward. "What the hell are you waiting for? Let's go and rescue Elif."

## 54

Gazing at the sky from the fortified flat above the *Valide Han,* Elif cursed. Why had Dervis betrayed her? What motive drove the pious archaeologist to support a gang of killers? What about Meryem? Why had the wiry socialist offered her home as a refuge for terrorists?

She had died for her pains.

The Groper had cut Meryem's throat as though he had performed the action a thousand times before. How bloodthirsty a life could a man lead? Savage, too, had experienced violence–some savagery in Moscow about which he refused to speak. He said he hated bloodshed. Yet sometimes, under stress, his body became as taut as one of the great cables on the Bosphorus bridges. Could he be somewhere in the city, searching for her, alongside Orhan?

A gull hung in the sky, wings motionless against the orange horizon. What did her kidnappers plan for her? Their scheme must involve the object. How else could an argument between Meryem and the Chief over an ancient relic lead to the woman's murder?

Perhaps the killers wanted Elif to explain the significance of the artefact to someone. They might have found a rich patron to buy the supposed handiwork of the goddess Athena for more money than a terrorist group could dream of. Could they want Elif to vouch for its authenticity? But how could she vouch for anything without examining the relic itself?

Nothing made sense. She could swear she had found the object in a long-sealed sarcophagus; and that, judging by the coins she found nearby, someone could have placed the object there in the fourteenth or fifteenth centuries. But to state the age with any certainty, she needed a carbon dating analysis.

Perhaps, like iconoclasts since time began, her captors planned to destroy what lay nestled inside the protective wrapping on the kitchen counter. Maybe they needed Elif to explain the meaning of whatever brutal action they planned.

She gritted her teeth and touched the back of her head against the chair, sending a spasm of pain through her body.

Her own pain, she controlled.

Her captors could block off all routes to escape. But they could never control the inside of her head or force her, Elif Mutlu, to do their will. Whatever twisted logic drove them to kill six innocent people at the building site and take her and Dervis captive, their efforts must fail. If an opportunity presented itself, she would kill them, or herself.

She shifted her arms and legs to try and ease the cramps. Since her betrayal by Dervis in the bathroom, they had again bound her arms behind her back. Her legs, too, remained taped together. They had placed her on a high-backed couch by the window where she could see outside. But she could not know what the Chief, the Groper, and Dervis might be doing behind her inside the flat.

"Woman." The Chief settled his bulk onto a chair next to her. He held in his hand a bowl of the soup Meryem had prepared. The smell made her mouth water. He dipped a spoon into the liquid and held a mouthful out to her.

Elif's stomach growled.

A few hours earlier, she had allowed the wrinkled socialist to spoon soup into her mouth.

Now, all cooperation must cease.

Instead of opening her mouth, she clamped her teeth shut.

The Chief tried to force the spoon between her lips. The metal clicked against her teeth. Hot liquid dribbled down her chin. She shook her head and the liquid spattered against her.

The Chief looked at her, his face expressionless. He did not speak or make another attempt to feed her, but stood and disappeared from her field of view. When he returned, he held a cloth, with which he wiped her face and neck.

He spread the cloth under her chin.

The Groper appeared. He looked down at her and smiled.

Elif's body stiffened. The young man's elegant features could have made him handsome. Judging by his actions, he must be angry, or cynical, or filled with hate.

*Yet he wanted to be friendly.*

What kind of twisted world did the man inhabit? In what universe could a woman he had seized by force, who had seen her friends murdered, who he had sought to molest at every opportunity, want to be his friend?

Maybe he lived in a world in which he had so little contact with the opposite sex that he barely understood women were not objects created to satisfy the pleasure, the sexual urges, and the thirst for power without which men seemed unable to live.

She shook her head and ground her teeth.

Without warning, the Groper grabbed her from behind, cradled her head in one hand, and pinched closed her nostrils with the other. When Elif struggled, the Chief sat astride her waist and pressed her bound body down into the couch.

Still she fought, arching her hips and throwing herself from side to side. The Chief tightened his grip.

Ten seconds. Fifteen. She needed air. She opened her lips a fraction and tried to breathe through gritted teeth, but no oxygen could penetrate. They rammed the spoon in again, hot soup against her lips. Elif closed her eyes and counted. Could she make herself black out? The impulse to breathe overwhelmed her. For a split second, she gasped for breath. The Chief rammed the spoon between her teeth and levered open her jaws. Using another, smaller spoon, he shovelled the warm liquid into her mouth.

She retched as the soup hit the back of her throat. The Groper gripped her head and nose tightly, keeping her face pointing upwards. She could not spit the soup out, yet when she tried to breathe, the liquid coursed down her throat. Tears of fury welled up in her eyes. She bit down hard on the metal spoon in her mouth and fought again to turn her head to one side.

She could not stop the two killers from force-feeding her. But maybe she could disrupt their plans by delaying them as long as possible.

## 55

P edestrians scattered as the police car careered towards the *Valide Han.* Two teenage girls leapt shrieking to one side. How could Savage have thought Orhan a reckless driver?

The woman at the wheel seemed to be actively trying to collide with other vehicles.

A moped roared straight at them. The police driver accelerated towards the rider, who eased aside at the last moment. Again, the woman put her foot down. Their convoy penetrated the maze of choked streets at the heart of the Old City with astonishing speed.

Towards the killers of Stuart Lamont.

Towards Elif.

"Turn the siren off," he said.

"Wrong," Orhan Mutlu said. "We gain more by arriving faster, with the sirens, than we lose by telling them we are coming." He paused to yell out the window at a slow-moving driver. "We have a hit on the *Valide Han.* A known political activist has an address on the top floor. We will go in hard. Korkmaz has buggered off to guard the American ship. This is my show." He pulled on a bullet-proof vest.

"Mind wasting one of those on a Brit?"

"Last time I heard, you were not a serving police officer. No vest. Stay at the back, you won't get hurt."

A scream rang out behind them. A stubby police bus, speeding through the alleyways a few yards in their wake, narrowly avoided an old woman, who shook her fist. Inside the bus, visible through the front window, black-clad police of the Special Operations Department pulled on their gear as they prepared for action.

Any moment now, overwhelming force would arrive at the *Valide Han*.

Suddenly the car braked hard. From a turn ahead, a filthy youth pulled out into the street a bulging, soft-sided hand-cart filled to overflowing with waste paper and boxes. The cargo rose high above his head: a van-sized bag of tough translucent plastic suspended in a crude steel frame mounted on two bicycle wheels, with narrow shafts projecting forward for steering and pulling. Seized by gravity, the cart plunged down the cobbled slope towards them, the boy running to avoid being crushed by his load. When the police convoy raced up the hill straight at him, he tugged and strained at the steering shafts to slow the cart. In the narrow alley, the police cars could not pass the hand-cart, or vice-versa.

The car slewed to a halt, almost touching the boy's knees. The youth stood transfixed, trembling, as if he had never seen a motor vehicle before.

The driver jammed her hand on the horn. "The child is simple," she said. The youth did not move. Orhan jumped out, shouting, his gun in his hand. The boy crouched down, trying to distance his body away from Orhan between the metal shafts of the barrow as if he feared being shot, but could think of no way of averting his fate. His eyes stretched wide, his mouth opened and closed without words, displaying rotten teeth.

An old, angular man, equally filthy and grappling with a second cart, turned the corner and surveyed the scene. He shook his head, pushed his cart back into the side-street, and came running towards Orhan and the boy. Without breaking step, he slapped the youth around the head with his bony hand and yanked him upright from where he crouched between the shafts of the cart. He pointed up the hill. The youth nodded and pointed the same way. He fought to turn the heavy cart around, wheels bouncing on the cobbles, while the old man raised his hand as if to strike the boy again.

Orhan climbed back into the car. "A lad from the East," he said. "Working for his uncle here in Istanbul. They collect waste paper and cardboard from the shopkeepers to recycle. He is punished if he does not deliver the cart to the foot of the hill on time. The cart is so heavy he can hardly push it up the hill in any case: only down is possible." He cursed, glanced at his watch, and gestured at the street. "Come *on*."

At last, with no help from the old man, the boy succeeded in manhandling the barrow as far as the turning and disappeared around the corner. The convoy accelerated forward and sped past.

"Two minutes," the driver said. "All ready?"

"What do you think?" Orhan growled. He leaned over towards Savage. "You: do not play the hero. We know they have weapons. It looks as if they enjoy killing people."

Savage said nothing. At last, after the altercation with the barrow-boy, the driver extinguished the siren. The ensuing silence amplified the sound of the car-tyres on the cobbled street.

"Thirty seconds," the driver said. "Twenty. Ten. We're here."

A high, blackened doorway loomed. A tangled spider's web of black wiring criss-crossed the pitted stonework. An oriel window projected over the street. Modern Turkish letters painted above the stone arch proclaimed the "*Buyuk Valide Han.*"

Orhan waited for the bus to disgorge a dozen special operations police, helmeted and armed with Heckler and Koch submachine guns.

"You." He picked out half the group, including two women. "Follow me. You others, disperse through the courtyard and block any escape routes. Take up protective positions in case they come out shooting. Do not let any person leave the *Han*, no matter if they say they are going to see their dying mother."

He led the first crew of black-clad officers up a steep flight of stone steps beneath the archway, Savage at the rear. In the cool air of the first floor, motes of dust hung in shafts of sunlight. The air smelled musty. Staircases and passageways plunged off in every direction. Sounds of hammering, the clink of crockery, and the whine of machine tools echoed from workshops and kitchens as they passed.

"Somewhere here." Orhan's hoarse voice echoed in the passage. He made a "down, down" gesture to the team behind him. They slowed and crept forwards, weapons trained on the doorways and passages to each side. Orhan pointed towards a narrow opening in the white-painted wall. Stairs led upwards, blocked by a thick metal gate. Orhan pushed and pulled, but the bars did not budge.

He shook his head. "We blow this, they know we are coming."

"Cut it," Savage said. "This whole place is full of craftsmen, no-one will hear a thing."

Orhan nodded. "Not a bad idea for an Englishman." He spoke to one of the officers, who ran back down the corridor. He returned seconds later with a giant bearded Armenian wearing a black singlet exposing his arms and upper chest. He carried in his hands a grinding tool.

Orhan pointed to the gate and raised his eyebrows. The bearded giant tugged at the metal bars, peered at the lock, and activated the tool. A hardened abrasive disk rotated with a piercing whine.

But instead of attacking the lock, the man applied the cutting edge to the thickest part of the gate, by the hinge.

The tool sliced into the metal, cutting a deep, clean gash. In thirty seconds, he cut through the frame of the grille below the bottom hinge. He attacked the bars above. In under a minute he had severed all connection between the lower hinge and the gate.

Orhan stepped forward and pulled hard at the bars but the gate still did not shift. The tall craftsman cut through the frame around the top hinge. The air filled with the pungent smell of scorched metal.

"One minute more," Orhan said. He picked out two of the team, both women, who removed their helmets. Both were tall, athletic-looking, and dark-haired. One had a scar above her right eye, as if a blunt instrument or projectile had gashed her face. "Are you ready?" Orhan said.

In reply the woman with the scar held up a thin green cardboard template holding in place two shaped charges of plastic explosive. The second held up two detonators and an armful of wiring.

"Come." The bearded craftsman pointed to where his bit had cut through the final metal support. Two police officers took hold of the gate and pulled. The structure fell away from the wall. Freed from its hinges, the grille fell towards the two officers, so heavy they struggled to slow the metal frame as it fell. At last they eased the remains of the gate onto the stone floor of the *Han*.

The two explosives officers ran up the stairs, around the corner, and into the darkness. Two others followed, crouching low on the steps to train powerful torches upwards.

"You have stun grenades?" Savage whispered. "Once they blow the door you'll have a couple of seconds to chuck a few in."

"You think we are amateurs? Or idiots?" Orhan frowned. "Will you people never learn the time of imperialists has ended? Observe and learn. The shock of the explosives to break open the door will knock them off their feet." He peered up the stairs. "Here they come. Stand clear."

The special operations officers who had climbed the narrow staircase reappeared. The woman with the scar emerged last, unwinding detonation cord from a reel. She waved at the waiting team to take cover. The gesture seemed unnecessary, as everyone had already backed away from the staircase. But when she moved a full ten paces along the wall away from the opening, ducked into a deep recess, still carrying her reel of detonator cord, and pulled protective goggles over her eyes, the remaining police officers scattered to more distant hiding places.

The explosives officer glanced around to ensure no-one remained in the blast radius. She raised her arm in warning. Savage ducked inside a room further down the corridor, covered his face with his arms, crouched down, and turned towards the wall.

The building shook with an ear-splitting blast. Windows across the passage burst inwards, and fragments blew down the narrow stairwell, debris raining down from the ceiling and dust filling the passage. Orhan shouted *"Go, go, go,"* hurled himself around the corner, and ran up the staircase, his pistol held out in front of him.

Savage jostled to enter the stairwell with the special operations police. Grit, smoke, and the acrid stench of explosives filled the air, but light streamed in from above. Two, three, four explosions roared in the space ahead. That must be stun grenades. Glass shattered as another blast rang out. Was anyone shooting? The din and confusion from the grenades hid any other sounds. He ran into the room and threw himself to one side behind a couch.

Had Orhan and his team shot the terrorists?

What had the kidnappers done with Elif? Could they have injured her? Or worse?

The evening light streamed through a haze of smoke and dust, creating a cloud of orange filled with looming helmeted figures. Savage longed for a weapon. If only he could see more.

"Gone." Orhan Mutlu pulled off his helmet. Perspiration streamed down his face like tears. "They have been here. But they are gone. We are too late."

## 56

Ali Aydin walked alongside Hussein and Dervis Basturk down the cobbled street, the object nestling under his jacket. He had The Protocol back on track. All around them, ordinary *Istanbullus* went about their business: shopping and trading, eating and drinking. Many of them mixed with people of different races, religions, and genders. Ali spat.

Right next to the road, in a jewellery boutique, three tourists, all young women with bare arms and short skirts, talked with a young salesman who laughed and grinned as he tried to make a sale.

The sight made Ali sick in the stomach. Why did the government or religious authorities permit such a mixing? Who allowed such godless behaviour to pollute the ancient traditions and faiths?

The nonbelieving citizens of Istanbul must be held to account and taught a lesson. The world must learn from the city's destruction.

Without Target One, they could move far more rapidly. The woman caused all their troubles. She had brought retribution on her own head. Her battles in the taxi had forced him to administer the chloroform. The drug had stopped her fighting back. But her appearance and her inability to walk had drawn the gaze of all those they passed. Ali had solved the problem. The quarrelsome woman could no longer resist. Nor could she attract attention. Who gave a second glance to three men walking down a busy street?

Target One deserved her fate.

But where should they go next?

In the old woman's apartment, Ali and Hussein had struggled to feed Target One a few mouthfuls of soup. Even bound hand and foot, she fought like a tigress, kicking and shouting and biting the spoon with her teeth. Ali could not deploy too much force. The Protocol stated Targets One and Two must not be injured, especially around the face, until the final moments of the operation.

After that, their value fell to nothing.

For now, if Target One injured herself, she damaged The Protocol. Even unhurt, she caused delay and disruption. But at last he had shovelled enough soup into her mouth to calm her noise.

At that moment, he had heard the sirens.

They evacuated the apartment in less than three minutes. They should have stayed longer. But they needed to escape, and The Protocol provided instructions for leaving the *Han* at speed.

The Protocol covered every eventuality. The Elders had set a clear path, yet also provided countless back-up plans in case of obstacles. They spoke truth when they said God had blessed The Protocol. The fall-back location at the *Valide Han* had served its purpose.

Hearing the sirens triggered the emergency escape.

But Target One presented a problem.

They could not move through Istanbul with a drugged or struggling woman without attracting attention.

Hussein had presented a solution to their challenge.

"The whore is rubbish," he said, as they struggled down the stairs from the apartment, grappling with the bound and gagged Target One wrapped in a blanket as she flexed her body and tried to squirm from their grasp. "We can treat her like rubbish." The slender young man touched his beard and turned to Ali. "I have the answer."

It took ninety seconds, and fifty dollars, to find the man they needed in the crowded *Han*. In a single action, they increased their chances of escaping many-fold. They also could move faster than Ali dreamed possible.

Further down the street, the two bulging handcarts zigzagged through the crowds. The boy pulled the first, piled to the brim with old cardboard and paper for recycling. His confusion when confronting the police convoy had almost led to disaster. When the plain-clothed cop leapt from the car, fear had paralysed the youth. The barrow containing the trussed-up body of Target One, weighed down by a full load of paper and cardboard, created a mass so great he could hardly push the cart back up the hill.

The old man had shown quick thinking. He deserved to be rewarded. When they reached their destination, Ali planned to invite him and the boy inside and give them a special bonus for completing the task, in return for help retrieving Target One from beneath the debris in the boy's handcart.

The street forked. Which way should they go? All day Ali had improvised: the Balat safe house was not available for another hour. Shoppers, hawkers, tourists, and the petty criminals who preyed on those tourists packed the alleyway towards the Egyptian Bazaar. Dozens of young Turkish men seemed content to stand around for hour after hour, watching the world pass up and down the street past the doors of their shops.

Standing around. As the two barrows approached the rear of the spice market, Ali wanted to laugh out loud. The handcarts solved the timing problem caused by leaving the *Valide Han* early. They kept the object safe. They tamed Target One. They made the team mobile and invisible.

Ali instructed the old man and the boy to proceed to the square at *Yeni Cami,* the New Mosque, and await instructions. To the police, the two men with their recycling barrows, like the thousands of other scavengers and vagabonds who roamed the streets of Istanbul, formed part of the invisible background to the city. Ali, Hussein, and Target Two, unencumbered by long weapons or a disabled captive, became three more men amongst the millions, fish swimming in Istanbul's great ocean of humanity.

Target One, crushed beneath the load in the boy's handcart, could stay right there for as long as Ali wanted. She could not move her body enough to struggle, and the strip of tape across her mouth kept her from crying out.

Ali and Hussein could roam the Old City until they reached the

Balat House. Then came the time to pay off their helpers, regroup, and activate the final element of The Protocol.

The pistol in his waistband reassured Ali. People thronged through the square, making the most of the warm evening. Ali and his team blended with the crowd. The Protocol protected them. They had left the enemy defeated and confused.

The Balat safe house lay close by, nestling in a neighbourhood of cafés, low-rent housing, and mosques. Their route took them through some of the quietest and least remarkable of Istanbul's thousands of streets: the police could not find or intercept them. Nor could the authorities identify, trace, or penetrate the safe house itself or guess the final leg of their journey.

Through Balat lay the glorious completion of The Protocol—and the destruction of the sinners of Istanbul.

## 57

S avage and Orhan stood on the flat roof of the *Valide Han* and
looked out at the city.

"You should never have turned the bloody siren on," Savage said.

"The boy with his waste paper cart," Orhan said. "I should have
shot him."

"That would have got us here much faster."

"Maybe I will shoot you."

Far below, the Galata Bridge sparkled as drivers turned on their
headlights. Skyscrapers loomed over the crowded tenements of the
city, filling the night sky with light. To the north, over the Bosphorus,
the LED illuminations of the first Bosphorus bridge depicted a giant
Turkish flag, fluttering in the breeze.

On the roof of the *Han,* the warm air carried the scents of
Istanbul: spices, sizzling meat *köfte,* fried fish, and the ancient, damp
stone of the *Han.* Savage breathed in deep. "We missed them this
time," he said. "But we haven't lost yet."

"Bullshit. The bombs at Besiktas and Taksim killed sixty people.
We still have no idea where Elif is." Orhan shook his head. "I know
none of this matters to you."

"Wrong. You and I analysed the threat and picked two targets
correctly. We saved lives. Maybe we can save more, as well as
rescuing Elif and finding the killers of Stuart Lamont. The dead
woman in the cupboard shows we are getting close."

"A dead Maoist who last appeared in our database in 1993?
Terrific."

"Get your brilliant problem-solving Turkish brain in gear.

Suppose the attacks so far were designed to sow confusion and tie up the security forces. Where might the true target be?"

"Look at this place." Orhan spread his arms to encompass the endless urban sprawl. "She could be anywhere."

"Where is Korkmaz?"

"He is with a squad at Kennedy Street, guarding the US warships. He says everything is quiet. Nothing that has happened so far points to an attack on the Americans."

"The phrase, 'End of the West' must mean annihilation on a vast scale. Hundreds of casualties. Thousands. No-one expected the 9/11 attacks in New York and Washington, using aircraft full of people as flying bombs. We have to look for patterns. What else has happened today around Istanbul that makes no sense?"

Orhan shrugged. "Every day a million things happen in Istanbul that make no sense. Like my sister wanting to sleep with you. But you are right. We need to look for coincidences and patterns, and ignore whatever the terrorists did last." He reached for his phone. "Maybe Korkmaz will listen to us now."

While Orhan called, the city below pulsed with life. The twenty million souls of Istanbul spread across Europe and Asia, a fusion of two continents, dozens of languages, and thousands of years of diverse history. A city in which somehow, in the twenty-first century, people of different beliefs lived and worshipped side-by-side.

On the European shore, a tangle of highways embraced a forest of brilliantly-lit office towers, stretching into the distance. Across the water in Asia, a jumble of constructions carpeted the hillsides, buildings of every shape and size jostling for space, taller structures rising beyond as if squeezed upwards by the sheer mass of people in the city. No wonder property developers like Arzu Pasha grew rich.

When a city's population reached the tens of millions, the opportunities to make money or mayhem became almost infinite.

Despite the warmth of the evening, Savage shivered. What if the masterminds behind the terror attacks did not plan to target the

*Gerald R Ford* or the *Queen Anne* or even the Besiktas-Liverpool game?

What if they planned to destroy all three targets and more? What if they had set themselves the goal of annihilating the city of Istanbul itself, as Misty Anderson said? But what weapon could terrorists possibly access to destroy one of the largest cities on earth?

Orhan lowered his phone. "Korkmaz says the stadium, the cruise ship terminal, and the military dock are quiet, and well protected. All the fans gathering at the stadium will be subject to body searches. The cruise liner has docked. Korkmaz is sure one of these will be the next target."

"What about my idea of scanning the airwaves for unusual coincidences?"

"Korkmaz thinks you are crazy. But I put a call into Police HQ." Orhan reached out and gripped Savage by the shoulder. "We had a hit right away."

"What kind of hit?"

"Two odd reports from different sources. Individually, neither adds up to much. But together they could mean something. One came from a coastguard ship in the Sea of Marmara. Another from a land-based station near Gebze."

"Gebze is part of Istanbul, isn't it?"

"Gebze is over sixty kilometres from here. But yes, Istanbul has engulfed the whole town. Mainly, Gebze is a port, with a giant LNG terminal attached. They import liquefied natural gas there on a grand scale to feed into the Turkish pipeline grid. The point is, a ship due to dock in Gebze sent out a distress signal a couple of hours ago. When the coastguard contacted them, they said they had set off the alarm in error–something about a pilot coming on board."

"When was this?"

"About three hours ago. What is weird is that after the coastguard spoke to the ship, it vanished. The navigation beacon, something called an AIS, seems to have failed."

"A faulty distress signal, then a faulty transponder. Might simply be a crap crew or a crap captain. What did the other report say?"

"The other report was about a coastguard ship intercepting a pilot boat, an hour or two before the distress signal from the ship heading for Gebze. The coastguard spotted an unidentified radar echo nearby and came to investigate. But when they arrived, they saw no sign of a second vessel. The pilot boat said they had not seen any other ship."

"Was the pilot boat heading for the ship that issued the distress call? What kind of vessel are we talking about?"

"I asked the Police Intelligence Department to send me the details. The ship is called the Royal Lion, delivering liquefied natural gas from the Middle East to Turkey. Designation is SMU1. SMU stands for Suezmax Ultimate, the first of a new generation of ultra-large LNG carriers. It is over four hundred metres long and can carry four hundred and fifty thousand cubic metres of liquified natural gas."

"Four hundred and fifty thousand cubic metres? Sounds like a monster. Where is the ship now?"

"We are trying to check. But based on the location of the Royal Lion when it sent the distress signal, if the ship is heading for Istanbul, it could enter the Bosphorus at any moment."

## 58

The diffuse light penetrating the plastic grew brighter and dimmed as the recycling cart trundled through the back streets of the Old City. Elif Mutlu could make out, on the edge of a brown cardboard box pressed against her cheek, the words *China Fancy Goods*. Reading the script gave her hope. It reminded her she still lived.

How long ago had the two thugs gunned down the students and labourers and seized her and Dervis at the dig? Nine hours? Ten? For much of the day they had kept her bound and gagged and subjected her to a series of humiliations. Yet she lay braced, taut, ready to fight. She could breathe, despite the strip of masking tape covering her mouth and the weight that lay upon her, crushing her body into the mass of paper and cardboard beneath.

The Chief had supervised her transfer to the barrow, placing her on her back, hands and feet bound, on a cushion of crushed boxes. He and the Groper had immobilised her by weighing her body down with a mass of waste cardboard and debris, leaving a space around her head.

They needed her for something. But for what?

Again, she cursed Dervis. How could the pious archaeologist believe their captors must have some good in them as people of faith? What faith sanctioned cruelty and barbarism? Even after seeing them gun down the students and the workmen, assault her, and slit the throat of Meryem, Dervis had betrayed her escape attempt. What motivated him?

In the apartment, Dervis had spoken of people contacting him through the internet. Meryem had talked about "The Elders." Could an organisation activate different individuals to contribute to a common project, by promising each of them their heart's desire?

What had driven Meryem, for her part? Had the old revolutionary believed helping anyone who wanted to overthrow the established order must be a good thing?

Whatever she believed, she had paid a high price.

The handcart jerked to a halt. People talked nearby: some kind of argument between a man and a woman about caring for their child. Squawks of seagulls rose above the roar of traffic. A shadow fell on the thick white plastic wall of the cart and disappeared as a pedestrian walked by. Again, she tried to move her body, but the weight of the paper and cardboard packed in around her immobilised her. Her moans and grunts through the gag sounded barely audible even to her against the background noise outside.

Turkish women never give up. Elif flexed her hands behind her, trying to loosen them, and kept up a stream of stifled groans as she lay in her claustrophobic hiding place.

## 59

Ali Aydin waited. A crowded rabble of infidels and apostates surged around the entrance to the Egyptian Market, jostling to enter the labyrinth of brightly-coloured stalls within. Seagulls soared around the towering, ornamented minarets of the New Mosque. Buses and trucks roared over the Golden Horn across the Galata Bridge, past hundreds of fishermen casting their lines into the water. On the lower level of the bridge, restaurants served food, along with alcohol in many cases, to diners looking out across the water. As dusk fell the sound of the *ezan* rang out over the city. Crowds of men, women, and children, mixed together regardless of gender and race, ignored the call to prayer, pouring off ships docking at the ferry terminals along the shore and streaming into the city.

A smattering of people entered the mosque complex as loudspeakers on the minarets amplified the *ezan*. Even those few included several who wore tourist dress, or carried cameras slung around their necks. Ali shook his head. The majority of people, whether on the docks, crossing the bridge, or in the markets, went on with their business as usual.

The Elders must be right. No city of such sin could be allowed to live.

Maybe that night long ago in the hospital, when Ali's mistake cost a life, had not been merely a test of his faith. The Almighty had wanted to send a message that he had more important work for him.

The time drew near for the name of Ali Aydin to live for eternity as one who taught the world a lesson in how a pious life should be lived—or face the consequences.

Between the Egyptian Market and the mosque, in a square

swarming with families visiting a warren of pet shops nearby, no-one paid attention to the old man and the boy as they stood next to their barrows, smoking Samsun brand cigarettes and staring into space. Watching from nearby, Ali wished he could smoke a cigarette to ease the tension. But the long day of running from place to place, caused by the unexpected early discovery of the object at Arzu Pasha's building site and the police raid on the *Valide Han,* had only a few hours left.

Ali fought to prevent joy shining from his face. Nothing must draw attention to him. Yet victory drew closer! He glanced towards their destination: the nearby district of Balat, where Arzu Pasha's first great shopping and entertainment complex rose like an alien spacecraft from a sea of decrepit low-rise housing. Arzu Pasha had replicated the boxy steel and glass structure for the *"Heart of Istanbul"* mall she planned to build above the archaeological site where they had captured Target One.

The tycoon had built her first mall five years earlier by demolishing a swathe of streets in an old Jewish neighbourhood of Istanbul. The Jews had left long ago; later, the area drew destitute immigrants from Anatolia and the Middle East. Now, a few westerners infested the area, believing the history, shabby chic, and central location ripe for gentrification. Arzu Pasha had grasped the potential of Balat, ramming through the permits and permissions at record speed to create a shiny new shopping paradise within walking distance of the Grand Bazaar.

The illuminated name of the complex ran in huge letters along the roof of the multi-storey car park: *"Istanbul Rising."* Where once the poor of the city ground out a miserable existence, a temple of commerce had grown up where thousands of staff served tens of thousands of customers every day.

How had The Elders bought the co-operation of Arzu Pasha to implement The Protocol? She, too, lived in Istanbul. Did she know The Protocol planned to raze all her malls to the ground before the day ended? Had they tricked her by appealing to her greed?

Ali checked the time. The Balat house awaited them.

He sent Hussein to the hand-barrows. The old man's face lit up as Hussein paid him a twenty-dollar bonus and told him about the additional cash that awaited him when they arrived.

Employing the two waste-paper scavengers to transport Target One speeded their way on every front. The old man knew every street and back-alley in the Old City. He and his nephew made their way westwards with confidence through a maze of narrow passages between run-down, painted tenements. They passed an ancient church, converted to a mosque, and climbed past a scrubby patch of grass where youths had sprayed graffiti on a wall, and children and dogs played around a derelict car. Behind, at a safe distance, Ali and Hussein followed with Target Two.

After half an hour they entered a street of traders and coffee-houses that, by day, formed the beating heart of the conservative neighbourhood. By day, pedestrians, café owners, or delivery drivers could all have betrayed Ali and his team of warriors. Now, the local merchants had long since shuttered their shops and cafés.

The two barrows halted at a gate leading into the backyard of a squat two-storey house. Inside, as The Protocol promised, a garage door gaped open. Hussein closed the gate to the yard. Ali led Target Two and the two scavengers into the garage.

"In here," he told the old man. "Please help us to unpack the goods."

The man grinned and pushed his barrow inside. The boy followed, his figure hunched. As he entered the garage he glanced back to where Hussein stood by the closed gate, blocking the exit.

Maybe the youth was not so simple.

"Start emptying the boy's cart," Ali said. He activated a control and the garage door descended. Hussein ducked inside at the last minute.

Target Two, Hussein, and the two garbage-collectors emptied the first barrow. In minutes, the head of Target One appeared amongst the waste paper. Her face gleamed, pale from the double dose of chloroform, her eyes blazing. Target Two and Hussein lifted her out and laid her on a bed of paper and cardboard.

"Wait," the old man said. "I need that stuff back in the cart."

"No," Ali said, "you do not."

The first shot from his silenced pistol hit the old man in the stomach. Ali fired a second shot to the head at point blank range, not because he wanted to save the man hours of bleeding and an agonising death, but because The Protocol demanded two bullets. Next, he walked around the second barrow to where the boy, crouching, tried to take cover. Ali shot him twice in the back of the head.

"Should we put the bodies in the cart?" Hussein said. "We can cover them with the rubbish."

"No need," Ali said. "We will be gone in ten minutes. After that, nothing matters." He scrolled through his address book and made a call. Seconds later came the sound of a key turning and bolts sliding back. A steel door opened at the back of the garage.

A tall, heavily-built, bearded man stood blocking the doorway, a black Heckler & Koch submachine gun in his hands. Behind him, almost hidden from sight, a slender young man with a few days of stubble peered around a turn in the passage.

The big man was muscle. The younger man provided the brains, perhaps as an explosives expert. Each of the five members of the group he and Hussein joined here had a specialist function. Ali beckoned to Hussein and Target Two, and they entered the front room of the house, leaving Target One lying in the garage with the corpses.

No-one had spoken since the bearded man opened the door to the garage. Why speak, when they all knew their role in The Protocol? At a table sat two further men: one muscular and squat with his head shaved and a Heckler & Koch slung around his shoulder, and a placid-looking youth with glasses, perhaps another bomb-maker. Ali blinked at the fifth member of the group. A young woman with bright blonde hair bunched into a ponytail with an orange hair-band perched on the end of the table, clutching a high-end camcorder.

Ali sighed. Another woman. Could they trust her to carry out one of the most important jobs of the entire project? But The Protocol must be right. She must have exceptional skills. Target One, helpless in the garage, had a role to play, too. In the right situation, even women had their purpose.

He glanced around the room. To give orders, he needed to know names. Even if the police could somehow have found and bugged the house in Balat, no leak of information could derail The Protocol at this late stage.

"I am Ali," he said. "This is Hussein. Tell me your names."

"Tolga," the bearded man who had opened the garage door said.

"Emre," said the squat, bald man at the table.

"I am Berat," the slim man with the stubble said. He pointed to the silent youth with the glasses. "And he is Zafer."

Ali grinned. The name meant "Victory." "And you?"

The blonde girl smiled. "You can call me Leni," she said. "Like the greatest cinematographer in history. My goal is to be the second best."

Ali frowned. Leni? Did the girl not know what The Protocol foresaw happening in the next hours? Why use a stage name now? He turned away. "Is the transport ready? And the equipment?"

Tolga nodded his great, bearded head. "Everything."

Ali said nothing but stood up straight, pushed out his chest, and nodded. At last they approached the goal they had worked towards for so long. For months they had trained and lived in secrecy. For months they had learned and relearned every aspect of The Protocol. All that groundwork had led to this, the climax, where he, Ali Aydin, took control of the main body of his soldiers, in this room.

Even with the woman digital technician, their team could not fail. The time had come to put the final stage of The Protocol into action.

## 60

"The largest conventional military bomb in use today weighs around ten tons." Ram picked out each word as he spoke on the phone. "Now try to imagine a bomb weighing around twenty thousand times as much."

"Wait." Looking down on Istanbul from the roof of the *Valide Han*, Savage closed his eyes to help grasp the magnitude of what the SIS man said. "Is LNG even flammable?"

"Listen carefully," Ram said. "The counter-terrorist chaps in London have sent through a briefing. The threat from liquefied natural gas is something people have studied for years. LNG is mostly methane, the same gas people cook with. Methane is highly flammable. But to transport the gas by ship or tanker you have to reduce it in size by freezing the vapour to make a liquid. Freezing concentrates the volume about six hundred times. LNG is a cryogenic liquid, meaning it boils into a vapour at room temperature. Actually, it vaporises at any temperature above minus one hundred and sixty-two degrees Celsius. Highly volatile stuff." The SIS man paused. He must be scrolling through the briefing on-screen.

"On board an LNG tanker," Ram went on, "the gas is kept super cold, so as to remain liquid, compact, and easy to transport. It is also pretty safe. If you could somehow stick a match into a vat of the liquid being transported, nothing would happen. To ignite, the LNG must first vaporise to a gas, and the gas needs to mix with oxygen. At that point, the risk profile begins to change rapidly."

"Speak in plain English, Ram. You mean the gas becomes flammable?"

"Not flammable. Explosive. The sequence is, first, for the liquid gas to escape and boil off into a vapour, expanding in the process around six hundred times. Second, the vapour mixes with oxygen, expanding further. Third, the mixture ignites. This is called *a boiling liquid expanding vapour explosion,* or a BLEVE. To get an idea of what a small BLEVE looks like, you can check out videos on the internet of when a road tanker carrying LNG exploded in China in 2012, or again in 2020.

"The 2012 video sums up the horror of what we face. You see a lot of people watching a fire in the distance. They could see the tanker had caught fire, but they did not understand the danger because the cargo of gas did not ignite at once and the vapour is invisible. Only after twenty tons of liquid gas boiled out and mixed with oxygen did the cocktail of gas and air detonate. At that point, you see a colossal explosion and the video cuts out. When a tanker blew up at a Spanish campsite in 1978, the fireball killed over two hundred people."

Savage opened his eyes. Far below, the dark stripe of the Bosphorus bisected the sea of lights, blanketing Europe and Asia. "Has an LNG shipping tanker ever exploded?"

"No. LNG tankers have a great safety record. They have super-insulated tanks and double hulls to prevent leaks and keep the gas at minus one hundred and sixty-two degrees. When the gas is being liquefied, and when it is transferred on and off the tankers, technical measures are in place to prevent and detect any leaks. If the gas does leak, the goal is to dilute the escaped gas with air to a point where the mixture is too feeble to cause an explosion."

"How would you get a—what was it? A boiling liquid vapour explosion?"

"Basically, LNG becomes explosive when diluted at a ratio of between five and fifteen percent—say, one unit of gas mixed with around nine units of air. Above fifteen percent, there is too little oxygen. Below five percent, there is too little LNG." Ram's voice shifted down a tone. "The problem is, all these scenarios assume an accident causing a small leak. No-one has modelled what would happen if someone blew up an entire tanker containing hundreds of thousands of tons of gas."

"Have we looked at the *Royal Lion*? Is the design of the ship vulnerable to an attack?"

"London have examined the construction of the ship. The story gets worse, unfortunately. The first LNG tankers were built according to something called the Moss method, after the company who invented the design. The liquid gas is stored in individual, spherical tanks. The trouble is, spherical containers are an inefficient way to transport anything. A sphere is strong, but you cannot cram them close together. Later generations of ships use what they call a membrane design: big, rectangular tanks built into the hull. The good news is, you can transport more gas, more cheaply. The bad news is that a breach of a membrane LNG ship would mean a much bigger leak. The *Royal Lion* is not only the biggest LNG tanker in the world. She is also a membrane ship."

"Are we sure Istanbul is the target? Could they sail through the Bosphorus to the Black Sea?"

"The *Royal Lion* cannot pass through the Bosphorus. The biggest ships that can navigate the passage are around one hundred and fifty metres long. The *Royal Lion* is four hundred metres. The goal—the target, if you like—must be Istanbul."

Savage gripped the phone. All around him, life in the city continued as normal. Somewhere out there, kidnappers held Elif captive. "I sense you're not about to tell me the terrorists have screwed up their calculations," he said.

"Work it out yourself. The *Royal Lion* carries four hundred and fifty thousand cubic metres of liquefied natural gas, weighing over two hundred thousand tons. If they sail the ship up the Bosphorus into the heart of the city and bring about a catastrophic breach of the membrane cells, the gas will leak out of the ship, boil into vapour, and create a cloud of gas spreading out over the entire city."

"How big are we talking about?"

"We consulted our US friends on this question. The answer is not reassuring. As I said, on a rough estimate, the gas expands by six hundred times when the super-chilled liquid boils off into vapour. So the load of the *Royal Lion* would be equivalent to around two hundred and seventy million cubic metres of gas."

"Two hundred and seventy million cubic metres." Savage tried to calculate. "Ten thousand cubic metres would cover an area one hundred metres squared in a layer a metre thick. A million cubic metres would cover a square kilometre..."

"You are thinking along the right lines, John. But you are missing the worst part of this. The LNG on the ship alone would be enough to create a three-metre thick layer of gas one hundred square kilometres in size. But that vapour would be more or less pure methane, which is not flammable. The gas would not ignite until it reached the right proportion of methane and oxygen."

The intelligence officer continued. "At first, people over a huge area would encounter concentrated gas, displacing the oxygen. They would be unable to breathe. Tens or hundreds of thousands could die of asphyxiation. The gas would continue to spread out, much further, mixing with the air as a gigantic cloud moved to cover the entire city on both the European and the Asian sides. By the time the mixture became flammable, i.e. when the proportion of methane fell below fifteen per cent, you would have a volatile gas cloud covering *over a thousand square kilometres*. That would mean all of Istanbul, particularly low-lying and coastal areas. That cloud would be ignited by a single spark, anywhere–a cigarette or a candle or even a gas cooker. Two hundred thousand tons of gas would ignite in a single cataclysmic explosion over the entire area. Forget a few thousand Americans on a cruise ship or some damage to an aircraft carrier. Forget the fans in the stadium. The whole of Istanbul would be incinerated. We could be talking ten, fifteen, even twenty million people."

"Twenty million?"

"We cannot be sure. But LNG has a high flame temperature, burning at around one thousand three hundred degrees Celsius. That is several hundred degrees hotter than gasoline, or petrol. Some experts in London are comparing the effects of two hundred thousand tons of liquid gas, vaporised and mixed with oxygen over an entire city and ignited, with the yield of a large nuclear weapon. The impact would be catastrophic."

Below, the lights of the city twinkled in the darkness. How did that song go? Eve of destruction? Something about the Eastern world exploding. The chorus repeated in his head.

"The end of all evil," Savage said. "End of the West. They think Istanbul, because of its position, its history, and its way of life, is a symbol of the tolerance and co-existence they hate. But where does Elif come in?"

"You tell me."

What had the American journalist, Misty Anderson, said? Could the terrorists believe that to destroy the city, they must destroy the Palladium? Or did they plan to use the object for some kind of propaganda? The idea the safety of a metropolis and the whereabouts of an ancient relic could be linked made no sense. Yet what religious beliefs did? What else explained the raid on the archaeological site that morning? Did they want to use Elif to amplify the terror they planned?

"Have they closed the Bosphorus to shipping?" Savage said.

"Yes. Since the bombings at the Dolmabahce Palace. The problem is, you cannot stop a ship that size from sailing anywhere it likes unless you are prepared to take the risk of blowing it up yourself. If another vessel tried to block *The Royal Lion*, the tanker would swat it aside."

"Are we sure someone has seized control of the ship?"

"We have no idea. But since a fully loaded LNG tanker is heading straight for Istanbul, we have to assume the worst."

"Could the Turkish military board the ship using helicopters?"

"In theory, yes," Ram said. "The problem is getting the police or military to make a decision quickly. Why mount a complicated airborne assault on a ship that might not be a danger, when they are investigating a string of attacks in the city and trying to protect targets on land? We saw during the 9/11 attacks in New York and Washington that government decision-making structures become overloaded and paralysed in a crisis."

"Paralysis is the natural state for government decision-making." Savage licked his lips. "So far as we know, Elif is somewhere in Istanbul. How would they get her on board the ship? With a boat?"

"No. LNG tankers have enormously high freeboards. Maybe they could board using a helicopter, assuming the terrorists controlled the ship. Or perhaps the terrorists themselves plan to fly an aircraft into the tanker to try and breach the membrane tanks."

"Would a helicopter break through the double hull?"

"No-one has ever tried it."

"Is airspace closed?"

"Yes. But that may not help us."

"In summary, we have a two-hundred-thousand-ton bomb sailing straight at us and we have no practical way to stop it?"

"Yes," Ram said. "That does seem to be the situation."

## 61

Ali Aydin sat in the front passenger seat of the black Mercedes minibus in the yard of the Balat safe house. The team loaded three heavy cases of explosives and ammunition. Target One struggled against her bonds as they carried her from the house. She seemed determined to fight, however futile her efforts, for as long as strength remained in her body.

What if Target One did not co-operate when the time came? The Protocol needed her to perform. In theory, Target Two could take her place in front of the camera. But the moral ambivalence he had shown since his capture this morning reduced his value as a witness. The fiery certainty of Target One would carry a stronger message. Ali felt the object snug against his body and smiled. No need to worry. The Protocol had overcome every obstacle so far. It stated that when the time came, Target One would play the part allotted to her. She had no choice but to perform that role.

Seconds later, Zafer, the diffident young bomb-maker with the glasses, pulled open the gate, and the shiny black bus nosed out onto the silent street. On the flank of the vehicle gleamed the logo of Arzu Pasha's VIP transport service.

Ali sat upright. After the confusion of the early start and the problems at the fall-back location in the *Valide Han*, everything was back on track. Even the transfer to the luxury minibus, with plush seats and tinted windows, seemed to signal an up-turn in their fortunes. Of course, they must use the prestigious vehicle because of their destination, to avoid raising suspicion. But did they not deserve to travel in style, tonight of all nights?

The journey to the *Istanbul Rising* complex took less than fifteen minutes. Hussein drove cautiously, observing traffic signals and allowing other vehicles right of way. When they approached the vehicle check-point at the foot of the ramp leading up towards the car park, a security official in the black and red uniform of an elite private security firm owned by Arzu Pasha stepped out and raised his arm.

Hussein leaned from the window. "We are travelling to the hotel heliport. Seventh floor. An important delegation. Friends of Arzu *hanim.*" He waved towards the passenger compartment in the rear, obscured by tinted windows.

"Okay." The guard glanced at the logo on the side of the bus. He opened the security barrier and retreated towards his booth. "You still have to take a ticket."

Hussein punched the machine and took the strip of card. He looked at Ali, who stowed the ticket in the glove compartment. No need to draw attention by discarding the token, even if he had no intention of ever paying the fee. They drove up a series of ramps, past floors crammed with luxury vehicles belonging to hire car companies and hotel guests, to reach the roof: an open-air platform high above the city. At the far end, beyond a chain-link fence, a dark blue helicopter sat waiting, washed with colour from the ground lights.

At first sight, everything appeared as The Protocol had promised.

Ali gripped his seat and gaped.

In front of the fence stood a police car, engine running and blue light rotating. A police officer climbed from the vehicle and walked to the brightly-lit booth, where two security officials greeted him.

"Slow down." Ali kept his voice calm, as though he had expected to find a dozen police officers on duty at the heliport. *I am Ali Aydin. I will prevail.* "Pull up at the gate and let me talk to them."

Hussein allowed the minibus to roll to a halt. Each of the private security officials carried a weapon. The police officer, with his holstered pistol, barely looked up when the van arrived.

Hussein wound down his window. "We have a flight booked," he said. "Friends of Arzu Pasha. We are due to leave in ten minutes."

The two security guards stood straighter at the words "Arzu

Pasha," but the police officer shook his head. "No-one is going anywhere. I came up here to tell them. The Governor has closed all Istanbul air space. Even the airports. You can imagine how Turkish Airlines are loving that."

Ali climbed down from the van and addressed the police officer. "What has happened? Nothing serious I hope."

"No idea." The police officer shrugged. "The order came through about ten minutes ago. No exceptions."

"That is unfortunate." Ali nodded towards the Mercedes. "The Sheikh will not be pleased. He is flying to visit Arzu Pasha herself. You had better explain the problem to him in person." He glanced at Hussein, who pressed the electric button to open the sliding door on the passenger side.

The officer and one of the security guards walked towards the van. Ali waited until they had nearly reached the open door, then stepped clear.

"Open fire," he said.

Two Heckler & Koch submachine guns roared in the confined space of the minibus. The remaining guard, by the office, tried to flee inside, but Hussein moved swiftly. Two shots from his pistol and the man lay flat on his face on the asphalt of the parking deck.

"Check the office," Ali yelled to Hussein. "The rest of you: load the helicopter. We are behind schedule."

The heavily-built Tolga and Emre, supervised by the technician, Berat, transferred the three cases and Target One to the helicopter. All three climbed aboard. They jammed the woman upright on the far side, against a window; there was no room to lie her flat. The silent bomb-maker, Zafer, walked around the aircraft examining the exterior. Satisfied, he sat down in the pilot's seat and activated the controls. Target Two, his face set in a frown of resignation, climbed aboard, followed by the blonde camera-girl who called herself Leni.

Hussein came out of the security booth. "No-one else inside."

"Come on board," Ali said.

"I have one more task, according to The Protocol." Hussein

climbed up into the minibus and backed well away from the helicopter. He got out and opened the luggage compartment.

"Come," Ali said. "None of this matters now."

"The Protocol must be right."

From the rear of the Mercedes, Hussein took a plastic water bottle and sprinkled liquid around the interior of the vehicle. Using a cigarette lighter, he leaned through the open door, set alight the edge of a gasoline-soaked seat, and sprang back.

For a few seconds, the flame trembled on the seat, comically harmless after Hussein's precautions. Hussein ran towards the helicopter then hesitated, looking back to ensure the fire caught hold.

"Leave it," Ali said. "Get on board."

The *whoomph* of the flames that filled the minibus rocked the vehicle on its wheels. By the time Hussein climbed on board the aircraft, tongues of flame reached into the sky and licked around the tyres.

"Doors closed," Zafer said. He waited a few seconds and engaged the rotors. The helicopter lurched.

Hussein sat next to Ali in the front seat. His eyes shone, and he stank of fuel. "So it goes," he said. "Are you not worried about the no-fly zone?"

"Not at all. Our journey is five minutes. They will not have time to locate us, let alone warn us and make the decision to shoot down a civilian plane."

The helicopter lifted into the air and swung out over the void. They had lost time killing the guards and the police officer. But nothing more stood in their way.

Below, the burning minibus illuminated the bodies of the three dead men. The craft turned, and the scene vanished. All around them, the skyscrapers and tenements of the corrupt, doomed city of Istanbul stretched glittering towards the horizon. Ahead, dividing Europe and Asia, the Bosphorus awaited them.

## 62

O rhan Mutlu's face turned pale. He ran his hand back over his shaved head. "One thousand square kilometres? A single explosion? Are you sure?"

"I'm trying to be bloody optimistic. That is a best-case scenario, assuming the gas spreads evenly," Savage said. Night had fallen on the roof of the *Valide Han*. "If the gas spreads in an irregular pattern, or makes a thinner layer, the explosion covers a greater area. LNG burns hotter than petroleum."

"Is that what your so-called experts say? Why should I believe you?"

"Because you want to save Elif. Because you want to protect Istanbul. Because you're not a prat. Take a look at this."

Savage held out his phone.

The first video showed the Chinese road tanker accident of 2012. A fire and a cloud of vapour appeared in the distance on a busy highway. After nearly a minute, as people stood and watched, came a huge explosion. The film ended in blackness.

A second clip showed more sombre, more graphic images. A film crew had recorded the aftermath of the Spanish campsite explosion of 1978. In those days, few people had video cameras. CCTV barely existed, and no record of the detonation survived. But the colour film showed rows of blackened bodies, limbs twisted and splayed like grotesque dolls, clothes burned off by the inferno. Families lay together in pitiful groups of charred remains where the flames had consumed them; the blackened shells of vehicles rested on burned-out tyres; smoke still rose from charred trees in the background.

"Allah, Allah," Orhan whispered. "That was twenty tons of gas?"

"More than two hundred dead, in a few seconds. The *Royal Lion* carries over ten thousand times as much. The gas will kill millions by asphyxiation, by explosion, and by fire." Savage seized Orhan in a two-handed grip. "For the sake of Elif. For the sake of the Scottish boy. And for Istanbul. We face the biggest Turkish kebab in history."

Orhan's fingers closed as tightly as if he wanted to crush Savage's hand. "I would break your nose for using that image if it were not thanks to you we have got this far. But we are alone."

"Do your bosses still think you're crazy?"

"Korkmaz says we have already wasted police resources raiding an empty apartment. He is fixated on land-based targets. He asked why anyone would attack a ship. He ordered me to join him in the Old City."

"Using the cargo of the *Royal Lion* to annihilate Istanbul makes sense of everything that has happened. A series of attacks to paralyse the city and send the police chasing their tails. When the security forces are run ragged, as night falls, the terrorists sail their weapon of mass destruction straight up the Bosphorus."

"Is the ship impossible to stop?"

"It would be easy to cripple the steering or even to destroy the ship with a well-placed missile or two, if you had missiles and someone willing to fire them. The challenge is to stop it without breaching the LNG tanks and releasing the gas. A missile attack would save the terrorists the trouble of blowing up the ship themselves."

Orhan struck his palm with his balled fist. "Even for that the Turkish armed forces would have to be prepared to listen, and deploy deadly force, on the word of an Istanbul police intelligence officer and an English diplomat. They will think we are laying a trap for them. In any case, they would have to decide, and launch an assault, within the next few minutes."

The two of them stood side by side, gazing at the lights of the city.

Orhan's phone rang. Savage looked south. Darkness swathed the Sea of Marmara: he could barely see the water, let alone any approaching vessel. Without the usual lights of marine traffic on the Bosphorus, or aircraft flying overhead, the city seemed bleak and exposed.

After the heat of the day, gusts of cool wind had sprung up. A fresh, earthy smell presaged a thunderstorm. Black clouds rolled in from the south. Might the ship, too, appear from there? As Orhan finished his call, his face white in the light of his phone screen, a bolt of lightning lit up the sky.

"A helicopter has breached the no-fly zone," Orhan said. "It took off from Balat, from a helipad on one of Arzu Pasha's hotels. It sounds as if they shot their way in. They flew north and turned over the Bosphorus. The pilot took the 'copter down low, along the wave-tops, to try and hide the radar signal. But they think he turned south, towards the Sea of Marmara."

"They're heading for the *Royal Lion*. How far is Balat from here?"

"Maybe half an hour's walk."

"They must be taking Elif to the ship."

Orhan said nothing. Nearby, in a restaurant, Turkish pop music played, a woman wailing about love, incongruous in the face of the approaching cataclysm. A few fat drops of rain swept across the rooftop and petered out.

The kidnappers had held Elif for the whole day. If she still lived, she would be tormenting them for sure, kicking and struggling even in the helicopter. A ship that size must be equipped with a helipad.

"We can't stop the ship before it reaches Istanbul," Savage said. "But we might be able to stop them blowing up the gas. Could the army or air force land some Turkish special forces on the ship and take control?"

Orhan gazed at him, the tiny dent in his forehead visible above his dark eyes. "Put some boots on the ship. Makes sense. I'm on it." He took out his phone and punched a pre-set. He outlined the threat and made a plea for a helicopter. Seconds ticked by. How long ago had the chopper from Balat flown towards the Sea of Marmara? Ten minutes? Fifteen? As he peered into the darkness, another bolt of lightning stabbed down on the Asian side, followed by a peal of thunder. Bigger rain drops splashed down on the ancient roof of the *Han*. Savage narrowed his eyes and searched the horizon.

There. As lightning lit up the mouth of the Bosphorus, the white bow-wave of an approaching ship stood out bright against a rank of black clouds. Someone had left the navigation lights burning. Perhaps they were impossible to turn off.

Maybe the terrorists didn't want an accident.

Savage gripped Orhan's shoulder and pointed into the night. Orhan redoubled his efforts, shouting into his telephone.

He sounded like a man pleading for his life.

The ship could only be the *Royal Lion*. The vessel steamed at full speed into the entrance of the Bosphorus. Two hundred thousand tons of liquefied natural gas had entered the heart of Istanbul.

## 63

From the ship in the Sea of Marmara, a sea of buildings and lights disguised the channel between Europe and Asia. The built-up mass of corrupt humanity swept down to the shore on every side, polluting both earth and water. In the distance, cargo ships moored, waiting to pass through the Bosphorus. Here, on the water, no vessels moved.

Beneath the black clouds, the sea seemed a desolate and lonely place.

"They will come soon," Saif al-Din said.

To express anxiety showed weakness. He wanted to ask how much longer it would be before the *Royal Lion* was in place. But he feared the contempt of Uzay, the Black Sea boatman, if he asked such a question. Uzay stood at the wheel, glancing from time to time at the radar screen, calm in the darkness. Since taking the wheel of the tanker, he had treated Ali less and less as his master and more like a simpleton child who did not understand the big world of DSC and AIS, navigation, coastguards, and technology.

Uzay did not see him as Saif al-Din, the Sword of the Faith, but as little Karim Ahmed, the taxi-driver from Istanbul.

The Black Sea man must have heard Saif, but he did not turn his head. "When does The Protocol say they arrive?" he asked.

"They will be here in good time," Saif said. "But we remain vulnerable, without reinforcements."

Uzay smiled. "We are sailing this brute of a ship into the heart of Istanbul. Already we have come too far for anyone to stop us. The Topkapi Palace is coming up on the port side, and Kadiköy and Haydarpasa to starboard. Even if they could make us put the engines into reverse right now, the momentum of the ship would take us all the way to the Golden Horn. No need to worry."

*No need to worry.* The boatman's insolence had grown intolerable. Saif glanced around. Kaan, too, smiled beneath the lump on his forehead where the second officer with the greasy hair had attacked him with the fire axe.

"What about the crew?" Saif said. "Could they recognise something is wrong?"

"Maybe. But most of their officers are here." Uzay jerked a thumb at the bodies, lying in the corner where Kaan had dragged them. "That fellow who tried to close the door to the bridge, he is the captain. The man who activated the alarm was the chief officer. I guess they both came up here to greet the pilot and enter port in Gebze. The one who climbed the stairs with us wearing the Pan-Arab socks was a second officer. The man with the fire-axe who tried to attack Kaan was a deck officer. We have cut the head off this ship.

"Maybe a chief engineer is working below deck. But the job of the engineers is to keep the ship moving, not to steer it. And if anyone from below decks tries to reach us here, they will have to get past two security doors." The Black Sea boatman placed a single finger on the ship's wheel and turned it a few degrees. "Best of all, we are almost at our destination. I have begun to slow the ship so we will come to a halt in the optimum position."

The radio telephone rang. Saif glanced towards the receiver. But Uzay placed his hand on the device. "No," he said. "Leave them in suspense." He pointed to the radar display. "See. They are sending a little coastguard boat to say hello."

The radio telephone fell silent. Then the bell rang again. Saif tried to ignore the sound and peered at the radar screen. What did the bright blue circle, filled with points of light, mean? Did one of the white dots represent the coastguard? What made Uzay think he could issue orders? Saif stood up straighter and tried to lower the tone of his voice.

"Stay on course. Their ship is too small to board us or block us. They dare not open fire."

"Yes," Uzay said. "Our ship weighs more than two hundred thousand tons. Their boat probably weighs less than two hundred."

"When the rest of the team arrive, Kaan and I will secure the helipad." Saif spoke with more confidence than he felt. "You will bring the ship to a halt at the spot defined in The Protocol. Join us at the appointed time."

"Yes, boss." Uzay did not even look around as Saif and Kaan left the bridge.

The metal stairs descending to the deck left the two of them exposed. Kaan leapt down two steps at a time, a Heckler & Koch slung over his muscular shoulder and his silenced pistol held out in front of him, sweeping from side to side as if desperate to find a target. Like Saif, he carried a rucksack filled with ammunition and spare weapons. Kaan's once-sullen eyes burned in anticipation of action. The bruise on his forehead made him look ferocious and unhinged.

They reached deck-level without encountering any crew members. Kaan unlocked the steel door. He and Saif stepped outside. Both men stopped.

Across the water, the lights of Istanbul looked close enough to touch. The city appeared immense, stretching along the coast as far as he could see in both directions. The rumble of the *Royal Lion*'s engines faded as the ship slowed. A cool wind whipped up the waves and swept over the deck; the air smelt salty and fresh. Something about the city had changed.

"I think I hear someone shouting," Kaan said. "Perhaps the coastguard." He moved towards the railing.

Saif heard nothing. No boats moved on the dark waters of the Bosphorus. He frowned at Kaan, who pointed over the railing, straight down the side of the *Royal Lion*. Then he stood back, his Heckler & Koch at the ready.

Far below, a white coastguard vessel bobbed like a toy next to the steel cliff that formed the hull of the gas tanker. A figure stood on deck, a megaphone to his lips. But from where Saif and Kaan stood, far above the patrol boat, the whistling of the wind and the crash of the waves drowned out the words. The coastguard could no more board the tanker than they could fly.

"Send them a greeting," Saif said.

Kaan unslung his Heckler & Koch, leaned forward over the rail, and unleashed a hail of bullets on the coastguard ship below. The man with the megaphone sprinted for cover.

"Enough. Now the helipad," Saif said to Kaan. The young man skipped ahead and climbed a metal staircase towards the centre of the ship. He held his pistol out ahead of him. Saif followed, his weapon at the ready. They emerged onto a broad, flat platform painted with a yellow circle and a huge letter "H."

Saif took a deep breath. From their vantage point they could see the front of the vessel and the city spread all around them. Ahead, half hidden by the steep hills that flanked the channel, the illuminated piers of the first Bosphorus bridge soared towards the heavens.

The sight of the bridge meant they had reached their destination. The stage was set for the final act of The Protocol.

Yet as Saif stood atop the vessel, at this moment of triumph, fear gripped his heart. The team from Istanbul should have arrived by now. What had delayed them? He searched the skies. The vastness of heaven and earth made the tanker seem puny, and Saif himself an insignificant speck of nothing.

He, Kaan, and Uzay could not implement The Protocol without reinforcements. Had they come all this way for nought?

"Look," Kaan said. He pointed towards the European side.

Saif turned. He knew what had changed about Istanbul. The stream of aircraft that flew over the city day and night, heading for the airport, had vanished. Only blackness filled the heavens.

With one exception. Approaching fast from the west, a helicopter swooped towards them, navigation lights flashing.

## 64

"**D**amn!" On the roof of the *Valide Han,* Orhan ended his call. "Korkmaz does not buy our story. Nor does anyone else. He says half the top brass believe the terrorists have shot their bolt. The other half think another attack is still planned, against a target in the city, and want to make sure they are well protected. No-one cares about some ship in the Sea of Marmara that changed direction."

"Can they not see the vessel of mass destruction?" Savage said.

Orhan gazed at the distant bow-wave. "If that is the *Royal Lion,* the ship will be opposite the Golden Horn in minutes. If they detonate the ship there, they will take out the Besiktas-Liverpool match, the *Queen Anne* and six thousand passengers, and the aircraft carrier, the *Gerald R Ford,* two destroyers, and everyone on board. Plus the rest of Istanbul. Yet no-one gives a shit. That leaves us. The Police SWAT team are still here in the old woman's apartment. We have to board that tanker. But how?"

"It's all about Elif," Savage said. "Why did they take her? Who needs an archaeologist on a gas tanker?"

In his pocket his fingers closed around a crumpled card. Misty Anderson. The American journalist had said the kidnappers might need Elif somehow to interpret the Palladium before launching their final attack. A helicopter, maybe carrying Elif, had set out to rendezvous with the *Royal Lion.* Could the journalist's theories about the Luck of Troy be right? *Call me if you get any more scoops,* she had said.

She answered at once. "Good to hear from you, Mr Savage. Do you believe me, now?"

"Do you want the biggest scoop of your life? We need transport. Your network must have a helicopter on stand-by."

"No dice. The whole of Istanbul is a no-fly zone."

"If you don't get your chopper in the air, it will be incinerated on the ground in twenty minutes, along with you and your entire bureau. Listen to me."

Savage spoke for two minutes. When he finished, Misty Anderson fell silent.

"Seems to me, I have a choice," she said at last. "I can keep my job, file the stories on today's Dolmabahce and Taksim bombings—with some fine footage of your good self, by the way—and get a good night's sleep. Or I can persuade our pilot to ignore the no-fly zone, put his licence at risk, and face prosecution from the Turkish authorities, based on the hunch of a deranged British diplomat. I don't think so."

"Misty. You are the leading exponent of the theory that the British diplomat and his Turkish colleague predicted the timing and location of both attacks earlier today and helped the police stop a massacre at Taksim. Also, the choice is not between a good night's sleep and taking a risk. The choice is between a scoop that will win you the Pulitzer Prize on the one hand, and a certain death by asphyxiation or a boiling liquid expanding vapour explosion, on the other. It's a no-brainer."

"A boiling liquid expanding vapour explosion? Can I quote you?"

"Do you record all your phone calls?"

"Only the important ones. If you're right, I'll make you a hero." The journalist paused. "But John, there is no way I am going to send a news helicopter into a no-fly zone in the middle of a thunderstorm. You're going to have to find some other sucker." The line went dead.

## 65

P art of Elif Mutlu longed for oblivion. The din inside the helicopter deafened her. Each time she tried to ease her position against the metal wall of the aircraft, the shoulder and arm of the heavily-built man from the Balat house crushed her towards the floor. The muscles of her neck and arms ached from hours of having her hands bound behind her back. Her captors had inflicted pain on her throughout the day. What drove them to such cruelty?

After the ether, the tension, the humiliation, and the violence, she longed to slide into unconsciousness. Each joint and muscle in her body protested. Each time the urge to vomit overcame her, the strip of tape across her mouth meant she must bite back the bile. As the helicopter rocked in the air, nausea threatened to overcome her once again.

Yet the day must be about to reach some kind of climax. She must not rest. She must fight.

She struggled to move her head towards the window. Her neck spasmed in fresh agony, but for a moment, she glimpsed the view.

The helicopter flew low over the European side of the city. They passed the Galata Tower, the Galatasaray School and Taksim Square. They swung low towards the Besiktas stadium, the stands packed with tens of thousands of football fans as the players trotted out onto the field. Did they plan to crash the helicopter, together with the contents of the heavy boxes they had loaded at the Balat house, into the crowds?

The city swayed and disappeared. Below, the waters of the Bosphorus glistened under a dark sky. The helicopter sank, skimming the waves alongside a rank of cruise liners, their multiple decks blazing with lights.

"Airspace is closed. They say we must land at once or be shot down." The young pilot spoke for the first time in a clear, educated voice like a radio presenter.

"Fly low and fly on." The Chief, sitting in the front seat, pointed ahead. "Our flight path will confuse them. Even a single crisis stretches the decision-making of the authorities. After a day like today, the police and armed forces will be chasing shadows all across Istanbul. They will never intercept us in time, let alone authorise anyone to shoot us down." He glanced back at Elif and addressed the bulky, bearded man squashed in against her.

"Tolga. Remove the tape. Gently. The time has come to start preparing her."

For hours, Elif had longed to free her mouth. When the big man's fingers touched her face, her gorge rose. But she could not flee. His eyes narrowed as his clumsy fingers picked at the end of the tape. At last he caught hold of an edge and peeled back the sticky band. She gulped in air through her mouth: deep, merciful breaths.

Should she scream? Why bother, in a helicopter over the sea? They controlled her. All her escape efforts had delivered only agony and indignity. What lay ahead? Had the Chief said something about *preparing her*?

The helicopter skimmed low over the water, above the tangled coil of currents where the mouth of the Bosphorus met the Sea of Marmara. The deep waters of the strait swirled, dark and forbidding.

The helicopter banked to one side. Her head shifted and she glimpsed a ship looming ahead, the bow rising from the water far above them. Elif blinked. The vessel's scale made no sense. They flew endlessly along a wall of reddish steel before rising above the deck. Along the centre bulged an immense yellow box festooned with masts and equipment, as if the ship were pregnant.

What had she argued with Savage about last night? Had Orhan received her text? Had he and Savage spent the day trying to find her? Or had they continued to fulfil their routine duties, oblivious to her agonies?

Next to the huge ship bobbed a second, white boat. The smaller vessel seemed so tiny as to be at risk of being crushed, or swamped.

"Coastguard," the Chief said. "They could fire on us. Move to port."

The helicopter dipped and the white boat disappeared beyond the bulk of the larger vessel. They hovered alongside as Zafer matched their speed to the forward movement of the ship then drifted sideways. The vessel was like an island in the sea. A yellow circle came into view on a black platform. Two men stood to one side.

Both carried weapons.

The helicopter sank towards the landing pad, settling so gently Elif did not realise they had landed until someone opened the door. Two men jumped out and took up position with drawn pistols, as if guarding them. A small blonde woman she had not seen before crouched to one side, filming everything. Two heavily-built men, including the one the Chief called Tolga, unloaded boxes.

The rotors of the helicopter slowed and stopped. As the engine fell silent, the roar of the wind and the waves surrounded them.

The Chief appeared at the door and looked at her. He smiled, as if he had achieved some lofty goal. *I own you,* he seemed to be saying. *Game over.* His white teeth gleamed, regular and symmetrical. Perhaps he was a dentist.

"The time has come," he said. "You will be famous."

"What time?" After so long without speaking, her voice sounded cracked and feeble. "Whatever you want, I will not do it."

"Strong words." He shook his head, still smiling. "But you are wrong. You will help us. You will have no choice." He reached into the helicopter cabin and touched her face. She tried to pull back but her injured head met the seat-back in an instant of agony. His slender fingers moved firmly across her skin, professionally almost, massaging her face as if he made a habit of examining human flesh.

"Your circulation is good," he said. "In a few minutes, all trace of the sticking-plaster will have disappeared."

"Why do you care what I look like? All day you have abused me. You have killed my students." Elif panted for breath. "You have nothing to offer except death."

The Chief shook his head. "You are wrong. It is you—all of you who live in this city of Istanbul—who are the destroyers. It is you, sinning, disregarding the faith and allowing others to do likewise, who have poisoned the world with your wrong living. For hundreds, for thousands of years this city has sinned. For this, Istanbul will pay the price. The world will see and understand how society must cure itself." He spoke in a low, confident voice, like a father explaining something to a child.

"You are mad," Elif said. How could the man be so certain of his cause? "I will have no part in this."

"Yes, you will." He smiled again. "Your role is to help the world to believe and comprehend. You will make history as the woman who announced the destruction of Istanbul."

## 66

"Misty Anderson refused to help." Savage fought an urge to throw his phone into the darkness. "Any joy with the military?"

"Nothing," Orhan said. "Korkmaz and the Special Operations Team have their hands full with Besiktas, the cruise ship terminal, and the Kennedy Street military dock where the warships are moored. They say anything happening at sea is a matter for the coastguard."

"Classic crisis paralysis," Savage said. "No-one making decisions. Who else has a chopper?"

"What part of *this is a matter for the coastguard* do you not understand?"

"What about Korkmaz himself?"

"Korkmaz who hates and distrusts both of us?"

"After we made him a hero at Taksim, he started believing us," Savage said. "Why doesn't he call a helicopter? If we load up the SWAT unit from here at the *Valide Han* we can reach the ship before they blow the gas."

"A few hours ago, both of us were trying to run away from Korkmaz. Now you want me to invite him over here."

"Better a punch-up than a human torch."

"You do not know Korkmaz like I do."

"What alternatives do we have?"

The Turk frowned and reached for his phone.

He could not get through to Korkmaz.

Orhan phoned again and again. He sent a series of texts. Finally, he tried a video call. Seconds later, the face of the huge superintendent stared out at them from the tiny screen. He seemed to be illuminated by a spotlight at a checkpoint, his face bright against the black sky.

"Mutlu? Is that you? What the hell do you want? Get over here."

"A ship carrying two hundred thousand tons of LNG is entering the Bosphorus," Orhan said. "If you were a hero saving hundreds of lives at Taksim, you will be president if you save the city of Istanbul. We need you here in a helicopter. To get us on board the ship."

Korkmaz shook his head. "It is not you giving the orders, Mutlu. I told you before I wanted you at the Kennedy Street wharf forthwith. Why are you still at the *Valide Han?* The job of the police is to secure the land, the coastguard have sent a cutter to intercept the tanker."

"Korkmaz," Savage interrupted. "If you do nothing, you, I and everyone else in this city will be burned alive within the next few minutes. Were we right at the Dolmabahce Palace? Were we right at Taksim? If we are wrong this time, you can lock us both up and throw the key in the Golden Horn."

Korkmaz peered at Savage, his deep-set eyes alert. "You again. The Russian English diplomat. You have been leading me by the nose all day. But you got it right at Taksim, I have to admit." The great head nodded. "I cannot leave here, and your theory about an exploding ship sucks. You have two minutes to persuade me."

"We need more than a helicopter," Savage said. "If that ship is a floating bomb, I need one other piece of technical equipment only you can provide."

## 67

The wind picked up, cool and damp. Between Elif Mutlu and the familiar sights of the Istanbul shore, white caps crowned the waves. The ship passed the red-brick bulk of the Haghia Sofia, the former Church of the Holy Wisdom, standing guard over the Bosphorus for fifteen centuries. The minarets of the Blue Mosque rose in the distance. Seraglio Point and the Galata Bridge receded behind them. The cruise ship terminal and the stadium came into view.

From the helicopter, a few minutes before, she had seen tens of thousands of fans packed into the game between Besiktas and the English club, Liverpool.

On a normal day, Orhan might be in that crowd, screaming at the referee. Today, the death and confusion her captors unleashed across Istanbul must have turned his life into a hell. Maybe John Savage, too. Had he thought of her?

What did the terrorists plan next?

As soon as they landed on the ship, the Chief had issued orders. Two of the men seized guns and accompanied two others towards the front of the ship. Each carried a heavy box of equipment.

A muscular, wild-haired man named Kaan, who had waited on the helicopter pad when they arrived, stood guard over Elif and Dervis. He had a huge bruise on his forehead and kept glancing around as though fearing attack. When a crewman appeared from a doorway, Kaan let loose a volley of automatic gunfire that sent the man ducking back inside. The petite blonde film technician, Leni, set up lights, a chair, and a camera tripod near where Elif sat on the deck, her hands and legs free, her back supported by a metal stanchion.

The chair sat in a pool of bright light in the darkness of the Bosphorus.

Dervis sat nearby, one hand handcuffed to the ship's railing. His face was as calm as if he were out for a boat-trip with some friends. From time to time he reached up to play with his earring. The Chief stood in the darkness nearby, clutching the bundle of cloth that held the object. He must be waiting for something.

"Dervis. Why did you help them?" Elif rubbed her mouth where Tolga had ripped off the tape. Pain throbbed at the back of her head. She dared not explore with her fingers the damage she had done herself on the floor of the car. The wind tore across the ship, carrying the threat of rain.

Dervis looked up. "It was right," he said. "It was my duty."

"Your duty? How? To allow thugs to kill our students and the workers and everyone else who has died?"

"I do not know who The Elders are. When they first made contact, I believed they were Hellenistic Polytheists: worshippers of the ancient Greek gods. They had a profound knowledge of Zeus, Athena, Aphrodite and what they stood for. They knew everything about me." Dervis touched his earring.

"I still believe they are men of faith." The archaeologist's voice grew louder. "They care for the *Xoanon*. For the Palladium. They protect it. To support their beliefs, they act. They draw the attention of the world to worshipping a greater power. Whatever we believe, we all need to find a way back to spirituality. To rediscover our souls. To praise and love our gods, whoever they are. There must be more to life than Arzu Pasha's shopping malls."

"What if people don't want to believe in God?"

"Everyone must believe. When the warrior Ajax believed he had achieved his victories without the aid of the immortals, the goddess Athena taught him a lesson."

"But how does killing innocent people help anyone?" Elif's voice rose.

"The philosopher Edmund Burke said, *'The only thing that is necessary for the triumph of evil is for good men to do nothing.'* When they contacted me through the internet, talking about freedom of religion and sexual orientation, I listened. I wanted to help."

Elif glanced up as Dervish mentioned sexuality for the second time. In recent months, he had lost weight and smartened up his appearance. How long had he worn that earring?

"I do not know who these so-called Elders are, any more than you do," Elif said. "But I do know they are playing you, and Meryem, and maybe even the killers on this ship, like a chorus of musical instruments. Meryem wanted to deliver the revolution: look what happened to her. What makes you think you can distinguish between people who are good and people who are evil?"

"I trust people with passion and with faith. People who want to support society, to build a better future, a new community. Many people think this way."

"The guards in the concentration camps also wanted to build a better society and a better future. Passionate leaders make ordinary people do diabolical things." Elif gestured towards Leni, whose video camera showed a red recording light in the dark. "Others are deluded narcissists."

"Thank you." The diminutive blonde woman stood up. "You will see who is deluded, now. It is not us." She turned to the Chief, waiting in the shadows. "I am ready," she said. "We are streaming live to the world. We should film as soon as possible; the rain could start any minute. That will ruin the sound. Okay with you?"

"It is time for us to reveal the truth." The Chief stepped into the light. In his arms, he clutched the object. "Sit in the chair."

"No." Elif did not stir from the deck. "I will never help you. Whatever nonsense you want me to say about some old piece of wood or ivory we dug up, I will never speak these words. You cannot make me."

The Chief looked at her. To her astonishment, he smiled. "That is good," he said. He turned to the camera. "As you can see, Professor Elif Mutlu of Istanbul University is objective and independent. She is one of the world's leading experts on the artefacts of ancient Greece. This is why we have invited her tonight. She is a woman of knowledge and conviction."

The light of the camera turned towards Elif as she leaned against the stanchion. She rose to her feet, shaking her head. People must see that she held her jaw tight and her teeth clenched, that the terrorists held her in their power. Nothing on earth could persuade her to speak on behalf of these maniacs. The ship seemed to have stopped, but the waves had grown larger, rocking the deck beneath her as the wind gathered strength.

"Our story begins in pre-history," the Chief said, "with the *Xoanon*—an ancient relic, believed by the Greeks to have been carved by the goddess Athena after she accidentally killed her friend Pallas, the daughter of Triton." He spoke loudly over the wind. "Hence the name *Xoanon*, meaning an object created by the hand of a god. According to legend, Zeus threw the *Xoanon* out of heaven, and the relic landed at Ilios, the site of what later became Troy. This is where the story of the *Xoanon*, also known at the Palladium, or the Luck of Troy, becomes relevant to today's events."

"None of it is relevant, because none of it is true," Elif shouted. "You are spouting illiterate mumbo-jumbo."

"You say this because you do not yet believe." Still the Chief smiled. "But wait a little. The story of Troy tells us how the Greeks failed to capture the city for ten long years until Odysseus and Diomedes stole the Palladium from the temple of Athena. This was the origin of the belief that the sacred *Xoanon* would make any city housing it invulnerable to destruction. True or false, this story is one of the most famous in the world."

The Chief patted the bundle in his arms. "From Troy, the Palladium travelled to Athens, and on to Rome. Neither city was ever invaded while the Palladium resided there. Finally, in the year 324, the Emperor Constantine took the *Xoanon* to the new capital of the Roman Empire, the city that would become Constantinople. Within decades the Empire fell into decline, and by 410 Rome had fallen–

sacked for the first time in eight centuries. Next, the Palladium protected Constantinople, this time for more than twelve hundred years, until the year 1453, when the Ottoman forces took the city after a long siege."

The Chief leaned forward towards the camera. "How did the Great Fatih Sultan Mehmet, the Conqueror, overcome the power of the Palladium? By sending a team of crack Janissaries into the city to steal the *Xoanon*, enabling the Ottoman forces to storm the walls and conquer Constantinople. They were the first army ever to do so. In the chaos that followed, the relic was lost, many believed forever. Until today.

"As has been reported, Professor Mutlu and her team stumbled across a cache of treasures, and bodies, sealed in a crypt during the events of 1453 and forgotten. These objects included the *Xoanon*. Initial analyses showed many of the relics found at the site were consistent with the date of the conquest. People of faith around the world heard these reports with joy and fascination."

The Chief paused, then continued in the same deep, calm voice, as though narrating a documentary. "We, and The Elders who support our enterprise, believe that the city of Istanbul, with its tradition of tolerating false religions, of permitting peoples of different beliefs and sexes to mingle freely, and with its worship of money, alcohol, drugs, self-indulgence, consumerism and other abominations, is a stain upon the earth. Istanbul teems with peoples and sins. The city is a cesspit; a Sodom and Gomorrah of our times. As those cities were destroyed, so we have come to destroy Istanbul. To show the need for a life of the spirit. To show the need for true belief.

"To demonstrate the totality of our victory, we have decided to show the world the Palladium, far outside the city, before we destroy it in our final act. That is why Professor Mutlu is here. To verify the sacred *Xoanon*."

Again, Elif frowned and shook her head. How could they be so foolish as to recruit her as their helper? Even if the object found at the dig came from ancient Greece, she needed radiocarbon dating evidence from a laboratory, preferably equipped with mass spectrometry, to give an opinion. Even if she believed the absurd assertions of a killer, no way could he persuade her to say anything to ease the path to a terrorist attack.

The Chief approached her, followed by the diminutive blonde camerawoman, filming his actions. Would he force the object in her face? Strike her?

"I will not do what you want," she said. She closed her eyes and braced herself.

But instead of any act of violence, he placed something in her arms. Her hostility lifted, and calm coursed through her.

Elif opened her eyes.

In her hands, resting in the protective fabric she had lifted from the withered arms of the mummified girl in the sarcophagus, lay the Palladium. A polished, abstract sculpture of a woman—a goddess—holding a stylised shield in one hand. The figure extended the other hand as if to hold a spear or sword, which must have vanished.

She held in her hands the most beautiful thing she had ever seen. The technique of the carving must be pre-Roman, almost certainly pre-Greek. But the artistry stole her breath away—a mixture of a pre-classical *kore* and something far older, maybe even Neolithic. The long-dead artist had carved the statuette out of something harder than wood—ivory, perhaps, stained dark, smooth and sensuous.

She reached out and ran her fingers across the face of the goddess. The power of the workmanship and the antiquity overwhelmed her. A wave of emotion rose in her at the significance of what she held and the fact of the relic lying hidden for so long in the embrace of a girl who had died with it in her arms. What else had this astonishing object witnessed in its thousands of years of existence? A tear trickled down her cheek.

A sound grew louder. Could that be a helicopter? Lightning split the sky and a peal of thunder rang out.

The thunderclap shook her out of her reverie. *The camera.* She opened her mouth to speak. She must scream that she held in her hands a worthless fake. But she could not utter a word. She had come to her senses too late.

Whoever had seen Leni's live stream, transmitted to the whole world, had witnessed the truth. Elif held in her hands the most magical thing on earth.

"Thank you," the Chief said. "Now we shall proceed."

The first drops of rain fell.

## 68

From Savage's cramped seat in the helicopter, the *Royal Lion* appeared like an island in a black ocean, stretching away into the darkness.

"That is the biggest bomb you will ever see," he said.

"It will be the last thing we ever see if we cannot stop the detonation," Orhan said. He turned to the captain of the SWAT team. "That coastguard ship hasn't a hope in hell of getting a man on board. Can we do better?"

"Visibility is shit." The captain gazed at the ship using high-powered binoculars. Rain had pursued them across the water; fat drops began to fall on the cockpit glass. "They seem to have placed men at intervals along the deck," the captain went on. "They are setting explosives to achieve a catastrophic breach of the gas tanks. Each team is armed."

"Any ideas?" Orhan took the binoculars. "We are out of time."

"Every option is suicidal." The captain, still clad in the assault gear he had used at the *Valide Han*, shook his head. "We cannot use the landing pad, because their helicopter occupies the space. This traffic 'copter is unarmoured and has nothing to which we can attach a landing rope. If we try to hover close to the ship to jump out, they will pick us off like sheep. Our team is only three, plus the two of you." He gestured at Orhan and Savage.

Savage gripped the door and tried to glimpse the deck of the ship. The wind buffeted the craft. One of the men on board the ship raised something to his face. A sharp crack rang out and a bullet-hole appeared in the glass by Savage's head. The pilot swung the helicopter away over the open water.

"We took a hit," Orhan said. "Everyone okay?"

"Roger that," the captain of the SWAT team shouted. "All good."

Savage cursed. Even without injuries, their force was small. The police traffic helicopter sent by Korkmaz had arrived at the *Valide Han* as a torrential rainstorm broke over the city from the west. In the deluge, Orhan had tried to cram as many of the SWAT team into the tiny cabin as possible. But only three had fitted into the craft.

The intelligence cop had tried to stop Savage boarding.

"You are not armed. We could trade you for another member of the SWAT team," he had said.

"Without me, you would be bulldozing the corpses at Taksim Square."

"Says who?"

Savage bared his teeth. "I will get on the chopper." He seized Orhan's wrist. "Do not try to stop me."

The flight to the tanker took less than five minutes. But now, in the thunderstorm, they could not get near.

To rescue Elif, or stop the terrorists, they must land on the ship.

"Look at this." Behind them, the second member of the SWAT team reached forward a phone, shouting over the noise of the helicopter. "It is on every news website and social media channel."

Savage peered at the screen. Someone was streaming video from the tanker.

Elif stared back at him. She held something. Astonishment and wonder shone from her face. Tears streamed down her cheeks.

Why had Elif done what they wanted?

Did she still live?

In the helicopter, surrounded by the din of the rotors and the blackness of the sky, Savage roared with anger. The kidnappers had somehow broken Elif. He closed his eyes. *Upturn opened her poor, frozen mouth in the woods outside Moscow, begging him to kill her with the scalpel in her hand. "That is the deal," she had said.*

He opened his eyes. The image of Elif on the phone changed to the smiling face of a good-looking, sophisticated man.

"*Thank you,*" the man said. The words appeared as subtitles on the screen. "*Now we shall proceed.*"

How had Elif suffered? What did the man mean by *proceed*?

He must mean blowing up the ship.

"They are going to detonate the gas." Savage fought for breath. "Have your people analysed this video?"

"No way we can ask," Orhan said. "HQ don't even know we have this helicopter. If we contact them, they will order us back straight away. Or shoot us down."

"The broadcast is trending everywhere," the man with the phone said. "Let me look at the video again." He stabbed at his device. "That's weird. My signal has gone."

Savage held his breath. Had Korkmaz come through with his second request? Perhaps they could still fight back. He peered out the window at the water below and bared his teeth.

A tiny vessel shot towards the *Royal Lion*, zig-zagging to avoid the mountainous seas, far smaller even than the coastguard ship toiling at the side of the giant gas tanker. The high-speed police rigid inflatable boat was designed to transport small loads swiftly. Each time the RIB disappeared behind a wave, only the radio aerial at the rear jutted forth, adorned with a tiny Turkish flag.

Korkmaz had delivered.

"Tell them to hurry," Savage yelled to Orhan, who held a VHF radio to his ear.

"The skipper says they will close with the *Royal Lion* as fast as they can," Orhan said. "Let them do their job, and we will do ours."

"They will shoot if we go closer," the pilot said. "One lucky hit and we are all dead."

"Open the side-door," the captain of the SWAT team said. "We will suppress their fire."

The door of the helicopter slid back. Driving wind and rain, overlain by the roar of the blades, filled the cabin.

"Wait until the SWAT team opens up," Orhan said to the pilot. "Then move in as close as you can."

"Roger that." The pilot frowned and tried to steady the craft parallel to the dark bulk of the ship.

"Fire!" the captain of the SWAT team shouted.

The helicopter swayed as three submachine guns opened fire in repeated short bursts. The SWAT team generated overwhelming firepower. But at this range, in the dark, wind, and rain, acquiring targets posed an impossible challenge.

The pilot let the helicopter drift sideways towards the ship as the firing continued. When the shooters paused to re-load, he grunted and swung the front of the craft around to head at the tanker, brought the nose down, and accelerated straight towards the bow.

A bullet slammed into the centre of the windscreen, burying itself into the seat next to Savage.

"Bugger this," the pilot said, "I can't risk it." Without waiting, he turned the craft away towards open water.

"Damn! We have to board that ship." Orhan put his face up close to the pilot, his expression grim. "They have used my sister to make her broadcast. They no longer need her alive. They could blow up the ship and release the gas any second."

"I am sorry about your sister," the pilot said. "But they have snipers on board. We cannot get close without being shot out of the air. I have no way to land you on the *Royal Lion.*"

## 69

Water soaked the fabric of Ali Aydin's shirt as raindrops streamed down his face. Target One cradled the object in her hands, her tearful eyes turned up towards the storm in the glare of the camera lights. A weight rose from Ali's shoulders.

The Protocol had predicted Target One's actions correctly.

He had never doubted she would do her job, as they all had done. The Protocol had brought together, trained, equipped, and financed a team whose actions fitted together like the parts of a machine, running accurately over days, weeks, and months.

Target One might have joined them against her will, but join them she had.

Next, the final act of The Protocol would come to a blazing, glorious conclusion.

The first of the two bomb-laying teams returned. The bomb-maker Berat, and Emre, the muscle who accompanied him, had laid six twin charges down the starboard side of the great tanker, each designed to tear a vast gash in one of the yellow, rectangular tanks of super-cooled LNG that made up the vessel. The second team, Zafer and Tolga, continued to lay their charges down the port side.

The Protocol foresaw that when the bombs tore holes the size of rail carriages in each side of every tank, four hundred and fifty thousand cubic metres of liquid gas would gush out of the ship, evaporating and spreading out across the water and into the streets of the metropolis.

As the liquid gas vaporised, a cloud of methane would blanket the entire city of Istanbul, stifling the unbelievers in their thousands in bars, clubs, villas, or wherever they carried out their corrupt and immoral practices. Panic would break out as people fell dying in the streets, their lungs starved of oxygen. Yet at first, The Elders stated, no-one across the vast area would grasp the magnitude of the terror they faced. Only when the four hundred and fifty thousand cubic metres of liquid gas dispersed into the air, across hundreds of square kilometres, would the mix of methane and oxygen reach the right proportions to explode. From then on, a spark or flame anywhere in Istanbul would set off a detonation The Protocol compared to a thermonuclear bomb: a super-heated rampant firestorm, unleashed against millions of sinners across a vast area.

Ali checked his phone. The signal remained strong. He had ordered Saif al-Din, the former taxi driver whose team had seized the *Royal Lion*, to call Uzay, the Black Sea boatman at the helm of the ship, down from the wheelhouse. The Protocol said the whole team must be together when he triggered the twelve twin charges to release the gas.

But the second bomb-laying team, led by the technician, Zafer, backed up by the bearded Tolga, had not yet appeared. Nor had Uzay.

Ali licked his lips. Zafer, the bomb-maker and pilot, had the meticulous nature of a master craftsman. He might take longer to complete his mission than Berat. But there he came. Zafer and Tolga pelted towards them in the narrow space between the hull and the gas tanks, their feet splashing in the puddles on the deck.

"It is done," Zafer said. He glanced at his fellow bomb-maker, Berat, whose smile split his damp, stubble-covered cheeks.

"Six double charges," Berat said. "Twelve, port and starboard. Twenty-four bombs in all. They will cut the tanker in two like a sword. We believe the membrane structure of the tanks and hull will collapse completely."

"But a helicopter is trying to approach the ship." Tolga held a sniper rifle and wore night vision goggles pushed back on his forehead. "That is why we are late. I shot three times. In the storm, I could not see if I hit them, but they flew away. If you permit, I will go forward with Emre into the darkness, where the goggles will be most effective, and stand guard."

"You will stay here," Ali shouted to make himself heard above the wind and rain. "You have done well. But we are ready to explode the ship. No-one can stop us now. You say a helicopter. Are they alone, or are more coming?"

"One so far."

"Good. Emre and Tolga: watch and listen, in case they try something, but stay close to us. The Protocol says we must celebrate the final act together."

Both men grinned, their teeth white in the darkness. "We are ready for martyrdom," Tolga said. They moved into position on the edge of the deck, their sniper rifles ready, and peered into the darkness.

"The time has come." Ali turned to Saif. "Where is Uzay?"

The little man shook his head and held up his phone. "He is not obeying. He is arrogant. First, he said he wished to be at the helm of the ship when we explode the gas. Now, I cannot get through to him. I think he is not answering."

"Your soldier is not obeying you?" Ali stared down at the man. After a day at sea, sweat stained Saif's white naval uniform. The downpour had left him bedraggled, twenty-four hours of stubble covered his chin. He held his small hands bunched at his hips as if he, too, longed to disobey an order. He looked less like the warrior Saif al-Din than little Karim Ahmed, the Istanbul taxi-driver. "Without obedience, we are nothing. Is Uzay not a warrior of The Protocol? Tell him to come instantly. Tell him it is my order."

"I am trying." Saif peered at his phone, soaking wet from the rain. "I have no signal."

Ali hesitated. The Protocol made clear they must all be together, with the object, when the bombs detonated. To disobey The Protocol was unthinkable. Yet Uzay's insubordination, or Saif's lack of leadership, had cost them precious minutes.

As a doctor, Ali had failed. Failure could not be an option now.

As the willing tool of The Elders, he stood on the brink of immortality.

They must wait no longer. He must act, with or without the rebellious Black Sea boatman. The heathen, sin-drenched metropolis of Istanbul and everything the city stood for must perish.

"All of you who are here," he said. "Come together. Turn on the camera lights and bring the woman and the object." He held up his phone. "It is time to complete The Protocol. Together we will bring about the end of the West."

## 70

E lif sat against the stanchion in the rain, the object in her arms. After hours of capture and constraint, every part of her body throbbed with pain. The back of her head was an open wound. She longed to sleep forever.

But her exhaustion and agony did not consume her.

How had she committed such a crime?

She had been determined not to do what her kidnappers wanted. She had fought them from the moment they first seized her in the Old City. When they pushed the camera in her face, she had not spoken a word.

Yet the whole world had seen her authenticate the object.

How had that happened?

The ancient relic comforted her. She stared into the blind face of the statuette, relishing its weight and smoothness in her hands. Who cared whether such an ancient, sacred relic bore the name of the Palladium or not? The object had survived through centuries, maybe millennia of human history. How many others had witnessed the relic or worshipped the legend behind those sightless eyes, over countless years? What hands before hers had touched the smooth surface? Byzantine princes? Roman emperors? Greek priestesses? Maybe Odysseus himself, or the goddess Athena. Neither of whom had ever existed. Despite the pain racking her body, she smiled at the desperate superstition of it all.

"Elif!"

The wind and rain threatened to carry the faint voice into oblivion.

"Elif! Over here."

Dervis stood, hair plastered to his head by the rain. He strained towards her, his big body filled with urgency, his arm still handcuffed to the railing. "Can you show me the object?"

Automatically, Elif wrapped the relic tighter in the protective cloth and hugged the bundle closer, as if Dervis might seek to harm it. "Why should I help you? If you had not betrayed us, none of this would have happened. In a minute we shall all be dead."

"If we are dead anyway, you have nothing to lose by showing me the object." Dervish smiled for the first time since the shootings in the tunnel. "I saw your face when you glimpsed it," the big man went on. "Even though you tried to keep control. You were in a rapture. Come. Let me share your joy."

Elif gripped the tightly wrapped object. Dervis's eyes blazed with energy. Beads of rain stood out on the hand he stretched towards her. What did she have to lose? Nothing remained of her attempts to stop the terrorists. Nearby, the diminutive Leni filmed a group of them, their fists held aloft in triumph. The cinematographer's bright lights illuminated members of the group grinning in the driving rain. Since Elif had fulfilled her role with the object, they seemed to have forgotten her.

She rose to her feet, as if sleepwalking, and shuffled across to Dervis. "Here," she held out the bundle. "Take a look. You may be the last person ever to see the Palladium."

Dervis reached out and took the relic, but made no attempt to unwrap the bundle. His eyes blazed. "I know I am a fool. What you said about them playing me like an instrument–that was so right. They said everything I yearned to hear about tolerance and faith and freedom. They even knew about my new relationship, and they accepted it," he smiled and shook his head. "Unlike my own mother and father. Now, I will lose him, too, along with everything else."

The archaeologist sighed and held the object close to his body. "When I heard that madman rave about destroying the whole of Istanbul, I realised what an idiot I had been. We all long for something good. We all yearn for change. But we never learn. The man or woman who promises you a simple, glorious future has learned to punch your buttons." He gestured to the clump of young people gathered on the deck. "Who knows what sweet words the so-called Elders used to persuade these poor fools to carry out such a slaughter? I am no better than them." Dervis raised his gaze to Elif. "My dear. I am so sorry. For everything."

Elif wanted to slap him. "It is a bit bloody late to apologise."

Dervis smiled again. "Perhaps I can do one last thing."

## 71

Ali Aydin checked the time. "Where is the woman? And the object?"

"Kaan and Hussein are fetching her," Saif said.

"Stand back! Stand back!"

Ali did not recognise the voice. A scuffle broke out by the ship's guardrail.

"Light!" He shouted to Leni. "Shine light on them!"

The tiny camerawoman grunted as she rotated the camera lights, illuminating a great cube of teeming rain. At first, the cube enclosed only empty deck. As Leni swung the lights further, a brilliantly-lit cast of players sprang into view.

Hussein, and Saif's muscle sidekick, Kaan, stood frozen, guns in their hands. The weapons pointed at Target Two, Dervis Basturk. Handcuffs still clamped the burly archaeologist's wrist to the railing. But in his other hand he clutched—*the object*, wrapped in the protective cloth, held over the side of the tanker above the water far below.

"You are madmen," Target Two shouted. "I will not be a part of your insanity! You tricked me!"

"No." Ali spoke with authority. "We want a better world. Like you. Give me the object."

In the shadows behind Target Two, Tolga, the bearded muscle from the Balat house, advanced silently towards him, his arms outstretched. Ali hesitated. Should he explode the bombs now? Or retrieve the Palladium so the cameras could film the destruction of the relic when the whole team assembled on the deck, as The

Protocol demanded? Surely no archaeologist could allow such a treasure to fall?

Target Two had not spotted Tolga's stealthy advance behind him. The muscle braced himself to spring forward and grab the object.

"Kaan! Hussein! Stand back," Ali ordered, staring in the other direction. "Do what he says."

"Do not try to trick me." Target Two leaned back over the railing, his hand holding the object further out above the water. His earring gleamed in the camera lights. "I—"

A volley of automatic fire rang out.

Ali stared at Kaan and Hussein and Tolga. All shook their heads.

The coastguard. The floodlit Target Two, leaning out over the water, must have made an irresistible target to the crew of the ship, bobbing frustrated in the shadow of the tanker.

Two bloody exit wounds flowered in the chest of Target Two. He gazed at Target One, who stared back open-mouthed, and shook his head. "Better this way, I guess," he said, and slumped backwards over the top of the railing. Before anyone could step forward, his feet rose off the deck and he toppled towards the water.

The handcuffs arrested his fall. For a second his body jerked back, suspended above the waves, one arm twisted back over the top of the railing to where the shackle bound his wrist to a steel support.

His other hand opened. The bundle containing the object, bright in the camera lights, tumbled into the waters of the Bosphorus.

Ali's mouth fell open. They had lost the Palladium. Target Two had breached The Protocol.

Around him on the deck of the ship, his comrades stared at him, seeking leadership.

Ali took a deep breath and stood taller. The ancient relic had fulfilled its role. They had taken the object far outside Istanbul. They had broadcast to the world the video of Target One, in which she confirmed the significance of the *Xoanon* beyond any doubt.

Nothing could stop them destroying the great sewer of depravity whose lights spilled down the shores of the Bosphorus towards the water.

"Everyone. To me." Ali held up his phone. "It is time. Leni. Film us." He forced a grin onto his face. "The world will witness the death of Istanbul. The end of the West. We are the ones who will change history."

They all came running. Hussein, who had helped and supported him all day. Saif and Kaan, who had captured the mighty *Royal Lion* with the rebellious Uzay. Zafer and Berat, the two bomb-makers. Emre and Tolga, the two fighters from the Balat house, who came clutching their sniper rifles, helped the exhausted Leni once again to rotate the camera lights towards the helipad where they gathered. A jagged bolt of lightning blazed overhead, followed by a peal of thunder.

"Are you recording this?" Ali said.

"Yes," Leni said. "I am not certain about the sound quality. No-one in Istanbul will be left alive to remember my work. But the rest of the world will watch and wonder." A smirk creased her face. "The visuals are great."

"Mankind will admire your work forever. Come. Join us."

The diminutive camerawoman fiddled to fix her camera to a tripod, and stepped into the circle of light.

What a team of lions Ali had built. Despite everything, they had completed The Protocol. By the handrail, in the shadows, Target One crouched close to the body of Target Two, hanging over the water. Maybe she mourned the loss of the object. Well, when the gas transformed Istanbul into an incinerated wasteland, the inferno would have destroyed the object along with everything else.

Ali dried the touchscreen of his phone with a corner of his shirt and shielded the device with his body. A new world dawned. His wet fingertips left droplets on the black screen. It took three attempts to bring up the app allowing him to call simultaneously the twelve other phones, each attached to a pair of bombs. Nothing could go wrong. The simple technology worked under all conditions. Saif and his team had already used a phone signal today to destroy a boat in which they had travelled.

To touch his finger to a phone to trigger the greatest liberation of souls the world had ever seen seemed almost trivial after so much sweat and preparation. Could anything be worthy of such a moment? He blinked and felt the raindrops fall on his eyelids. Of course, The Protocol stated exactly what he must say next.

Ali took a last look around the proud faces of his team, gathered on the helipad. He smiled. Some of them beamed back; others looked anxious, or tense. Joy overwhelmed him. Everything in his life led to this instant of salvation.

Nothing stood in his way.

"The Protocol is complete," he said. "Praise God." He looked into the lens of Leni's camera and pressed the button.

Nothing happened.

## 72

The police traffic helicopter hung low over the dark waters of the Bosphorus, rain streaming in through the open door. Ahead, a blaze of light shone from the stern of the great LNG tanker.

The glare reminded Savage of the corpse-strewn tunnel at the archaeological site. The killers had gunned down Stuart Lamont, helpless on his cushion.

Could he avenge that injustice?

"They are gathering." The SWAT captain peered through his binoculars. "They are preparing for something."

"They are getting ready to blow up the ship." Buoyed by the sight of the RIB and tense from the memories of Moscow and Stuart Lamont, Savage leaned forward. "How many of them? See any long guns?"

"Eight people. Maybe nine. I cannot see their weapons."

"This is our chance." Savage seized the binoculars and gazed at the pool of light. "It looks like a ritual, everyone together for the final act. They have withdrawn the snipers from the front of the ship. We expected ten attackers. If one or two control the ship from the wheelhouse, that would leave eight or nine on deck."

"I can see no-one further forward," the SWAT captain said.

"At best, the snipers can cover the flanks," Savage said. "Approach from the bow. If the gas blows, we're all toast anyhow."

"Hell is too good for these people," the SWAT captain said. He gripped the pilot's shoulder. "Fly to the front."

"I am not paid for this." The pilot did not move. "I am a commercial pilot, and this is not an Apache."

"Do you want to die a nobody? Or fight like a hero?" Orhan punched the pilot on the arm. "Be a man."

"Yeah, like I am motivated by machismo. That is how it works if you are a commercial helicopter pilot."

"Do you want me to take the controls?" Orhan said. "I cannot believe you prefer to wait here until you asphyxiate and burn when the ship explodes."

"Okay, okay. You are all heroes. With a death wish." The pilot swung the craft in a long, smooth arc towards the front of the tanker. "But for the record, if I save Istanbul, I want a raise."

"I promise not to have you court-martialled for stealing a helicopter," Orhan said. "Do we have a deal?"

"Terrific." The pilot grimaced. "Thanks."

"It will be like landing on a porcupine." Savage peered through the binoculars. "Most of the deck is obstructed by masts and equipment. But there is a small flat area at the bow, ahead of the gas tanks. The zone is sheltered from the rear of the ship where the terrorists are. The open space is too small to land. But if you can hover there close to the deck, we can exit the chopper."

"Sure, hover there close to the deck, no problem." The pilot shook his head and peered into the rainstorm. But he continued to pull the helicopter round, low over the water, until the craft hung in the air ahead of the bow of the vessel.

"In we go," the pilot said.

They closed on the tanker fast, the wipers battling the rainstorm. The pilot flew low, skimming the waves. Rain sheeted down. A bolt of lightning revealed the prow of the ship, looming over them like a cliff.

"No-one at the bow, or they would be blasting us at point-blank range." Savage peered upwards. "The body of the ship is shielding us. Bring us close in, then come up over the front rail so we can exit fast."

The pilot said nothing. But the helicopter rose.

The ascent to the level of the deck seemed to last forever. Even the rain fell in slow motion. Why had they not yet breached the gas tanks? Had Savage's reserve plan worked? Or did whoever had seized Elif have something else planned entirely? Close up, the name of the ship loomed into view, painted in tall white letters.

*Royal Lion.*

## 73

A li Aydin stared at the screen of his phone. *NO SIGNAL,* the display read. How could that be? Could the storm have disrupted the service? He prodded at the touch-screen with his finger.

This time the display read *CALL FAILED.*

When he last looked, the signal had shown five bars. Something had gone wrong. He remembered Saif, trying to call Uzay on the bridge, and failing to get through.

"What has happened?" Hussein approached him. The rest of the team waited on the helipad. Earlier, as Ali prepared to trigger the bombs in the rain, his team had seemed invincible. Now, their pale faces looked vulnerable and young. Had he let his valiant soldiers down? Could he have stopped the object from tumbling into the sea? The premature loss of the relic left a part of The Protocol unfulfilled.

They had come too far not to complete the operation.

The Protocol provided a Plan B for every eventuality.

"Zafer! Berat! The bombs have a secondary trigger mechanism in case the phone signal is not working. Explain it to us."

"The devices are built with a fall-back switch," Berat said. "A manual override. But the bombs do not have a timing device. If any of us engages the manual switch on a bomb, the charge will explode immediately, killing that person. I am ready to die." The wiry, stubble-chinned young bomb-maker glanced at the silent Zafer, who nodded fiercely. "But one or two bombs may not release enough gas. We need four, minimum."

"We are all ready to die. And we are nine," Ali said. "Can you teach us how to trigger the bombs?"

"It is a simple relay to disconnect the phone circuit." Berat sprang forward and rummaged in one of the equipment cases. "Come forward. Everyone."

Under the brilliant lights, Berat drew a package from the box. "This is a part-assembled device, without the explosive," he said. "This switch is set by default at Position A. This is designed to ensure primary Circuit one will be completed when the device receives a phone signal, detonating the explosive." He held up the bomb to demonstrate the action. "If we move the switch to Position B, thus, we complete the secondary circuit, Circuit two. This will detonate the explosive, with immediate effect." He stood up. "That is all. Any questions? I suggest you all try out the mechanism." He passed the package around.

Ali took the device as it reached him and activated the switch. A child could operate the mechanism. Whatever blocked the phone signals could not stop manually activated detonators.

"Berat. You take Emre, Saif, and Leni down one side. You can detonate four bombs. Tolga, you take Kaan and Hussein. Berat, you will give a visual signal to detonate the seven bombs simultaneously."

"What about me?" Zafer, the placid bomb-maker who had flown the helicopter, said. "I, too, am ready to die."

"You will remain here and construct all remaining explosives into an additional bomb," Ali said. "As a back-up."

"The remaining explosives are not enough to make a big hole." The rainstorm nearly drowned out Zafer's voice. "I want to go with the others."

"No," Ali said. "The Protocol always has a backup plan, and a backup to that. I need you here. Build another device. The charge will be enough to puncture at least one tank. The rest of you, go forward. You will take a few minutes to reach the furthest bombs, at the end of the ship. Be ready to detonate the seven devices as soon as you are all in place. Good luck."

"The blast from those bombs will hit us here, even before the methane ignites," Zafer said. "You and I must move behind the shelter of the upper deck." Without waiting, he took a few steps forward and settled down alongside his equipment box against the bulkhead. He set to work, his face a mask of concentration.

The seven brave warriors marched forward, three on one side of the ship and four on the other, to detonate their explosives in a final, valiant act of suicide.

Ali moved against the protective steel of the bulkhead, alongside Zafer, and counted down the seconds until the blasts.

## 74

"Going up and over the bow now," the pilot said. "Hold onto your seats."

Savage had experienced turbulent helicopter insertions in Afghanistan, but his stomach lurched as the craft jerked upwards, soared past the ship's name and over the guard-rail, and rocked to a halt above a green-painted steel wilderness of winches, vents, and deck machinery. The craft swayed as a gust of wind caught the rotors.

"If I go any lower we'll hit something," the pilot said. "Everyone out."

The captain of the SWAT team jumped, landing with a curse. The second and third black-clad officers landed on the deck, rolling to break their fall.

"Take care," Orhan said. "That steel deck will take no prisoners." He jumped, landing gracefully.

Savage jumped last. This time, he wore the bullet-proof vest Orhan had grudgingly given him. But he had no weapon. He rolled once and threw himself behind a wall of yellow-painted steel that he guessed formed the front end of the gas tanks.

By the time he looked round, the helicopter had disappeared.

After trailing the terrorists all day, he and Orhan could at last strike back.

But what had the killers done with Elif after forcing her to make the video? Had they executed her and thrown her body into the Bosphorus?

How many minutes, or seconds, remained before they ignited the explosives?

Orhan sprinted forward to join the SWAT captain, who

crouched at the head of a flight of stairs. Beyond, a gangway ran the length of the yellow superstructure. Two other black-clad figures crouched to port, peering aft through the rain. Orhan beckoned to Savage.

"No sign of anyone," he said. "But I can see six IEDs on this side. Maybe double charges." He gestured along the superstructure. The dim lights illuminating the walkways revealed dark, glistening objects against the yellow of the giant gas tanks.

"This side, too," a SWAT officer to port shouted over the rain. "That makes twelve bombs. Or twenty-four."

"Ten minutes since they transmitted the video with Elif." Savage flashed a grin. "Let's hope they are having ignition problems."

Orhan punched him on the arm. "I guess they tried to detonate the bombs using a phone signal and failed. The phone jammer you asked for on the RIB must have screwed up their plans. Nice work."

"It had to be a phone signal. Impossible to explode multiple IEDs any other way on a ship this big, unless you had a hell of a lot of wire. They will take a while to reset the bombs with timers, even if they have them."

"Wait. Someone is coming."

Four people ran through the rain along the starboard walkway of the ship towards them. They reached the first bomb within seconds. A small, blonde woman stopped by the explosive device. The rest ran on. The woman was so short she could barely reach the unit.

"They do not know we are here," Orhan said. "The storm drowned out the noise of our landing. They are moving without precautions."

The stationary ship pitched. Savage peered along the walkway. The rain stung his eyes. He glanced at the SWAT captain on the opposite side, who held up three fingers.

Seven people approached them.

Orhan handed Savage the binoculars. The improvised explosive devices projected from the yellow gas tanks at regular intervals along the ship. The length of the vessel meant that while someone already stood next to the two bombs furthest away, other terrorists still ran to reach those nearest to the bow.

"Are they setting the bombs off with timers?" Orhan said. "How can they blow the charges simultaneously, if they were wired for a phone signal?"

"They have no timers. They are on a suicide mission. See how they are leaving one person at each bomb? They will co-ordinate a manual detonation by a visual signal. Each will set off the explosive next to them."

"The nearest man has reached the last bomb." Orhan's voice rose.

"Open fire. Take them all at once. Go!"

Without hesitating, Orhan raised his hand and brought it down.

The bold rattle of automatic weapons rang out on both sides of the ship. Orhan fired his pistol.

The straight, exposed walkways formed a shooting gallery. On Savage's side, three figures fell to the deck. The fourth, the tiny blonde woman, lunged towards the closest IED, only to be cut down by a fresh burst of firing. She fell to the deck and crawled for cover around the corner towards the far end of the ship.

The bombs still waited, mute, along each side of the gas tanks. But no bombers remained.

"All clear this side," the SWAT captain said. "We will move forward along the top of the tanks. These gangways are a death trap."

Orhan rose and climbed a ladder up to the raised section of deck between the two walkways. Savage and the three black-clad police officers followed. They made short dashes, seeking cover from the machinery and masts crowding the central part of the deck. The SWAT team members moved further ahead in the downpour, scanning potential hiding places and blind spots for trouble.

Savage kept a watchful eye on the walkways. None of the shot terrorists moved. He passed the first bomb, clamped to the surface of the tanker. What if a timer did control the charges?

At any moment the devices could detonate, ripping open the

metal and releasing hundreds of thousands of cubic metres of choking, explosive gas.

Ahead, the SWAT captain raised his hand and paused behind a mast. "It is too quiet. Where are the other terrorists?"

"How many people do they have?" Orhan said.

"The chopper they flew out had space for eight people, maybe nine at a pinch," Savage said. "Three or four people must have already been on the ship, to take control. So, maybe twelve all together. Minus Elif and Dervis, makes ten. That would be consistent with the intelligence. If we hit six or seven of them, they still have another three or four."

"Their first priority will be to set off the charges, not to worry about us." Orhan peered through his binoculars. "I see no-one."

"Every second we don't control the ship, they can blow the whole bloody package to kingdom come," Savage said. "All they need is a phone signal. Where are the cavalry?"

"I told the pilot to head back to HQ and show them the damaged helicopter," Orhan said. "I hope he will mobilise the military to send some special forces. But they may arrest him and lock him up for breaching the no-fly zone. Even if he succeeds, they will not be here in time to help us."

"I know where the attackers are," Savage said. "Maybe Elif, too. Remember the low, flat deck at the bow, where we landed? They are holed up in a section at the rear, by the helicopter pad, shielded from the upper deck or side walkways. They will have more explosives. They can still breach the tanks. We must reach them fast. If we stay on the upper deck, we shall be looking down on them." Savage reached out to Orhan. "Give me a gun."

"Are you crazy? You are a diplomat. You cannot use a firearm in Turkey."

"Suppose Elif dies because you did not give me a weapon? Are you ready to live with that?" In the rain, Savage clenched his fists. "*Give it to me.* I know you have a spare."

In the dim light, Orhan reached out and seized Savage by both arms. "You are as crazy as a Turk. You know I hate you, John. But I will love you forever if you save Elif. And Istanbul."

"Crazy as a Turk." Savage smiled. "I guess that's a compliment. What about a gun?"

"I do not have a spare pistol, so the question does not arise." Orhan embraced him. "Maybe you can kill a terrorist with your bare hands. Take care."

Savage hugged Orhan in return. "Thanks, you stubborn Turkish bastard. You too."

"Let us finish this." Orhan took a deep breath and stood, rain streaming down his face. "Come."

In a single movement, all five men stepped out of cover and ran along the top of the gas tank towards the rear of the vessel, the SWAT team drawing ahead.

An explosion shook the ship. Savage fell to the deck, his ears ringing, a dull pain piercing his chest. A jagged fragment of metal protruded from his bullet-proof vest. The protection had stopped the shrapnel from tearing his body apart.

He rose to his feet. Orhan crouched near him on all fours, shaking his head like a dog. All three of the SWAT team, further ahead, lay sprawled on the ground. One of them pulled himself up on his elbows and pointed towards the captain, who lay motionless, his thigh a bloody mess.

"A bomb. To breach the tanks." Savage peered forward through the rain. "Can you hear that?"

"A whistling sound?" Orhan climbed to his feet and knelt by the SWAT captain. Savage helped him apply a tourniquet to the man's leg; the third SWAT team member lay nearby, his leg bent at a grotesque angle, his arm raised to show he still lived.

"The captain's pulse is fine," Orhan said. He helped Savage roll the man over into the recovery position, then rose. "Is that noise the gas escaping? I can see nothing."

"The gas is boiling off," Savage said. "But the noise means the hole is small. The LNG is shooting out under pressure. We must ignite the gas before vapour gathers and causes an explosion that destroys the ship and releases the whole cargo. If we set the gas alight before enough collects to explode, the LNG will burn off as it escapes."

"You want to make the gas catch fire? But that is what the terrorists want."

Savage tried to remember what Ram had told him, and what he knew about gas and explosions. He took a deep breath.

"I am sure. We must shoot at something metal near the back of the ship. We need a spark."

Orhan unholstered his pistol. He fired once, without result. Twice.

"Nothing."

"Try the rear mast. Anything steel. Shoot, damn you. The gas could be spreading towards us right now."

Orhan took careful aim and fired. Once. Twice. He gritted his teeth and fired repeatedly in quick succession, reloaded, and blazed away again.

A flash and the crump of an explosion answered. A bright blue wall of flame rushed towards them and disappeared. A searing blast of heat washed over them. Savage smelled his own burnt hair.

He lived. Too little gas must have escaped to form a critical mass.

Yet something had changed. Light filled the sky, illuminating every detail of the deck, the masts, and the superstructure.

Savage raised his gaze.

Above, a gigantic sword of fire soared into the heavens, burning with an intense, other-worldly heat.

The figures on Ali Aydin's timer counted down. Twenty seconds remained before the bombs exploded, releasing a cloud of gas ready to ignite in a super-heated fireball across Istanbul.

Ali smiled. The Protocol provided for everything, even a problematic phone signal. The initial detonation might end his life, too. But he did not care. Glory awaited, whether he died in seconds, minutes, or hours.

Ten seconds remained. Nine, eight. A crackle of gunfire rang out. Had the coastguard opened fire again? In the din of the storm he could not place the source of the sound. He peered down at Zafer, his face swathed in concentration as he constructed the final device.

"Soldiers are on the ship."

Ali whirled around. Leni lay slumped against the bulkhead. Her slight figure looked as if the rain could sweep her away. Blood soaked her clothing. "They shot our people."

"How?" Ali said. "Why did you not activate the switch?"

"We were about to detonate all seven bombs when they opened fire. I tried to reach my device, but they shot me." She shook her head. "I am hit. In the arm. And in the leg. I am sorry."

Ali scowled at the tiny girl. Why had The Elders recruited a woman to his team? Instead of detonating her device, she had fled at the first sign of danger.

"Help Zafer with his work," he barked. "Where is your weapon?"

"I lost it," Leni said. "All the others are dead."

"I need no help." Zafer did not look up. Leni did not move.

"Stay with him. Show your honour, not your cowardice. Defend him. Die with him if necessary," Ali shouted at Leni.

What had gone wrong? In the space of moments, his certainty of success had vanished. In place of joy, an aching horror had sprung up. This greatest and most honourable of all missions could end in failure.

How had his phone malfunctioned? How had someone gained access to the ship in the middle of the storm? Most important, how could he complete The Protocol?

Zafer had enough explosive left to puncture one of the six giant tanks that contained the liquefied gas. The single hole might be smaller than the massive multiple breaches they had planned, but given time, a sixth of the gas could still escape, evaporating and expanding in volume.

Ali calculated. The explosive mixture could still cover an area of hundreds of square kilometres–vast enough to envelop the whole of central Istanbul in a fireball that would char a man's flesh from his bones. Such a detonation might well destroy the ship, too, releasing the gas in the other five tanks.

His breathing slowed. Zafer worked in the glare of the lights, fighting to produce a viable device. They could still complete The Protocol, with or without the so-called Luck of Troy.

Thinking of the lost object reminded him of Target One. Could she have thrown herself into the water? It would be no loss. He ran towards the railing.

The woman lay where he had left her, on the deck next to the pale corpse of Target Two. Somehow, single-handedly, she had hauled the body of the burly archaeologist back over the railing, from where the corpse had hung above the water, and onto the deck.

The effort seemed to have exhausted her. She gazed up at him, her half-closed eyes smouldering.

Before he could speak, he heard Zafer shouting out through the rain.

"The final bomb is ready!"

Ali whirled round. "Detonate it."

Zafer blinked at him. "When I press my hand against the switch, the bomb will explode at once."

"What are you waiting for? Are you afraid?"

The quiet boy's face clouded with anger. He shook his head. "No."

A squall of rain swept the deck. A gust of wind cleared the rain. Zafer, lit by the TV lights, held a package against the outer skin of the gas tank with his bare hands.

The girl, Leni, had vanished. Of course, she had fled–a coward, like any woman.

Ali ducked behind a stanchion on the deck.

Even behind the steel upright, the shock of the explosion took his breath away. The stanchion shielded Ali and Target One from the blast. The TV lights blew out.

A roar of rushing, whistling, escaping gas filled the air, boiling out into the Istanbul night.

Ali peered past the stanchion. Euphoria swelled in his breast.

He, Ali Aydin, had fulfilled The Protocol.

Zafer had done his job well. He had designed the charge so the blast tore through the wall of the gas tank. The explosion had ripped a ragged hole, not much bigger than a man's hand, in the metal surface. The shape of the cavity blurred and swam as Ali tried to focus his gaze. That must be good. Thousands of cubic metres of super-cooled, liquefied gas were warming, expanding, and vaporising, as pressure within the tank forced the volatile mixture out into the night air.

The mangled chunks of flesh that had been Zafer sprinkled the deck. The explosion had ripped his body into fragments.

Ali raised his face to the heavens. Zafer had died nobly, to complete The Protocol. To staunch the escaping gas would be impossible for whoever had come on board the ship, or anyone else.

He slumped to the deck. When his life ended, eternal glory beckoned. The Elders spoke the truth.

He stared at Target One, slouched in the shadows next to the corpse of Target Two.

She looked back, her gaze expressionless, and shook her head.

For some reason the gesture reminded him of the old revolutionary, Meryem, in the *Valide Han*. The Elders had recruited her, too, but by promising something quite different to what they had pledged Ali. Target Two, for his part, had believed The Elders wanted something else again. They had found his weak spot. They had even induced the tycoon Arzu Pasha to fight alongside them, little realising their goal was literally to reduce her property empire to ashes.

What if The Elders had lied to Ali, also? Had they played him, too, as a useful idiot? What if The Elders had identified the weaknesses and dreams of every one of his team of lions, every hero martyred today, to recruit them?

Ali shivered as a gust of wind hit him. From the day The Elders first reached out to him on the darknet, they had seemed to know more about the doctor, Ali Aydin, than he knew himself. They had fuelled his desire to serve the faith. They had empathised with his loss of belief at the hospital as though they had stood by him in the operating theatre, the dead baby cradled in his hands, knowing his own error had caused the child's death. As if they, too, had seen the mother's face turn to stone. The Elders had understood Ali's thirst for salvation better than anyone. They told him the Almighty had a more important task for him.

The Protocol must be true. He nodded to himself, trying to recall his first contacts with The Elders on the darknet.

Or had he based his entire quest on a deception?

Target One held his gaze. Her eyes bored into him, as if she could see the doubts in his mind.

The whistle of the gas bursting out of the tank rose a tone. The vapour must be pouring into the air around the ship. LNG had no smell. He took a deep breath of the cool, salty air. Could the gas steal his oxygen without his knowledge? Or might the force with which the deep-frozen liquid evaporated and escaped from the tank carry it far up into the sky? He heard something else. Was that the crackle of pistol shots?

Target One smiled.

Everything turned white. A searing blast of air pressed in on him, an instant of scorching heat replaced in a split second by the drumbeat of the rain.

A light shone down on Target One, highlighting a face beaded with moisture, a mouth open in fear and wonder.

Where had the light come from?

Ali rose to his feet. A flame blazed from the hole made by Zafer's final bomb: a jet of fire soaring high into the thunderous sky. In answer, lightning stabbed down through the blackness, as though seeking to connect with the colossal blaze.

Somehow, the enemy had lit the gas, too soon for anything more than a tiny fraction of the cargo in the ship's tanks to have escaped.

The gas burned as soon as it vaporised and mixed with the air. The flame consumed the LNG before enough could accumulate to cause an all-consuming explosion.

Ali Aydin stared at the catastrophic blade of fire, and his shoulders sank. His dream of bringing justice and order to the sinful aberration that was Istanbul had been consumed by fire. The Protocol had failed. Should he end his own life, too? Or should he first take revenge? He closed his fist around the reassuring bulk of the pistol in his waistband, drew the weapon forth, and turned towards Target One.

## 76

E lif blinked up at the brilliant jet of flame. Surely the terrorists had hoped to achieve more than this. The outcome seemed laughable after the death and suffering she had witnessed throughout the day.

Had she misunderstood? Might the flame lead to a greater, more cataclysmic event?

She ran her hand over her face. The blast of heat when the gas ignited had seared and cracked her skin. She touched the back of her head and cringed. The mess of flesh felt as if someone had smashed her skull in with a brick. But the pain meant nothing. What mattered was that the people who had unleashed the day of terror upon the great city of Istanbul had suffered a defeat.

Elif rested her hand on the cold forehead of Dervis. The poor, misguided man had paid with his life for his blind belief in the healing power of faith.

At least she had given him dignity, lying on the deck instead of dangling over the water from his handcuff like some macabre fender.

Something moved in the darkness. Elif climbed to her feet. Her back and legs ached from hauling Dervis's body back over the railing.

The Chief stood in the shadows a few paces away.

He stepped into the light, a gun in his hand.

The Chief. That morning in the tunnel he had gunned down the students and workers before stepping forward to execute them in cold blood with a bullet to the head. How many more had died?

Energy poured into her from the burning gas in the sky.

Let him shoot her.

"You pathetic bastard!" she yelled. "You caused all this. Why?

√hat can you achieve? Even if you destroy Istanbul. How will that make the world better? How?"

She took a step closer to him. Then, with all her might, she slapped him across the face.

The man's head jerked round at the force of the blow, towards the front of the ship. His body stiffened. He lunged forward, his arms crushing her chest, pulling her between himself and the bow of the ship.

Elif gasped.

Orhan and John Savage stood on the green-painted deck, their backs to the yellow superstructure of the gas tanks. Orhan held a pistol, extended in front of his body. Savage wore an expression she had never seen before, his eyes blazing with energy. He seemed to be unarmed.

"Shoot!" she shouted. "Shoot! It does not matter if you hit me."

"Shut up." The Chief gripped her tighter and slapped the back of her head with his hand.

Elif cried out at the pain.

Could she use her own agony against him?

Before she reacted, the blonde camerawoman, Leni they had called her, hobbled into sight on top of the yellow painted superstructure behind Savage and Orhan. One arm hung limp, the other gripped a rail to steady herself as her leg trailed behind her.

"Look out!" Elif could barely whisper.

Orhan swung round. The tiny woman lurched forward off the top of the gas tank towards the two men. Savage spun away but Orhan raised his gun to shoot and the momentum of the woman smashed him to the steel deck. The woman scratched and tore at Orhan's face with her good hand as he tried to lash out, but the impact against the deck seemed to have knocked the fight out of him.

Two shots rang out. The blonde terrorist slumped back, her body jerking in death. What had motivated her to join in this plan of senseless destruction? Nearby, a camera on a tripod lay broken.

Orhan sprawled on the deck, his face twisted in pain, his pistol in his hand.

He looked up at Savage. "I am hurt. I'm out of ammo. Do not fail me."

The Chief tightened his grip around Elif.

"You are coming with me." His voice was harsh in her ear. "It is time we followed your precious Palladium into the water."

He backed towards the railing, high above the turbulent waves of the Bosphorus.

## 77

The tiny form of the blonde woman plummeted past Savage, smashing Orhan to the metal walkway. She clawed at the police intelligence officer's face. The shots from Orhan's pistol ended the struggle.

Even before Orhan cried out, Savage knew his partner had emptied his magazine. He had counted as the Turk blazed away to try and ignite the gas. He knew Orhan had fired his last round even before the tell-tale click of the action confirmed the fact.

At his waist, Savage touched the sheathed combat knife he had taken from the injured SWAT captain.

If only he had taken the man's firearm.

Yet a gun might have provoked his opponent to open fire while he protected himself with a human shield.

The killer holding Elif was the same sophisticated-looking man he had seen on the video. Had he tortured her? Why else had she authenticated the Palladium? Elif had turned pale as marble. Her hair looked matted with blood, something dark oozed down the base of her neck. What had they done to her? When the terrorist slapped her on the back of her head, she had flinched.

The man had one foot on the railing as if preparing to leap into the water with his hostage. Yet his arm, crooked around her neck, made any kind of shot or assault impossible.

Savage pulled the knife from his belt. The black serrated blade, speckled with rain, gleamed in the glare of the fire jet. He gripped the hilt. At the slightest move, the other man might open fire or hurl himself and Elif into the water.

Elif's captor pulled her closer, preparing to jump.

ELIF FELT the Chief's arm tighten around her neck as he stepped up onto the railing. Did he plan to drown himself? Minutes before, he had tried to raze an entire city. Savage stood across the deck, a knife in his hand, watching.

At any second the Chief could send them tumbling into the darkness of the wave-torn Bosphorus.

Her head throbbed from where the Chief had slapped her.

Elif gritted her teeth. On the floor of the car in Sultanahmet, she had smashed her head against the steel seat support.

The act of self-harm had given her power. The way she seized control had driven her two captors half mad.

Turkish women had the hardest heads on earth.

She jerked her head forward and with all the hate in her heart, slammed her ruined skull back into the face of the man holding her.

The Chief cried out as an excruciating pain ripped through her head. His grip slackened. Elif ignored the agony from her own wound. She leaned forward and smashed her head back again with added ferocity. Nausea swamped her senses. But the Chief staggered back, clutching the rail for support.

Elif threw herself forward on the deck.

---

SAVAGE HELD the knife in his hand. Elif's face twisted in agony as she pounded her head back against her captor. Blood streamed from the man's face. The impact of her skull must have smashed his nose.

Or was that blood hers?

*Upturn had rammed the scalpel into her own neck to end her suffering. Savage had seized the handle and jerked out the blade, blood splashing across his hand, warm despite the icy temperature. He had raised the scalpel, as she begged him, and plunged the short blade again and again into her exposed flesh. Upturn's own actions had taken her life. Savage had made a show of killing, for the FSB video cameras in the Moscow wood, to save her family.*

Elif delivered another crushing head-butt to the man's face. The killer staggered back. Elif fell forward. Savage leapt and smashed the base of the knife down on the hand holding the gun. As the pistol clattered to the deck, he punched the jagged blade up hard into the centre of the stomach, under the rib-cage, an eviscerating, fatal blow delivered with such fury that he lifted the man's feet off the ground and pushed him over the top of the railing. Savage thrust further with all his strength, his hand warm with blood as his knuckles entered the wound in the man's chest. He rammed the knife further, for Elif and for Upturn and for Stuart Lamont, until the body toppled back.

He withdrew the knife, his hand bloodied to the wrist. The kidnapper's dying body tumbled over the railing and somersaulted into the waves. Savage weighed the murder weapon in his hand, smiled, and threw the blade into the sea.

He turned. Elif had crawled to where Orhan lay. She cradled her brother in her arms. Both of them gazed at Savage.

Orhan's face wore a look of triumph.

Elif stared at him with horror.

## 78

I stanbul was a city of views, like Barcelona on steroids, with a thousand years more history. Something splashed in the water next to Savage and a cormorant appeared, bobbing in the Bosphorus. A warm breath of wind washed the tangy, fresh smell of the sea over him. He poured himself another glass of red wine.

"Hallo? Have you forgotten me?" Across the table, Elif raised her glass of *raki*. "I know these things are difficult to discuss. But if you want to look out to sea all night, I may as well head home."

"I never saw the beauty of the Bosphorus." Savage lifted the wine to his lips and put down the glass half empty. "The Russian song? Yesenin? *In your eyes, the sea. Blazing blue fire.* Pretty bloody appropriate, I thought."

Elif stared at him.

Savage drained the glass. "I know you saw a darker side of me, that night on the ship. I saw another side of you, too. The difference is, what I saw, I admired."

"The surgeon admired my head." Elif Mutlu lifted her hand to where a scarf covered her bandaged scalp. "It seems my skull actually is thicker than average. But when you killed that man." She sipped the *raki* and peered at him over the glass. "You looked like a psychopath."

"Your brother said the same. But he meant it as a compliment."

"I never dreamed you were capable of such butchery. You're not the only man on earth who is a bit awkward around women. But your face, as you pushed in the knife." She shook her head and hesitated. "You seemed excited by killing."

"Orhan said he would love me if I helped save Istanbul and save you. I guess he must love me, now. As well as hating me. Now you are scared of me. What a mess." He tipped the end of the bottle into his glass.

"The day was not easy for me." Elif poured an inch of fresh *raki* into her glass, turned the clear liquid milky with a dash of water, and chilled the mixture with ice cubes. "That is British understatement, by the way. To round it off, I see my brother nearly killed by a kamikaze terrorist. Then you, whoever you are, kill a man, rip him to pieces, with a knife." She looked down at her drink. "Have you any secrets you want to tell me? About what made you who you are? About Moscow, maybe? If I knew more, it might help me make sense of you." She sipped her drink. "Talking about Russia might even make you feel better."

"No." Savage broke off a piece of *lavas* bread and chewed on the hot, soft dough before replying. "I don't think it would help me, or you, to talk about Moscow. But I am still the same man I was before the killers appeared at your dig."

She smiled. "That is what I am afraid of." She reached out and stroked the back of his hand, her fingers moist from the chilled *raki* glass. The breeze caressed his face.

"Orhan's case against Arzu Pasha looks solid."

"Yes." Elif shook her head. "What did she think she was she doing, supporting a bunch of terrorists?"

"She is a property developer. Obviously, she has no moral compass whatsoever. She puts her finger into every pie, twenty-four seven, to try and increase the value of her assets or to buy something on the cheap. When someone told her they could speed up construction of the shopping mall in the Old City and at the same time depress property prices elsewhere in Istanbul through a terrorist attack, she was hanging out the flags."

"You are starting to talk conspiracy theories like a Turk. But seriously, she supported a terror attack to make money?"

"She wouldn't be the first. She had no idea of the scale of what they had planned. They knew which buttons to press: power, secrecy, and greed. Like everyone else involved, like Meryem and Dervis, she thought she could use them to achieve her goals. In reality, they used her."

"Poor Dervis. He learned the hard way." Elif touched the back of her head again. "But who was behind the attack?"

"No-one knows," Savage said. "It seems some central organising group or individual, codenamed The Elders, used the darknet to persuade different people to take a series of independent actions. They must have studied each person online, before presenting an offer tailor-made to their beliefs or way of life. Like an online fraudster who persuades people to send money by exploiting their dreams. Maybe the killers were fooled like everyone else."

"Did any of them survive?"

"No. They found one more man lying by the ship's wheel when special forces stormed the bridge. He had shot himself in the head. I guess he figured things weren't going too well."

"Who are The Elders? What do they want?"

"Who knows? They hide behind the darknet, VPNs, and encryption. You can buy most of the technology off the shelf. They could be anywhere in the world. Or in many places. Maybe they have an ideology, or maybe they just like breaking stuff. There are plenty of people who think the world would be better if the system came crashing down. They have a kind of snow day mentality: if it snows enough, nothing works, and everyone gets a day off. They think a snow day that lasted forever would be a great thing."

"Sometimes, I think I know how they feel." Elif peered at Savage. "Making sense of life can be hard. Where is the ship now?"

"In the middle of the Sea of Marmara, surrounded by a fifty-kilometre cordon. The flame is still burning: the gas will take days to evaporate and burn out. As soon as the pressure drops, they will try to plug the hole to stop any flame from entering the tank they breached."

"Fifty kilometres?"

"If flames enter the void and explode, the blast could breach the other tanks."

"At least I can complete my dig, now. Who knows what else we will find down there?"

Salt from the pistachios had dusted Elif's lips. Antep nuts, they called them in Turkish. Would he ever kiss those lips again? The two of them seemed unable to discuss themselves or their future. But she had touched his hand. He sighed. "I am sorry about the Palladium."

"The one thing that relic could not have been is the Palladium, because the Palladium is a mythical object. But it was an incredible, ancient piece." She turned and stared out across the water. "When I held the statuette in my arms, it seemed almost to comfort me." Elif wiped her eyes. "I cannot believe I held one of the finest archaeological finds of all time in my hands, and now it is at the bottom of the ocean."

"The gang believed the Palladium protected Istanbul. Misty Anderson was the first person to work it out."

"Superstitious nonsense." Elif emptied her glass.

"Maybe the Palladium never left Istanbul. The city covers both sides of the Bosphorus, so why not the middle? Or perhaps the Luck of Troy is still providing protection from the bottom of the channel."

"I tell you. Istanbul doesn't need protecting."

Savage put down his glass. "In my experience, everywhere and everything needs all the protection it can get."

"Don't tell me you are turning superstitious."

"People believe many strange things. Who knows what the future will bring?" He reached across the table and stroked the back of her fingers. "The first thing is to decide what we want."

"Yes. Knowing what we want isn't easy to decide, John. Nothing worthwhile is ever easy."

Elif Mutlu looked down at the table and gently withdrew her hand.

# EPILOGUE

The fisherman Mustafa Parlak rubbed his eyes and yawned as he turned his small boat towards the rickety wooden berth at Yenikapi. Overhead, the sky grew pale as dawn approached. He frowned and blinked as he tied the boat up; his eyes had grown dim with the passing years.

The night had been long and dark. But the sea had teemed with fish. It was as if they, too, had welcomed the lifting of the ban on boat traffic in the Bosphorus after the bomb attacks in the city, and had decided to celebrate by gathering in great numbers to greet Mustafa and his fellow fishermen.

But the swirling, multi-layered currents of the Bosphorus were famous for their unpredictability. You never knew where the fish might show up—or not.

As Mustafa stepped from his boat onto the wharf, something bobbing in the water caught his eye.

All kinds of debris washed up at Yenikapi, brought south from the Bosphorus or north from the Dardanelles. Even after endless land reclamation and transport projects had cut off Yenikapi from the sea, beyond desolate car-parks and bustling highways, Mustafa always kept an eye open for what the tide brought in.

He peered at the drab bundle sitting low in the water. He had enough to carry already. His back ached. But something about the surface of the object, what looked like a piece of embroidered fabric, caught his attention.

He knelt, reached down, and grabbed the bundle. The object rose from the water, almost as if it wanted to be found.

Blinking at his discovery, Mustafa pulled back the covering.

Something like a face gazed back at him. He squinted at the features, eyes narrowed. Perhaps someone had lost a doll of some sort. He scratched his grizzled chin. His grandchild, who he called Fistik, or peanut, loved to play with dolls when she visited.

Then he remembered that Fistik had thrown away her toys long ago. She had children of her own. Fistik seemed too busy ever to come to see him, now.

Still, Mustafa smiled. The doll, or carving or whatever it was, would remind him of Fistik as a child, giggling as he lifted her up in his arms.

He stowed the bundle in his bag, with the fish, and walked home. He crossed a patch of scrubby waste ground and climbed a flight of steel steps to a bridge over the busy coast road. No trace remained of the original Yeni Kapi, or New Gate, known before the conquest of Constantinople as the Jewish Gate.

At a local fish-merchant's, he exchanged his night's catch for a gratifyingly large cash sum, no questions asked. He considered showing the fishmonger the object he had found in the water, but something held him back. At a grocer's shop and a bakery, he bought himself fresh vegetables and bread for breakfast.

The road climbed steeply from the fish-market through low-build apartment blocks towards Laleli Caddesi, Tulip Street. Mustafa stopped at a café for a refreshing glass of Turkish *cay* before entering the front door of his block and climbing the narrow flights to his two-room apartment.

Outside, the rising sun painted the Old City of Istanbul a pale pink. With a sigh, Mustafa sat down at his kitchen table and pulled the package from his bag. Carefully, he opened the wrapping. The material had two textures: partly cloth with embroidered stitching, partly leather, stamped or embossed with a pattern he could not make out. The leather must have kept the package afloat, by trapping air in its folds. How long had the object floated in the water?

He spread the fabric out to dry on a shelf above his cooker. The colours had faded, but he liked the patterns. Perhaps he could use the wrapping to cover the end of his bed.

Should he keep the object itself? He had never seen such a thing. When he ran his thumb across the face he felt a nose, but hardly any mouth or eyes to speak of. An arm stuck out on each side, one bigger than the other. The body had smooth, simple contours. Fistik might have given the figurine short shrift, had she ever got hold of it. He weighed the object in his weathered hands, wondering whose tools had carved the soft curves. For a moment, peace descended on the tiny kitchen. The little figure felt cool to the touch. Perhaps it, too, would fit well on the shelf.

He reached up and propped the statuette on top of the wrapping, so the sightless face stared out the window.

Mustafa smiled. The new arrival seemed at home with him. Perhaps he or she enjoyed the view. He walked over to the window and peered out as the breaking dawn lit up the minarets of the Bodrum Mosque, built over a thousand years before as a Byzantine church known as the Myrelaion.

# REFERENCES

1. LNG vessel cascading damage structural and thermal analyses – Jason P Petti et al, Sandia national Laboratories, Albuquerque, New Mexico, 2013.
2. The Turkish straits and LNG: private paper prepared for Author by IBS Research Consultancy, Istanbul, 2013
3. LNG Information Paper No.1, Group International des Importateurs de Gaz Naturel Liquefie.

# AUTHOR'S NOTE

This is a work of fiction. None of the politicians, officials, security operatives, or terrorists who people its pages are based on anyone I've met, or even seen on TV. Nor does this book contain any information I think might endanger the security of real individuals. There is no "Heart of Istanbul" mall in Turkey's largest city, nor is there one called "Istanbul Rising."

If you would like to learn more about my writing, do have a look at my website rleighturner.com.

Thanks again for reading.

Leigh Turner
Vienna, 5/17/2022

# DISCUSSION QUESTIONS

1. How did you enjoy *Palladium*?
2. Which parts of *Palladium* did you enjoy most?
3. Which characters did you find most sympathetic? Which did you dislike? *? None describe well so no view*
4. Place yourself in the action of *Palladium*. Which character would you like to be?
5. Which twists in *Palladium* surprised you? Why?

## RELATIONSHIPS

1. Before *Palladium* begins, Elif and John have quarrelled. What do you think they quarrelled about?
2. John has told Elif he can never love her. How true do you think this is?
3. Why does John join Orhan in trying to rescue Elif? What drives him?
4. How does the relationship between John and Orhan develop during *Palladium*? How does their relationship affect their ability to rescue Elif and save Istanbul?
5. What do you think happens to the relationship between John and Elif after the final scene?

## THE CHARACTERS

1. Elif struggles to free herself from her captors. Could she have done more?
2. What part does Elif play in saving Istanbul?

3. Are the terrorists trying to destroy Istanbul evil? Or are they as much victims as those they seek to kill? Who might "The Elders" be?

4. Why do you think Arzu Pasha, the property developer, and Meryam Shah, an idealist, helped the terrorists? *Money?*

5. What do you think motivates the journalist, Misty Anderson, to behave as she does? *Fame?*

## THE PLOT

1. How important is superstition to the plot of *Palladium*?

2. Is the object discovered in the tomb really the Palladium? Does it matter? What did you think of the object's fate in the epilogue? *immaterial, unless you feel it did protect Istambul!*

3. Did the title *Palladium* capture the essence of the book? *No* What would work better?

4. How realistic is the plot of *Palladium*? Is it more or less realistic than other thrillers?

5. How did the final scenes, on the ship, make you feel? *too much* *Bored with shooting* When did you realise how the *Royal Lion* would affect the plot?

# ACKNOWLEDGMENTS

Special thanks go to David Tonge, IBS Research & Consultancy, for advice on tankers, dangerous cargoes and the Bosphorus. Elif Safak, Orhan Pamuk, Ahmet Umit, Buket Uzuner and Elcin Poyrazler showed me some of the great writing coming out of Turkey. Arzu Sekirden Döven worked tirelessly to teach me Turkish. My great team at the British Consulate General in Istanbul were brilliant for my four years in that great city – special thanks to Yasemin Baser for helping me so much. Thanks also to all at the British Embassy in Ankara for supporting me, including on countless visits there.

A host of inspirational people introduced me to Istanbul adventures, including Akin Bayraktaoglu, my host in Baltalimani; Chris and Gulten Gaunt; Pinar Kartal Timer of the Pera Palace; Jonathan Beard; Denny Caouki; Owen Matthews; Ahmet and Cigdem Ongun; Pelin Akin; Gunes Savas and Yucel Yemez who saved my life with crucial hospitality; Dan Dombey; Hugh Pope and Jessica Lutz; Benjamin Harvey and Hande Ataizi; Amberin Zaman; Tilda Tezman; Mustafa Suzer; Ender Mermerci; Rahmi Koc; Demet Sabanci; Nurtac Ziyal; Zuhal Seker; Cansen Basaran-Symes; Basak Akdemir; Fulya and Stephen Fraser; Unal Cevikoz; Paula Domzalski; Cem Kozlu; Refika Birgul; Princess Esra Jah; and Nilgun and Hakan Kavur, of Gali Wines.

My fellow Consuls-General in Istanbul: Chuck Hunter, Muriel Domenach, Jens Odlander, Monika Schmutz, Robert Schuddeboom, Federica Ferrari Bravo and Christine Wendl.

Without Immortal Works, none of this would be happening. Thank you, Staci Olsen for finding me, Holli Anderson for liking and editing Palladium, Ruth Mitchell and Megan King for the publicity, and Rebecca Barney for the maps and the cover art.

Above all, thanks to Gözde for taking me to Istanbul in the first place, and explaining so much.

# ABOUT THE AUTHOR

Leigh Turner is a writer and former British ambassador to Ukraine and Austria. He grew up in Nigeria, Lesotho, Swaziland and Manchester, England and attended Cambridge University.

In 1979, Leigh hitch-hiked through 27 states of the continental US. His diplomatic career took him to Vienna, Moscow, Kyiv, Berlin, Hong Kong, Vladivostok, Miami, St Helena, Buenos Aires, Beijing, Bermuda, Samarkand, Istanbul and Las Vegas.

In Berlin, Leigh took four years off diplomacy to look after his two children and became a travel writer for "The Financial Times". You can find the results at his rleighturner.com blog. His other books include the Berlin thriller *Blood Summit*, his satirical thriller *Eternal Life* and his darkly comic *Seven Hotel Stories*.

Leigh is also working on a diplomatic handbook, *The Hitch-hiker's Guide to Diplomacy*.

This has been an
Immortal Production

DERVIS - archeologist, religious | "the
protect the paladium. Give orders | elders
Ed Burke - philosopher = "the only thing for the
triumph of evil is for good men to do nothing"
Dervish = Gray?
LENI - small woman filming everyone
P296 - Philosophy like Hitler - kill to make
a better world?
Leni etc wanted Elif to give validity to views to
kill for their cause - E refused but was filmed
P298 - EXPLANATION of the PALADIUM
"XOANON" = Paladium
P 300 - Description of the Palladium!
Sounds like BAFTA statue!
Elif under the power of the Paladium =
[A why] - Elif touched back of her head
she felt mess of flesh as if someone
had smashed head with a brick

Who was "the chief" A woman?
a Bodrum Mosque built over 1,000 yrs
ago as Byzantine + called Myrelaion.
(Haghia Sophia) = 1,500 yrs!

'The killing in Sebastopol'
previous book. Savage's
traumas

Eternal Life - Leigh Turner.

Janissany warrior – YUSEF ALI-BEY-HASSAN his pal.
ORHAN MUTLU – Soldiers – ORE siblings
ELIF – excavator. } ex lovers.
JOHN SAVAGE

"SATRANC" = Chess!

= calls savage for help. –
YUSUF = Soldier, took P. metrochites = Soldier, revealed
hiding place of PALLADIUM,
Pasilica = a canon. without palladium city would
P.41 fall.
R20 PASHA – woman wanting to Bulldoze site!
ARS – co excavator, irritating German.
Ely finds mummified child in a sarasfagus in
yuseft Halil, Yazid – got PALADIUM, wrapped fabric
so Constantinople now unprotected & it fell!
Elif abducted in Taxi, phone taken, Savage
searching for her
MY RELAION – A cistern.
Terrorist attack @ football match – Savage
trying to stop – Elif involved?
Protocol" dictates the action if Palladium is
missing.
WHAT IS the PROTOCOL? A large BOAT!

Sailp was called Kaan before "protocol"
Terrorists will strike in the sq. Savage
. Terrorist attack in Istanbul predicted it
Elif prisoner in a hand cart – bound &
gagged. I felt claustrophobic! Author
tapped Info human fears well city of
PROTOCOL? Istanbul must 'go' = Sin
P263
get RID of GREED!
LNG – Gas on ship could ignite & blow up
all Istanbul like NUCLEAR explosion
out! paralysed I can't make decisions.

Haghia sophia – church of Holy wisdom
stands guard over Bosporous for 15 centuries

FMRI = Can see brain activity g super
ages.
visual cortex - visual source g supapers
roll eyes left → Right ( head still) before a
memory test.
2 NUTRIENTS = eye memory conection
= "CHOLINE" → ACETOCHLORINE
- Alpha GPC - v. g. = no memory probs
GABA" - eyg memory comunication
Ayurverdic = BACOPA = Eliminates brain tangles
= "AGELESS BRAIN" pills
TYROSENE as well = Good.
"SMOOTHIES for a HEALTHY MIND"

Lightning Source UK Ltd.
Milton Keynes UK
UKHW010745260522
403565UK00002B/217